Praise for

Easy

"Webber weaves an intricate layered plot that leaves us wanting to see what happens."
—*USA Today*

"A truly memorable story about such deep, emotional, and delicate subject matter . . . One of my favorite books I've read this year."
—*The Book Vixen*

"Truly unique."
—*Harlequin Junkies*

"This is a gritty book as well as a satisfying romance."
—*All About Romance*

"Easy to love. Easy to recommend. Easy to want more. From start to finish, I didn't want to put it down, and I especially didn't want it to end."
—*Maryse's Book Blog*

"It's just extraordinary."
—*Once Upon a Twilight*

"A profound story about empowerment, healing, and moving on . . . Webber created a cast of memorable and stunning characters."
—*Tina's Book Reviews*

"Webber's characters . . . are extremely real."
—*A Book Vacation*

"You get some really sexy scenes . . . you get to watch the evolution of a relationship from virtual strangers to lovers; and you get to meet a fiercely guarded, damaged boy and girl blossom into something new."
—*I Love YA Fiction*

"*Easy* will grab your attention from the very first page and will take you on an intense and emotional roller coaster that will leave you emotionally drained, but completely satisfied."
—*Mostly YA Book Obsessed*

Berkley titles by Tammara Webber

EASY
BREAKABLE

tammara webber

Breakable

B

BERKLEY BOOKS, NEW YORK

Published by the Penguin Group
Penguin Group (USA) LLC
375 Hudson Street, New York, New York 10014

USA • Canada • UK • Ireland • Australia • New Zealand • India • South Africa • China

penguin.com

A Penguin Random House Company

BREAKABLE

This book is an original publication of The Berkley Publishing Group.

BERKLEY® is a registered trademark of Penguin Group (USA) LLC.
The "B" design is a trademark of Penguin Group (USA) LLC.

Berkley trade paperback ISBN: 978-0-425-26686-1

An application to register this book for cataloging has been submitted to the Library of Congress.

PUBLISHING HISTORY
Berkley trade paperback edition / May 2014

PRINTED IN THE UNITED STATES OF AMERICA

10 9 8 7 6 5 4 3 2 1

Interior text design by Jeanine Henderson.

To GWK

When I was a child, I sometimes wondered
if you were my guardian angel. Now that I'm older
I know that you are.

chapter *One*

LANDON

Eight years ago

I woke with a jerk, screaming.

"Nurse!" someone called out. "Nurse!" A face leaned over me. Cindy Heller, Mom's best friend. "Landon, honey—it's okay. You're safe. Shh, you're safe."

Safe? Where?

I felt her cool fingertips on my arm and tried to focus as her red-rimmed eyes filled with tears. She bit her lower lip so hard it was colorless and trembling. Her whole face was crumpled, like paper wadded up tight and then smoothed back out.

Her husband, Charles, appeared next to her, one arm slipping behind her back to pull her tight. She slumped against him as if she'd have tipped right over without his reinforcement.

His opposite hand was warm on top of mine, then, enveloping it. "You're safe, son. Your dad is on his way." His voice sounded grainy, and his eyes were red, too. "He'll be here soon."

A nurse materialized on the other side of the bed with a huge syringe, but before I could pull away, she stuck it into a bag suspended from a metal stand, not into my arm. A clear cord extending from the bottom of the bag looped down. I knew it was attached to me when I felt whatever she'd just injected into it, like I'd been shot with a tranquilizer gun.

Gun.

Mom.

"Mom!" I said, but my mouth wouldn't cooperate and my eyes kept trying to close. "Mom! Mom!"

Cindy couldn't bite her lip hard enough to stifle the sob that escaped. Tears overflowed and trailed down her cheeks. I couldn't feel her touching me anymore, and she turned into her husband's chest, hands flying up to cover her mouth—too late to muffle another sob.

The pressure of Charles's hand diminished bit by bit as everything grew fuzzier. "Landon, sleep now. Your father will be here as soon as he can. I'm here. I'm not leaving you."

His face became less and less distinct, finally fading altogether, and I couldn't keep my eyes open.

Mom! I screamed her name in my head, *Mom! Mom . . . Mom . . .*

But I already knew she wouldn't have heard me, even if my voice was as loud as a jet engine.

LUCAS

In a lecture hall of 189 students, it's unusual for one of them to stand out the first day, but not unprecedented. When one separates from the herd that early, it's typically because of something negative. Like asking stupid questions. Or talking during the lecture—and missing the evil eye from the professor. Excessive body odor. Audible snoring.

Or my personal anathema: being a trendy douche.

So I wasn't too surprised when I became aware of such a guy during the first week of fall semester. Typical previous BMOC of his high school—used to toadies toadying. Still expecting it, still getting it. Frat guy. Casual but affluent clothes, expensive haircut, self-important smile, perfect teeth, and the requisite cute girlfriend. Likely majors: econ, poli sci, finance.

He annoyed me on sight. Biased of me, sure—but it's not like my opinion mattered. He paid attention in class and asked competent questions, so he was unlikely to need tutoring, though that didn't preclude him from showing up to the study sessions I administered for Dr. Heller three times a week. Often the brightest students made up most of the group.

The first semester I did supplemental instruction—last fall—I paid close attention during Heller's lectures. I'd made an A in his class, but it had been a year since I took it, and economics isn't a stagnant field. I didn't want a student asking me a question in the middle of a tutoring session that I couldn't answer. By the third semester—my fourth sitting through the class—I didn't really need to be there, but class attendance was part of the tutoring gig, and it was easy money.

So there I sat—bored off my ass on the back row, working on assignments from my senior-level courses, sketching out design project ideas, keeping an ear on where the lecture was going so I could stay on topic during my sessions, and resolutely ignoring my pointless dislike of the conceited sophomore sitting in the center of the class with his accessory of a girlfriend.

But by the end of that first week, my attention was straying to her.

Since childhood, drawing has been a comforting diversion, and sometimes an escape. My mother was an artist, and I don't know if she discerned that I had a natural aptitude for it or if it was a learned skill resulting from her early encouragement and plenty of practice. All I know was that by the time I was five or six, paper and pencil were my way of relating to the world. My personal form of meditation.

Once I began college, most of my drawings became mechanical or architectural in nature—probably unavoidable, given my mechanical engineering studies. But even in my free time, I rarely sketched bodies or faces anymore. I had little desire to do it.

Until her.

Entering and exiting class, her boyfriend sometimes held her hand. But it was like he was holding a lead, not the hand of a girl he cared about. Before class, he talked football, politics, music, and frat particulars like rush or upcoming parties with other guys like him and guys who wanted to be like him. Nearby girls bestowed sidelong glances he pretended to ignore.

Somehow, while he was preoccupied with everything and everyone around him *except* her, I suddenly couldn't see anything else. She was beautiful, sure, but in a university with thirty thousand undergrads, that was hardly riveting. If not for my initial annoyance with her boyfriend, I might never have noticed her at all.

Once I realized how often my gaze drifted over her, I consciously fought the inclination—but it was no use. There was nothing in the room as interesting as this girl. What fascinated me first and foremost were her hands. Specifically, her fingers.

In class, she sat next to him, wearing a loose smile, sometimes quietly conversing with him or others nearby. She didn't look unhappy, but her eyes were almost vacant at times, like her mind was elsewhere. During those moments, though, her hands—her *fingers*—were performing.

At first I thought she had a nervous habit, like Heller's daughter, Carlie, who'd never stopped moving since the day she was born. Carlie was forever tapping a fingernail or a foot, jiggling a knee, talking. The only thing I've seen calm her was petting Francis, my cat.

This girl wasn't tapping her fingers restlessly, though. Her movements were methodical. Synchronized. Sitting far enough to the left of her to study her profile, I watched her chin bob, so subtly it was almost undetectable—and at some point, I realized that when her expression was remote and her fingers were moving, she was hearing music. She was *playing* music.

It was the most magical thing I'd ever seen anyone do.

• • • • • • • • • •

According to Heller's seating chart—received with the rest of my tutoring support materials for the semester—the douche's name was Kennedy, assuming I was reading the scrawl of his print correctly. Sitting on the sofa in my apartment, scanning the chart, I murmured, "No fucking way," when I read her name, neatly printed in the square next to his: Jackie.

Jackie and *Kennedy*?

He couldn't be going out with her because of her name. No one could be that shallow.

I thought back to this morning at the end of class. He'd handed her his homework and said, "Hey, babe—take this up to the front with yours? Thanks." Flashing an entitled grin, he'd turned to continue some debate about what should and shouldn't be considered hazing while she placed his paper on top of her own, rolling her eyes as she spun to walk down the steps to the front of the classroom.

Yeah. He could absolutely be that shallow.

I touched a finger to her name. Every letter she'd printed was rounded, feminine. Even the "i" had a slight bend and a right-swerving tail. The dot over the "i" was a dot, though. No open circle. No little *heart*. And there was the eye roll after his *Hey, babe*. Maybe she wasn't hopelessly caught in his web.

What the hell was I even thinking? This girl was a student in the class I tutored. She was off-limits, at least for the remainder of the semester. Which was a long goddamned time, considering we'd just entered the second week of class.

And aside from the fact that I couldn't touch her if she was available . . . she wasn't available.

I wondered how long they'd been going out. They were both sophomores, according to the roll sheet. Worst-case scenario, then: they'd been a thing for a year.

So I did what any normal stalker would do. I looked her up online and found a locked-down profile. *Damn*.

But his was wide open.

Kennedy Moore. In a relationship with Jackie Wallace. No anniversary listed, but there were photos tagged of her—not just over the past year, but before that. I worked backward, growing progressively pissed off for no good reason.

The summer before college. High school graduation. Prom. Skiing over spring break. A surprise party on her eighteenth birthday. A distance shot of an orchestra with more performers than the population of my entire high school. A close-up of her wearing that orchestral attire plus a Santa hat—but no instrument in her hands, so I wasn't sure what she played.

Thanksgiving with his family. The two of them horsing around with friends on a football field just outside a high school that reeked of moneyed suburb. *Previous* summer break. Junior prom. Yet another Christmas.

The earliest photo of her with him was taken at a fall carnival nearly three years ago.

They'd been together three years. *Three years*. I couldn't even wrap my mind around it.

A yowl at my door signaled Francis's return from whatever trouble he got into between dinner and sleep. Like any good domesticated companion, I put my laptop aside and went to let him in. When I opened the door, he sat on the mat, licking a paw.

"C'mon, then," I said. "I'm not gonna refrigerate the whole neighborhood."

He shrugged into a standing position, stretched indolently, and darted into the apartment as I made to shut the door in his face. Just before it snapped closed, I heard, "Lucas!" and pulled it open.

Carlie was halfway up the wooden staircase that led to my apartment over the Hellers' garage. It was late. She'd developed an uncomfortable crush on me last spring, which I'd thought was over months ago, after I pretended not to notice her prolonged stares and excessive giggles. I'd known her since she was born, so she and her brothers were like cousins or siblings to me, especially considering I didn't have either. She was also five years my junior—a kid, really. The last thing I wanted to do was hurt her.

I moved fully into the doorway. "Hey, Carlie. Shouldn't you be in bed?"

She wrinkled her nose and scowled, insulted. "I'm sixteen, not *six*. Sheesh." When she got to the top step and moved into the semicircle of light over the small landing, I noticed she had a plate in her hand. "I made cookies. Thought you might want some."

"Cool. Thanks." I took the plate but didn't move into the apartment.

She shuffled one foot and stuck her hands in the back pockets of her shorts. "Lucas?"

"Yeah?" I said, thinking, *Oh, shit.*

"Are you ever gonna . . . have a girlfriend? Or do you have one, but you just don't bring her around here? Or is there, you know, something else you haven't *revealed* yet . . ."

I swallowed a laugh. "If you're about to ask if I need to come out of the closet—the answer is no. I'd have done that a long time ago." That question was, weirdly, a lot easier to answer than the other.

"I figured you would have. I mean, you kind of don't mind being controversial."

I quirked an eyebrow. "Because of the lip ring?"

She nodded. "And the tattoos." Her eyes widened as she realized what she'd just said. "I mean—obviously, you have your reasons for those. Most of them . . ." She shut her eyes. "God, I'm so stupid. I'm sorry—"

"It's okay, Carlie. No worries." My teeth scraped over the sliver of metal threaded through my lower lip, while I fought to keep my eyes from skimming over the tattoos wrapping my wrists. "Thanks for the cookies."

She huffed out a sigh. "Yeah. No problem. Good night, Lucas."

Girlfriend question averted, I sighed, too. "Good night."

Carlie was the only Heller who never had a problem remembering to call me Lucas. When I left home for college three years ago, I wanted to change everything, starting with my name. My mother had given me her maiden name—Lucas—as my middle name. I supposed lots of people went by their middle names, and bonus—no legal proceeding was required to use it.

My dad refused to call me Lucas, but what he chose to call me hardly mattered. I didn't live with him anymore, and when I went home, we barely spoke. Carlie's parents and both of her brothers remembered sporadically—but they tried. I'd gone by Landon for over eighteen years, after all, so I usually let it slide without correcting them. Old habits, *blah*, *blah*.

From that point on, though, I was Lucas to anyone new. I wanted to make Landon disappear for good. Nonexist.

I should have known it wouldn't be that easy.

chapter Two

LANDON

Since kindergarten, I'd attended a small private school just outside DC. We wore uniforms: girls in white blouses with pearl buttons, pleated plaid skirts, and cardigans; boys in starched white oxfords, pressed slacks, and blazers. Our favorite teachers turned a blind eye to unauthorized scarves and colored shoestrings and ignored ditched cardigans and jackets. The stricter instructors took up contraband items and rolled their eyes when we argued that hemp bracelets and glitter-coated headbands were expressions of individual freedom.

Victor Evans got suspended last spring when he refused to take off a Bottega Veneta dog collar, claiming that wearing it was his right under the First Amendment and wasn't technically against the rules. Administration cracked down after that.

We all looked the same on the surface, but during the two weeks I was out of school I had altered completely—beneath the skin, where changes count. I'd been tested and I had failed. I had made a promise that I didn't keep. It didn't matter if I was still outwardly identical. I was no longer one of them.

I was allowed to make up work missed, as though I'd been out with a severe case of flu, but the special considerations didn't stop there. Teachers who'd challenged me before patted my shoulder and told me to take my time on new classwork. They granted unearned passing grades on crappily written essays, extra time on incomplete lab assignments, automatic do-over offers on bombed exams.

Then there were my peers—some who'd known me since we were five. All of them mumbled condolences, but they had no idea what to say after. No one asked for help on algebra homework or invited me over to play video games. The other guys didn't shove my books off my desk when I wasn't looking or hassle me when my favorite football team got their asses handed to them by the Redskins. Sex jokes cut off mid-sentence when I walked up.

Everyone watched me—in class, in the hallway, during assemblies, at lunch. They gossiped behind their hands, shook their heads, stared like I couldn't see them doing it. As though I was a wax figure of my former self—lifelike, but creepy.

No one looked me in the eye. Like maybe having a dead mother was contagious.

One overly warm day, I rolled up my sleeves in Mr. Ferguson's US History class without thinking. I heard the telltale whispering, moving person to person, too late. "His *wrists?*" Susie Gamin hissed before someone shushed her.

Tugging the sleeves back down and re-buttoning the cuffs made no difference. The words, unleashed, were an avalanche of tumbling boulders. Unstoppable.

The following day, I wore a watch with a thick band on my left wrist, even though it chafed my still-raw skin. I stacked silicone wristbands on my right, banned unconditionally by the principal the previous spring. These became part of my daily uniform.

No one made me take them off. No one mentioned them. But everybody stared, eager to catch a glimpse of what was underneath.

• • • • • • • • • •

Things I stopped doing:

1. *Hockey*. I started playing when I was six, shortly after attending my first Capitals game with Dad. Mom wasn't thrilled, but she tolerated it—maybe because it was a bonding point for Dad and me. Maybe because I loved playing so much.

Though right-handed in every other situation, something happened when I laced my skates and took my left-wing position. Powering a puck to the goal, I was ambidextrous. Between breaths, I shifted positions to dig a puck from the corner or freaked out opponents by switching hands in the middle of a play, sinking goals before they could catch up. My select team didn't win every time, but we'd made the finals last year. I began eighth grade certain this would be the year we'd take home the championship trophy. Like that was the most significant thing that could ever happen to me.

2. *Participating in class*. I didn't raise my hand. I wasn't ever called on. Pretty simple termination.

3. *Sleeping*. I still slept, sort of. But I woke up a lot. I had nightmares, but not obvious ones. Most often, I fell. Out of the sky. Off a building, a bridge, a cliff. Arms windmilling and legs kicking futilely. Sometimes, I dreamed about bears and sharks and carnivorous dinosaurs. Sometimes, I dreamed about drowning.

One thing was constant: I was always alone.

LUCAS

On hot days, I missed having the beach right outside my door. Even if the air had been saturated with humidity and the sand had been grassy and irregular, the gulf had always been there, cool waves lapping against the shore like a come-hither murmur.

For the past three years, I'd lived four hours inland. If I had the desire to submerge myself in a body of water, I had two choices: the Hellers' pool or the lake. There was little solitude to be found at either.

The lake was perpetually crowded with tourists and townies alike, and Carlie's friends still hung out at the house almost daily, lounging in the pool's deck chairs as they had all summer. The utter last thing I needed was a gaggle of very underage girls trying to net my attention just because I was the only non-dad male in the vicinity. Cole had been the object of their interest all summer, much to his sister's disgust. But he left two weeks ago to follow in his mom's footsteps at Duke, and Caleb was only eleven—as young to all of them as they were to me.

They failed to perceive the correlation.

Growing progressively paler over the past few years made my ink stand out even more. I'd begun with the complex patterns that wrapped my wrists, and they'd become sleeves, primarily composed of my own designs. Combined with the pierced lip and the longish dark hair, I more closely resembled a guy who thrives on depressive music and darkness than the beach-dwelling adolescent I was when I first *got* the tattoos and piercings.

In high school I'd sported multiple piercings—an ear stud, a barbell through an eyebrow, a nipple ring—in addition to the lip ring. Dad hated them, and my small-town high school principal alleged they were all signs of deviance and an antisocial disposition. I didn't bother arguing.

Once I left home, I'd pulled them all out but the one through the edge of my lip—the most conspicuous one.

I figured Heller would ask me, *Why leave* that *one?* But he never did. Maybe he'd known the answer without me vocalizing it—that I was categorically messed up and far from concerned with *fitting in*. To ordinary people, my lip piercing indicated the opposite of approachability. It was a self-erected barrier, and it served as a warning that pain wouldn't deter me—that I welcomed it, even.

Class had been in session for two weeks. Against my better judgment—what was left of it—I studied Jackie Wallace. Her brown hair fell in soft waves several inches past her shoulder, unless she twisted it into a knot with a hair tie or a clip or glossed it back into a ponytail that made her look Carlie's age. She had large blue eyes—an unclouded, wildflower blue. Brows that furrowed deeply when she was annoyed or concentrating, and arched in repose—which made me wonder what they did when she was surprised. Average height. Slim, but still curvy.

Her fingernails were short and unpolished. I never saw her chew them, so I decided she must keep them filed down intentionally, the better to conduct those symphonies in her head and allow her hands to simulate the instrumental movements. I wanted to put on earphones and plug into her and know what she was hearing when her fingers performed. I even grew curious about which instrument she played—as though I'd know the difference between a cello and a viola by ear.

There's this fallacy that if you're artistic, you're arty and creative in your approach to everything. True for some—like my mother—but not for all. When I was younger, people were confused that I didn't play an instrument or paint or write poetry. But I've only ever been artistic in one way. *Drawing*. That's it. Even my tattoos are the result of paper and pencil sketches transferred from my notebook to the tattoo artist's ink, injected under my skin.

After absorbing a mind-numbing chapter about sensor calibration for measurements lab, I returned my textbook to my backpack and pulled out my sketchpad. Fifteen minutes of Heller's class remained. My eyes strayed to Jackie Wallace, sitting several rows down, chin in hand. Without conscious intention, my hand began sketching her. The sweeping rudimentary lines were there before I knew what I was doing. I couldn't capture her moving fingers within the confines of a sheet of paper, so I caught her paying attention to the lecture—or seeming to.

"Those of you who aren't planning to major in economics might ask yourself, 'Why should I waste my time studying economics?'" Heller said. I sighed, knowing what came next. I knew his whole routine inside out. "Because when you're filing for unemployment, *at least you'll know why.*"

A few predictable groans rose from his captive audience. I admit that I held back an eye roll, stemming from the fact that I was now four semesters familiar with this particular spiel. But Jackie smiled, the corner tip of her mouth just visible from my spot in the back, along with the upward arch of her cheek.

So. She liked corny jokes.

And her boyfriend was one of the groaners.

· · · · · · · · · ·

My first tutoring session of the semester was this afternoon. Two weeks into any given semester, most students are still full of early-semester optimism, even if they're already falling behind. It was possible I'd only have a handful of students show today—or none.

My very first semester as Heller's tutor, only one person showed up on the first day—the roommate of someone I'd hooked up with two weeks before. I could barely recall the girl I'd spent a couple of hours with, but I recognized the roommate instantly, because there'd been an enormous bulletin board full of exhibitionistic selfies over her bed. They'd been . . . distracting. Like being watched by half-naked spectators. I'd found myself wondering—during the most awkward moment possible—what she did during Parents' Weekend. Tacked posters of the periodic elements and Albert Einstein over them?

So during my first tutoring session ever, I drew charts on a whiteboard while explaining the difference between a downward shift in demand and a decrease in demand to *one* student. One student who was oblivious to the fact that I'd seen her topless selfie gallery. I couldn't look her in the eye, or anywhere else, really, the whole hour, which was pretty damned awkward since she was the only other person in the room.

I had four students show today, all of them surprised that they were the only attendees out of such a huge class. None were Kennedy Moore or Jackie Wallace. I was relieved and disappointed—and I had no right to feel either of those things.

"This is my third semester tutoring for Dr. Heller," I said, facing them. Four pairs of eyes watched me raptly from their front row seats in the tiny classroom. "Last year, every person who attended supplemental sessions two to three times per week for the entire semester made an A or a B in the class."

Eyes widened, impressed. Clearly, I was a miracle worker.

Truth? Regular session attendees were usually the overachievers—students who only missed class for emergency surgery or when someone died. They did the assigned reading and the optional chapter quizzes. They turned in extra-credit assignments. Education was a priority, and most of them might have aced the class without me.

But the statistical data gave me job security, so I used it.

Every week, I allotted at least fifteen hours in class, in sessions, making up worksheets, and providing individual assistance, either on campus or through email. Those hours added up to a quarter of my tuition, paid. Being Heller's tutor wasn't as lucrative as Job One—parking enforcement officer for the campus PD, or Job Two—working the counter at the campus Starbucks, but it was way less stressful than either.

Well.

Until her.

chapter *Three*

LANDON

Dad didn't seem to notice I'd quit hockey. He didn't notice my detachment from friends or the collapse of my social life. He'd only arranged for a car to pick me up from school each day because I'd stopped to ask him how I was getting home just before exiting his car on my first day back.

His Ray-Bans hid his eyes, so I didn't have to witness the agony that scorched through them every single time he realized that Mom was gone, so she couldn't do a thing she'd always done. Things *someone* had to do in her place. Like pick me up from my private school, because home was a twenty-five minute drive or a Metro trip I'd never taken alone followed by a several-block walk.

In my mouth were the words, *I'll just take the Metro—I'm thirteen, I can do it*, when he answered, "I'll . . . call a car to take you home. You're dismissed at three o'clock?"

"Three thirty," I said, shouldering my backpack and stepping out, anger building. I felt myself fracturing down deep, straining to contain it.

Mornings were still cool, not yet cold enough to see your breath. Kids who'd already arrived were hanging out front, waiting for the first bell while others exited their parents' cars. No one was rushing inside. Heads swiveled, watching me. Parents, too, none of them pulling away from the curb. Everyone slowed—suspended, watching. I felt their eyes like dozens of tiny spotlights.

"Landon?"

I turned back to my father's voice, irrationally hoping he'd tell me to just get back in the car. That he'd take me back home. Take me to work with him. Anything but leave me here.

I didn't want to be here. I didn't want to do this.

"You have your house key?"

I nodded.

"I'll have a car here at three thirty. I'll be home early. Five thirty, latest." His jaw hardened. "Lock the door when you get home." *And check the windows.*

I nodded again and shut the passenger door. He looked at me through the glass, and again, the crazy wish that he wouldn't leave me here sprung up and grabbed me by the throat. He raised a hand and drove away.

So I'd never reminded him about hockey practice. I just stopped going.

When my coach finally called me, I told him I was quitting. He suggested that keeping previous routines in place would be good for me. Told me I could return at my pace, build back up. Said the team was ready to support me—that some of the guys had discussed having decals of Mom's initials added to our helmets or sewn onto the sleeves of our jerseys. I sat stonily on the other end of the line, waiting for him to realize that I wouldn't argue, but I also wouldn't go.

I don't know if Dad continued to pay or if they stopped billing him, and I didn't care.

• • • • • • • • • •

There was this girl I'd liked, before. (Everything now was either *before* or *after*.) Before-girl's name was Yesenia. I hadn't seen her since the last day of seventh grade, but we'd texted a couple of times over the summer and had been friends online, trading cryptic social media comments, which is sort of like flirting in semaphore. *Cool shot. Haha awesome. Pretty eyes.* This last was from her, one comment of a dozen on a pic Mom had taken of me on Grandpa's beach, standing in the surf at sunset.

Hers was the only comment that mattered. It was also the boldest thing either of us had ever said to each other.

I'd grown over the summer. A good thing, because Yesenia and I had been the same height in seventh grade, and there's this thing about girls and height—they want to wear heels and not be taller than the guy. I'd added three inches and had hopes for more. Dad was over six feet. Neither of my grandfathers was.

The only daughter of an ambassador from El Salvador, Yesenia was beautiful and dark, with short, silky black hair and huge brown eyes that watched me from across classrooms and lunch tables. She lived in a brownstone off Dupont Circle. I'd talked Mom into letting me ride the Metro to her place alone two weeks before, but hadn't yet built up the nerve to ask Yesenia if I could come over.

That second week of school, I managed to catch her without her mob of friends—a rare occurrence with thirteen-year-old girls. "Hey, do you wanna go see a movie Saturday?" I blurted the invitation and she blinked up at me, hopefully noticing those three inches. She was the tallest girl in our grade. Some guys had to look up to *her*. "With me?" I qualified when she didn't answer right away.

"Um . . ." She fidgeted with the books in her arms as my heart thudded out *dammit, dammit, dammit*, until she said, "I'm not really al-lowed to go out with boys yet."

Huh. My turn to fidget in response.

"But maybe . . . you could come over and watch a movie at my house?" She was hesitant—like she thought that maybe I'd turn her down.

I felt like I'd been dunked headfirst in cold water, yanked back out, and then kissed, but I just nodded, determined to play nonchalant. So I'd asked a girl out. No big deal. "Yeah, sure. I'll text you."

Her friends showed up at the end of the hall, summoning her and eyeing me curiously. "Hi, Landon," one of them said.

I returned the greeting with a smile and turned, hands in pockets, mouthing *yes, yes, YES* under my breath, as though I'd just fired a puck into the goal right past the goalie's padded knee. Saturday was only five days away.

Twenty-four hours later, my life had shifted into *after*.

LUCAS

"You. Are. An. *Asshole!*"

My lips pressed into a thin line, I struggled to contain the retort flashing across my brain: *Wow. There's one I've never heard.*

I continued filling out the parking ticket I was thankfully nearly finished recording.

I feel sorry for people whose meters run out before they get back to the car. I feel sorry for people parked in admittedly ambiguously labeled lots. I do *not* feel sorry for a student who parks directly under a FACULTY PARKING ONLY sign.

When she realized that her appearance and predictable insult hadn't motivated me to quit writing or even glance up, she tried a different tactic. "C'mon, *pleeease?* I was only in there for like ten minutes! I swear!"

Uh-huh.

I tore the ticket off and extended it toward her. She crossed her arms and glared at me. Shrugging, I pulled out an envelope, placed the ticket inside, and stuck the envelope under her windshield wiper.

As I turned to get back into the cart I drive lot-to-lot around campus, she yelled, "Son of a monkey-assed *whore!*"

That, on the other hand, is new. Well played, Ms. Baby Blue Mini Cooper.

Man, I wasn't sure they paid me enough to compensate for this type of abuse. I sure as hell wasn't doing it for the *prestige*. For this, I tucked my hair under a polyester-coated, navy hat that made the top of my head feel like it was on fire when I stood out in the sun too long on hot days, which described 70 percent of the year. I replaced my lip ring, its piercing thankfully several-years-healed, with a clear retainer for the duration of my shifts. I wore a uniform that was the direct opposite of anything else in my wardrobe.

Granted, these three things kept every student I've ever ticketed—even, in a couple cases, people I sat right next to in class—from recognizing me while I was in the process of ruining their days.

"Excuse me! Yoo-hoo!"

This is the sort of summons usually delivered by someone's grandma—but no, it was my thermodynamics professor from last spring. *Hell.* I pocketed the ticket pad, praying he wasn't Mr. Brand-New Mercedes, who I'd just ticketed for parking across two spaces at the back of the lot. I wouldn't have thought Dr. Aziz capable of being such an asshat—but people were weird behind the wheel of a car. Their personalities could morph from stable, sane citizens to road-raged dipshits.

"Yes, sir?" I answered, bracing.

"I need a jump!" He panted like he'd sprinted across a football field.

"Oh. Sure. Hop in. Where's your car?" I ignored the girl in the Mini Cooper, giving me the finger as she squealed by us.

Though he didn't comment, Dr. Aziz wasn't as inured to the gesture that was all too routine for me. Brows elevated, he climbed into the passenger seat and held on with both hands after fumbling for the non-existent seat belt. "Two rows over." He pointed. "The green Taurus."

I slowed to keep from flinging him out the cart's open side while making a U-turn at the end of the row, reflecting that my usual, less-approachable incarnation would've been way less likely to get flipped off in the middle of a parking lot. I was a walking target, patrolling the campus in this damned costume.

Once I got his car started, I removed the cables and dropped the hood. "Be sure to get that battery charged or replaced—this box provides a jump, not a charge." I knew my engineering professor didn't need this advice . . . but I assumed I was unrecognizable.

Wrong.

"Yes, yes, Mr. Maxfield, I think I am quite familiar with auto charging by this point." He laughed, still wheezing a bit. "This is a fortunate meeting, I think. I was mentally reviewing former students just this morning. I'll be contacting a handful of these, inviting them to apply for a research project that begins next semester. Our objective is the development of durable soft materials to replace those normally damaged by thermodynamic forces—such as those used in drug delivery and tissue engineering."

I knew all about Dr. Aziz's proposed research project—it had been animatedly discussed at last month's Tau Beta Pi meeting with the sort of enthusiasm that only a bunch of engineering honor society nerds can supply.

"You're a senior, I believe?"

My brows rose and I nodded, but I was too stunned to reply.

"Hmm. We're primarily interested in juniors, as they'll be around longer." He chuckled to himself before pursing his lips, watching me. "Nevertheless, the founding team of a project is critical, and I believe you could be an asset, if you're interested. The position would be reflected as a special projects course on your transcript, and we've received a grant, so we're able to provide a small stipend to those ultimately chosen."

Holy shit. I shook myself from my stupor. "I'm interested."

"Good, good. Email me tonight, and I'll forward the official application. I am obliged to inform applicants that spots on the team are not guaranteed. They'll be quite sought after, I imagine." He wasn't kidding. A few of my peers would seriously consider pushing me into traffic to secure one of those spots. "But . . ." He smiled conspiratorially. "I think you'd be a top candidate."

● ● ● ● ● ● ● ● ● ●

When Heller gave the class their first exam, I had a day off from attending. Instead of sleeping in like a normal college student, I'd stupidly signed up for an extra campus PD shift. It was like I no longer had any idea how to chill out and do nothing. Between paid jobs, volunteer jobs, and studying, I worked all the damned time.

The skies opened up around seven A.M., deluging the area with a surprise thunderstorm just in time to negate sunrise, so I bummed a ride with Heller instead of enduring a soggy, miserable drive to campus on my Sportster. After helping tote a box of books from his car to his office and agreeing on a time to leave for the day, I headed to the side exit.

The sun had emerged in the few minutes I'd been inside, granting a short reprieve from the rain, though trees and building overhangs still dripped fat drops onto the students trudging through puddles and hopping over miniature streams. Given the low, gray clouds gathering visibly overhead, I knew the sunburst would last five minutes tops, and hoped I could make it to the campus police building before the next downpour.

If the rain kept up—and all forecasts said that it would—I'd be stuck inside, answering phones and filing stacks of folders in the department's wall of file cabinets instead of issuing parking citations. Lieutenant Fairfield was *always* behind on filing. I was half convinced he never filed anything. He simply waited for rainy days and unloaded the mind-numbing task on me. Strangely, I'd rather brave irate students, staff, and faculty than be stuck inside all day.

And I won't see Jackie Wallace at all today.

I willed my brain to shut up, sliding my sunglasses on and holding the door open for a trio of girls who ignored me, continuing their conversation as though I was a servant or a robot, installed there for the express purpose of opening the door for them. *Damn this uniform.*

Then I saw her, splashing through pools of water in aqua galoshes covered in yellow daisy outlines. I stood like a statue, still holding the door ajar, even though she was yards away and hadn't noticed me—or anyone around her. I knew she'd be entering this door. She had an exam in econ in about one minute. There was no Kennedy Moore in sight.

Her book bag threatened to slide down her arm, and she hitched her shoulder higher while fumbling with an uncooperative umbrella that matched her galoshes. Her agitated body language and the fact that she'd never been late to class before—or arrived without her boyfriend—told me she was running behind this morning. Her umbrella refused to close. *"Dammit,"* she muttered, giving it a hard shake while pushing the retract button repeatedly.

It folded shut a moment before she looked up to see me holding the door.

Her hair was damp. She wore no makeup, but the tips of her lashes were spiky—she'd clearly been caught in the rain on the way from her dorm or car. The combination of her wet skin, her proximity, and the breath I took looking into her beautiful eyes nearly knocked me over. She smelled like honeysuckle—an aroma I knew well. My mother had encouraged a wall of it to vine over the tiny cottage in our backyard that she'd made into an art studio. Every summer, the trumpet-shaped blooms had infused the interior with their sweet scent, especially when she'd cranked the windows open. While Mom worked on projects for fall gallery showings, I sat across the scarred tabletop from her, sketching video game characters or bugs or the innards of an inoperative appliance Dad gave me permission to take apart.

An astonished smile broke across Jackie's face as she glanced up at me, replacing the scowl she'd given her wayward umbrella. "Thank you," she said, ducking through the open door.

"You're welcome," I replied, but she was already rushing away. Toward the class where I was the tutor. Toward the boyfriend who didn't deserve her.

I hadn't let myself want anything so impossible in a very long time.

chapter *Four*

LANDON

Hours after Dad brought me home from the hospital, he'd totally lost it, using a box cutter to rip out the bloodstained carpet and pad from the room, all the way to the structural floor. Without a mask over his eyes or nose, he'd switched on the sander and scoured the floor until the wood dipped like a bowl in the middle of the room. Sawdust wafted from the doorway like smoke, coating the room and everything in it, including my dad.

I sat in the hall with my back to the wall and my hands covering my ears, sick from the sound of his grief and rage, his hoarse tears and roars mixing with the deafening sander, all of it useless because none of it would bring her back. When the motor stopped, I crawled to the doorway and peeked inside. He knelt, crying and coughing, the hated stain fainter but still visible under the now-silent sander.

The day of her funeral, I woke to the sound of his footfalls in the hallway outside my door, trudging back and forth. My room was dark in the predawn, and I lay motionless, barely breathing, identifying the screech of hangers shoved together and the drag of drawers opened and shut before he tramped past my room and back again, over and over. An hour later, the door to their room snapped shut.

He'd moved into the small guest room downstairs. By unspoken agreement, neither of us entered their sealed and haunted bedroom after that.

· · · · · · · · · ·

Cindy stopped by a lot to check on Dad and me, bringing food or straightening up. Usually Charles came with her, or Cole—who said all the wrong things, even though they were the exact same things everyone else said.

"Sorry about your mom," he'd said last night as we sat side by side on my bed, game controllers in our hands.

I'd nodded, staring at the screen where we drag-raced down some famous street—I couldn't remember which one—mowing down trash bins, trees, other cars, and the occasional hapless animated pedestrian. I tried not to hit the people. Cole seemed to aim for them, especially if his little sister Carlie was around, because she freaked whenever he did it.

"You hit a *kid*! You just hit a *kid* on *purpose*!" she'd say when his car jumped the curb and ran over a skateboarder.

I forgave Cole for hitting the people deliberately, and for saying what everyone else said, because he was ten, and because he treated me the same as always. He was the only person I knew who did that.

Murmuring voices drew me from my room and down the stairs one Saturday morning. Cindy and Dad sat at the kitchen table, coffee mugs gripped between them. Their voices reverberated in the room and spilled into the hallway, as quiet as they were. I knew they were discussing me before I heard what they were saying.

"Ray, he needs counseling."

Cindy had always joked that she'd happily trade both her sisters for my mom, who was her "true" sister. Like a meddling aunt who'd known me my whole life, she'd always treated me like I was partly hers to raise.

For a long moment, Dad didn't answer, and then he said, "Landon is imaginative—you know that. He draws all the damned time. I don't think a few sketches are cause for a *shrink*—"

"Ray, I've watched your child, *her* child, since he first picked up a pencil. Of course I'm familiar with how he expresses himself artistically. But I'm telling you, this is . . . different. It's disturbing, violent—"

"What the hell do you expect?" he hissed, and it was her turn to go quiet. He sighed. "I'm sorry, Cin. But . . . we'll deal in our own way. We don't want to talk about it. When I think about that night—" His voice broke. "I won't make him talk about it."

I heard what he didn't say. That he didn't want to hear what I had to say about that night.

But he was right. I didn't want to talk about it.

"He's withdrawing, Ray. He barely speaks anymore." Her voice was choked with tears.

"He's *thirteen*. Reticence is normal for thirteen."

"If he was this way before, I'd agree. But he wasn't. He was happy and communicative. Watching him with Rose gave me hopes of having sons who'd still talk to me and laugh with me and kiss me good-bye when they become teenagers. This isn't normal behavior for *Landon*—thirteen or not."

My father sighed again. "His mother is dead. How can he ever be normal again?"

She sniffed, and I knew she'd begun crying softly.

"I can't discuss this anymore," he said. "I appreciate your help, and Charles's—but I just can't—"

"What if I find a therapist for him? What if I take him, and you don't have to be involved, until you want to—"

"*No*. Not . . . yet. Give him time."

"But—"

"Cindy." That was his *I'm done* voice. I was all too familiar. When I wanted something my parents didn't want me to have, Dad had always been the one to deliver the final no, and that was how he said it. *Landon*, and that scowl. No use arguing once I'd gotten that.

• • • • • • • • • •

Before I was born, the Maxfields and the Hellers began celebrating Thanksgiving together. They did it every year—through postdoc assignments on opposite coasts, Charles's acceptance of an assistant professor position at Georgetown, and my father's decision to take his PhD and work for the government instead of some university. After I came along, they kept the tradition, settling twenty minutes from each other in Arlington and Alexandria—both inside the Beltway.

This year was supposed to be our year to host. Instead, Dad and I drove to their house, each silent, hating and enduring the stupid Christmas carols on the radio. Neither of us moved to change the station.

My mother had loved holidays—all of them. For her, none were spoiled by too much hype or commercialism. She made heart-shaped cookies in February, oohed and aahed over fireworks in July, and sang along the moment Christmas carols began playing, no matter how many weeks it was until December 25th. I would never hear her voice again. My stomach heaved and my jaw clamped tight, my body launching a protest against the meal we were about to have. Without her.

I sat in the front seat with a store-bought pumpkin pie on my lap and a can of whipped cream in a bag at my feet. We'd burned the edges of the crust, and Dad had scraped off the blackened parts, leaving the pie looking as though squirrels had broken into the house and sampled it. It had to be the most half-assed contribution the Maxfields had ever made to Thanksgiving dinner.

I was smart enough to keep this thought to myself.

The meal was bearable, but grim and pretty quiet until Caleb—who was almost four and still considered silverware optional—stuck his finger through the whipped cream and pumpkin filling and then sucked it off.

"Caleb—*fork*," Cindy said gently, for the fourth or fifth time since we'd begun eating. She rolled her eyes when Cole copied him. "*Cole,*" she said, less gently. I couldn't help smiling when both brothers stuck their pie-coated fingers in their mouths. Carlie snorted a laugh.

"Wha?" Cole asked his mother, faking innocence, unapologetically sucking whipped cream from his finger.

Giggling, Caleb copied his older brother. "Yuh—wha?" Then, for some inexplicable reason, he glanced around the table, popped his sticky finger from his mouth, and lisped, "Where's Wose?" Everyone froze, and his eyes filled with tears. "Where's *Wose*?" he wailed, as though he'd just figured out that when your parents tell you someone has gone to heaven, that person is never, ever coming back.

All the food in my traitorous stomach surged up at once. I leaped from my chair and ran to the guest bathroom, the memory of that night condemning me. The sounds I would never forget. The futile screams I'd shouted until I could do no more than rasp her name, until the tears stopped because I literally couldn't produce them. The useless son I'd been when she needed me.

I puked up everything I'd eaten, gagging on sobs when nothing was left in my stomach.

A month later, Dad quit his job, sold our house, and moved us to the Gulf Coast—to my grandfather's house—the last place he'd ever intended to live again.

LUCAS

I had dinner with the Hellers once a week or so—whenever Charles barbequed or Cindy made a huge pan of lasagna. The Hellers always tried to make me feel like I belonged to them, like I was one of them. I could pretend, for the space of one or two hours, that I was their son, their big brother.

Then I returned to reality, where I had no connection to anyone, except a man who lived hundreds of miles away and couldn't look me in the eye because I was a reminder of the night he lost the only person he ever loved.

I knew how to cook, but I'd never moved beyond a basic range of meals, most of which I learned from my grandfather. He'd been a simple man with simple tastes, and for a time, I wanted nothing more than to be like him.

During meals with the Hellers, I steeled myself for the inevitable semi-veiled queries, especially from Cindy—lines of subtle interrogation her daughter had recently taken up. I wondered if Carlie had been deployed last month to find out if I was secretly gay or just perpetually girlfriendless. She was her mother's daughter—interfering where she believed she was needed, and often too uncomfortably close to target.

I couldn't be upset with either of them for trying to draw me out, but there was usually little, if anything, to tell. I went to school and I worked. Sometimes, I went downtown to hear a local band play. I attended monthly Tau Beta Pi meetings. I studied and worked some more.

I sure as hell wasn't going to bring up Jackie Wallace, Charles's student—and mine—who'd progressed from capturing my attention during class to stealing into my conscious and unconscious fantasies.

This morning, my alarm began blaring in the middle of a dream about her. A vivid, detailed, solidly unethical dream.

She had no idea who I was, but that fact didn't stop my mind from imagining that she did. It didn't stop the sweeping disappointment when I woke fully and remembered what was real—and what wasn't.

Purposefully arriving late to econ, I slid into my seat, pulled out my programming text, and forced myself to read (and reread and reread) a section about transfer functions so I couldn't watch her tuck a strand of hair behind her ear or stroke her fingers across her thigh in a measurable rhythm that progressively drove me crazy.

Definitely nothing going on in my life that would make it to dinnertime conversation.

I arrived to find that I wasn't on the agenda, which was all good until I knew why. Carlie, who'd always been a wisp of a girl despite her hearty appetite, sat poking at her food with her fork and eating almost nothing. Cindy always made a small, separate dish of meatless lasagna in deference to her daughter's refusal to eat "anything with a face." It was Carlie's favorite meal, but she wasn't eating.

A worried glance passed between her parents, and I wondered what the hell was going on.

"How did volleyball practice go, Carlie? Any more talk of moving up to varsity?" Heller asked in an *everything is normal* voice.

Carlie's eyes filled with tears. "I'm done," she said, shoving half-heartedly at her barely touched dinner and rushing away. Her bedroom door slammed shut, but the thin lumber couldn't block the sound of her sobs.

"I'd like to kick that punk's ass," her father growled.

Caleb's eyes widened. He was constantly encouraged not to say *ass*.

"I understand the sentiment, believe me, but what would that solve?" Cindy set her plate on the granite counter and turned toward the staircase leading to her daughter's room.

"It would make me feel a damn sight better," Heller muttered.

Carlie's pitiful wails grew louder when Cindy opened the door upstairs, and all three of us winced.

"A breakup?" I guessed. Obviously, this wasn't about volleyball. I hadn't even known she was dating anyone, unless— "The homecoming guy?"

He nodded. "Ditched her for one of her friends, no less. Two-for-one heartbreak."

That smug little asshole. I'd only met him once—when he arrived to pick Carlie up for the dance. Sliding an orchid onto her wrist and posing for pics, he'd seemed cocky next to her wide-eyed artlessness, inevitably reminding me of Kennedy Moore . . . which made me think of Jackie Wallace. *Dammit.*

"Brutal," Caleb observed, his mouth full of noodles. "I'll help with the ass kicking, Dad. We can give him a two-for-one *ball* breaking."

Heller harrumphed. "Don't let your mother hear you say that, or we'll both get our asses kicked." His words admonished gently, but he offered a closed fist in solidarity, and Caleb snickered and bumped it.

I'd always defined jealousy as coveting what someone else has. Like me, wanting Kennedy Moore's girlfriend. There was only one of her. If she was mine, she wouldn't be his.

So I didn't know what to call how it felt to watch Charles with his sons, or with Carlie. A form of jealousy, I guess. But they all shared him as a father, and they shared their mother, too. If I'd been born a Heller kid, none of them would have lost a parent for it.

They'd never begrudged me my relationship with their parents, and I was more grateful for that than I could express. Yet as often as we all pretended I was part of their family, Cindy wasn't my mother, and Charles wasn't my father. Neither of them could take the place of what I no longer had, as much as they strove to fill those empty spaces.

Upstairs, the sobbing had calmed. Barely audible sniffles were all we could hear between Cindy's empathetic murmurs and her daughter's muffled replies. Caleb chortled at another of Charles's opinions concerning Carlie's ex—who would be wise to never show his face near the Heller men again if he wanted to keep his nuts intact.

Carrying my plate to the sink, I crushed the envy I wasn't entitled to feel with the only weapon on hand—my shame.

You're the man of the house while I'm gone. Take care of your mother.

• • • • • • • • • •

I've never faulted anyone for wanting to be part of a group. Just because I shied away from frats and other campus organizations—exception: those with career geek networking potential—didn't mean other people felt the same, and that was fine.

Still, some people on this campus couldn't seem to dress themselves in the morning without their Greek affiliation stitched or glued onto some article of clothing. The girl speaking with Kennedy Moore before class was one of these. She was doll pretty—but every time I'd seen her, she wore a T-shirt, pants, shorts, jacket, or *shoes* with the letters of her sorority prominently displayed. Sure enough, today was a lettered baseball cap with a sleek ponytail pulled through the back.

She leaned in to say something to him, laying a hand on his forearm, and he cast a glance over nearby socializing classmates. His gaze glided right past me—and everyone else, so I assumed he was looking for Jackie. He caught sight of her just after I did. Back to him, she was laughing with a friend across the hall, out of earshot.

He removed ZTA girl's hand from his arm but held on to it a degree past appropriate. I'd seen this girl talking to Jackie before. Maybe they weren't close friends—but she had to know that what she was doing was out of line. As I came closer, their conversation became audible.

"Come on, Ivy," Moore said, glancing toward Jackie again, "you know I have a girlfriend." There was a note of regret in his voice. *Regret*. Son of a *bitch*.

The girl flicked a sidelong glance toward Jackie and back, too, before batting her eyes at him. "I wish you didn't."

As little as I thought of the guy and as much as I didn't believe he was worthy of the girl I couldn't get out of my head, I hoped he'd surprise me and say something to explicitly dismiss this girl's ill-mannered *wish*.

But no. His eyes grazing over her head to toe, he murmured, "You know you're too sweet for me. I can be kind of a dick."

Her eyes sparked. "Mmm. Promise?"

I turned sharply into the classroom and dropped my backpack on the floor. *Not my business*. I clenched and unclenched fists that wanted to pummel him. How could that lucky bastard have a girl like Jackie committed to him and *see* anyone else, let alone entertain that kind of suggestion?

Five minutes later, he and Jackie entered the classroom together, his hand at her lower back as they moved down the steps toward their seats. Ivy slid into her chair a dozen seats away and a row up from them, her gaze lingering on Moore. When Jackie twisted to grab her textbook, he turned to smile over his shoulder. Ivy's expression altered to a quick, saccharine smile when their eyes connected.

I returned my stare to the sketchbook on the desktop in front of me, pulling the pencil from behind my ear. Shading the illustration of a guy I'd seen skateboarding up the drag this morning, I made every effort to convince myself of the thing I knew to be true: Jackie Wallace's heart was not mine to defend or protect against treacherous friends or disloyal boyfriends. Nothing about her, in fact, was my business.

I flipped a few pages back to the second drawing I'd allowed myself to do of her, during my rainy-day filing shift. Hearing her soft *thank you* in my head all morning, recalling her smile, I hadn't been able to banish her face from my brain until I consigned her to paper. Even then, I couldn't forget her bright blue gaze, so close, or the friendly expression I seldom got from any student when wearing that goddamned uniform.

I turned back to the unfinished skateboarder, but minutes later, made the mistake of glancing down the slope of desks to where she sat three days a week, unaware that I watched her. Unaware of my continual internal battle not to. Unaware of me.

Her fingers stroked metrically across the side of her leg—one-two-three, one-two-three—and I imagined that if I was the one sitting next to her, I'd open my palm and let her trace the music she heard onto my skin.

Then Moore reached over and placed his hand over hers, stilling her. *Stop,* he mouthed. *Sorry,* she mouthed back, self-conscious and curling her hand into her lap.

My teeth clamped together and I concentrated on breathing slowly through my nose. *Stupid, stupid bastard.* It was good I had a sparring session scheduled at the dojang tonight. I needed to hit something. Hard.

chapter *Five*

LANDON

The fact that my grandfather and my dad didn't get each other was weird, because they were like the same person born thirty years apart. I'd never noticed that before we moved in with Grandpa. Maybe because Dad had done everything he could to escape who he'd been, or who he might have been. He'd grown up here, in this house, on this beach, but he didn't have my grandfather's drawl, or any accent at all, really. Like he'd worked at obliterating it.

Grandpa quit school at fourteen to work the fishing boat with his father, but my father completed high school, left home for college at eighteen, and hadn't quit until he had a PhD in economics. People in town seemed to know Dad, but he hadn't lived here for over twenty years, and whenever we'd visited, he hadn't hung out with any of them. Those people kept their distance now and he kept his, spending his days on the boat with Grandpa. I imagined them out there, all day, saying nothing to each other, and I wondered if that was how Dad and I would be. If it was how we already were.

He'd given away his nice suits before we moved—all but one. We left our furniture and electronics, dishes, cookware, and his library of finance and econ and accounting books. I brought most of my clothes, my video games, some books, and all my sketchpads—anything I wanted that was mine—but only what would fit into the car. Cindy boxed all the scrapbooks and framed photos, and wrapped Mom's paintings with brown paper and lots of packing tape. She and Charles took some of them to their house.

Whenever we'd visited Grandpa before, it had been summer. I'd slept on a sleeping bag on the screened porch, or on the shabby, stale-smelling sofa in his living room—which was actually the only room in the house besides the kitchen, two bedrooms, and a bathroom. I didn't really think about where I would sleep until we got there, two days before Christmas.

A three-foot-tall, fake Christmas tree sat on a rickety table in a corner window, looking as pathetic and unfestive as possible. Non-blinking, multicolored bulbs were affixed to it. The only ornaments were a few actual candy canes, still in their cellophane wrappers, hooked over branches, a dozen shiny silver glitter-coated bells, and eight felt-enclosed school photos of me, from kindergarten through seventh grade.

There was no star. No angel. Nothing on the top at all. No gifts beneath. Just the plastic stand, sitting bare on the wood.

Our trees had always been tall and fresh, chosen at a Christmas tree farm twenty miles out of the city. Mom and Dad always let me choose the tree, and then Dad would pay the tree farmer before cutting it down and strapping it to the roof of our car, where it would hang out over the windshield in front and poke out from the back like a roof-mounted rocket. Last year, the tree I chose was so tall that Dad had to climb to the top of the ladder to circle the top branches with twinkly white lights and add the star.

The tree skirt Mom used looked like a tapestry—trimmed in gold braid and embroidered with gold-threaded words like *Noel* and *Merry Christmas* and *Ho Ho Ho*. There were always lots of gifts on top of it, and most of them said *Landon*.

I'd been spoiled, and though I'd been somewhat aware of the fact, it didn't seem to matter, because every kid I knew was the same.

Grandpa grabbed a suitcase from my hand and turned to walk toward the kitchen. That was the moment I wondered where my room would be.

He opened the door to the pantry. Only, it wasn't the pantry anymore. The lower shelves had been removed, and a twin mattress and frame was somehow, impossibly, crammed wall-to-wall inside. From the ceiling, an overhead light hung on a chain—a three-bulb type of light usually found over a kitchen table. I recognized that it had, in fact, hung over the kitchen table the last time I'd been here, months before. The world's most compact, narrow chest stood crammed into the entry corner. I had to shut the pantry door to open any of the drawers. There was no window.

I had become Harry Potter. Except I was thirteen and not magic, and my destiny, whatever it was, held no profound purpose.

"Spruce it up or not—whatever you'd like. It's just for sleepin' and holdin' your stuff. You aren't obliged to stay in here." People as old as Grandpa forgot a lot of things, obviously. If he'd have remembered being a teenager, he'd have known we live in our rooms.

Grandpa was commonsensical, Mom always said. "He's like your dad. They see the world in black and white."

"Why are they always mad at each other?" I asked.

"They aren't really mad—just in a disagreement about what's black and what's white. Problem is, they're fighting over something in between."

Dad believed Grandpa was disappointed in him for leaving, instead of staying and working on the boat. I wasn't so sure. Maybe Grandpa just wanted to be allowed to do what he wanted to do with *his* life, instead of being judged as not educated enough—not good enough.

"So they're fighting over the gray stuff?"

"Yes, but more like—the colors. Gray tones in black-and-white photos are the colored things in real life—the green grass, a pink scarf, a yellow rose. I think they sometimes don't understand how much falls in the middle. How much will never be black or white." She smiled. "Maybe they're artistically challenged. Like I'm math challenged. You know?"

I nodded. But I was comfortable with both, so I didn't really understand.

• • • • • • • • • •

Lying on my new bed, I stared up at the three faux-flame bulbs of the only light fixture in my microscopic room. The switch was on a cord that hung down the wall by the door. The fixture and arms were a sort of oxidized brass, but so corroded that I couldn't tell what it was supposed to look like. Maybe the metal had been shiny once—like fifty years ago. Probably, brass wasn't made to be this near the ocean and never polished.

I stretched my arms out to either side and touched the walls, then reached behind me and touched the third wall. The fourth wall was mostly the pantry door, with a tiny bit of wallboard around and above it.

Going up on my knees, I groped along one of the shallow shelves Grandpa had left attached to the wall and grabbed my iPod from its new home next to a stack of my sketchbooks. A few months ago, these shelves held canned goods and preserves and boxes of cereal and macaroni and cheese. There had been a basket of potatoes by the door that Grandpa called tubers, and a basket of onions next to it that I could still smell even though they'd been moved somewhere else—to a drawer in the kitchen, I guessed.

I shoved my earbuds in and dialed to a playlist of a new band I'd just discovered before we left Alexandria. They'd been local, getting some play on the college stations. I was thinking I might go see them, live. Now, unless they got really famous and started touring, I'd never see

them. Even if they started touring, they'd never come here. No one came here.

I wasn't sure what happened to the boxes of ornaments and decorations Mom dragged from the basement closet every year—the strands of lights, twistable green garland, velvet stockings, and the advent calendar with its tiny hinged windows.

I hadn't expected any gifts, but Grandpa gave me a pearl-handled pocketknife with a blade longer than my middle finger. It looked old, but well maintained and wicked sharp. Dad, having failed to remember to buy me a gift on a major holiday, handed me a few bills, and I stuffed them into my wallet without looking at them. "Thanks," I said to each of them, and then Grandpa pulled an ancient waffle iron from a low cabinet and a box of waffle mix and plastic jug of maple syrup from a high cabinet.

First Christmas without Mom, over.

. . . .

I'd grown a bit more since summer but hadn't been shopping for new clothes. I hadn't gotten a haircut. Honestly, I sort of forgot about how I looked until the first day I had to go to a new school.

In this town, there was one elementary school, one junior high, and one high school, all housed at the same address. Sort of like my private school back home—or what used to be home. Most of the kids here had known each other most if not all their lives, just like we had. Newcomers were mistrusted until they made friends or became outcasts. I knew this, but even so, I didn't think about how it would apply to me, until it did.

My T-shirts still fit okay, but my jeans didn't. My shoes squeezed my toes. I'd outgrown my North Face jacket, and the sleeves of my hoodies were all too short. I tugged them down my arms until the knit cuffs stretched out like too-wide mouths and stayed that way.

I wore my wide-banded watch and my rubber wristbands every day, relieved they weren't banned here, because my teachers quickly decided that I was a delinquent. They wouldn't have bent any rules for the introverted and possibly unstable new kid with ill-fitting clothes, too-long hair, and no desire to participate in class.

The other kids mostly agreed with the teachers.

In class, I took whatever seat the teacher pointed me to and did as little as possible. In the halls, I kept close to the walls of lockers, eyes on the floor, ignoring any insults or "accidental" shoves. Sometimes I imagined myself reacting. I remembered the scuffles and shoving matches we'd had on the ice—the rush of putting an opponent face-first into the acrylic wall when he'd injured a teammate or talked a little too much trash. No skates or glassy ice beneath my feet, I could have smashed noses and popped shoulders from joints before most of these guys knew what hit them.

But then they'd know I gave a crap what they did to me. So I didn't bother.

At lunch, I was sentenced to the outcast table with a couple of guys from my grade, Rick and Boyce, and a seventh-grade girl, Pearl, who slumped into her seat and read while hiding behind a head full of scraggly, dark hair and glasses. None of them were inclined to talk to me, but they didn't toss bits of food or hateful comments, either, so I ate my lunch, as silent as I was the rest of every day, and then I pulled out my sketchpad and hunched over it. I'd learned to keep my backpack with me all day. Lockers weren't secure, even though everyone was warned to guard their combinations. The supposedly confidential codes of those built-in locks had long since spread through the student body.

On my fourteenth birthday, I'd endured two weeks at a new school, and I had four months to go. Next fall, I'd move up to the high school. I had no delusions that it would be an improvement. Sometimes I stood on the weathered planks of Grandpa's back porch and stared out at the water, wondering how long it would take to drown, and what it would feel like.

Like Christmas, I woke certain of no gifts. I wasn't sure Dad or Grandpa would even remember, and I sure as hell wasn't going to remind them.

Pulling the door to my pantry room open, the smell of frying pork and cinnamon greeted me. Most mornings, Dad and Grandpa were already gone when I got up. I'd emerge from my cocoon, get ready in the one bathroom we all shared, and walk to school. January was chilly here, but nothing like what I was used to. Grandpa laughed when I asked if it ever snowed. "Once in a blue moon," he said. "Don't hold your breath or blink."

I missed the seasonal changes and the blanketing white from the window, but I wouldn't miss trudging through it when the new wore off, or the bite of the wind slicing through my clothes and making my eyes water to keep my eyeballs from freezing over.

Dad was gone, but Grandpa was in the kitchen, sliding sausage links and French toast onto two plates. I usually ate cold cereal or microwaved a packet of oatmeal, so I didn't waste time beyond mumbling a barely awake *thanks* before grabbing a fork and digging in.

"Thought we'd head over to the Thrifty Sense today," he said, and I glanced up, mouth full of toast and syrup. "You're lookin' like a scarecrow in them short pants. Unless that's some sorta new fashion with your demographic. I'm not exactly up on all the trends." He plunked his plate across from mine and angled a brow, waiting.

I shook my head in answer while confirming what day it was in my mind. Thursday. "But, school?"

He waved a hand. "Bah. They can do without you for a day." *They could do without me every day.* "I'm gonna call you in sick. We got some birthday shoppin' to do." We shoveled a few bites in silence before he added, "Don't suppose you'd go for a birthday haircut?"

I shook my head again, fighting the smile that pulled at the edge of my mouth.

He huffed a long-suffering sigh. "Thought as much." Patting a hand over his short, silver bristles, he added, "If I had it, I guess I'd flaunt it, too."

I came home with several pairs of worn jeans and pants, two pairs of grungy sneakers and battered-to-hell western boots, and a faded black hoodie. Nothing cost more than five bucks. Everything fit.

Dad had come and gone while we were out, leaving a small case on my bed containing a dozen good quality charcoal pencils in different degrees of hardness, two erasers, a sanding block, and a sharpener. I recognized the case; it had belonged to Mom. Under it was a new sketchpad with finely perforated pages, the type Mom gave me for drawings I wanted to remove from the pad and display.

I pulled my tattered sketchbook from my backpack and opened it to a drawing of a seagull sitting on the hull of Grandpa's boat. I spent the rest of my birthday testing the pencils, recreating the simple sketch and shading it until the seagull looked a little sinister—more like Edgar Allan Poe's raven from a poem we'd read in English last fall, my first week back.

The raven had tormented a guy who was going crazy over the death of someone he loved. Everyone was supposed to write a short essay analyzing the poem, but my teacher, staring at a point right between my eyes, gave me permission to choose something else, though I hadn't asked to be excused from the assignment.

I chose an Emily Dickinson poem about the balance life keeps between bad things and good. I'd had thirteen years of good. I wondered if I would survive the thirteen bad required to pay for them.

LUCAS

A week or two into any given semester, overall class attendance falls off, especially in large intro courses like history or economics. This semester was no different. Unless there was a scheduled quiz or exam, the classroom exhibited an ever-changing pattern of empty seats. But Jackie, and her boyfriend, I admitted grudgingly, didn't cut class. Not once in the first eight weeks.

Which made her first disappearance noteworthy, and the second—the very next class period—significant.

During a homework break, I checked Kennedy Moore's social media status, which now stated: *single*. Jackie's profile no longer existed—or she'd temporarily deactivated it.

Holy shit. *They'd broken up.*

I felt like a complete dick for the jolt of straight-up joy that gave me, but the guilt didn't prevent me from hypothesizing one more step: she'd stopped coming to class. Maybe she was planning to drop economics . . . at which point she'd no longer be a student in the class I tutored.

By her third absence, Moore was openly flirting with the girls who'd been fawning over him the last several weeks. The following week, Jackie missed the midterm. I waited for an updated status to come through the system, telling me she'd officially dropped the course, but it never did. If she forgot to officially drop by the end of the month, she'd get an F at the end of the semester.

I knew damned well she wasn't my responsibility or my concern . . . but I didn't want her to fail a class, in addition to whatever that douchebag had done to her by ending their three-year relationship. But after more than a week of scanning and dismissing every girl on campus remotely resembling Jackie Wallace, I started to believe I'd never see her again.

BREAKABLE

· · · · · · · · · ·

Francis gave me a *How'd that get there?* look as I lifted his butt off my buzzing phone.

It was Joseph, one of the full-time maintenance technicians at the university who scored me occasional extra income doing odd jobs on campus—usually legit contract labor, sometimes under-the-table cash. I wasn't choosy; I'd take either. "Hey, man."

"Duuuude . . . you busy tonight?" *Stoned.*

I shook my head. Joseph was fond of his recreational pharmaceuticals, especially at the end of a crap week of dealing with some of the more condescending academics, harried admins, or bosses on power trips of their own.

"Just studying. What's up?"

Francis took advantage of my distraction, plopping his fluffy, twenty-pound body on top of my textbook and half my class notes. I shoved at him halfheartedly and he swiped my pen off the sofa in retaliation.

"On a Friday night? Dude, you have got to *stop* that shit." This was a frequent assertion of Joseph's. He knew I wasn't going to change—he just felt like he had to restate his objection from time to time. "When are you going to *live* a little?"

"Soon as I graduate, man," I promised. "Soon as I graduate."

Sighing heavily, he turned to the purpose of his call. "I've got a little . . . proposition for you."

If I had a best friend, Joseph was probably it. The weirdest thing about our friendship was the fact that we had only two things in common. First, our nearly identical tastes in music, and second, an affinity for compartmentalizing our lives, something we did with equal compulsion.

After spotting me alone at several shows last spring, he'd walked up and stuck his hand out. "Hey, man—Joseph Dill. Don't you work on campus?"

"Yeah." While we shook hands, I tried to place him. He wasn't an engineering classmate, but he seemed a little young to be a professor. One of the slightly older students from one of Heller's classes, maybe?

"Campus cop, right?" His tone wasn't contemptuous, but it wasn't complimentary, either.

I cursed that job for the millionth time, for all that those ten hours per week paid enough to cover nearly half my tuition. "Oh, uh—not really," I said. "I just write parking tickets. It's a work-study position. Still have to wear the dumbass uniform, though."

"Ah," he nodded, sizing me up. "So . . . you're a student."

Though we inhabit the same small realm, maintenance and groundskeeping personnel don't generally interact with students. He gestured to himself after the merest pause, stepping across that invisible border. "Building maintenance." He smiled. "Thought I'd buy you a beer and ask what are a couple hot guys like us doing going to concerts alone?"

I smiled, but it abruptly occurred to me that Joseph might be interested in more than a conversation, because my gaydar was blaring.

"You're legal, right?" he asked.

"Uh, yeah . . ." Raising my red-banded wrist, I told myself this would be no different than turning down a girl when I wasn't interested or in the mood—something I'd done often enough the previous three years.

"Cool." After paying for two beers, he handed me one and clinked the necks before taking a long swallow.

I thanked him guardedly, not wanting to shoot him down before he asked a question.

He picked at his bottle's label, finally coming to some conclusion. "So, my boyfriend is a musical theatre guy. And fuck if I wouldn't rather be chased by starving zombies than be forced to endure *Rent* ever again. He has no problem getting a friend to go to that shit with him, thank Christ. I don't have the same luck with my musical tastes in our circle of friends, ya know?" He eyed me then, waiting for either confirmation or a prejudiced response.

Relieved, I smiled at the thought of this guy, who looked as if he'd be more at ease in a biker bar than a Broadway show. On the heels of that thought, a buried memory pushed to the surface—my father, standing awkwardly next to Mom at one of her gallery showings, clutching a fluted glass of champagne. Dad was a sports-watching scotch/rocks guy, not an art enthusiast. But he loved and supported my mother.

"I don't really *know*, but I can *imagine*," I said.

Joseph's mouth pulled into a half-smile, and we'd been friends since then.

"Okay," I said now. "Proposition away."

"You, uh, have experience fixing AC systems, right?"

"Yeah?" I'd worked for Hendrickson Electric & AC my last year of high school, assisting old Mr. H on hundreds of maintenance calls and repairs—but I'd never been in charge of diagnosing a disorder. After a year of working with him, he joked that I'd learned just enough to be dangerous, which summed up my level of expertise perfectly.

"Here's the thing. I just got an after-hours call to fix the AC at one of the frat houses. And dude, I totally forgot I was on call this weekend . . . and I am *baked*."

I smirked. "You don't say."

"Yeah . . . There is no way I should be operating heavy machinery. Like. My truck."

"That's undoubtedly true."

"So I was thinking *you* could go do the job, and I'll pay you—I get overtime for this shit. That way, I don't get caught stoned on the job, you make some extra cash, everybody's happy."

Going to a frat house to identify and repair an issue with a major appliance that I might not know enough to fix wasn't exactly an upgrade from sitting alone in my apartment. "Er. I don't have the tools and equipment—"

"Come over, take my truck—it has everything you need in the box. Those dumbasses won't ask you for ID or anything. They just want their AC fixed. Why the emergency, I don't know. It's like seventy-five degrees out. Probably a party or something."

I sighed. I didn't want Joseph driving high or getting his ass fired showing up to make a campus repair while high and paranoid. Plus I could always use extra cash. "Okay, man. When?"

"Uh. Now?"

The subterfuge included wearing one of Joseph's official maintenance staff shirts—his name stitched in navy blue script into the white rectangle on the left side of my chest.

"They probably need Freon or a wiring repair." He patted my shoulder and dropped the keys to his truck into my hand. "Call me if you get stumped. I'm stoned, not comatose."

He was right about everything—the guys were gearing up for a party, and no one blinked an eye at me showing up in one of his shirts. Some guy answered the door and showed me that adjusting the thermostat didn't change the temperature in the house. Luckily, Joseph was also correct about it being a simple wiring issue. The unit was close to twenty years old and would have to be replaced soon—but not yet.

"Oh, man—*sweet*." D.J., the frat's VP, threw his head back and closed his eyes, exhaling a relieved breath. "We blew a wad on this party. It's supposed to be nice tomorrow, but you never know around here."

"True." I loaded the tools into the box.

"Thanks for coming out, Joseph." It took me a beat longer than it should have to realize he was speaking to *me*.

"Oh, sure thing."

At the door, he offered a folded twenty.

I waved it off. "No problem, man. All part of the job." The real Joseph was paying me fifty bucks for doing an hour's worth of work, and I was apprehensive enough doing this at all.

D.J.'s brows drew together briefly, probably unused to a blue-collar worker turning down an offered tip. "Okay, well—if you're free tomorrow night, we're having this Halloween party."

No shit, I thought. The whole house was decked out with imitation cobwebs and black lights and all the furniture had been pushed to the walls, freeing space for dancing or socializing in the center of the main room.

"It's technically for students, but you're obviously not old, and this one's not Greek-exclusive, so stop by if you're open."

With effort, I kept from smirking. "Yeah, sure. Thanks . . ." *But no thanks.*

Then I looked up and saw Kennedy Moore across the room, talking to another guy. That's when it hit me—this was his frat. Jackie might be at this party, even if they were broken up.

Well, damn. Guess I was going to a frat party.

· · · · · · · · · ·

I'd spotted Jackie the moment she walked through the door. Even with the dark and the crush of bodies, I never lost sight of her in the crowd for long. She was dressed in red. Shiny, sparkly red. Perched on top of her head was a headband sporting two pointy red horns. A thin, forked tail was affixed to the back of her skirt, and it swayed behind her as she walked or danced.

Her legs were smooth and bare, and seemed longer than usual. Geometry suggested that her short skirt and impossibly high red heels were responsible for that effect, but no amount of math could lessen my visceral reaction to seeing her again—especially in such a mind-blowingly hot costume. That outfit on this girl was riveting to more guys than just me, though—as proven by how many asked her to dance. She either didn't know or didn't care, because nine times out of ten, she shook her head *no*.

She and her ex—and I was sure, now, that this was the case—remained apart as though they were polarized. He held court on one side of the room, and she made noticeable efforts to ignore him from the other.

I devised and discarded two dozen opening lines.

Hey, I've been watching you in econ class, which—I couldn't help but notice—you stopped attending a couple of weeks ago. I hope you're planning to drop, because then I won't be violating campus not to mention personal ethics when I ask you out. Brilliant. And not at all creepy.

I think red just became my favorite color. Lame.

I can tell you the square root of any number in ten seconds. So, what's your number? Ugh.

I've never wanted to go to hell so bad. No.

Is it hot in here, or is it just you? Jesus Christ, *no*.

A couple on the dance floor were amusing everyone with an over-done drunk twerking demo—the only time I'd seen Jackie smile in the hour or so I'd been watching her. My view of her was blocked when a girl in cat ears and penciled-on whiskers stopped right in front of me, peering over the rim of her cup. When I raised an eyebrow, she said, "Aren't you in my econ class?"

One of the twerkers bumped into her, sloshing her drink onto her face. She lurched forward and I grabbed her arm to keep her from going straight to the floor. Turning, she shrieked, "Back off, *skank*," to the twerking girl, though it was the guy who'd bumped her.

When she turned back to me, the ugly sneer dissipated. She smiled prettily, like the past ten seconds hadn't happened. Scary.

"What'd I just say?" She sidled closer and I dropped her arm. "Oh, yeah. Economics. With what's-his-name . . ." She snapped her fingers a couple of times, trying to remember, while I glanced over her head at Jackie, dancing with a guy wearing a long, dark cape. He laughed at something she said, showing off his white plastic fangs. There were at least a dozen vampires in attendance tonight.

"Mr. Keller?" Econ girl said.

"Dr. Heller," I supplied.

She smiled again. "Yeah, that's him." She poked me in the chest with a metallic silver fingernail. "You sit in the back row. Not paying attention. Tsk, tsk."

Wow. I have got to extricate myself from this conversation. "I'm actually the supplemental instructor for that class."

"The who-de-whaty?"

I looked down, pursing my lips. *Christ.* "The tutor."

"Ohhhh . . ." Then she told me her name, which I forgot immediately, and launched into a monologue of enmity concerning the girl who'd bumped her. I didn't know either of them, and I couldn't have cared less about their blood feud, which concerned either a guy or a pair of shoes—I couldn't determine which in my state of *I don't give a shit.*

When I visibly located Jackie again, she'd pulled her bag over her shoulder and was heading out the back door to the concrete lot shared by several of the Greek houses. I'd come to the party hoping to see her, though I had no business stalking her like this. It was just as well I hadn't asked her to dance or spoken to her. I could leave now, no harm done. Just follow her out the door and go home.

Except I'd squeezed my bike into a small space between a couple of cars out front. No reason for me to go out the *back* door.

Vampire guy had been watching the back door, too. He slung the cape over a chair and spat out the plastic fangs, shoving them into his front pocket. Exiting right behind Jackie, he didn't seem rushed, but he wasn't dawdling, either—like he had somewhere to be. Or someone to meet.

chapter Six

LANDON

The wooden block on the desk read *Mrs. Sally Ingram*——black lettering set into a polished brass plate. It sounded like a nice enough name, and she'd seemed nice from a distance during the mandatory orientation assembly last week. *Nice* was the first thing my high school principal seemed to be and wasn't.

I hunched into a hard vinyl-seated chair in front of her massive desk. The top was a solid slab of wood that seemed built for the specific purpose of preventing someone from lunging across it easily. I couldn't imagine how they even got a desk that size into this office. It must have come into the room in pieces, because it sure as hell couldn't have fit through the door.

Mrs. Ingram leafed through an open file, shifting pieces of paper like I wasn't sitting there, waiting to find out why I'd been called to the principal's office on my first day of high school. Her glasses sat at the end of her nose, the way Dad wore his when he was reading or updating the books——the only concession to his previous career I'd seen since we moved here eight months ago.

At first, there'd been arguments and accusations——my father spitting out criticisms concerning Grandpa's lack of business sense or planning or record keeping with the fishing enterprise that had supported him for decades . . . which was Grandpa's line of reasoning.

Finally, they'd come to some sort of agreement, and my father took over the financial aspects of the business. While entering numbers in the ledgers or transferring them to his laptop, Dad still mumbled the occasional cuss word or yanked his glasses off and pinched the bridge of his nose as if his frustration might trigger a nosebleed. But he'd ordered the "office"—which consisted of a cupboard crammed into the hallway between the living area and kitchen (which held log-books instead of dishes), and the built-in kitchen table . . . over which drooped a single lightbulb on a cord. The work space was a long way from Dad's office in Washington or his home office in Alexandria.

Mrs. Ingram cleared her throat and removed her glasses, staring at me. Her eyes were dark and close set. I would sketch her as a dragon—beady reptilian eyes sizing up her prey and fixing it to the ground, wordlessly taunting it to run. This was the first day of school. I couldn't have done anything to piss her off already. Not that I ever tried to piss anyone off. I just wanted to be left alone, and for the most part, I'd managed to make that so.

"Landon *Maxfield*." She said my last name like it was something slimy, and I couldn't help the defiance that forced my eyes to narrow. Maxfield was my grandfather's name, and I didn't like anyone insulting it. Leaning onto her elbows, she steepled her fingers. "I've heard about you, and I thought we should become acquainted, since you're in *my* house now."

I blinked. She'd *heard about* me—from who? And what did they say?

"Your inauspicious academic beginning in this exemplary school precedes you, you see." Her fingers tapped at the tips, like we were simply having a constructive first-day chat. "And I make it a habit, as the principal of this school, to take notice of all potential . . . deficien-cies, before these defects transmit themselves to the rest of the student body. A bit of preemptive damage control, if you will. Do you understand?" She gave me a mocking smile, lips pressed tight and barely turned at the ends.

I doubted she expected me to follow a single thing she'd just said. But her patronizing vocabulary was no match for my previous education or the well-read parents who'd raised me. I wished I hadn't followed what she'd said. I wished I didn't know what she thought. My heartbeat thumped in my ears, and I dug my fingernails into my palms to stop angry tears before they even gathered. Glassy eyes would make me look weak.

"You think . . . I'll contaminate the other students." My voice scraped its way out of my throat, betraying the emotion I'd intended to suppress, but she didn't seem to notice. She was too startled.

Her eyes widened, but somehow, that didn't counter the beadiness. She was the scariest woman I'd ever met. Her hands flattened on the desktop. "Well, let's not get ahead of ourselves. I'm merely making certain you understand the notion of *zero tolerance*, Mr. Maxfield." My back teeth ground against each other. She stood, so I did, too. I didn't want her staring down at me. "Simply follow my rules while you're in my house . . . or you'll be out on your butt, mister."

My first day of high school, and I'm being threatened with expulsion?

I decided not to give her any more information about what I could or couldn't follow. She was the type who shot first and asked questions later. If ever.

I nodded once, a jerk of my head, and she dismissed me.

It had been 339 days since my mother died.

It felt like years. It felt like hours.

LUCAS

I stood unmoving, eyes on the back doorway, while my conscience and an obsession I couldn't seem to bring under control began a throw-down battle in my head.

This might be my only chance to ever talk to Jackie Wallace. I'd not seen her—on campus or off—a single time since she quit coming to class.

But what the hell would I say to her?

And then there was the guy who'd followed her outside. She clearly knew him. Maybe they'd decided to meet up, away from prying eyes. Or he'd been waiting for a chance with her, too, and unlike me, he was taking it—instead of wasting time with pointless internal arguments.

Maybe she'd just decided to leave early, and so did he, with no relation between their actions.

Or maybe I was squandering valuable seconds doing nothing.

My inner adolescent was growing enraged at my reticence. *Put that rancid cup of crap down, follow her outside, and* say something—*anything, dammit.*

First thought—I could tell her I was the tutor in the class, and I noticed she'd missed a number of class days, including the midterm, but hadn't dropped. *Right after trailing her into a dark parking lot.* I'd be lucky if she didn't knee me in the balls first and ask questions later.

The last drop date *was* three days away, though. I could save her from an F on her transcript, if nothing else. Propelling my ass off the wall, I abandoned the supposed conversation I was having with the whiny semi-bombed chick in the middle of her rant.

Walking straight to the back door and out, I told myself that if Jackie Wallace and the meathead vampire were getting chatty—or worse—I would arc around to the front, get on my bike, and forget she ever existed.

Sure you will. All those meticulous details you've spent the past nine weeks analyzing and burning into your brain will just dissolve away. No big deal.

Shut up.

For a few seconds, I was afraid I'd missed her. There was a threat of storms overnight, and the wind blew the gathering cloud cover, deepening shadows and making illuminated areas infrequent and short-lived. I spotted her by her glowing cell phone. She was texting someone, winding through the cars and trucks at the far end of the lot. Her vampire friend was between the two of us, and he sure looked like he was shadowing her. He didn't call out to warn her, though, the jackwad. He was going to scare the shit out of her if he just popped up out of nowhere.

I took a deep breath, shuffled down the back steps, and started slowly in her direction, prepared to turn around on a dime.

Likelihood I was about to regret this entire night? Ninety-five percent.

On the very back row, she unlocked the door of a shiny dark truck. Interesting. I wouldn't have pictured her driving a pickup. Maybe a little sports car or a compact hatchback. Her friend came up behind her and they both moved into the space on the other side of the open door. I couldn't see either of them clearly, and I had *zero* desire to witness them tonsil-checking each other.

Time to turn around. Except—the fact that he'd never called out to her bugged me. At best, he thought scaring women in deserted parking lots was funny. At worst—

She screamed. Once, cut off abruptly.

I stopped dead. And then I ran.

I've rarely allowed my temper free rein in the past three or four years, because I know too well the potential consequences of doing so.

But when I saw his body on top of hers across the seat of her truck and heard her sobbing, begging him to stop, I lost it. No amount of self-restraint would have prevented the outcome—assuming I'd been inclined to calm myself.

I wasn't.

Grabbing two handfuls of his shirt, I yanked him from the truck. He was kinda drunk. The degree of drunk that makes idiots think, *I'm cool. I can drive—no problem.* Just enough to slur a word here or there. Just enough to render him ineffectual in a fight against anyone who knew what he was doing.

I knew what I was doing.

I was going to kill him and worry about the consequences later. This was not a hope or an opinion. This was a fact. He was a dead man.

My first two punches were, somehow, a total surprise to him. His head snapped back, as he stood there, baffled at how the predator had become the prey in the space of two heartbeats.

Fight me, asshole. Go ahead. Fucking fight me.

He swung a fist, finally, but missed my head by a good foot, losing his balance as a result. I hit him twice more, my arms warming up from the adrenaline pounding through my bloodstream. A streak of moonlight lit the scene black and white for a split second. Blood gushed from his nose, dark and gratifyingly abundant. *Bleed, asshole.*

He wiped at his mouth with his forearm, staring at the result. With a short roar, he ducked his head and bolted forward.

Uppercut with the right, just under his chin. Elbow to the head with the left. Openmouthed, he crashed against the truck, bouncing off—the alcohol making him too stupid to fall down or run. He flailed toward me and I grabbed his shoulders and provided a skull-jarring knee to the jaw.

He was lucky. I could have crushed his windpipe instead. He went down, arms flung over his head, knees pulling to his chest.

Get up. Get up. Get up. I started to lean down to jerk him back up and hit him again, but a soft sound broke through the haze of rage.

I glanced up and peered straight into the truck, where Jackie cowered against the far side door, chest rising and falling with short, shallow breaths.

She was a terrified, feral thing, recoiling from him. From me, perhaps. I knew it wasn't possible to feel the pace of her heartbeat, to smell her panic, but I swear I did both. My fists were covered in her attacker's blood. I wiped the back of my hands on my jeans, slowly, stepping carefully to the door—no sudden movements.

Her eyes widened, but she didn't move a muscle otherwise.

"You okay?" These were the first words I ever uttered to this girl I'd watched and sketched and lusted after and dreamed about. She didn't answer or nod. Shock—she was going into shock.

Very slowly, I drew my phone from my pocket. "I'm going to call nine-one-one." Still no response. Before dialing, I asked if she needed medical assistance or just the police. I didn't know what he'd done to her in the seconds it took me to cross the lot. His pants were still up, though unzipped—but he had hands. Another red haze threatened to descend. I wanted him *dead*, not just whining and bleeding at my feet.

"Don't call," she said. Her voice was so soft and small that I could barely hear the words.

I thought she didn't want an ambulance. But no, she clarified that she didn't want me to call the *police*.

Incredulous, I asked, "Am I wrong, or did this guy just try to *rape* you, and you're telling me not to call the police?" She flinched, and I wanted to pull her out of that truck and shake her. "Or did I interrupt something I shouldn't have?"

Damn my temper. Damn it to hell. WHY did I say that?

Her eyes glassed with tears, and I wanted to punch myself in the mouth. I forced my breathing to slow. I had to calm down. For her. *For her.*

Shaking her head, she told me she just wanted to go home. My brain ticked off a hundred reasons why I should argue with her, but I'd been on campus long enough to know how it would go. The frat would close ranks around him. Someone would swear she went willingly. She was a woman scorned, trying to hurt her ex's frat. She was a liar, a tease, a slut. Administration wouldn't want it to leave campus. He hadn't succeeded, so it would be he-said-she-said. Slap on the wrist for him. Social exile for her.

I would testify . . . but I had a juvenile record for assault, and I'd just beat the shit out of the guy on the ground. A smart attorney would have me arrested for assaulting *him*, discrediting anything I might contribute.

The piece of shit on the ground turned over and cussed, and I rolled my shoulders and took slow breaths—in, out, in, out—attempting to convince myself not to stomp his head under the heel of my very solid boot. He'd not bled enough to satisfy the monster inside me.

It was a close thing.

She breathed along with me, and I concentrated on her soft breaths. She was trembling, but she wasn't crying, yet. If she started, I didn't know what I would do.

"Fine. I'll drive you," I said.

Without a beat between my words and hers, she said that no, she'd drive herself.

How many shocks could I handle in one night? It appeared that I was about to find out.

Like I was going to let her drive. *Right.* I reached down and picked her keys out of the items strewn across the floorboard. Her bag was on its side—knocked there, no doubt, when that shithead shoved her face down into her truck.

Holy. SHIT. I've never wanted someone to jump up and throw a punch at me so badly. I wanted an excuse—any sort of excuse—to end him.

Scooting closer, she held her hand out for her keys. I stared at her slim fingers. The fingers I'd watched from a distance for weeks. They trembled.

"I can't let you drive," I said.

These words confused her. I rattled off my justifications: the visible fact that she was shaking—reason enough on its own. I wasn't sure if she was uninjured. And I assumed she'd probably been drinking, though I hadn't actually observed a cup or bottle in her hand.

"I have not," she said, her brows furrowing and her tone indignant. "I'm the designated driver."

I shouldn't have looked over my shoulder and back, asking her who, exactly she was designated *for.* I shouldn't have berated her for walking across the parking lot alone, paying no attention to her surroundings—even though these things were true. I definitely shouldn't have implied that she'd acted irresponsibly, which was the same as telling her she was responsible for the attack.

I knew who was responsible. He was lying in a bloody heap at my feet, moaning as if either of us should give a shit.

"So it's my fault he attacked me?" she spat, furious. "It's my fault I can't walk from a house to my truck without one of you trying to *rape* me?"

One of you.

"*'One of you'?* You're gonna lump me in with that piece of shit?" I gestured to the guy I'd put on the ground, indignation bubbling to the surface like a chemical reaction, instantaneous and unrelenting. "I am *nothing* like him." I heard my words push into the space between us, hostile and defensive. As I spit them out, her eyes slid over my mouth—and the ring in my lip. I saw the fear she tried to swallow before I could see it.

My anger was not for her. Her fear should not be for me. But I was making it so.

She asked for her keys again, hand out, her voice breaking mid-sentence—but she stared into my eyes, determined. I was astounded at her bravery in the face of this night. And here I stood, another man trying to bully her into doing something she didn't want to do.

One of you.

She was wrong, but not entirely. The sensation that washed over me at this realization wasn't pleasant.

"Do you live on campus?" I asked, allowing the gentleness she deserved back into my voice. This was her choice, not mine. Saving her didn't give me the right to dictate to her. She could drive across campus without me, though I'd prefer she didn't. "Let me drive you," I coaxed. "I can walk back over here and get my ride after."

Relief swept over me at her surrendering nod. As she gathered her personal effects from the floor of the truck, I helped her, returning items to her bag, braving an unjustified twinge of jealousy when I handed her a condom packet.

As though I'd offered her a scorpion instead of a harmless square of cellophane, she retracted her hand and said it wasn't hers.

So he'd thought it out far enough to try to keep himself "safe" from evidence?

Don't turn around. Don't look at him.

Ignoring my mind's warning, I glanced back to make certain he was still on the ground. He was. I may have mumbled something about his intent to conceal evidence, which made me wish she'd let me call the police, because intent like that could point to fully cognizant plotting. I'm not sure if I said it out loud. She didn't reply, if I had. I shoved the condom into my pocket, wondering if a condom could go through a shredder, because I would be trying that little experiment when I got home.

In my imagination, he'd be wearing it at the time.

I climbed into her truck, shut the door, and turned the key in the ignition. "Are you sure you don't want me to call the police?" Resolved as I was to let this be her decision, I had to ask one last time.

She stared at the back of the house and the party within through the windshield, silent for a full minute. "I'm sure," she said.

I nodded and backed out of the lot, headlight beams showing the damage I'd done to her attacker. It wasn't near enough. I forced myself to keep the truck in reverse. I'd have rather put it in drive and flattened him beneath the tires.

It had been years since I'd felt this level of violence roiling through my blood.

Staring at the road, I pretended an artificial composure to force myself to become calm, knowing that it would work, albeit slowly. At the intersection, I asked the name of her dorm and turned right when she gave it, her voice weaker and quaking, now that the danger was past.

I gave her as much privacy as I could, keeping peripheral watch while she strained to regroup. She hugged herself as though she was freezing, even though the night was more perfect than October had a right to be. A little warm, even. She shuddered in waves, her body throwing off the need to defend itself while her mind couldn't escape the degradation she'd just experienced.

I wanted to reach across the cab and touch her. I didn't.

It could have been so much worse.

But I would never, ever say that to her.

In her dorm lot, I parked and locked the truck, handing her the keys and walking with her to the side entrance. She was still shaking, and I fought to keep my hands to myself. I wanted to comfort her, but a stranger's touch was the last thing she needed. Though she was familiar to me—unique and fascinating, I was unknown to her.

She didn't even know my name.

I asked for her ID at the door, figuring she'd have a difficult time swiping the card, the way her body was shaking. I wondered if I should walk her all the way to her room, or if that would feel like a threat. It was a miracle she'd allowed herself to trust me this far.

Then she gasped when she handed over the card, her eyes on my knuckles. "Oh, my God. You're bleeding."

"Nah. Mostly his blood," I said. *Like that's comforting.* Jesus.

I swiped the card and handed it back, staring down into her face, now fully visible under the dome light of the entryway. My eyes touched what my fingers couldn't, tracing the visible tracks of her tears, the smudges of mascara beneath her eyes. I wanted to smooth the anguished furrows from her brow with my thumbs, pull her within the circle of my arms and press her face against my chest, let my heartbeat calm her.

"You sure you're okay?" I asked, and her eyes filled instantly. My hands curled into fists at my sides. *Don't touch her.*

"Yes. Fine," she said, gaze falling from mine. What a horrible little liar she was.

She would tell a friend what happened. A roommate, maybe. Someone known and trusted. I couldn't be her confidant and I knew it. I'd served my purpose, and I only wished I'd served it better. Faster. I'd be pissed at myself forever for my initial hesitation in following her out tonight.

I asked if I could call someone for her, and she shook her head no, skirting around me, careful to avoid any physical contact—even a brush of fabric. Further evidence of my anonymous status.

I watched her walk to the stairs, the heels of her shoes tapping against the tile floor, the glittered, forked tail swaying absurdly behind her, no matter how stiffly she moved now. Her costume's horns were long gone.

"Jackie?" I said, carefully, not wanting to startle her. She pivoted, her hand on the rail, waiting. "It wasn't your fault."

She bit her lip, holding herself together, nodding once before gripping the rail and running up the stairs. I turned and left, certain those four words would be the last thing I'd ever say to Jackie Wallace.

It was a good last thing to say.

chapter *Seven*

LANDON

Boyce Wynn, previous fellow occupant of the middle school outcast table, had become my nemesis. If I'd have called him that, he'd have had no clue what I meant and would call me a pussy and/or threaten to kick my ass. In other words, the same as what happened when I said nothing to him.

Contrary to some things adults like to say, responding to bullies—if you can't beat them—gives them power, because then they know you care. I didn't intend to do that. Principal Ingram had threatened me with her *zero tolerance*, and Wynn probably *could* kick my ass in addition to getting me expelled. He was big and mean, clomping around like one of the upperclassmen, who put up with him because he was rumored to have access to drugs, alcohol, and stolen car parts. Also, he didn't threaten *them*. He only screwed with those he perceived as smaller or weaker.

Which meant me.

There wasn't an outcast table in the high school lunchroom, so choosing where to sit required an impromptu decision, two seconds after paying. A wrong move could be fatal.

On crap days, social lepers ate outside in the quad, but when it was nice out we stayed in, relinquishing the quad's sunny tables and benches to guys like Clark Richards, the youngest son of a developer my grandfather hated, and girls like Melody Dover, Clark's popular blonde girlfriend.

There weren't many crap days here, weather-wise—rain or high winds, the occasional hail and tornado threat. Otherwise it was warm and sunny, even in the winter . . . which meant I spent most lunch periods inside. The safest spots were at vacant ends of tables where no one semi-popular or Wynn-like sat.

But that didn't stop them from finding you when they went looking for entertainment.

Example 1: It's surprisingly easy for someone to propel a lunch tray across a cafeteria table—sending it crashing to the floor and launching food in every direction—without slowing his stride or acting as if he had anything to do with it.

I began grabbing a foil-wrapped, suspiciously preserved sandwich and bottle of water in the line instead of a tray of hot food.

Example 2: Whoever invented locker rooms—where several rows of solid metal and concrete block whatever happens in the back from the coach's sight—was a dick. Thanks to an ambush, I lost a pair of secondhand Chucks and my vintage camo cargo pants. Because I wasn't mental enough to ID the assholes, the coach's remedy was to have me choose something to wear from the lost-and-found barrel—which gave off an odor suggesting something had died at the bottom and was currently decomposing.

I smelled like literal shit during last period, every girl nearby wrinkling their noses and scooting their desks as far from me as possible, while guys made brilliant observations like, "You *reek*, Maxfield. Try telling your handler to hose you off occasionally." Et cetera.

I tugged it all off as soon as I got home and threw it all in the burn pile out back after taking a scalding shower.

I borrowed five bucks from Dad and asked Grandpa to take me back to the Thrifty Sense, where I unearthed a pair of like-new Vans in my size. They were marked seven dollars.

"I know where ya live," Grandpa said, passing me the additional two bucks.

I stopped changing clothes for PE, which earned me demerits every day until Coach Peterson realized that penalizing me wasn't having any effect.

But I had three classes with Wynn—PE, World Geography, and Auto Shop.

"Wash up!" Mr. Silva called, his thunderous voice booming over the noise of operational motors, machine tools, country music, and conversations about cars and car parts, girls and girl parts.

Most of the stuff guys said was harmless. Even if the entire town full of moms threatened to wash our mouths with the abrasive Lava soap we used to get the clingy streaks of oil and grease off our hands and arms, it was usually just talk.

Sometimes those words didn't feel like just phrases or expressions, though. They felt like memories and nightmares, when I was doing my best to avoid both. My hands closed into greasy fists as I stood in line for the sinks, captive to the exchange going on behind me, in which Boyce Wynn played a major part.

"Dude, her tits are like two juicy *watermelons*." His drawl crept up the back of my neck and I imagined the hand gestures I knew he was making.

"Yeah, I'd do her," his friend said, and they both laughed. "She doesn't put out though."

"*Yet*, Thompson. *Yet*. I'd teach her to put out." Staring straight ahead, my vision hazed at the edges.

"Riiiight. You wish, asshole. She wouldn't give your white-trash ass the time of day."

"Who needs the time of day? Time of night, man. Under cover of darkness, she'll be begging for more."

His friend laughed. "Dude, seriously, she'd be all like, '*Nope*.' Plus she's not *that* hot."

"Naw, man, are you crazy? I'd rape that so fast—"

Before I knew what I'd done, I had spun around, my tightened fist planting itself right at the edge of Boyce Wynn's mouth. His head jerked back a little with the impact and his eyes went wide with shock. By instinct, I knew better than to stop there, but suddenly there was a circle of guys chanting, "Fight! Fight!" and my limbs immobilized while his whole body rolled forward, preparing to pound me into the cement floor.

Before either of us could move, Silva gripped us both by the upper arms, separating and immobilizing us. "What the *hell* are y'all dumbasses doing? Trying to get yourselves *expelled*?"

I didn't take my eyes from Wynn, and he stared back with murder in his eyes. A trickle of blood glistened at the lower corner of his lip.

"What'd you do, Wynn?" Silva growled, shaking him. Our shop teacher was two hundred fifty pounds of *pissed*.

Wynn's eyes narrowed, still glaring at me, and he seemed to come to some sort of vindictive conclusion. He shrugged his free shoulder, as if indifferent. "Nothin', Mr. Silva. Everything's cool."

Silva whipped his gaze to me, and Wynn slowly raised his free hand to smear the bead of blood from his face with a knuckle. The churning adrenaline sent a tremor through me.

"And you—Maxfield? That your story, too? What happened here?"

I shook my head once and echoed Wynn. "Nothing. Everything's cool."

Silva ground his teeth and rolled his eyes up to the corrugated ceiling, as though God might peel it back and tell him what to do with us.

Jerking our arms once more, harder, he almost popped them from their sockets. "There will be *no fighting*. In. My. Shop. Is that understood, men?" He spat the word *men* as though we were anything but.

We nodded, but he didn't drop either of our arms. "Do I need to talk to Bud about you causin' trouble?" he asked Wynn, who shook his head, eyes widening. Whoever *Bud* was, his name inspired fear in the guy who inspired fear in most of the student body.

The bell rang, and our audience scrambled belatedly to the oversized aluminum sinks. Silva released us but didn't budge, crossing muscular arms over his beefy chest and staring holes into the backs of our heads while we scrubbed up. I grabbed my backpack from its cubby and made for the side door as Wynn exited the front with two friends.

My escape was temporary. That much I knew.

• • • • • • • • • •

In an effort to torture her students, my World Geography teacher announced a team project as soon as we returned from winter break—during which everyone who remained in town for Christmas had enjoyed an unprecedented half foot of snow covering the beach, palm trees, resort hotels, and fishing boats.

In Alexandria, winter began before Christmas and continued into March—surprise bouts of rain, sleet, and occasionally snow—piles of it plowed into corners in parking lots, shifting from white to gray if left to melt rather than bulldozed into trucks and hauled away. By February, everyone was sick of scraping frost from windshields, sick of shoveling sidewalks and driveways, sick of waking to the rumble of gravel trucks or snowplows, sick of the constant wet cold.

Here, snow was a dusting, if that. Any measurable quantity of it inspired awe. Six inches was deemed a *miracle*. People walked around *oohing* and *aahing*, shaking their heads. Parents sent kids out to build snowmen and make snow angels with socks on their hands, because no one owned gloves or mittens.

"In light of our 'Christmas Miracle'—we're going to *miraculously* team up to examine the effect of climate shifts on environments and people." Mrs. Dumont's tone was much too cheerful for the second period of the first day back. No one wanted to be there, and no amount of enthusiasm would change our minds after two solid weeks of sleeping in and doing nothing. "In the interest of showing how people adapt to unexpected change, we're all going to pick a letter from the hat and pair off." She beamed, as if the knowledge that fate was choosing our partners would improve the assignment.

As one, we all groaned. Unperturbed, she handed an upside-down baseball cap bearing the school mascot—surprise, it was a fish—to Melody Dover, who drew a slip of paper and passed it to the girl behind her. From the last seat of Melody's row, I watched the cap come nearer. I drew an F. Appropriate.

When the cap reached the last row, Dumont called over the din of voices, "Now—find your partner, and move seats! You'll be sitting with that partner for the first three weeks of class this semester, at the end of which we'll be presenting our projects to the whole class!"

You've got to be kidding me. I'd only been assigned one class presentation, last spring—on which I took a zero. Oral presentations were painful to do, and painful to witness others doing.

I considered standing up and walking out the door. Then I heard, "Okay, what lovely lady has an F?" from the opposite side of the room, and I couldn't move.

Boyce. Wynn.

Oh. *Damn.*

He got up and started snatching the bits of paper from students to find out who his partner was. "You got F? Who the fuck's got F?"

"Mr. Wynn," Mrs. Dumont said, scowling darkly.

He shrugged. "I can't find my partner, Mrs. Dumont." His eyes lighted on Melody, who sneered a little. "Is it you?" He snatched the paper from her hand as she objected.

"No." She snatched the paper back, raising her chin. "I got *Clark.*"

Her boyfriend was already sitting next to her. They didn't even have to move from their front-row seats to work together. So I got stuck with Boyce-fucking-Wynn, while privileged Clark Richards gets stuck with his *hot girlfriend.* Naturally.

"Oh, *no no no*—that won't work." Mrs. Dumont rushed over, her eyes on Melody. "You can't be paired with your . . . er, friend. I want us to all experience a shift in culture and environment! Relocation diffusion in action!" As the three of them were trying to figure out what she meant, she grabbed Boyce's and Melody's slips of paper and swapped them. "There. Now Clark, run along with Boyce. I'll be passing out project assignments in a moment!" She seemed to think this would soothe Clark from having to replace a hot girlfriend partner with a hulking bully partner.

"What the——" He scowled, clamping his jaw. "Why can't Mel and I work together?"

Mrs. Dumont smiled benignly and patted his shoulder. "Now who has F?" she called, ignoring his question entirely.

I raised my hand a few inches off my desk without saying a word. Four pairs of eyes found me. Only Mrs. Dumont smiled. "Come on up to the front, Landon. You can take Clark's seat for the next three weeks."

From the look on Clark's face, she might as well have said, "You can screw Clark's girlfriend for the next three weeks."

"Dumb fucking luck, Richards," Boyce said, pinning me to the corner with an unblinking stare. Somehow, being involuntarily paired with some other guy's girlfriend was one more strike against me.

I shouldered my backpack and walked up the aisle, feeling as if I'd been condemned to lethal injection instead of forced to complete a project with a girl I'd fantasized about at least once. As Dumont handed out the packets, Melody pulled out a spiral notebook and began dividing our responsibilities—*Melody* on the left, *Landon* on the right, both underlined. She penciled a thick line down the middle, using the edge of her textbook to keep it straight.

"I'll do the maps," I volunteered, my voice low.

She pressed her lips together and held herself bolt upright, clearly irritated. Great.

She started to print *maps* under my name and stopped midway, turning to level big, pale green eyes at me. "Do you . . . draw? Because I can do them, if not."

I fixed her with a stare of my own. "Yes."

When I didn't elaborate, she rolled her eyes and muttered, "Fine. I'd better get a decent grade on this."

We exchanged phone numbers and addresses, though she made it clear she didn't intend to set foot outside either the school building or her parents' house with me. The Dover McMansion was just down the beach from Grandpa's place. "Oh, yeah. *Maxfield*. Clark said—" She went silent, probably at my black expression.

Clark was son to John Richards, our town's biggest developer of residential monstrosities and vacation condos. He'd been hounding my grandfather to sell his prime beachfront property forever. Things came to a head a few years ago, Grandpa said, when Richards tried to get the city to invoke eminent domain, claiming Grandpa's "shack" was an eyesore and his fishing business was a front. Grandpa told him where he could stick it right there in the middle of the city council meeting. The intimidation attempts had slowed since Dad took over the financials for Maxfield Fishing, but the hostility was potent as ever.

Melody cleared her throat somewhat delicately. "Uh. So, call me tonight, after I'm home from dance class."

Dance class. What did girls like Melody wear to dance class? Spontaneous images threaded their way into my imagination. I twisted one of the rubber bands on my wrist. "K."

"Like, eight o'clock?"

"K," I repeated.

She rolled her eyes. Again. The bell rang and she shot up to exit the classroom with Clark, who narrowed his gaze on me as he slung an arm over her shoulders. Boyce came just behind him and shoved me back into the desk. "Freak," he said. "Richards will probably have you killed if you touch her."

I hadn't had any intention of touching her. Funny how that threat made me want to.

LUCAS

I guess my brain rebooted during the four hours of sleep I finally got, because I remembered the nagging thing I hadn't been able to recall since Saturday night.

If Jackie didn't drop the class, she was going to fail it, and she had exactly one day in which to do it—because the last undergrad drop date was tomorrow.

The likelihood that I could find her again, *today*, was low. I only had one choice—I could email her as the class tutor—like a courteous, informative reminder of the drop date. *Dear Student: you might want to take care of this important thing—hint, hint.*

Never mind that no one else on campus would receive this kind of individualized dire warning. Administration didn't believe in sending many specific alerts, especially about dropping courses. They preferred to include them on web pages of department requirements, or nestled somewhere in that registration documentation everyone scrolls through without reading it, right before clicking the button that says *I agree.*

The generally held belief: students are responsible for their own scheduling maneuvers. Because they're adults. Technically.

Ms. Wallace,

I'm the tutor for Dr. Heller's intro economics course, which it appears you've stopped attending—according to attendance records and the fact that you were not present for the midterm last week. As such, I wanted to remind you that students are not dropped automatically for non-attendance, but must initiate the course withdrawal process themselves. Drop forms and instructions are available online; I've included the links below.

Please note that the last drop date is TOMORROW.

L. Maxfield

I hit *save* and closed my laptop, planning to send it later, after adding the links. I had to swing by Starbucks before class to turn in a copy of my food handler renewal card, or I wouldn't be allowed to work my shift this afternoon. She probably had other classes this morning as well. I had time.

"Hey, Lucas," Gwen said, wiping a small ground coffee spill from the granite countertop. Gwen had a Monday morning smile that no one I knew could replicate—certainly not our coworker, Eve, who pretty much never smiled. "You're still working for me this afternoon, right?"

I nodded, grabbing a cup of coffee. "Soon as I get out of my tutoring session. It ends at two."

"You're such a sweetie!" She beamed, following me to the back. "I'll be back in time for you to get to your lab."

I couldn't help but smile in response as I stuck the photocopy in my file and left a note for my manager that I'd done so.

"We need to find you a girl," Gwen said, out of nowhere. I choked on the sip of coffee I'd just taken, and Gwen thumped my back.

"Uh . . ." I stammered once I could speak. "Thanks, but I'm good."

One of her pale brows rose, telling me without words what she thought of that statement. "You're a good guy, Lucas." I must have made some expression of disbelief, because she shook her head. "Trust me. I'm an honest-to-God expert at finding dickholes, and you aren't one."

• • • • • • • • • •

Kennedy Moore was in his usual center-of-attention position, laughing and clueless as to what his ex-girlfriend of *three years* had been through two days prior. I wondered if he was even friends with the guy I couldn't picture without having to do taekwondo forms in my head to calm down.

I slid into my back-row seat and pulled out a textbook, preparing to study for a quiz in my eleven o'clock class. Waiting for Heller to arrive so Moore and his buddies would sit down and shut up, I sketched something violent in the margin of my text. I'd often wondered what people who ended up with my used textbooks thought when they turned the page to one of my doodles. Usually, they were just designs—the product of momentary woolgathering. Sometimes, they were personal illustrations for the printed material. Rarely—very rarely—they included faces or body parts.

Heller entered by the door at the front of the classroom, snapping my attention from my pointless musing. Since Jackie quit coming, class had grown incredibly boring. I knew the material inside out. I knew all of Heller's jokes and humorous anecdotes. The personal touches he incorporated into his lectures made him an awesome instructor, but even so—three times was plenty for most of them, and four was bordering on torture.

"If everyone will be seated, we'll begin," he said. From my vantage point in the back row, everyone was sitting down, but he was clearly addressing someone with that statement—

Oh, God. I stared. I couldn't do anything but stare.

Jackie—cheeks flushed, eyes wide and fixed on Heller—stood feet away from me, just inside the back door of the classroom. Suddenly, as if prodded from behind, she scampered three rows down, sliding into the only empty seat . . . except for the one next to me. Which would have been closer.

Maybe she hadn't seen it. Or me.

Maybe she had.

What was she doing here?

Good thing I'd been through this lecture three times and could comfortably regurgitate it for my session later, because I couldn't focus on a single word Heller said the entire fifty-minute lecture. It was all *blah blah blah* and swishes of lines on the whiteboard. Jackie didn't appear to be faring any better, though I assumed her inattentiveness was caused by altogether different reasons than the shock I'd received from seeing her. She couldn't seem to look up without glancing at the back of her ex's head, which left her staring at the board—whether or not Heller was writing or diagramming graphs on it, or at the empty page in her spiral notebook—which remained unfilled the whole lecture.

She was there to drop, I thought, finally, relaxing. That's what she was doing—dropping the class. She'd arrived too late to speak with Heller before class began, so she was sticking around to get his signature on the drop slip after it was over. Reinforcing my conclusion, she stepped down to the front at the end of class (once her ex had passed in the center aisle—without even noticing her). After a quiet exchange with

Heller, she waited for him to chat with two other students, and then followed him out the door.

I should have been relieved. No need to assume any further responsibility for her. No need to send that email I'd written this morning.

No need to ever see her again.

So why this conviction that I would surrender something irreplaceable if I let her vanish from my life?

The answer was just another question. What other choice did I have?

• • • • • • • • • •

Just like the Halloween party, I saw her the moment she entered, taking her place at the back of my line. She was an invisible force, dragging at something equally hidden inside me. I wondered at the magnetic field we'd managed to create between us, and whether she'd feel the pull of it as she moved nearer. Maybe it was just me who felt it.

She was with the pretty redhead I vaguely recognized from the party, where they'd arrived together—Jackie in her red-hot devil costume and her friend dressed as a wolf—fuzzy ears and bushy tail, requisite skintight leotard . . . and granny glasses on the end of her nose. Which I didn't get until a tall, shirtless guy in jeans and a hooded red cape jogged over, picked her up—literally—and carried her onto the dance floor.

Whenever it rained, people elected not to leave campus between classes, and the student center Starbucks was besieged. Snaking around two displays and trespassing into the miniscule seating area where every seat was taken, the end of the line trailed down the hallway. The rush showed no sign of letting up. I didn't have time to be distracted, but I was, watching Jackie and her friend inch closer, one step at a time.

Her friend leaned out of line to check the wait and decided it would be too long. I thought they'd both leave, but she enfolded Jackie in a hug and darted off alone.

Jackie hadn't noticed me, not that she'd fully focused on anything at all. Her empty gaze drifted over the other patrons or stared out the far window. Her mouth was a flat line, her pensive expression a contrast to the rainy day smile in my sketchbook. Watching her made my heart ache, as if that organ had become linked to her emotional state, rather than targeting its primary task—keeping me alive. She checked her phone and scrolled through messages or some web page for a minute or two, before resuming her aimless gazing, shuffling forward behind a tall guy who blocked her view of me, for which I was grateful. I knew instinctively that if she looked up and saw me now, she'd turn and head for the exit.

Finally, the guy in front of her gave his order, paid, and moved to the pickup area.

"Next," I said gently, rousing her from her musing.

Her lips parted, but whatever she was about to say dissolved, unsaid. A blush ignited under her skin. I held her eyes—which I noticed, now that I was staring straight into them at close range, were a bit bloodshot, as though she'd been crying, recently. Surely Heller hadn't made her cry? As much of a hard-ass as I knew he could be when necessary, I couldn't imagine him making this girl cry because she wanted to drop a class.

My heart constricted again, attuned to her. I'd be forever associated with that night in her mind. Nothing would eliminate that fact. I scared her or reminded her—either way, she wanted to escape it. How could I ever blame her?

The girl in line behind her cleared her throat, impatient.

"Are you ready to order?" I grounded her with this question, pulling her back to where we were. *It's over.* I wished she could read my thoughts. *He's not here. We're not there.*

She gave her order then, her voice a distorted hum that I somehow understood. I printed it on her cup, along with her name, and passed it to Eve. Late Saturday night, it occurred to me that I'd called her *Jackie*, when I had no cause to know her name, but there was no reason to pretend ignorance of it now.

When I looked up, she was staring at my right hand—still swathed in a light layer of gauze. Most of the blood Saturday night had been his, as I'd told her—but not all of it. Once I got home and cleaned up, I could tell how hard I'd hit him by the split, abraded skin on both sets of knuckles. The injuries were gratifying. Proof that I'd not held back. Little wonder he'd gone down and stayed there.

I rang up her drink and she handed over her card—the one I'd used to swipe her into the dorm. The smiling girl beneath that protective laminate was incongruous with the expressions I'd seen her wear over the past few days.

"Doing okay today?" I asked, not recognizing the cryptic meaning until the words were between us. *Damn.*

"I'm fine," she said, her voice still warbled.

When she took the card and receipt, my fingers grazed over hers of their own volition. She jerked her hand back as if I'd burned her, and I recalled how Saturday night, she'd made sure we didn't touch when she moved past me into her dorm.

Was it me she feared touching now, or every guy?

I wanted to be the one to relax and unravel her, to show her the gentleness and respect she'd not received at the hands of the would-be rapist or, frankly, her ex.

I would never be that man for her, and I was all kinds of idiot to hunger for it.

"Thanks," she said, her eyes confused and wary.

BREAKABLE

The girl behind her leaned too close, stating her order over Jackie's shoulder, though I'd not asked for it yet. Jackie shied away from the physical contact. Biting back a retort to the impatient twit and taking the order, I reminded myself that I was at work, we were busy as hell, and as much as I wanted to make all of these people disappear, there was no doing it.

Our eyes met once more before she was swallowed by the crowd on the other side of the barista counter, where Eve worked her magic with manic speed and narrow-eyed ire toward anyone who grumbled about the wait time. When Jackie picked up her drink, she left without a backward glance, and I began to wonder how many times I would lose sight of her, certain it would be the last time.

chapter *Eight*

LANDON

The day started out for shit and went downhill from there. I was half-way to school when the humid morning morphed into an unforecasted thunderstorm. One minute, my clothes felt like warm, damp rags in the clammy air, and the next minute, a mass of clouds rolled in, opened up, and dumped rain on my stupid ass the rest of the way to school.

When I pushed through the double doors, I cursed myself for not having turned around and headed home the minute it started raining. I couldn't have been more lock, stock, and barrel soaked if I'd jumped into the ocean, shoes and all. The ends of my hair fixed themselves into dripping points, like a faucet that wouldn't turn off. The drips became streams pouring from the hem of my saturated hoodie, and from my jeans into my Vans. They squeaked and squelched as I slogged down the hall.

I blamed my bad judgment and yeah, *desire* to go to school—a first in the past year and a half—on Melody Dover.

The first two weeks of our project, we'd only worked together in class. And by together, I mean we sat next to each other. We barely spoke, not that I could blame all of that on her.

I had a cell phone, but not a computer, so she'd penciled *PowerPoint* under her name. While we read up on climate patterns and geographic distribution individually, I began sketching maps and she scoured the Internet for images. Finally, we needed to get together to begin combining our individual sections, work on the written portion, and practice the presentation.

Last night, she'd grudgingly invited me over to her house. I showered and changed clothes before setting out down the beach. The wind whipping off the gulf was cold and dry, swirling my still-damp hair into cowlicks and tangles. It riffled the pages of the sketchpad I'd used for topography sketches, threatening to tear it to pieces and fling my work into the water. I hunched into my hoodie, arm locked over the sketchpad and hands in pockets, hating Mrs. Dumont and Melody Dover and whatever jackhole decided geography should be part of ninth-grade curriculum.

Melody answered the door in pink sweats and fuzzy white socks.

"Hey. Want a Coke or something?" Without waiting for an answer, she pushed the door closed behind me and walked into the house.

I followed, wondering at the word *PINK* spelled out across her ass. I arched a brow at the redundant label while eyeballing her slim hips, swinging smoothly, drawing me along until I realized we'd entered a bright kitchen the size of my grandfather's entire house. She bent to pull two cold sodas from a lower shelf of a huge fridge and I pulled to a stop, staring. *PINK* was my new favorite word.

Leading me toward the granite countertop, she handed me a can and plopped her perfect ass onto a leather-topped barstool. Turning her laptop toward me, she indicated the adjacent stool and I sat, struggling to shift gears. Geography held even less allure than it had before. I hadn't thought that possible.

She said words, and I didn't understand them. The wind must have scrambled my brain. The wind, or the word *PINK*. "Landon?"

"Huh?"

"Let's see your maps." Her tone said she was anything but excited at the prospect. I opened the sketchbook to the first map. Her mouth dropped open. "Oh, my God."

"What?"

Her lashes swept up and then back down as she turned the page. "Wow. You're . . . you're an artist?"

I shrugged, releasing a relieved breath.

She turned another page. "Oh, my God," she repeated. "These are *amazing*. Are these figures tiny little people? And trees? Wow." She flipped slowly through the rest of them, until she turned to a blank page. Then she did something I hadn't expected her to do. She turned back to the front of the notebook and opened it.

I reached for it, unwilling to snatch it rudely from her, but apprehensive of her examining sketches I'd never shared with anyone else. "Uh, that's all the maps . . ."

Her mouth had fallen slightly open again, and she shook her head a little, like she couldn't believe what she was seeing. I felt my face heat as her finger ran over a detailed sketch of a seagull cleaning its feathers, and then one of Grandpa, sleeping in his favorite chair.

Returning my hand to my lap, I waited while she examined each drawing, until she'd come back to the first map.

"You should do me."

I blinked and cleared my throat, and she reddened slightly.

"Uh. Sure."

"Who's this?" a woman's voice said then, startling both of us. We sprung apart and I nearly fell off my barstool.

Melody's jaw set tight but her voice was all passivity. "This is Landon, Mom—he's my partner on that geography project?"

Her mother's gaze swept over me, and I was acutely aware of my recycled clothes, my shaggy hair, the cheap leather-banded watch on one wrist and the faded gray bandana I'd wrapped around the other. "Oh?" One brow arched as her eyes, the same pale green as her daughter's, turned back to Melody. "I thought Clark was in your geography class."

"Mrs. Dumont assigned partners." A slight bit of defiance. Also an excuse—*It's not my fault or choice that he's my partner.*

"Hmm," her mother said. "Well. Let me know if you need anything. I'll be in my office across the hall." Spinning, she disappeared through a doorway we could see from the counter.

Melody rolled her eyes—but this time, not at me. "I swear to God, she's *such* a pain in the ass. Parents suck."

I smiled, and she smiled back and my heart stuttered. *Damn.* So pretty. So out of my league. So girlfriend of some other guy.

We worked on the project for two hours, during which time she texted with Clark five times and was called by two friends. We were also spied on by her mother every fifteen or twenty minutes. Finally, she walked me to the door and glanced over her shoulder as I zipped my hoodie. "So maybe . . . I'll walk down to your place next time?" Her voice was soft. *This* defiance was to be a secret between us. "Mom can't walk in on us every five minutes there. Unless your mom is worse? Which I doubt is even possible."

I swallowed thickly and shook my head. "No. I mean, *yeah*, you can come over."

Had I just invited Melody Dover to my house—where I had no real bedroom? Was I a total jackass? Yes and *yes*. But I couldn't take it back. And I couldn't get the idea of her in my bedroom—which was really a bed and nothing else—out of my head.

I leaped out of bed this morning, the first time my phone sounded an alarm. The sudden storm hastened the already rushed pace I'd set when I walked out the door, so I arrived way early—ten minutes before the first bell. Students weren't usually allowed inside the building until first bell, but it was raining. They'd look like total dicks making us stand around outside.

My shoes squeaked against the linoleum, echoing in the near-empty hallways, and I knew without glancing back that I was probably leaving a trail of watery footprints. My strident footfalls were loud enough that I didn't hear anyone come up behind me, and I was so distracted thinking about second period geography that my usual self-preserving instincts were muted.

"Take a dip in the ocean, Maxfield, or just piss yourself?"

I didn't stop or turn, but I also didn't run. Something about rabid animals and power-hungry assholes makes them chase what runs.

He grabbed my backpack and I almost shrugged out of it and kept going, but something wouldn't let me kneel that far. I jerked around to face him and of course, he was flanked by two friends. He was almost as soaking wet as I was.

"What do you want, Wynn?" I sounded more composed than I felt. My heart was hammering, but I wasn't shaking visibly.

"What do I want?" He stepped closer, the strap of my backpack still caught in his fist, the muscles in his neck bulging and his nostrils flaring like a bull on the verge of charging. "I want to make you pay for that little stunt in Auto Shop. I want to bring the pain and make you bleed and cry like the little bitch you are."

I narrowed my eyes. *The hell.* "You might be able to make me bleed, but you'll never make me cry. Crying is for cowards who can't fight without the help of their *bitches*." I indicated his mates with a jerk of my chin, and they bristled. One of them growled.

Then a teacher rounded the corner. She slowed a bit, like she was assessing the details of the scene from a distance before judging what was taking place.

Wynn dropped my strap and sneered. "I'll be watchin' you, ass-face. There won't always be someone around to save you from the whoppin' you deserve." He bumped my shoulder as he passed.

LUCAS

I checked my email, expecting nothing important. Mostly, I planned to scrap the draft to Jackie about dropping the class, since that no longer applied. I did delete that message—but not for the expected reason.

Two emails stood out from the half dozen others, as if they'd been highlighted. One was from Heller—subject line: Jacqueline Wallace. The other . . . was from JWallace.

I opened Heller's first.

Landon,

The above referenced student is currently enrolled in the econ section you tutor. She's missed a couple of weeks of class, unfortunately including the midterm. She intends to salvage her grade, and to that end, I'm allowing her to replace the midterm grade with a research project (information attached). I've given her your email address and told her she must contact you to get started. Before your sense of justice goes into overdrive, know that the project will require quite a bit more work than the missed exam, so she's not escaping easily. (Neither am I, since I'll have to grade the damned thing when she's finished. She's apparently suffered something comparable to Carlie's recent trouble, though, and after watching my daughter self-destruct a bit before finally bobbing back to the surface, I have renewed sympathy for emotionally distressed students.)

I imagine she'll need individual tutoring to catch up on the new material before the third exam. If she fails to do what I've asked of her, she'll simply receive whatever grade she's earned at the end of the semester. I'm requesting that you assist her insofar as your tutoring duties extend, but she must complete the work alone. Hopefully she'll give her academic career precedence over some idiot boy in the future.

CH

I reread Heller's email. Twice.

She and Moore *were* broken up, but she *hadn't* dropped the class.

She was no longer Moore's girlfriend, but she was *still* my student.

She'd nearly thrown a gear when she saw me across the counter at the Starbucks this afternoon—which didn't exactly indicate awareness that the guy who'd beat up her assailant Saturday night was also the tutor in her economics class. My email address was an ambiguous LMaxfield.

"*Son of a bitch,*" I said to Francis, earning me a yawn combined with a meow.

I shouldn't care. *I shouldn't care.*

But I did.

Dear Mr. Maxfield,

Dr. Heller told me to contact you regarding a research project for macroeconomics that he wants me to complete. I missed two weeks of class after an unexpected breakup, which means I also missed the midterm. I know that doesn't excuse me for skipping classes, however. I'll do my best to complete the project and catch up on the new material as quickly as possible. Please let me know when you're available and what additional information you need from me.

Thank you,

Jacqueline Wallace

I shot an answer back immediately, informing her that I didn't need to know the reasons she'd skipped class, and suggesting when and where we could meet.

Things my answer shouldn't have done, but did: (1) It made me sound like an asshole. An insensitive, superior asshole. (2) Who didn't care that her heart had been broken by an actual asshole. (3) It was signed *LM*. (4) It made me sound like an asshole.

I shut my laptop and paced around the apartment, earning a dirty look from my cat, who'd probably never had girl problems—because he accepted that he was a self-governing asshole who refused to become emotionally attached. I'd aspired to that since I was sixteen, and thought I was something of an expert.

Pulling to a halt, I realized I'd slid halfway down the rabbit hole before I knew I was falling. I didn't just want this girl. I *cared* about her. I'd wanted to destroy that guy Saturday night—I wanted to hit him until he'd never get up, and if she hadn't made a noise in the truck, I might have done just that.

Fucking hell.

I sat back down and reopened the laptop. Minutes later, my inbox alert chimed.

I'd pissed her off. That much was clear. She told me she tutored at the middle school, but didn't say what she tutored. Then she wrote: I'm sure I can catch up on the regular coursework on my own. She signed off as *Jacqueline*, not *Jackie*.

Throwing on shorts and a T-shirt, I assessed and reassessed every nuance of her message, looking for an opening—a place to change course. My thoughts in a jumble, I laced up my running shoes and jogged down the steps. I would pound the pavement under my feet until I either eliminated her from my mind or came up with a solution.

• • • • • • • • • •

I couldn't tell her through email that I was the guy from Saturday night. She was afraid of that guy, but she needed me to pass econ. She'd know as soon as we met up, of course. My only hope was to convince her, as the class tutor, that she could trust me.

Switching to *Jacqueline* instead of *Ms. Wallace*, I suggested a meeting time and added a postscript: What do you tutor?

Her next email kicked my ass, because it opened with *Landon*. She must have gotten that from Heller. No one else on campus called me by the name I'd discarded when I left home at eighteen. *Shit.*

I concentrated on the rest of her message, where I learned she played the upright bass. The thought of her magical fingers coaxing music from an instrument that was roughly my height made my body tighten.

I needed another run and a much colder shower than the one I'd just taken.

After discovering that our schedules wouldn't coordinate easily, and in the interest of not scaring her away completely—at least, that's what I told myself—I offered to send her the information through email and conduct our tutoring sessions online for the time being.

I didn't tell her I went by Lucas, not Landon. I didn't tell her I'd been watching her, guardedly, for over two months. I didn't tell her that I was the guy who witnessed the attack she'd just as soon forget, and also the one who stopped it. I didn't tell her I was the guy whose touch made her flinch—even across a Starbucks counter, two days later.

We conversed via email over the next couple of days. I sent her the packet from Heller, clarifying a few things where he'd used a bit much econ jargon for a first-semester student. We joked about college bartering systems where beer is the currency for helping friends move. I began to look forward to her name in my inbox: JWallace—and then Wednesday morning came, and reality crashed down around me, firmly, and right on target.

chapter *Nine*

LANDON

I would be alone when Melody came over, because Dad and Grandpa had an appointment in town to see Grandpa's accountant, who Dad referred to as a swindler and a con man. When he wasn't calling him something way more insulting.

"I've been seein' Bob since you were in diapers!" Grandpa growled this morning.

"Then he's had several decades to skim his share of your profits," Dad shot back. "It's time to cut him off."

"I'll do no such! Maybe if you'da stuck around, you'd know that most people aren't criminals like the type you meet in *Washington*." As far as Grandpa was concerned, Washington was a "teeming cesspool of shady dealin's," and the fact that his son had chosen to live and work there had tainted him. I didn't stick around to hear Dad's answer. I was pretty sure I'd already witnessed this argument. Multiple times.

I grabbed a protein bar after slugging some OJ from the carton while they were too busy one-upping each other to notice and headed out for school. Watching for Wynn or his thug friends as I got closer, I almost slowed to a stop as I crossed in front of the elementary school. A little kid was hopping out of his mom's pickup, but he misjudged the curb and tripped forward, flat onto his face. His head bounced off the pavement as his mother screamed his name. I jogged straight over and went to one knee, lifting him while he sucked in air for the coming shitfit he was about to let loose. His nose was gushing blood and the tip of it was scuffed raw, but he looked pretty intact, considering. No forehead gash. No teeth on the ground.

"Ohmygod, Tyler, ohmygod!" his mother said, rushing up and yanking tissues from her purse, eyes wide. She slammed a tissue against his nose, which released the delayed wail I'd been bracing for. The kid's lungs were certainly working okay.

"So much blood! Oh, God—I should have pulled closer!" she said, shaking and crying, tears streaming down her face.

"Uh, I think his nose might be broken—you might not wanna press so hard on the bridge."

She snatched the wad of tissues away, her hands trembling. "B-but the blood—"

I grabbed a couple of the tissues from her and pressed them under the kid's nose. "Hold that right there, dude." He stared at me, but obeyed, sobs subsiding slowly. "You're gonna be fine. I broke my nose a few years ago, playing hockey. That rink was a bloody *mess* and I nearly gave my mom a heart attack, but I was fine. No big deal."

The kid reached for his mother, who gathered him close.

"Thank you," she said. "Your mother should be real proud of you. Not many boys your age woulda done that."

I nodded and stood, mumbling, "No problem."

• • • • • • • • • •

The rest of the day felt fairly uneventful, consisting of me dodging Boyce Wynn and purposefully not staring at Melody Dover in class, though she whispered that she'd walk over after school. Hesitant about the whispering and the secrecy—we were project partners, after all—I slid a glance at her boyfriend. He glared from across the room, and Wynn grinned like he knew something I didn't. Not an expression I wanted to see on him.

Just before four o'clock, Melody knocked on my front door.

I let her in, tense from the awareness of how she must view the place her boyfriend's dad called a shack and an eyesore and worse. Her parents probably felt the same way. And her friends.

I'd spread my project materials out over the kitchen table in hopes she wouldn't ask about my room—but that plan bombed. "So where's your room?" she asked, right after I offered her a soda and she followed me to the kitchen to get it. *Fuck,* I thought, opening the pantry door and bracing myself for ridicule.

"Whoa!" Her eyes went wide. "This is so *small*! And . . . cozy . . ."

She hopped onto the edge of my bed, and my heart thudded. *Melody Dover is sitting on my bed.* Her eyes roved over my textbooks and novels, stacked on the shelves. She turned around to study the opposite wall, half-covered in drawings like the ones she'd flipped through a couple of nights before—but better.

"This is the coolest thing ever. It's like this . . . artist's cave." She smiled. "Can we work in here?" Without waiting for my answer, she slung her laptop bag over her head and crawled toward the head of the bed.

"Uh, sure . . ."

When Dad and Grandpa came home, we were sitting side by side against a mound of pillows, working on the citations page. They were arguing, as though they'd picked up right where I left them this morning, like a paused movie. My face burned when they each stopped right outside my door and peered in with mirrored expressions of shock. For what felt like eternity, neither said a word.

"Makin' dinner," Grandpa said eventually, turning away. Dad grunted and turned in the opposite direction.

Melody's pale gaze shifted from the empty doorway to me. "So your mom . . . ?"

I shook my head. "She . . . she died."

"Oh. That's terrible. Was it recent? Is that why you moved here?"

I nodded, unwilling to elaborate or make eye contact or speak at all. My hands were fists in my lap. *Please don't ask.*

I almost jumped out of my skin when she laid her hand on my arm, right over the wristbands I was wearing today. Her fingers grazed the top of my hand. "I'm sorry."

She was apologizing for the fact that I lost my mother, like everyone did. I couldn't say, *It's okay.* Because it wasn't, and it never would be.

But I couldn't dwell on the loss of my mother with Melody's soft hand on mine, her fingernails painted an electric, metallic blue, like a sports car. I couldn't think of anything but where her hand rested, and its proximity to other, wide-awake parts of me. Angling her fingers, she rasped her nails along the back of my hand and inches away, my body responded, hardening fiercely. I prayed she couldn't see. I was afraid to move.

"She stayin' for dinner?" Grandpa said from the door, and we both jumped, snatching our hands apart. The laptop bounced on her lap.

"Oh, no, thank you. I have to get home soon." Her face was as red as mine.

Then her boyfriend texted to ask where she was, and she lied and said she was home.

"I'm real sorry about your mama, Landon." She leaned over and kissed my cheek, and my whole body caught fire. It was uncomfortable and amazing, paralyzing me like a poison-tipped dart and filling me with flares and embers. I couldn't think straight. Sliding to the end of my bed, she stuck her laptop in her backpack. I followed her to the front door, silent, her kiss a brand on the side of my face.

BREAKABLE

· · · · · · · · · ·

The fight, when it came, was quick and dirty and unwitnessed by any teachers. It was raining again during lunch, and I wasn't in the mood to get banished outside, so I had the asstastic idea to hang out in the library computer lab and check out the PowerPoint Melody had put together. Our presentation was two days away.

I rounded a corner and there he was—with a posse, one of whom was Clark Richards. Wynn's lead moron, Rick Thompson, was acting as lookout.

"Hey, Maxfield. Time to pay your dues," Wynn said, as unemotionally as if he'd just delivered a weather report. Then his fist flew at my face, almost slow motion, but so were my movements. I couldn't reel back fast enough to avoid the blow, and he caught me square in the jaw. My teeth rattled and fireworks exploded behind my eyes.

I staggered back and he followed. "You sucker punched me in shop, motherfucker. That shit was *not cool*. Just *try* to hit me, now that I'm payin' attention."

I got lucky and blocked the next punch, but as he threw an arm around my neck and pulled me down into a low headlock, I knew he'd make up for missing. Twisting from his grip, I turned and slammed my right fist into his chin and my left into his kidney, determined not to make that payback easy. Another wrestling move from him and I was back in deep shit. He cuffed the side of my head and then punched me in the stomach.

"Whatsa matter, mama's boy? Useless piece-a-shit weirdo." My ears rang and his taunts almost grew unintelligible, but he kept dispensing them like he was looking for a panic button. "Daddy never taught you to fight, huh? Is he as big of a pussy as you are?" I couldn't rotate into the right position to get a grip on him or throw a punch, and I'd lost count of how many he'd landed. "Maybe your mama needs a real man. Maybe I oughta pay her a little visit."

And there it was.

With a roar, I threw both arms wide, breaking his hold, and then I hooked a foot behind his ankle and sent him sprawling to the ground. Jumping on top of him, I didn't bother to hold him immobile before I began using both fists to hit him over and over. I couldn't see. Sounds were muted. I could only feel the rage, and it drowned everything else. Striking his face and the side of his head repeatedly, my fists grew numb. I wanted to pound him flat, but his hard skull prevented me. I grabbed him by the hair and slammed the back of his head into the floor.

He bucked me off with a roar of his own, swinging wildly, one eye already purple and half shut. I rolled and stood, breathing heavily, but before I could launch myself at him again, Thompson hissed, *"Teachers!"*

Our altercation had gained an audience, I noted then. Fellow students surrounded us, inadvertently hiding us from view. We both stood, eyeing each other, slowly straightening, hands tense but at our sides.

"What in tarnation is going on here?" Mrs. Powell said, pushing through. "Fighting is an expellable offense!"

Mr. Zamora parted the spectators and came to stand behind her as Wynn, his face as battered as mine felt, deadpanned, "We weren't fightin'."

Narrowing his eyes, Zamora pointed down the hall. "Principal's office. *Now.*"

I tried to care that I was about to be expelled but couldn't. Truth be told, it took every shred of self-control I had to walk calmly toward the office instead of leaping onto Wynn and thrashing him into dust.

Minutes later, my entire body was beginning to ache. My face hurt. My ears were ringing. My abdomen felt like I'd done crunches for four hours straight. My hazy vision was due to blood in my eye, which began to clear as I blinked. I fought nausea as Ingram stared at us from across her huge desk, where not a single file folder or receptionist's message dared to be out of order. On the surface, the boy next to me seemed indifferent to the threat sitting feet away from us, but his hands dug into the arms of his chair.

"There is zero tolerance in this school for fighting." She paused, letting this sink in. My clammy, blood-streaked hands pressed into my thighs and gripped hard, reminding me to remain silent. "I assume both of you are aware of this policy?"

I nodded. The dumbass next to me shrugged.

"Mr. Wynn? Did you just shrug your shoulders in answer to my politely stated question? Perhaps you need it stated in more . . . understandable terms?"

"No, thanks." Oh, man. This guy was an even bigger idiot than I'd imagined.

Ingram's eyes narrowed farther—which I hadn't thought possible. "Excuse *me*?"

"No, *ma'am*," he mumbled.

"*No, ma'am*, I didn't just observe you shrugging your shoulders, or *No, ma'am*, you aren't aware of the policy?" she asked, knowing exactly what he'd meant, trying to get him to say or do something with expellable consequences.

"*No, ma'am*, I don't need it stated in more understandable terms. *Yes, ma'am*, I understand your policy. But I wasn't fightin'."

It took everything I had to keep my jaw from dropping. If he thought I was going to take the fall for this shit alone, he could think again. I wanted to turn that black eye into a matched set, though intuition kicked in enough to warn me that that reaction would definitely get me expelled—something this bitch had wanted all year.

Her mouth contracted into the type of pucker someone has after sucking on a lemon. "You weren't . . . fighting." Her contemptuous tone carried a clear-cut warning. Somehow, I knew Wynn wasn't going to heed it. "Then why all the blood and bruises?" She leaned forward, her lips stretching into the beginnings of a gotcha grin.

"I fell down the stairs."

Her stare should have iced him over. "You live in a *trailer*."

"I didn't say I was at home."

Her gaze whipped to me. "And you?"

"He fell down the stairs, too." *Christ on a cracker*, as Grandpa would say—Wynn was answering for both of us. I was so screwed. "We both did. It was epic. Pretty sure it's on YouTube by now."

Her eyes didn't budge from me. "Mr. Maxfield? Care to tell the *truth*?"

No matter what I thought of Wynn, Ingram was not on my side and I knew it. I took a breath. "I think we were pushed."

Her eyes flared wide. "By *whom*?"

"I don't know. They were behind us."

There was a long silence as she figured out that neither of us was willing to give up the other to benefit *her*. "You are both"—she paused to harden her already-sharp jaw—"expected to follow *my rules* while you are in *my house*. If I find one teacher who will say they witnessed a single punch being thrown by either of you, I will toss both of your ill-bred carcasses back into the streets and on your butts without a moment of misgiving! Do. You. Feel. Me?"

I bit the inside of my cheek to keep from laughing, because one, I had no doubt she wanted nothing more than to rid herself of both of us, which was anything but funny, and two, my lip was split in two places and would hurt like a motherfucker if I so much as smirked. But a middle-aged woman asking us *Do you feel me*? What the hell?

Wynn, fingering his chin, said, "This sounds familiar . . . Have you considered making a handout?"

I cough-laughed into a fist, wincing at the pain. *Son of a bitch.* My heart hammered as hard as it had when I'd first swung my fist at his face.

Her face mottled, and all I could think was the dragon was about to breathe fire. "*Get out.* I'm calling your parents. You are both suspended for a full week. Sit in the outer office until called. *Do. Not. Talk.*"

Under his breath, Wynn muttered, "Shit."

Luckily, she didn't hear him over my, "Yes, ma'am."

We jumped up and exited her office, slouching into hard lobby chairs that did nothing for my sore back. I hoped Wynn was hurting even worse than I was. Facing the front counter of the main office, we left an empty chair between us.

I didn't know what Dad would do or say. He barely spoke to me as it was.

"Maxfield?"

Surprise, surprise, Wynn defied the *do not talk* command before the first minute was up. I ignored him.

"Sorry about what I said. You know, about your mother." As if it needed qualifying.

Scratching at a splotch of dried blood on my jeans, I wondered if it was mine or his.

"It was a dick thing to say."

I looked at him, confused. "Yeah. It was."

LUCAS

I almost began thinking of myself as two different people, at least where Jacqueline was concerned. I was the guy who'd been mesmerized by her for weeks and had regrettably earned her fear in saving her from an assault, and I was the guy who was the opposite of a threat—trading quips and stories through email while helping her catch up in class.

On one hand, I wanted her to know I was both the class tutor and the guy from Saturday night. Mostly, though, I wished I could be someone else altogether. Someone unrestricted by an otherwise sensible ethical line, and someone untied to possibly the worst night of her life.

Instead of entering the classroom when I arrived, I leaned on the wall across the hall and waited for her to show up. Without intending to be, I was a grudging witness to some banter between Kennedy Moore and Ivy. Leaning on the wall just outside the door, they swapped phone numbers and contact pics. She giggled the entire time. *This* was the sort of girl this guy thought could replace *Jacqueline*? There were plenty of intelligent women on this campus, including sorority girls, if that was his thing—but this girl?

No.

I turned my eyes away, and that's when I noticed Jacqueline, standing in the middle of the hallway, watching them. From her stationary posture and the quiet hurt on her face, her motivations for skipping two weeks of class were all too clear. Not only had he ended their relationship without warning, he wasn't wasting any time moving on. Only a masochist would want to watch that in action.

Some clumsy dickhead bumped into her then, and I pushed off the wall as her backpack slid down her arm and hit the floor. She righted herself, twisting down as I picked it up. Her eyes flashed up to mine and I wanted nothing more than to shield her from every injury or discomfort she might ever encounter.

So not possible—this I knew.

"Chivalry isn't really dead, you know," I said, sliding the bag back onto her shoulder.

"Oh?" Her cheeks were tinged pink. It was cool outside this morning, but I gathered that her flush was due to embarrassment, not the slight November chill.

"Nah. That guy's just an asshole." Lifting my chin toward the jerk who'd run into her without even a proper apology, I couldn't help fixing her dick of an ex in my sights, too, before returning to her. "You okay?"

In her eyes, I read her recognition of this recurrent question, and I hated myself for constantly reminding her of that night, even if that was the last thing I wanted to do.

Maybe she couldn't help but be reminded, no matter what I said or did. I needed nothing to trigger my personal nightmares, after all. They came indiscriminately, regardless of what I did to avoid them.

"Yes, fine." Her voice was a deflated whisper as she glanced toward the doorway. Moore and his would-be conquest had gone inside, and she moved to follow her classmates. "Thank you."

Her *thank you* reminded me of the rainy day I'd held the door for her. The first time I'd seen her up close, looked into her eyes, and admitted to myself that I wanted her.

Damn.

She didn't glance back or notice that I entered the classroom behind her. From the last row, I leaned back in my seat and watched her takes notes as Heller covered the whiteboard with new material, her furrowed brow and general body language screaming *not getting this*. I shouldn't have wanted her to need Landon Maxfield, but I knew she'd be emailing me later, and I was already anticipating the questions I wanted to ask her.

Then, leaning down to reach into her backpack, she looked directly back at me.

So, she knew I was in the class, and where I sat. She must have noticed me on Monday before I'd seen her standing there. She must have chosen not to sit next to me. She'd preferred to take a seat that required her to climb over the outstretched legs of a guy who napped in class at least once a week.

But she knew where I was, and she was curious enough to glance back. I tried to keep my expression level, but the edge of my mouth pulled into a smile, even as I fought it. She whipped her face forward, and didn't look back again.

When Heller wrapped up for the day, I hightailed it out the back, while Jacqueline thumbed through her spiral and turned it toward the guy next to her.

Before I could escape the building, a student stopped me. She'd been in Heller's class last spring, but had dropped. She'd signed up to try again, but wasn't doing any better this semester. She never came to tutoring sessions, and the only time she'd asked for individual tutoring, she'd wanted to meet off campus. I'd said *no* to that, as we'd been trained to do.

"So we can't meet at my apartment?" she asked, as if we hadn't had this *exact conversation* a few months prior.

I sighed. "Nope. Sorry. On-campus tutoring only—university rules."

Catching a strand of her long hair and winding it around her finger, she pouted her lower lip out. That act must work on some guys, or her parents, but it sure as hell had the opposite effect on me. My phone buzzed in the front pocket of my jeans. Jacqueline hadn't left the classroom yet, and I wanted to leave the building before she came out. That probably wasn't going to happen, now.

"So it's a group tutoring thing? And it lasts an hour?"

That hair wound tight around her finger, the girl in front of me swayed from one foot to the other, adding to my annoyance. I wanted to grab hold of her shoulders and make her stand still for the thirty seconds more I was giving this exchange. "Yeah. From one to two."

She asked what I was doing after the tutoring session. As if she knew I wouldn't *tutor* her off campus . . . but maybe I'd be game for hooking up. *Jesus. Christ.*

"Work."

"You're always working, Lucas."

I couldn't remember ever having the actual feeling of someone watching me before, so I wasn't sure if that's what it was. Maybe it was merely the fact that I knew she could be there. But I'd swear my skin heated and my muscles contracted and my breath hitched. I couldn't keep my eyes from pulling up and zeroing in on Jacqueline Wallace in the crowd of people zigzagging through the hallway, as though I knew exactly where she'd be. As though she was the only other person in that hallway.

She was close enough that I could have taken four strides to reach her. I knew she'd heard my name. Now she thought I was *Lucas*, while she was emailing *Landon*. There was no reason for her to reconcile the two. In that split second, I was utterly relieved and then disgusted with myself and then torn right down the middle. Again.

Before I could move, she turned and disappeared into the flow of people, and I swear I felt her leave.

chapter *Ten*

LANDON

I walked to Melody's house to give her the maps I'd drawn and the citations page I'd finished. I didn't take into consideration what my face looked like before I went. Even though I'd showered away the blood and Grandpa had patched me up with a couple of bandages, my lip was swollen and split all the way through. The bruises would be there for a while.

Her older brother answered the door. I recognized him from school. He was a senior, on student council. Popular.

"Who the fuck are you?"

"Evan," a woman's voice said, and her mom's face appeared behind him, scowling.

"Oh . . . my. Landon, is it? What—what do you want?"

Evan didn't move. He stood glaring at me while his mother moved to his side as if the two of them were blocking me from entering. Which they were doing.

"I, uh, was bringing these to Melody. For the presentation." I hadn't thought this out well. I hadn't texted her to say I was coming. I wanted to explain in person that I didn't want to let her down. That the only reason this consequence—the suspension—bugged me at all was that fact.

Mrs. Dover's brow arched. "And you can't just bring it to class yourself?"

I shook my head, eyes sliding to her shoulder. "I . . . won't be at school Friday."

"I see." She sighed as though she'd expect no different from someone like me. She stretched out her hand. "I'll see that she gets them."

I swallowed and looked her in the eye. "Maybe I could see her? She'll have to do my part of the presentation, too. We should discuss it."

Her son crossed his arms over his chest, while her hand remained outstretched, waiting for me to hand over what I'd brought. "I don't think so." Her smile was full of the fakest kindness I'd ever seen. Her voice was ice. She said nothing else.

I handed her the folder and left.

By the time I went back to school a week later, everyone had returned to their usual seats in World Geography. Clark Richards smirked at me from his reclaimed chair next to Melody. Melody didn't look at me at all. The presentations were all done, and Boyce Wynn and I had received zeros. Mrs. Dumont gave the two of us a pop quiz to "make up for" the missed grade, but with no knowledge of the material and no chance to study, I bombed it. She stuck us in the hallway, sitting on the floor on opposite sides of the door, to do it.

We weren't supposed to talk. Of course, Wynn broke that command like it was a suggestion he could choose to follow, or not.

"Hey, Maxfield. We're doin' a bonfire thing tonight, over by the inlet. Rick's older brother—we call him Thompson senior—scored some extra weed from a deal, and he's payin' Rick to do his chores. In *weed*." He chuckled.

I looked over at him and frowned, like *And?*

"We're meetin' up at like eleven. Once the rest of this loser town shuts down, nobody will see us to report it." The bruises on his face looked like mine. Yellowing. Almost gone. His eye was still a little fucked up, and so was my lip. I wondered if this invitation was some sort of trick.

"We friends now or something?" I asked, peering at him skeptically.

He shrugged. "Yeah, why not. You, uh, know Richards paid me to do it, right?"

A million jumbled thoughts lurched through my head. "No."

He smirked. "Yeah, he found out you had his little piece of ass at your place, and when he texted her she said she was home. He figured you were either tappin' that shit or about to."

"So he *paid* you to jump me—"

"Guy's a rich dick, right? I was happy to take his money. Truth, though, you'd sorta pissed me off already. Gotta own up to that, man." He angled his head, thinking. "So that day in shop—that thing I said about Brittney Loper right before you punched me—you like her or somethin'?"

I stared at the floor, shook my head. "No. Don't really know her." I didn't really know anyone. I thought I was getting to know Melody, but that had been a pathetic illusion.

"Then what? Because *dude*."

My heart pounded. I had to say it. It was stuck in my throat, but I forced it out, an uneven murmur in the empty hallway. "You said you'd *rape* her."

"What?" He frowned, confused. "That's just an expression—I don't mean anything by it—"

"*It means something.*" I stared at him. "It's a—sort of . . . trigger word for me."

"No shit," he said, and I stared at the floor between my knees. "Okay, well. Sorry? I'll remember that's your apeshit word, man."

He had no idea.

I left home around midnight, after Dad and Grandpa were solidly asleep, which eliminated the need to explain where I was going. The air was just cold enough that I could see my breath, misting in front of me and curling over my shoulder with each step I took down the beach. The inlet wasn't far, and it was impossible to get to without meandering through private yards or beaches. All the more reason Clark Richardson's daddy wanted Grandpa's beachfront property.

I heard, "Maxfiiiieeeeld," as I rounded a jut of rock and happened upon the bonfire, which was more like a campfire—probably in the interest of dodging attention from local authorities. There were less than a dozen people around it, though, so its size was adequate. Popping up from the sand, Wynn slapped my palm and bumped my knuckles as if we were lifelong bros, and I let out a breath. *No ambush.* I hadn't realized I'd been expecting it until it didn't happen.

There was a first-quarter moon and the sky was clear, and my eyes had completely adjusted to the semidarkness during the walk. I recognized a few of the people there—like Thompson, who was giggling like a hyena and slapping his thigh over something one of the other guys had said.

There were also girls, and a couple of them were watching me curiously. Or maybe they were so stoned that I could be anyone or anything.

Wynn threw an arm over my shoulder. "Everybody know Maxfield?"

Thompson jutted his chin in my direction. "Hey." As if he hadn't egged Boyce Wynn on to beat the *ever-lovin'* shit out of me a little over a week ago.

"Come sit by us," one of the girls said. She and her friend—Brittney Loper, she of the watermelon-sized boobs—were huddled inside a large blanket that looked more like a comforter yanked off one of their beds. It was floral and downy and smelled like pot—but that was probably because everything smelled like pot. The sweet, potent scent floated over the whole scene, a cloud of it hovering and dispersing, hovering and dispersing. I wondered if I'd even have to smoke a joint to get high.

The girls shifted apart, inviting me to sit between them. When I did, they huddled close on either side, sighing with contentment and pulling the blanket back over the three of us. My hoodie was suddenly a furnace. I unzipped it, and the girl on my right helped me strip it off. "Ooh, you are *so warm*." Her hands caressed my forearm and slid up inside the sleeve of my T-shirt. She gripped my bicep and I made a mental note to begin doing push-ups to exhaustion every single day, not just three or four times a week.

"I'm Holly, by the way." She pressed closer and offered the joint, which I took.

"Landon," I said.

"Mmmm," Brittney said, as if my name alone was something appetizing. She pressed her chest against my arm and my body answered, like it knew from experience what to do next. It didn't.

I watched Thompson take a hit off his joint, and I parroted his movements—after which I coughed like I was choking up a lung. Or dying.

"Slow down, Landon," Holly said. "You don't have to suck it all down in one go."

"That's what he said," the guy next to us quipped, and the blood in my body didn't know whether to heat my face or continue hardening my dick.

"You wish," Holly said to him, sounding more amused than insulted, and the guy patted his lap in invitation. She shook her head. "I'm fine right here." As she peered up at me, dark tufts of her hair drifted up from a slight gust of wind, one loose tendril moving across my mouth and sticking there. She ran her fingers over my lower lip, pulling it free.

Harden it is.

I put the joint to my lips and pulled a more measured, careful hit, staring back at her.

"There ya go," she encouraged, taking it back, placing her mouth where mine had just been and sucking a little deeper than I had before passing it to Brittney.

For the next half hour, the three of us took slow turns, their hands roaming over my arms, chest, and back. Occasionally pressing into a thigh. Unless I was holding the joint, my fingers dug into the sand behind me, because I didn't trust what I wanted to do with my hands.

Somewhere during that half hour, Holly leaned in and pressed her mouth to mine, just as I began to feel like the ground beneath me was a big, soft pillow, and everything sharp had muted—the talking and laughter around us, the stars in the sky, the nearby crash of waves on the sand. Between hits, I kissed her back, hoping I was doing a credible job of it. She licked my lower lip and I opened my mouth and touched my tongue to hers. Grabbing my shoulders, she lay back and pulled me down on top of her. Brittney sighed and abandoned the blanket to us, tossing it over our heads as our legs tangled under it, and I had no knowledge or care where I was after that.

Several hours later, I stumbled home, ate all the leftovers in the fridge, fell into bed, and had weird, scorchingly dirty dreams about Holly's hands and mouth on me. I turned off my phone's alarm when it alerted me that it was a weekday and time to get up. Having never skipped school, I felt a twinge of guilt. But I was too exhausted to give a shit, and I told myself it was just this once.

Forging a note from Dad, I showed up by third period. I didn't want to miss Auto Shop—the only class I enjoyed. Before lunch,

Wynn and Thompson caught me in the hall. "Hey, Maxfield, c'mon. Thompson senior said we could pile in the back of his pickup. Whataburger for lunch, baby."

After the last twelve hours, going off-campus for lunch—which only upperclassmen were allowed to do—would be the least of my transgressions. Thompson's older brother Randy and two of his senior friends were in the truck's cab, packed shoulder to shoulder, while Boyce, Rick, and I held on for dear life in the bed, trying to look cool and pretend like we wouldn't be thrown twenty feet to our deaths if Randy had to slam on the brakes for any reason.

"Man, I'm still starvin'," Rick said, wolfing down his burger and large fries minutes later.

"Bet Maxfield is some needin' fuel after Holly got done with 'im," Boyce said. They laughed at my tight-lipped expression. "Dude, Holly likes to initiate the new guys. It's like her *thing*. We've all been there, if you get my drift."

Ah.

"Yeah, Holly's cool—just *don't* fall for her." Rick popped a handful of fries in his mouth and kept talking. "She hates that. If you don't go mushy on her, she'll be your little snake charmer for a while, man."

They both guffawed while I regrouped. "Good one, man," Boyce said to Rick.

The bonfire parties were every weekend and sometimes during the week, with a shifting group of regulars and out-of-towners. Weekends were wilder, but nothing beat spring break for crazy. Heedless of what the guys had said, I'd gotten more than a little attached to Holly, though at school, she acted like we were just friends and no more.

On the beach, though, and high—she became my first everything.

Then came spring break. There were new guys all over the beach, and all over Holly. Her desertion stung, for all that I'd been warned that what we had was no relationship.

"Holly gets a cut from Thompson senior—she's like . . . a tourist trap," Boyce explained.

My jaw hardened, but Rick laughed. "Man—seriously. We told you. Holly's her own girl. She doesn't do committed sappy shit. If you want a stand-in, how 'bout *look around*." I obeyed, glancing at the dozens of girls in bikinis, dancing around the fire, everyone drunk or stoned or getting there. More than one of them sent promising glances my way. "Put your new skills to use, man."

Then I spotted Melody, perched on a tall rock. Alone. Clark stood twenty feet from her, cigarette in one hand and beer can in the other. Talking to a bunch of guys, his back was to her.

"Oh, man—not *there*." Boyce groaned, but it was too late. I was already moving toward her.

When I climbed onto the rock, her lips fell apart. She glanced at her boyfriend, who wasn't paying any attention, and I made a quick, discreet examination of her. Legs smooth and pale in the moonlight, they stretched out from her cuffed baby blue shorts, and she was wearing a skimpy little bikini top under her thin white tank. Her blonde hair hung down her back in a heavy braid, loose curls floating around her face. How Clark Richards could ignore her was a mystery to me.

I sat next to her, and we watched and listened to the goings-on just below.

"You looked kinda bored up here," I said, finally. "Wanna go for a walk?"

Her eyes swept over Clark, who remained with his back to her. She nodded. "Okay."

I took her hand to help her down, and she let go once she hit the sand. I checked over my shoulder, but no one followed. We walked down the beach, and it didn't take long before we could no longer hear the party. Strolling past my house, we ended up in front of hers. She

walked to the side yard, where there was a weathered wooden struc-
ture I'd never noticed.

"Cool fort."

She turned a latch and tugged the rope handle on the drawbridge,
and we went inside. There was a ladder to a platform that sat even
with the top of my head, but no roof. "Evan and I used to play cowboys
and Indians with neighbor kids, or hero dragon fighter and imprisoned
princess." She climbed up, and I followed.

"Who was the dragon?"

She smirked and sat, tucking wisps of hair behind her ears and
pulling her knees to her chest. "The dragon was imaginary. Sometimes I wanted to be the dragon, though. Or the hero. But Evan
wouldn't let me."

I lowered myself near her and lay back, hands behind my head.
"That seems mean. I don't have a sister, so I don't know how that
works. But if you wanted to be a dragon, you should have got to be a
dragon." I thought of Carlie Heller, who at ten would make a kick-ass
dragon, and who would have booted her twelve-year-old brother—
literally—right off a castle wall, were he to suggest that she play a
princess. Unless the princess wielded a sword.

Melody looked up at the stars. "Yeah, well. Evan was always basically
a Dad clone, even when we were little. They get their way. Every time."
She paused, sighing, and I wanted to pull my fingers through her hair
and loosen her braid. Guide her mouth to mine and kiss her and make
her forget the condescending guy who treated her like crap. "My mom
is like this really strong woman to everyone but Daddy," she said then.
"She says that's what marriage is supposed to be. It's give and take, but
if there's a real disagreement, the husband makes the decision."

I thought about my parents and their relationship. My dad had
never been expressive, but he'd been completely devoted to my mother.
She could have asked for anything and he'd have given it to her, or

tried to. *Whatever you want, Rose.* How many times in thirteen and a half years had I heard that?

He knows I'll never ask him for anything that would hurt him, because I love him, Mom told me once. *I trust him the same way, because I know he loves me, too.*

"Or the older brother?" I asked Melody, who lay back beside me.

"Or the older brother," she conceded. "Or the dad."

I could see how Clark Richards fit into this picture more clearly than I had before. "In other words, the man."

She shrugged, watching me. "I guess."

I frowned and peered at her. My mother was the most giving person I'd ever known, but she wouldn't have tolerated someone making decisions for her, just because he was her husband. Or boyfriend. "That doesn't seem right to me."

She smiled. "Maybe not. But it doesn't matter now. I don't have to be anyone's princess if I don't want to. You can ask my mom—I'm definitely a fire-breathing dragon if I don't get something I want."

She didn't even see it. She was her boyfriend's captive princess. She would never be the dragon or the hero in his story. Those roles were already filled.

LUCAS

As expected, Jacqueline emailed and requested extra help with catching up. She thanked me for translating Dr. Heller's instructions, which could be unintelligible. His grad students could follow him, but he often lost a few of the undergrads. That's why he had me.

I corrected her assumption that I was an economics major, attached several of the worksheets I'd created for the sessions she couldn't attend, and ended with asking how her orchestra students had done at regionals. Then I added: btw, your ex is obviously a moron, and pressed *send*.

What the *hell* did I mean by doing that? It was beyond out of line to say that about any student—in an *email*, no less—*to another student*. Regardless if it was true.

I breathed a sigh of relief when she didn't refer to that impropriety in her reply, though she seemed to believe that helping her was a nuisance for me. I wanted to convince her of the wrongness of that impression. It had been a long time since I felt the sort of breath-stalling anticipation I experienced waiting for her name to appear in my inbox or the sight of her in class. She was the opposite of a nuisance, infiltrating my dreams and stealing into my waking desires.

She told me about her two freshmen students, who'd each cornered her privately to ask which one was her favorite. I laughed out loud at her answer to both of them—You are, of course—and her question to me—Was that wrong??

When I returned the worksheets, pointing out her minor mistakes, I confessed that a bass-playing college girl would have rendered me speechless at fourteen. I closed my eyes and imagined her as she was now, alongside the quiet disaster I'd been at fourteen, needing someone to just *see me*. I'd have fallen for her immediately, and hard.

And in case you're wondering—yes, you're my favorite, I added to the end of that message.

Totally inappropriate flirting, but I didn't care. I wanted Landon to win her over, so that when she found out who I was, she would forgive me for being part of that night.

This was doomed. But I couldn't stop now if I tried.

· · · · · · · · · ·

Friday afternoon shifts were often monotonous as hell—it had been ten minutes since we'd even had a customer. There were only two of us working the counter. If Gwen had been there, I would have welcomed hearing anecdotes about her kid's teething or crawling or colic for the hundredth time just to break the boredom. I was working with Eve, though, who was texting nonstop, setting up weekend plans and leaving me far too much time to ruminate over my Jacqueline Wallace dilemma.

Absorbed in conversation, two girls strolled up to the empty counter. I recognized one of them as the redhead who'd come in with Jacqueline on Monday, then hugged her and sprinted away before they'd reached the front of the line.

From their Greek-lettered T-shirts, I deduced these two were sorority girls. In spite of her attendance at that party and her frat boyfriend, I hadn't thought that pertained to Jacqueline—but it was entirely possible that she was in a sorority. Not like I hung out with that crowd enough to know who was or wasn't part of it. Or care.

Until now.

Eve stepped up to the counter while I cleaned the decaf canister, inadvertently eavesdropping and unable to stop once I heard the subject of their conversation.

". . . if Kennedy wasn't such a dickhole."

"Your order?" Eve intoned, without a hint of affability.

"He's not totally horrible—I mean, at least he broke up with her first," the dark-haired girl countered before answering Eve. "Two venti skinny iced green tea lemonades."

My coworker punched the register buttons and gave their total. With 2G gauges in her earlobes and more piercings and tattoos than I'd seen on a girl in years, Eve wasn't a fan of Greeks. I'm not sure if she had a reason. If so, she'd not shared it with me. I figured we were cool because she assumed, as most people did, that my own visible piercing and tats meant I was equally antisocial. I suppose that much was true . . . I just happened to have a weakness for one particular socially active girl.

I wondered what Eve might do if some hunky frat boy took a liking to her and got too close.

She'd likely stab him with a brow barbell first and ask questions later.

"I beg to differ," the redhead said. "He's a total fucking ass. I saw it often enough, even if she didn't. He took the *high road* because in his mind breaking up with her before fucking around excused him from all responsibility for breaking her *heart*. They were together for nearly three years, Maggie. I can't even comprehend being with someone that long."

Maggie sighed. "Seriously. I've been with Will for three weeks, and if he wasn't hung like a—"

"Your *card*," Eve interjected as if repulsed, and I escaped that too-clear mental picture of *Will*, whoever he was. Thank Christ.

"—I'd be bored out of my mind. I mean, he's sweeter than choco-late, but ugh, when he starts talking. Zzzz."

Jacqueline's friend laughed. "God, you're such a bitch."

I pulled the lemonade from the fridge while Eve pumped syrup into a shaker.

"Yeah, yeah. Nice girls finish *never*. Speaking of, what are we going to do about Jacqueline?"

Her friend sighed. "Hmm. Well, she left the party early last week, so that was a major fail—but that was probably because Kennedy was douchebagging it up with Harper right in front of her. Harper's been after him since last spring—I'm sure she flaunted the shit out of bag-ging him. God. I never should have taken J to that fucking party . . ."

Eve slid their drinks across the counter, rolling her eyes—which went unnoticed. Poking straws through the lids, they turned to go, caught up in plotting.

"We should dress her like *dessert* and take her somewhere Kennedy won't be, so she can get her groove back."

When the redhead suggested a club known for blasting crap music—overplayed on every top-40 station in existence—I knew I'd reached a new level of personal idiocy, because I was going to go. I had to see her on neutral ground, and I was willing to endure almost anything to make that happen. Even pop music.

I'd barely looked at her in class today, trying to fight the attraction I'd been feeling weeks before I'd become the guy who prevented her from being raped in a parking lot. I'd been her savior that night, yes, but I also bore witness to the humiliation she must still feel. I was eternally linked to that night—an inevitable reminder of it.

That was clearly how she thought of me—as evidenced by the wide-eyed shock on her flushed face when I asked if she was ready to order on Monday. Evidenced in her quick, "I'm fine," when I asked if she was okay. Evidenced in the way she jerked her hand back when I handed her the card and my finger grazed hers.

But then she looked back at me in class on Wednesday, and the hope I knew I should discourage reignited. It was a dull glow in the pit of my heart—that somehow this girl was meant to be mine. That I was meant to be hers.

Avoidance would have been the smart thing, but where she was concerned, all logical thought was useless. I was full of irrational desires to be what I could never be again, to have what I could never have.

I wanted to be whole.

• • • • • • • • • •

Watching from a distance as her friends pressed drinks into her hand and encouraged her to dance with whatever guy popped up to ask, I suspected she'd not told them about that night. They'd brought her here and pushed her into the arms of new guys to get over her breakup, not to recover from an assault. Smiling and performing silly dance moves, they coaxed smiles from her, and I was glad to see that happiness on her face, no matter what put it there.

I knew I should leave her alone. She was a lure I couldn't resist, though she had no way to know it. No way to know I'd watched her relationship crumble from a safe distance. No way to know that I was as attracted to the sense of humor and intelligence she revealed in our email exchanges as I was to those captivating movements her fingers made when her mind was on music and not what was going on around her.

Her ex had chided her once for her inattention to some gibberish he was spouting, and I wanted to throat-punch him. What a fucking idiot he was, to have had her so long and somehow to have never *seen* her.

I finished my beer and vacated my seat at the bar, torn. I didn't want to betray Charles's faith in me. This wasn't my scene, so there was no denying the knowledge that I was there for *her*, in deliberate disregard of the fact that she was my student. I would keep to the edge of the club and head straight out the door. Or I would just say hello and leave.

I walked up behind her, noting that she was taller in her heeled boots. Even so, I towered over her. Stroking a finger over the soft skin of her arm, I knew that all pretense of fighting this attraction was suspended, at least for these few moments. I vaguely noted her friends, both facing me, but couldn't tear my eyes from her bare shoulder long enough to acknowledge them.

Jacqueline turned, and my eyes were drawn straight to the plunging neckline of her top. Holy. Hell. I snapped my gaze back to her face.

Brows raised at my quick but blatant inspection of her chest, she seemed to hold her breath, and I let myself be caught by her mesmeric gaze. I wanted her trust. I didn't deserve it, but I wanted it. This was no time to be sidetracked by *dessert*.

She'd yet to release the intake of breath, while I recalled our engaging email exchanges—her comical admission of friends who bartered the use of her pickup for beer, and the way she'd talked about her students—boys who must have been crushing out of their minds during every music lesson. I couldn't stop the stupid smile stealing across my face, but I wasn't the one who'd shared those exchanges with her.

Way to not be creepy, dumbass.

I leaned in, intending to take a moment to compose myself as well as avoid yelling the *Hello* I meant to say before leaving. Instead of expressing an innocent greeting, I found myself drowning in her scent— the subtle honeysuckle that had etched itself onto my olfactory sensors that rainy day weeks ago. *So sweet.* My body tightened, and with enormous effort, I murmured into her ear, "Dance with me?"

I pulled away, watching her. She didn't move until her friend poked a finger in her back and gave her a firm nudge in my direction. She reached her hand forward as I reached to take it, and I escorted her to the dance floor, telling myself, *Just one dance. Just one.*

Yeah. That didn't happen, either.

The music of that first song was loud, but slow. As long as I'd been watching her, she'd refused invitations to dance every slow song. She'd flinched from the touch of every guy, almost inconspicuously, but none of them seemed to notice. Maybe alcohol had dulled their senses. More likely, they simply didn't sense her anxiety at all, and wouldn't have known the grounds for it if they had. They didn't have my knowledge of what she'd experienced. In addition, years of martial arts had trained me to discern the barest of physical reactions. Hers were clear to me, as were their origins.

I hated the fear that asshole had instilled in her, and I wanted to dispel it.

As we danced, I took both of her hands, gently, and brought them together behind her back. Her breasts brushed my chest and it took every sliver of willpower to keep from crushing her closer. She moved perfectly with me, closing her eyes. Earning that fragment of trust from her only made me want more.

She swayed, probably more affected by the cheap tequila in the half dozen margaritas her friends had furnished than being in the circle of my arms. When I released her hands to hold her body more firmly, she grabbed on to my arms like she was falling. Inching upward, those hands tracked a slow path to link behind my neck, and I waited for her eyes to flicker open. Her chin lifted, but her eyes remained shut until she was fully pressed against me—and then they flashed open, and she stared up at me.

She swallowed like she was summoning courage and stretched closer, curiosity in her unguarded eyes and lightly puckered brow. She didn't know me—a fact evidenced by her question: "S-so what's your major?"

Ah, fuck.

I wasn't ready for this fantasy to end—and end it would, as soon as I told her I was the guy she'd been emailing with all week—her tutor, who wasn't supposed to touch her like this, let alone the ways I really wanted to touch her.

"Do you really want to talk about that?" I asked, knowing she didn't. It was just an opening for more. More that I couldn't give.

"As opposed to talking about what?"

This was what you got, when you became too cocky about how principled you were, walking that straight and narrow. You slammed right into the one thing you couldn't have, just because it crossed your path while you were focused on your almighty integrity. Jacqueline Wallace wasn't mine to take, and her needs weren't mine to uncover and fulfill.

"As opposed to *not* talking," I said, wanting one slice of time with her, unspoiled by the secrets between us.

"I don't know what you mean," she said, a slight blush in her cheeks. But she didn't let go. And she didn't pull away.

I drew her closer still and leaned to inhale the scent of her again, committing it to deeper memory. "Yes, you do," I breathed, my lip grazing the soft skin just behind her ear. She gasped gratifyingly, and I couldn't decide if that reaction was the most enchanting or the most unfair thing I'd ever heard. "Let's just dance," I said, holding my breath, waiting for her answer.

She nodded once as another song began.

chapter Eleven

LANDON

When I started racking up detentions for tardies from sleeping in and my grades began slipping, the consequences I'd expected didn't happen. I thought Dad would try to ground me or yell at me. I thought he'd set up a parent conference with Ingram or take away my allowance. But nothing changed.

Sometimes Grandpa grumbled at me, but most of his griping happened when I didn't pick up after myself or pitch in on chores, so I figured out how to run the washer and help cook, and I kept most of my crap stuffed into my room.

Over dinner one night, Grandpa said, "You need to learn a vocation, son. Might as well be fishin', what with the gulf so handy and all."

As he plopped a spoonful of potatoes onto his plate, Dad scowled, but didn't contradict him—which was weird. So when summer came around, I was conscripted into working on the *Ramona*—which had been named for my grandmother. Getting up early sucked, because most nights I partied on the beach with the guys and staggered home late, no longer bothering to sneak out or in. I only got three or four hours of sleep before Grandpa woke me up, which he'd taken to doing with a pan and serving spoon when my alarm didn't do the trick. Nothing echoes like a metal pan in a tiny room with no windows.

Dad never took a day off. He was gradually transforming Grandpa's commercial fishing business into chartered fishing and sightseeing tours only, setting up a lame website with pics of rich tourists in front of the *Ramona*, showing off their catches—guys willing to pay a thousand bucks to spend a day drinking and being pointed to a boat-attached pole whenever it jerked from some poor fish taking the bait. All summer long and into the fall we transported skilled and wannabe fishermen to the best sites to throw down lines for redfish in the bay or kingfish offshore—fathers and sons or couples who bonded or spent the day trapped and pissed at each other, elite executives who came alone or brought VIP clients, frat guys who did more drinking, cussing, and sunburning than fishing.

I baited hooks, filled the tanks and supplies, cleaned and gutted fish, hosed down the deck, and took photos. By the end of the summer, I was darker, harder, and at least an inch taller than my grandfather, unless the wispy white hair drifting above his head like fog counted as height. (Grandpa claimed it did.)

Grandpa nearly came unhinged when Dad added sunset cruises for couples, dolphin-sighting tours for families, and whooping crane excursions for groups of little old ladies. But the money increased, and the workload was easier—especially with me for free labor, so there was only so much he could protest.

· · · · · · · · · ·

"I was thinking."

I feared Boyce was about to turn philosophical, and I was way too tired for that shit. I'd only had one beer before nearly falling asleep while making out with a hot chick who'd be gone tomorrow, so I decided to quit drinking before I ended up face-first in the sand. Boyce stopped in solidarity of the fact that we were the only two in our pack who worked our asses off during the day. Me on the boat, him at his father's garage. We carried threadbare beach chairs down into the surf to escape the others, who could be annoying shitheads, especially when they were high and we weren't.

"Dangerous, Wynn."

"Ha. Ha."

I focused on the cool waves lapping over my feet and the ceaseless, lulling hum and crash of the rolling water. The tide was still coming in. If we remained in this spot, we'd be waist deep by midnight.

"*I was thinking* that I've never seen you without your wrists covered."

I tried not to react, but my hands clenched the aluminum arms of the chair. As tan as I was, my wrists were as white as my ass—they never saw the sun. Ever. I wrapped them in bandanas and wristbands or the watch I seldom wore anymore. No one here had ever noticed the fact that all that stuff was masking something else. At least, I'd assumed they hadn't.

I turned my head to look at him. "And?"

He chewed a bit of dry skin on his lip. "I was thinking you could probably get tattoos to cover—y'know—whatever you're . . . hidin'." He shrugged, closing his eyes.

I stared out at the moon's reflection rippling across the water and felt my insignificance to my core. Nothing was important enough to strive for—nothing but the need to keep my past pushed too far down to feel. There was nothing else to be done with it. No other way to avoid it.

I'd never considered his idea, which seemed abnormally genius for Boyce. "Don't I have to be eighteen?"

He laughed, low. "Nah, man—don't you know me at all? I know a girl who'll do it."

"I don't know. Maybe."

He shrugged. "Let me know. I'll hook you up."

BREAKABLE

· · · · · · · · · ·

Her name was Arianna, and she was in her mid-twenties. One arm was sleeved in colorful ink, and the other had only two scripted lines on her inner forearm that read: *New beginnings are often disguised as painful endings ~ Lao Tzu.* We'd come an hour after the studio closed, since I wasn't old enough to get a tattoo without parental approval.

"If you want the tattoo to sort of cover the scars, like a smoke-screen, then the scar tissue is inked. But you could also incorporate the scars into the design—leave them inside the negative spaces. They'd be hiding in plain sight—like camo." She examined my wrists, turning them to and fro and brushing her fingers across the disfigured pink tissue. I felt nauseated and exposed, but I couldn't move. Boyce was uncharacteristically silent. "We could also tat all the way around. Make it look like wristbands."

I nodded, liking that idea. We looked over a few designs from a scrapbook before I pulled a sheet of paper from my back pocket. "Um. I sketched a couple of ideas . . . I don't know if you can use them."

She unfolded the sketch and smiled. "I can absolutely do this, if it's what you want."

I nodded.

She sketched and transferred the two designs onto my wrists—one for the right, one for the left, and then readied the equipment and snapped on latex gloves. It hurt like hell, but it was a bearable pain. Boyce was so skeeved out—I assumed from the blood, though my blood all over his fists a few months ago hadn't bothered him—that she ordered him to go sit in the waiting area until we were done.

"So why are you doing this?" I gritted my teeth as she worked over the bone at the side of my wrist, and tried not to think about the needle stabbing me over and over. "For me, I mean." I knew Boyce had filled her in. She hadn't batted an eye when I removed the bandanas.

Her eyes didn't waver from her work. "Because having the ability to make my skin my own again saved my life." She wiped the blood away and examined the link she'd just filled in. Her eyes met mine. "Some of us can begin to heal the damage people have done to us by escaping the situation, but some of us need more than that. Tattoos make statements that need to be made. Or hide things that are no one's business. Your scars are battle wounds, but you don't see them that way. Yet." She pumped the machine back to life with her foot.

I felt the burning prick of the needle as she began another link. "This ink will make your skin yours again. Maybe someday, you'll see that your skin isn't you. It's just what houses you while you're here." She paused as a roll of chills ran over me. "You're an old soul, Landon. Old enough to make this decision. Just like I was."

I went home with bandages around both wrists and strict care instructions. "This is like a wound of its own," she warned me. "Do *not* get a sunburn on top of it."

For the rest of the month, I kept them hidden, same as always. When the sun touched the bare skin of my wrists for the first time in almost two years, I felt naked. The reactions of most of the people I knew was some variation of *Cool tats, man.* Some people assumed I'd been hiding them under the bandanas all along, which made me laugh. *Yeah. The tattoos are what I've been hiding.*

Girls thought they were sexy. Sometimes they asked, "Did it hurt?" I'd shrug. "A little."

Dad and Grandpa had similar reactions—a quick flash of the eyes to the ink when it was noticed. A grunt of disapproval. No words spoken.

My next tat didn't cover a scar—not a visible one. Arianna put a rose directly over my heart. I didn't need to add her name, *Rosemary Lucas Maxfield,* to say who it memorialized. Dad didn't need her name, either. His face mottled purple the first time he walked into the kitchen and saw me in my board shorts and no shirt. He stared at the tattoo, still new and shiny with medication, and his hands fisted. Slamming through the back door, he hadn't said another word about it until a couple of weeks later, when we were out on the boat.

I'd just baited a kid's hook. He was ten or so and looked like he would pass out if he had to do it himself. Poor kid. He'd probably rather be building sand castles or slurping a snow cone on the beach than fishing with his dad and uncle. Instead, he would be stuck on this boat all day. I knew how he felt.

As I turned to open another bucket of bait, Dad said, voice low, "It's illegal for you to get those without parental consent. I checked." He stared where a dark red petal peeked out from the neckline of my white tank.

I waited, silent, until his eyes, ghostly silver in the bright sunlight, met mine. "It's *my* skin, Dad. Are you going to tell me I'm too young to mark it *on purpose?*"

He flinched and turned away. "Dammit, Landon," he muttered, but didn't say anything else. Every few months, I added something new. Black flames licking over my delts, following the sharp lines of my biceps. A gothic cross between my shoulder blades for my maternal Catholic ancestry, with Psalm 23 scripted around it. Mom hadn't been full of religious devotion, but she'd possessed an innate spirituality I envied now, and we'd attended mass often enough for me to have an idea of what it was about. I wondered if it would bring me peace to think of her in heaven, instead of in the ground.

Probably not.

On the second anniversary of the day we buried her, I got my eyebrow pierced. Dad railed satisfactorily while my grandfather seemed baffled that anyone would pierce a body part deliberately. "I've gotten enough hooks through various parts of my anatomy to not wanna put a hole through m'self on purpose!" He had a scar near his eye where a hook at the end of an inexperienced fisherman's pole had almost rendered him half blind. "Half an inch more and he'd have yanked my eyeball plum out!" He was fond of telling the story, and I'd heard it enough times to *almost* keep from pulling a squeamish face at the imagery.

· · · · · · · · · ·

Come fall, the Hellers were suddenly much closer, because Charles accepted a tenure-track position at the top state university—two hundred fifty miles inland. While their new place wasn't the twenty minutes we'd been accustomed to when we all lived in Virginia, it wasn't an impossible distance for a weekend trip. Except to Dad, who refused to make a four-hour drive to see his best friends in the world. His excuse was work, same as always.

I figured then that people never change. Dad might have quit his high-powered banking job, but he brought his workaholic personality with him when he left Washington.

Even though the teaching position was a step up for Heller's career, Cindy had to look for a new job, and Cole and Carlie had to make new school and neighborhood friends. I knew they'd done it with us in mind, but Dad closed his eyes to the sacrifice they'd all made. For him. For me.

His silence seemed to blame them for what had happened, though maybe just being around them reminded him. Maybe my presence— which he couldn't ditch as easily—reminded him, too.

I didn't need a reminder. I knew who to blame for us losing Mom. Myself, and no one else.

Dad dropped out of Thanksgiving at the Hellers' place—big surprise. Since I was fifteen and carless, he drove me to the bus station pre-asscrack of dawn. I could have refused to go by bus, alone, just to be an asshole, but that would have been a pointless rebellion. I wanted to go, even if I had to board a bus with a collection of broke degenerates who took one look at me and concluded that I was the most menacing guy on board. Silver lining: no one sat next to me.

The bus stopped in four piece-of-shit towns to pick up more transportation-challenged losers before arriving in San Antonio, where I transferred to an identical crap bus with a matching set of losers. The total trip would have been less than four hours by car—straight shot, no stops. Instead, after six hours, I arrived at a station that smelled like the combination of a poorly run rest home and areas of Washington, DC, that my friends and I had been forbidden to venture into on our own. Charles was waiting to pick me up.

"Happy Turkey Day, son," Charles said, wrapping me in an easy hug that pinched my heart with a single, abrupt awareness—my father hadn't touched me since the funeral. Even then, I remember clinging to him, unleashing my grief into his solid chest, but I don't recall him reaching for me on purpose.

He'd never uttered a word of blame, but there were no words of pardon, either.

Remaining within Charles's embrace a beat longer than comfortable to clear the moisture from my eyes, I shoved at the never-ending guilt in my mind and wished it would fall silent, just for today. For an hour, even. For a few minutes.

"You're gonna be Ray's height, I think," Charles said then, drawing back to take my shoulders in his hands and inspect me. I'd grown since I'd seen him last; we stood eye to eye. "You favor him quite a bit, too—but you got Rose's dark hair." He crooked an eyebrow. "And lots of it."

Charles had been a military guy before he went to college. I'd never seen a hair on his head longer than an inch. If it even got close to that, he joked that he looked like a damned hippie and went to get a haircut. It amused the shit out of him to harass Cole and me about our hair length whenever he got the chance.

"You're just jealous that we *have* hair," Cole smarted off the last time his dad had grumbled that he couldn't tell him apart from Carlie. I'd spit milk through my nose.

• • • • • • • • • •

My parents met the Hellers at Duke. Dad and Charles were PhD track in economics—worlds apart from Cindy and my mother, who were undergrads and best friends. None of them would've ever met their future spouses if not for my mother's decision to stroll through a doctoral student get-together held by her father—a distinguished economics professor and a member of Charles's and Dad's dissertation committees.

I was eight or nine the first time I heard the story, but the telling I remember was when I had my first real crush—Yesenia, in eighth grade. Love and destiny had suddenly become essential things to comprehend.

"I saw your dad from my bedroom window and thought he was so cute." Mom laughed at my eye roll. I couldn't imagine my father ever having been *cute*.

"I was sick of the pretentious artist boys I usually dated, and I thought someone like my father might suit me better. He always listened to my opinions and spoke to me like I had a brain of my own, and he spoiled me rotten, too. But his students were all so nerdy and awkward—until your dad. I thought if I could get his attention, I could get him to talk to me. Of course then he'd fall in love with me and ask me out." Her eyes crinkled at the corners, remembering.

"I must have tried on a dozen outfits before settling on one. Then I waltzed down the stairs and nonchalantly cut through the living room on my way to the kitchen. My clever little plan worked, of course, because I was pretty cute myself back then."

This time, I was the one who laughed, because my mother was

beautiful. There were times I caught my father staring at her like he couldn't believe she was standing in his kitchen or living in his house. Like she shouldn't be real, but was, and somehow belonged to him.

"He followed me into the kitchen to refill his iced tea glass." She nodded at my confused expression. You couldn't pay Dad to drink iced tea. "I didn't find out until later that he *hated* iced tea. He leaned against the counter, watching me make a sandwich. 'So are you Dr. Lucas's daughter?' he asked, and with a perfectly straight face, I said, 'No. I just wandered in off the street to make a sandwich.' I turned and looked him in the eye to give him a smirk, and I almost stopped breathing, because he had the most beautiful eyes I'd ever seen."

I had my father's eyes—clear and gray as rain, so this compliment was for me. I hadn't known yet that I'd also inherit his height, his analytical abilities, and the watertight way he could disappear into himself.

"Then, Charles strolled into the kitchen. Your dad glared at him, but he grinned and said, 'You must be Dr. Lucas's daughter! I'm Charles Heller—one of his many acolytes.' One of them asked me what I did, and I said I was an undergrad at Duke. 'What major?' your dad asked, and I told him, 'Art.' And then, Landon, he almost kept you from ever being born."

I waited, stunned. I hadn't heard *that* part of the story before.

"He sputtered, *'Art?'* and asked me what I was going to do with such a worthless degree."

My mouth fell open.

"Right? I wanted to punch him right in his handsome, arrogant face. Instead, I told him I was going to make the world more beautiful—*duh*! I let him know how unimpressed I was that all *he* was going to do was 'make money.' I stomped back upstairs, spitting nails and determined to never look at one of my father's students again, no matter how cute he was. I even forgot to take my sandwich with me."

The rest of the story was familiar: an impulsive invitation——passed through Charles in a chance meeting——to her very first gallery showing. Her best friend, Cindy, was there for support, in case Raymond Maxfield was insufferable. But my father was the opposite of insufferable. Appraising her work, he was awed. My mother always pouted that it was actually her paintings and not her charm, her beauty, or her sass that made him fall in love with her.

He'd always insisted that it was definitely her sass.

I knew the truth. He fell for all those things, and when she died, it was like someone had extinguished the sun, and he had nothing left to orbit.

LUCAS

Hours after I came home from the club Saturday night, I still couldn't stop thinking about holding Jacqueline——how she'd fit against me, bracketed by my arms. Her eyes, dusk blue in the smoke-thick club. Her nervous swallows. Her stuttered questions. As if everyone else had disappeared the moment I pulled her close, I didn't smell the mixture of sweat and cologne from the crush of bodies around us——just her sweet scent. I could no longer hear the music, shouts, or laughter. I was only aware of the beat, pounding vigorously, like the blood tearing an endless loop through my body.

Once home, I lay in bed and stared unseeingly toward the ceiling as my imagination ran rampant. I pictured her stretched out on top of me, knees astride, her body meeting my measured thrusts, her mouth open to the stroke of my tongue. My hands kneaded my thighs and every nerve in my body blazed. I felt her soft, bare skin. Her silky hair brushing the sides of my face. Her complete trust.

I pulled a pillow over my face and groaned, knowing anything I did now to relieve the building pressure would be a goddamned inferior rendering of what I really wanted. I could not have her, for so many reasons. She was off-limits, as a student in my class—which she didn't know. She was emerging from a breakup after a *three-year-long* relationship. I was the witness to a humiliation no one should have to bear, and she was afraid of me.

But maybe a little less so, now, my mind murmured.

I couldn't contain the thrill that shot through me, so I let it run its course.

Then I stamped it out and gave myself that second-rate release so I could get some sleep.

• • • • • • • • • •

Sunday night, Joseph and I met up at a bar in the warehouse district to see a fledgling alternative band from Dallas that we both liked. Though I'd barely slept the night before and had put in two hours of training at the dojang that afternoon, I was both wired and weirdly contemplative—two things I can usually dispense with in one good sparring session.

Master Leu had agreed to spar with me, since no one else was there, which had kicked my ass. For a smallish guy, he was the biggest badass I'd ever met. At a training expo, I'd watched him—in two moves—put a larger but equivalently trained opponent in a choke hold that could cause a real-life adversary to pass out. Or could crush his trachea.

Jacqueline's attacker had no idea how lucky he was that I was still a few levels away from being allowed to learn that move.

"Dude, you are not in Kansas anymore." Joseph's voice broke through my reverie.

I smirked. "I've never been to Kansas, actually."

He shook his head. "What—or *who*—are you thinking about? Never seen you so distracted. I've asked you three times if you're going home for Thanksgiving and you haven't so much as purposefully ignored me. You just aren't *hearing* anything."

Shaking my head, I sighed. "Sorry, man. Yeah, I'm going home. You?"

He shook his head and tossed back the rest of the tequila shot he'd been sipping. "Going home with Elliott. His mom loves me." His lips twisted as he leaned an elbow on the bar and looked at me. "Mine—does not."

Joseph had dropped hints about his family's rejection before, but he'd never stated it outright. I didn't know what to say.

"So . . . you're not welcome to bring Elliott home with you?"

"No, man. I'm not welcome home, period. It's a *no fags allowed* zone."

"Jesus. That sucks."

He shrugged. "Is what it is. Elliott's family is more than fine with us being a couple—his mom makes up a guest room for us that would rival any bed-and-breakfast, but they've had to deal with him bringing home a blue-collar guy. They're all educated and shit—whole family. His little sister is in fucking med school. The first time I met them, all he'd told them was where I worked. Imagine their surprise when they found out I keep the campus plumbing in order instead of teaching history or math or, you know, women's studies." He laughed. "I can't catch a break, man. I'm too gay to be redneck and too redneck to be gay."

Whatever my dad thought about me, whatever I did to piss him off—even purposefully, he'd never told me I was unwelcome to come home. I knew without thinking about it that I could move home right now if I wanted to. I wouldn't. But I could.

The band took the stage, and Joseph and I enjoyed sound that was neither pop nor musical theatre, a few drinks, and more than a few attentive glances from girls. "Yep," he said, angling a brow at a boisterous trio of coeds who kept looking our way. Hands behind his neck, he popped his guns from the sleeves of his white T-shirt. "I still got it, even if I don't want it."

Chuckling, I shook my head and signaled the bartender for one more round. I never picked up a girl when I was with Joseph, but I knew the ground had shifted beneath my feet when I found myself not even the slightest bit curious whether any of those girls were cute. There was only one possible reason for that disinterest.

I couldn't stop thinking about how to get Jacqueline Wallace back into the circle of my arms, come hell or high water. I was all too familiar with both.

· · · · · · · · · ·

Monday morning, I was nursing a slight hangover and a dampened outlook. Every time I saw Charles, I felt guilty. Every time I thought of Jacqueline, I felt more so. She hadn't emailed me over the weekend. I had what felt like a premonition about her figuring out that I was Landon, and told myself, *again*, that I had to put a stop to this. Now.

She dropped onto the edge of the seat next to me.

I was so thrown that I didn't say anything. Just stared.

"Hey," she said, knocking me from my stupor. Fearing my earlier gut feeling was about to go down, I focused on the subtle smile teasing the edge of her mouth.

"Hey," I returned, opening my textbook to shield the sketch I was working on.

"So, it occurred to me that I don't remember your name from the other night." She was nervous. Not angry. Nervous. "Too many margaritas, I guess."

Here's your chance. Sitting in economics class—what better place to clear up the . . . mix-up about your name.

I stared into her big blue eyes and said, "It's Lucas. And I don't think I gave it."

Dammit.

Heller came slamming and cursing through the door down by the podium, and Jacqueline's smile grew a little wider. "So . . . you, um, called me Jackie, before?" she said. "I actually go by Jacqueline. Now."

I called her Jackie? When . . . Oh. That *night*. "Okay," I answered.

"Nice to meet you, Lucas." She smiled again before hurrying to her seat while Heller was arranging his notes.

She didn't turn to look at me the entire lecture, though she seemed distracted—given the way she squirmed in her seat, unless she was talking to the guy next to her. They both laughed softly a couple of times, and I couldn't help smiling in response. It wasn't the first time I'd heard her laugh—but I was wired to her now. I felt the sound of her laughter all the way to my boots and back. I wanted to make her laugh—something Landon had undoubtedly done.

As absurd as it was to be envious of *myself*, I was. She responded to Landon's teasing emails with teasing of her own. When he told her he was an engineering student, she'd replied, No wonder you seem so brainy. Flirtatious words to direct at a tutor. Careful, possibly innocuous words . . . but flirtatious in context.

Dammit. I was jealous of *Landon*. Of all the stupid-ass reactions I could have right now, that was the most ludicrous.

At the end of class, she shot from her seat and rushed out the door before I could even get my backpack loaded. Some primitive, predatory impulse urged me to leap up and chase her out the door, as if that would be the most sensible reflex to her cut-and-run exit. I consciously slowed the process of sliding my texts and notebooks into the pack, stunned.

She was driving me crazy. And I was loving it. Goddamn, I was in trouble.

· · · · · · · · · ·

I'd agreed to take a couple of hours of Ron's shift so he could meet with an architecture professor who only had office hours once a week. I also had a parking enforcement shift this afternoon—after the group tutoring session and after my two-hour team project course. I wouldn't have time to study until after ten P.M. This day, with the singular exception of Jacqueline initiating that one-minute conversation this morning, was going to suck.

I glanced at my phone in between orders. Half an hour to go, and we were busy. Both canisters were running low. As soon as there was a break in the line, I closed my register. Just in time, too—because a group of students materialized and joined Eve's line.

"Eve—I'm going to the back to get coffee. It's low."

"Grab me a bottle of vodka while you're at it," she replied. Eve was grouchier when we were busy. Which was about 90 percent of the time.

"Grab one for me, too, Lucas!" The mechanical engineering admin was next in line. Dark-skinned and white-haired, Vickie Payton was an organizational wizard for professors, a valuable source of campus information for students, and a shoulder to cry on for everyone.

"Little early in the day, isn't it, Mrs. Payton?" I chuckled, backing through the door.

"Spring registration," she answered with a smirk. *"Oy vey."*

"Ah." I winked at her. "Two vodkas and one bag of Kenyan, coming right up."

"I wish," Eve mumbled, taking Mrs. Payton's order.

I brought the bag out and sliced it open. The line had grown, but Eve—whose apathy toward people in general didn't hinder her proficiency, luckily—had everything under control. Unthinkingly, I scanned the line, searching for Jacqueline. During the two weeks she'd missed class, looking for her on campus had become ingrained—something I did whenever I entered a room where she might have the smallest possibility of being.

The likelihood of her showing up here was better than most. Despite that fact, I was still mystified at the sight of her. My eyes swept over her, slowly, devouring every detail as if she were a last meal that I wanted to simultaneously consume wholly and savor.

She was with her friend, again, and that friend was watching me. Jacqueline was decisively *not* watching me. But they were talking, animatedly, and Jacqueline was blushing so hard I could see the blotchy pink of her cheeks from a dozen feet away. With effort, I turned to make the coffee, but the hairs on my arms stood up. My entire body was aware of her eyes on me.

My forearms were fully visible, and she hadn't seen my tattoos before. That night, in her truck, she'd stared at my lip ring and I'd known that she was one of those girls who shied away from guys like me on principle. I looked like a poster boy for a bad life choice. From her mode of dress, I knew she was a preppy sort of girl, as were her friends. And her ex. Hell, if someone stood me next to that asswipe who'd attacked her and asked the general populace which one the rapist was, I'd get a helluva lot more votes.

Even so, she was watching me now. On the dance floor Saturday night, she'd come into my arms as though she felt safe, against all better judgment. She was confused, but curious. Interested. I felt that one truth in the pit of my stomach, and it was gripping and unnerving. I wanted her attention. Her full attention. And I meant to get it.

I popped *start* on the coffee and turned to the register next to Eve without looking up. As soon as Eve took the guy in front of Jacqueline,

I shifted my eyes up to meet hers. "Next?" She blinked as though I'd caught her misbehaving, but came closer. "Jacqueline," I said, as though I'd just noticed her. "Americano today, or something else?"

She was surprised I'd remembered what she'd ordered a week ago. I would happily catalogue her likes and dislikes. Every one of them. From how she took her coffee, to how she liked to be kissed, to what stroke to use where to make her shiver from head to toe.

She nodded. I grabbed a cup and a Sharpie, but I pulled the espresso and made her drink myself.

Eve cocked a double-pierced brow at me, because she knew what I'd just done. "In the habit of handing out your digits to sorority chicks?" she murmured. *"Lame."*

"There's a first time for everything."

Shaking her head, she wiped the espresso valves and dumped two shots into a grande cup. "No, actually, there's not."

I shrugged. "True enough. Is it acceptable if she's not a sorority chick?"

Her lips twisted, and I got the feeling she was making a concerted effort not to smile. "No. But less *un*acceptable."

As Eve and I took orders and began to whittle the line down, I didn't allow myself to watch Jacqueline cross to the condiment stand to get her three sugars and splash of milk. I knew exactly where she was, every second, but I ignored her until she walked through the door, at which point I couldn't watch anything else.

"Oh, dear God. Someone's got it bad." Eve laughed, which made the guy across the counter smile at her.

He was wearing a Pike T-shirt.

"What?" she barked, glaring at him.

His smile disappeared and he threw up his hands. "Nothin'— just . . . nice laugh. That's all."

She rolled her eyes and spun to grab a new carton of soy milk, ignoring him.

When he looked at me, blond brows arched, I shrugged. I didn't know the girl's history, but there was no crossing that explosives-laden barrier. She was barely civil to me half the time, and she *liked* me.

chapter *Twelve*

LANDON

When spring semester began, I found myself in fourth period biology with Melody Dover and Pearl Frank—who'd been Pearl Torres, fellow occupant of the middle school loser lunch table, when I was in eighth grade and she was in seventh. Then her mom married Dr. Thomas Frank, prominent local surgeon and one of the town's most stubborn playboy bachelors—until he met his match in Esmeralda Torres, who wanted a big diamond on her finger and her daughter set for life.

She got both.

Pearl, who'd been a nerdy, awkward kid when I knew her, took a few summer school courses to skip ninth grade altogether, got a makeover and a shitload of brand-name clothes, and arrived in tenth grade hotter and richer than she'd ever been.

Melody lost no time in making Pearl her new best friend.

They exchanged a less than euphoric look when they were assigned to the only half-empty lab table—Boyce's and mine.

"So why are y'all in bio this period now? Get kicked out for bein' too sexy in class?" he asked.

They both rolled eyes at him and I shook my head and stared at the scarred black table, trying not to crack a smile. He'd been batshit for Pearl the minute he'd noticed her in the hallway last September. Too bad he hadn't paid her any attention in middle school, when she had no friends. She was returning the favor now.

"No, *dumbass*," Melody said, cocking her head at him. "We both made the dance squad, which meets last period. That's when we had bio last semester, so we had to switch. Lucky us."

Her glance flicked over me then, taking swift inventory of the tats peeking from the sleeves of my thermal henley, the bar through my eyebrow, and the stud in my ear. For the space of one second, our eyes met before hers slid away.

"Jesus, Dover—no need to be hostile." Boyce chuckled.

She glared, objecting to being called by her last name, I'd guess— especially by Boyce, who'd admitted to me that he'd called her Rover Dover all through elementary school. Having pretty much burned every bridge he crossed, our friendship was like a malfunction of his usually deficient people skills.

Our table was at the back of the classroom. Boyce and I leaned against the wall, stools tipping onto two legs in defiance of classroom policy. Mr. Quinn either didn't notice the infraction or didn't care to confront us. Melody and Pearl had to turn around to face the front of the classroom, leaving their notebooks and bags on the table, vulnerable to Boyce's inspection.

The girls had been writing back and forth in Melody's spiral, and when they turned their backs, Boyce slid the notebook to our side of the table to read it.

"Cut it out, man," I whispered. "What the fuck." I moved to push it back, but he held an elbow up, blocking me.

Eyes wide, he pointed to the feminine scrawl that I recognized as Melody's. I shook my head, and his brows elevated. "*Look*, dude. *Seriously.*"

I scanned the page and read, *Is it just me, or is Landon Maxfield OMFG HOT this year??? Holy. HELL.*

But you have CLARK, Pearl had written beneath this pronouncement.

Melody replied, *I can look, can't I?* ☹ *Switch chairs with me. I want to sit across from him.*

I glanced at the back of Melody's head, her silky blonde hair hanging straight and heavy down her back to brush the tabletop. It covered her ears today, hiding the side of her face from view. She remained diagonally across the table from me. Pearl had shaken her head, frowning, at some point in this written conversation—probably here. There was no reply from her in the notebook.

Dangit, Pearl. What kind of wingwoman are you? Melody wrote.

The kind that will keep you from making a big mistake. Duh, Pearl replied.

I rotated the notebook and pushed it back where it had been, my thoughts spinning, while Boyce pretended to grab his dick and whack off, complete with facial expressions of ecstasy. I punched him in the arm and his stool unbalanced itself and slid out from under him, crashing to the ground and making us the center of attention. Landing on his feet, he tried to punch me back, but I brought my stool forward and leaned out of his reach.

"Mr. Wynn has decided to demonstrate what happens when someone violates the class rule concerning keeping all four legs of our lab stools firmly and *safely* on the ground." Mr. Quinn sighed loudly. The rest of the class chuckled as Boyce righted his stool and sat, scowling.

"Assclown," Melody muttered.

"Do you need *medical* assistance, Mr. Wynn?" Mr. Quinn pressed, enjoying the moment of interest and popularity his lectures never generated.

"No, sir, Mr. Quinn. My ass—and other important parts—are all in working order. It's just OMFG hot in here. Holy *hell*." The class roared with laughter and Mr. Quinn attempted to restore order.

Melody narrowed her pale eyes at him, and one second later they went wide in realization. Her gaze snapped to me and her lips fell apart as her face flamed red. I stared at her glossy pink lips and then back into her eyes. Grabbing her notebook, she slammed the cover shut and turned around with it in her hands.

I punched Boyce again, he fell off his stool again, and Quinn sent us to the office with yellow slips that would result in detention.

"Jesus, Wynn." I twitched the hair out of my eyes as we left the classroom.

"What? You didn't wanna know that your favorite little piece of ass thinks you're—"

I turned and slammed him into a locker and he threw his hands up. "Fuck me. Dude, don't go losin' your shit over a girl like her—"

"And Pearl Frank is any different?" I shot back, turning to march toward the office—and Ingram, who'd be thrilled shitless to see the two of us, no doubt.

He sighed and followed, our boots echoing in the otherwise empty hallway. "I'm realistic, man. I just wanna do her. I know I can't have more than that."

I rolled my eyes. "Oh, but *doing her* is completely possible."

He grinned. "Hell, yeah. I'm Boyce Fucking Wynn. Anything is possible."

I couldn't help but laugh, pulling the office door open. He didn't even hear what he'd just said. In one breath he insisted that all we were to girls like Melody and Pearl was a good fuck, and in the next, anything was possible.

I was holding out for the latter.

• • • • • • • • • •

"Ain't you 'bout to be sixteen?" Grandpa said to me, the night before my birthday.

"Yeah, Grandpa." I waited for the punch line. With Grandpa, there was almost always a punch line to these sorts of queries.

"I didn't know if you were wantin' a flouncy pink dress or somethin' to go with that earring." He chuckled to himself and I smirked.

"Pink's not really my color. But thanks."

He was showing me his secret weapon to chewy box brownies—adding one less egg.

"Your grandmother never could figure out how my brownies came out better'n hers," he said, and I laughed.

"You kept your secret a secret from Grandma?" My father's mother had died when Dad was in high school, so I'd never known her.

"Hell, yeah, I did! She did try to wheedle it outta me, God love her." His eyes glazed over, reminiscing. I stared into the bowl and beat the ingredients together, giving him his private moment. As I stirred, he leaned closer. "The ladies love chocolate. Don't ever forget that, boy. If you can provide *homemade* chocolate, all the better. This secret will getcha out of the doghouse, guaranteed. Mark my words."

"Grandpa—this isn't actually homemade."

He harrumphed. "Close enough." I layered the creamy mixture into the pan he'd made me butter with my bare hands—which was kind of gross. "That butter'll crisp it up. Get it into all the corners," he'd said.

Once they were baking, he asked, "What were we talkin' about? Oh, yeah. Your ever-advancin' age." He snickered and I rolled my eyes when he wasn't looking. *Still waiting for that punch line.*

"I was thinkin' that tomorrow, we ought to start you learnin' how to drive." My mouth fell open. When I didn't reply, he said, "'Less you don't want to."

"I want to!" I answered, jerking out of my stupor. "I just . . . I didn't think you and Dad would—"

"Don't get too excited. Ain't no muscle car behind this proposal.

Just my old Ford truck, when I'm not using it. Figured you might wanna go on a date or somethin'—as long as it's not with that Boyce Wynn. You can do better'n him." He laughed to himself again, and this time, I joined in, shaking my head.

"Thanks, Grandpa. That'd be awesome."

He shuffled down the counter and pulled a driver's handbook from the drawer next to the silverware, full of secrets tonight. "Start learnin' the rules, and I'll alert the populace to vacate the back roads this weekend." He grinned and patted my shoulder, leaving the kitchen, and I stepped into my pantry room, flopped onto the bed, and opened the book, listening for the brownie timer.

• • • • • • • • • •

Mr. Quinn walked table to table, assigning diseases. "Each team will identify how their particular disease is caused—genetic, viral, bacterial, chemical, et cetera. I want to know if there are methods of prevention, if there are known or debated treatments, and whether or not it's contagious."

The table next to us was assigned anthrax. We got lactose intolerance.

"What the hell kind of lame-ass—"

"Mr. Wynn, I'll thank you to keep your language deficiencies to yourself."

"But Mr. Quinn—*lactose intolerance*? What kinda *disease* is that? People who get the sharts when they drink milk?" The class erupted into howls while Melody stared at Boyce with homicidal intent and Pearl covered her eyes, elbows on the table, sighing. Our teacher's face screwed into a knot of exasperation. Predictably, none of that deterred my friend. "Stop drinkin' milk—problem solved! Can't we have something like, I dunno, Ebola?"

Quinn returned to the front as the bell rang. "Start your research tonight, and be ready to debate your findings within your team tomorrow!" he called over the shuffling as we all headed for lunch.

"*How* can you be friends with that idiot?" Melody asked as we pressed toward the exit.

I lifted a shoulder and smiled down at her, catching the edge of the door and holding it open. "He's entertaining?"

She conceded with a tilt of her head. "If you're amused by complete idiocy." She started to return my smile, but it vanished when her boyfriend dropped his arm over her shoulders the moment we entered the hall. He was usually waiting for her after class.

"Hey, babe." He fixed me with a look. "Hey, emo freak. Get your dick pierced yet?"

"*Clark.*" Melody gasped as we entered the flow of students, most of us eager to escape campus for half an hour.

"Why are you so fascinated by my dick, Richards?" I asked.

He turned around and then glanced over my shoulder, where I knew Boyce was. "Fuck off, freak," he said, leading Melody down the east hall, toward the parking lot.

"I think Richards needs a new repertoire." I watched the sway of Melody's hips, her boyfriend's arm around her neck like a collar.

"Huh?" Boyce arched a brow. "You know he's buyin' from Thompson now, right?"

I laughed. "Perfect. So he's a hypocrite as well as a douche."

"Dude. Coulda told you that years ago." He knocked knuckles with a friend over the heads of a couple of girls as I watched Melody and Clark disappear through the far door. "Did I tell you he tried to pay me to fuck you up again?"

I pulled to a full stop and a freshman slammed into me, bounced off, and sprawled on his ass. Reaching down, I grabbed his hand and yanked him to his feet, guessing he had every textbook he'd been assigned in that backpack. He weighed twice what he should.

"What'd you tell him?" I asked Boyce as the freshman stammered a thank-you and scurried away.

Boyce grinned, one brow arched. "Told him to go fuck himself, of course."

LUCAS

Jacqueline didn't text or call me, so I concluded that either (a) she hadn't seen the number on her cup or (b) she saw it and wasn't interested in talking to me.

Considering that she'd volunteered her name and asked mine, I didn't think she was indifferent.

She emailed Landon, but her message was economics-related only. Or so it seemed on the face of it. She mentioned going out with friends Saturday. When I replied, I referred to that comment: I hope you enjoyed your night out. A night out I knew all about. She wouldn't tell *Landon* any more about her Saturday night, of course . . . but I wanted her to. With every exchange, I dug myself a bigger hole, but I couldn't stop digging.

Then I alluded to her breakup, and the fact that I'd never meant to be rude by acting as if I didn't want to know the details. Between the written lines, I urged, *Tell me,* but I didn't expect her to answer that unwritten directive—to reveal such an unprotected part of herself.

With one paragraph, she laid it all at my feet—the amount of time they'd been together. The fact that she'd followed him here to school, instead of auditioning for a prestigious music program far away. The way she blamed herself, completely, for being stupid. For believing in him.

She thought she was stuck somewhere she wasn't meant to be in consequence of that decision.

I wasn't a believer in fate or higher powers, as much as I wanted to be. I had faith in taking responsibility, and clearly, so did this girl. But I couldn't fault her for following someone she'd loved for three years—it pointed to a loyalty she wasn't giving herself credit for. If she believed in responsibility, then the best thing for her to do would be to take control again. To own the decision she'd made, however she'd made it. To make the best of it.

So that's what I told her.

• • • • • • • • • •

Wednesday, she arrived in class early, and I made an impulsive decision—all I seemed to be capable of where Jacqueline Wallace was concerned. I slid into the seat next to her and said her name. She startled a little when she looked up, expecting the guy who usually sat there, probably. But she didn't lean away from me.

"I guess you didn't notice the phone number on your coffee cup," I said.

"I noticed." Her voice was soft for such a smart-ass retort, candid curiosity in her steady gaze.

I asked for her number in return, and she asked if I needed help in economics. I almost choked, strung out between a now-familiar guilt trip and amusement at the absurd corner I'd backed myself into. *Do you need help in economics?* I asked why she'd think that, wondering, for two heartbeats, if she knew and was screwing with me.

If so, I completely deserved it.

"I guess it's not my business," she said, miffed.

I needed to move the conversation away from this line of thought. I leaned closer and told her the honest truth—that my wanting her number had nothing to do with economics.

She picked up her phone and sent me a text: Hi.

Her classmate walked up, wanting his seat. (Benjamin Teague, according to the roll sheet. I'd checked his campus address, schedule, grades, and any possible disciplinary notes—there were none. He seemed harmless, his fondness for *bro* T-shirts aside, and he made her laugh—both a point in his favor and a reason I sort of wanted to clock him cold.)

I surrendered the seat, holding back a jackass-level grin. She hadn't called me . . . but she had programmed my number into her phone.

And now she'd given me hers.

Toward the end of class, I glanced up to find her watching me—a first. I hadn't paid enough attention to the lecture, because I'd been immersed in devising and sketching alternative tissue engineering designs for Dr. Aziz's research project next semester. Nothing but thoughts of Jacqueline could break through my excitement after getting his email yesterday, telling me I'd been accepted. I would be working with two of the university's top engineering faculty members, and my final semester of tuition would be paid by the project's grant. I would still tutor for Heller and work the occasional parking enforcement shift, but I could quit the coffee shop, which currently sucked up fifteen hours of my week.

For the seconds Jacqueline and I stared at each other, Heller's voice receded and everyone else in the room disappeared. I couldn't return to Aziz's project, or recall the mass of ideas swirling through my brain one minute ago. My past evaporated. My future plans blurred. Every cell in my body was aware of her, and her only.

I knew I could be careful with her. Her trust would be hard-won, because she was afraid of being hurt again, but I could win it. I knew, from these few seconds of staring and from the one time I'd held her that she would respond to me, under me. That I could coax her body to levels of pleasure she couldn't possibly have received from her narcissistic ex, regardless of how long they'd been together.

And then I couldn't offer her anything more. At the end of this year—mere months away—I intended to take a job somewhere far away. To escape this state, and my father. To build a career and a life for myself, with no emotional entanglements. Not for a long time, if ever.

I wanted this girl, but I wasn't going to fall in love with her.

She deserved someone's whole heart. She deserved someone honest and loyal.

And I was not that man, no matter how much I wanted to be.

Landon,

We're making steak fajitas tomorrow night—come if you're free. Also, I'm giving a quiz over CPI first thing Friday morning, in case you want to work that into your Thursday worksheet. The quiz should take fifteen or twenty minutes of class, so feel free to grab a cup of coffee first and come in late.

CH

Jacqueline and I hadn't gone over CPI, so as soon as I created the worksheet, I emailed it to her. I also questioned her interpretation of meant-to-be as it related to her decision to follow Kennedy Moore to college: Can you prove you'd be better off somewhere else?

I asked her major, wondering if she'd given up music altogether, hoping she hadn't.

Her answer, music education, was a relief, but she lamented the thought of teaching, as if that would prevent her from performing. I couldn't see the correlation. Woe to anyone who tried to tell Heller he wasn't *doing* economics because he was teaching it. They'd get an earful about how he conducted research for respected peer journals, stayed current on global economic events, and participated in influential economic conferences.

I added a stern postscript *ordering* her to do the worksheet before Friday.

She emailed me back and called me a slave driver.

I closed my laptop and went for a run, but it didn't lessen the uncontrollable effect of her impertinent little replies. I paced the apartment for half an hour before grabbing my phone and pulling up her number. Shoving all misgivings aside, I sent her a text: Hi. :)

She answered in kind. I asked what she was doing, and commented on her quick disappearance at the end of class. I told her to come by the Starbucks Friday afternoon, when it was usually dead, adding, Americano, on the house?

She agreed to come, and I had a moment of exhilaration followed by the desire to beat myself into a bloody pulp.

"Why did you just sit there and let me do that?" I asked Francis.

He supplied a steady feline stare.

"You could have at least *attempted* to stop me."

He licked a paw, ran it over his face, and stared again.

"Is this how schizophrenia begins? First, talking to a girl as two different guys, and then talking to my cat. This is a new low."

"Meee-ow," he answered, tucking himself into a circle.

• • • • • • • • • •

Whenever Charles and Cindy were barbequing or making fajitas, I didn't have to ask what time dinner was—I just waited for the smell of grilled meat to permeate my apartment.

I grabbed the pan of brownies I'd made and headed over.

Dinner conversation concerned Cole, who would arrive in a couple of weeks for his first visit home from Duke, only to be stuffed into a car with the rest of us and driven to the coast. If Raymond Maxfield wouldn't come to Thanksgiving, Thanksgiving would go to him.

"Cole will be a cranky, stinky a-hole—three hours on a flight and then four hours in the car? Ugh!" Carlie protested.

"He's eighteen," Charles said. "He'll sleep."

"Good idea. Drug him," Carlie said, scooping a corn chip an inch high with guacamole. *"Please."* Her appetite had returned and then some after she got over her breakup. During dessert, her parents exchanged a smile when she took a brownie square. "Mmmm. These are like sex on a cloud," she commented, licking a finger, and her father's face turned to granite.

"Carlie Heller," Cindy said. "You're going to kill your father with statements like that."

"What? Dad, I'm *barreling* toward adulthood." She spoke while chewing. "You're around college students all day. That's less than two years away for me! Get real. I can't be a kid forever."

Caleb's eyes swung back and forth between his sister and parents. He hadn't been the center of conversation once during the meal. As the baby of the family, that was tantamount to invisibility. "Stephen Stafford kissed a snake," he said.

"I hope that's not a euphemism, because *eww*," Carlie said.

"What's a euph—"

"The snake in your science classroom?" Cindy asked, focusing on her youngest kid. Caleb nodded. "And how did this happen?"

"Dale Gallagher dared him."

"Ah." She looked at Charles across the table. "Well, I feel very sorry for Stephen Stafford's parents."

Caleb frowned. "Why? He probably didn't tell them he kissed a snake."

"Still getting mental pictures and trying to eat, *thank you very much*," Carlie mumbled, wrinkling her nose.

"Also Dale Gallagher had to pay him five bucks to do it."

"Then I suppose we can feel sorry for Dale Gallagher's parents as well," Charles said, arching a worried brow at Carlie. "If he's dumb enough to *pay* someone to kiss a reptile."

• • • • • • • • • •

When I'd first moved into the apartment above the Hellers' garage, I hadn't known what to expect—from how much interaction I would have with them to what the apartment would look like. No one had lived there since they moved in. They'd only used the space for additional storage. But I figured that whatever it looked like, it would beat sleeping in a pantry.

Carlie ran up to the SUV when Charles and I drove up. She'd been a preemie baby, so she had been small for her age all her life. Next to my eighteen-year-old body, she'd never seemed tinier. Still, she nearly knocked me over when she launched herself at me, as wide-eyed as a little kid on Christmas morning.

"Landon, you *have* to come see!" She grabbed my hand and pulled me along the driveway. After the four-hour drive, I was ready for a bathroom, a meal, and a nap, plus I had a carful of shit to unload, but there was no stopping a fully energized Carlie.

Her brothers and parents followed us up the steps, where Carlie presented a key ring with a single key attached. The ring's logo was that of the university where I would, unbelievably, be an official student in a week's time. As she bounced on her toes, I unlocked the door and found a sparsely furnished apartment. I hadn't expected furniture. Or newly painted walls, newly installed blinds, dishes in the cabinets, towels in the bathroom. An entire wall of the bedroom was covered in cork, ready for the drawings I might want to pin to it. Sheets were stacked at the foot of a platform bed.

With effort, I struggled to swallow. I couldn't turn and look at any of them. I couldn't speak. It was too much.

I walked to the window and twisted the rod, opening the blinds and flooding the room with light. My bedroom view was treetops—thickly leaved live oaks, and sky. The view from the living room would be the Hellers' backyard, pool, and house. They would be feet away. Steps away.

Charles and all three kids disappeared without my notice, and Cindy moved to stand beside me as I stared sightlessly out the window. "I'm so glad you're here, Landon," she said, her hand coming to rest on my back. "Charles and I are proud of what you've done to make this happen for yourself."

The Hellers were like family to me. They always had been. They always would be. But they were just that—*like* family. They weren't really mine.

chapter *Thirteen*

LANDON

"The frog is dead. It can't hurt you."

Melody batted her lashes from behind a huge pair of goggles. "That thing is disgusting. I'm not touching it." The one-size-fits-all lab apron fell to her knees and wrapped all the way around, and she held her forearms up, elbows bent, to keep the gloves from falling off her small hands. She looked like a child playing operating room nurse.

Don't think about her hands right now.

I crooked an eyebrow at her—the one with the barbell she was staring at last week when Pearl snapped her fingers in front of Melody's face to get her attention. "Would you have said that to Pearl?" I asked.

She shrugged one shoulder, her eyes on my eyebrow. Her dark green sweater looked as soft as her hair. The color darkened the edge of her irises and contrasted starkly with the pale strands forked over that shoulder. "Yes," she said.

Don't think about her eyes. Or her hair.

I sighed. "Okay. I'll dissect. You pin and label."

She thrust her plump lower lip out in a pout that should have looked ridiculous on a sixteen-year-old girl. *God. Damn.*

I was grateful for the heavy canvas apron I was wearing. And the high table between us. "Fine. I'll *dissect* and *pin* . . . and you label?"

She picked up a pen and smiled—awarding me positive reinforcement for caving so easily. "What's first?"

Like a lab rat, I itched to discover where she hid that lever. I'd push it over and over to have that smile directed at me.

"Uh . . . well, let's see . . ." I checked the instruction page. "Um. First we're supposed to determine the sex."

Melody caught her glossy lower lip with her flawlessly white, straight teeth, and I felt that bite—as though I was made of a single nerve ending—in one concentrated place. My dick twitched like a flag caught in a sudden gust of wind. *Jesus, what am I—eleven?*

Damn Boyce and his stupid mono. Damn Pearl and hers, too. They'd both been out for a week. Without Pearl's dampening presence or Boyce here to irritate Melody every five seconds, we'd begun to talk every day like we hadn't done in over a year. Since the doomed geography project. Since her boyfriend paid Boyce to kick my ass.

Melody leaned over the dissection pan and stared at the poor dead frog, which looked like it had died dancing—nose in the air and jazz hands. "I don't see a thingy. So it's a girl?"

I laughed. "Frogs don't have external *thingys*."

She scowled, the back of her gloved hand covering her nose to block the embalming fluid's eye-watering odor. "Then how the hell are we supposed to tell?"

I looked at the sheet again. "Says here the male has an enlarged thumb pad."

Heads together, we both stared at the frog for one long moment.

"C'mon now, he's not doin' it with his thumb!" she said.

Oh. My. *God*. I stared at her. She blushed and giggled, and then we were both laughing and Mr. Quinn was scowling in our direction. Apparently, dissection was not supposed to be fun.

"Let's skip that part for now," I said.

Don't think about your own goddamned thumb, either, for fuck's sake.

Melody dutifully inscribed tiny labels and stuck the pins through them while I sliced the frog stem to stern and pointed out internal organs. We grew accustomed to the formaldehyde and she made less and less gross-out protests. She began sticking the pins through the parts I removed, though she refused to even pick up her scalpel or tongs unless Mr. Quinn was making rounds to confirm that everyone was participating.

"Aww, everything is so tiny," Melody said, in complete seriousness. As though the parts inside a six-inch-long amphibian could be anything else. She looked at the diagram and back at the frog. "Ooh, are those his little nut things?" She picked up the pin with the *testes* label.

I chuckled. "Yeah. That's his nut things. Congratulations, we have a boy."

She frowned. "So he doesn't have a . . ." She trailed off while my brain filled in the blank: *dick, penis, cock, boner, phallus, beast.* That last was Boyce's designation.

"Er. No." Caught between regret and intense relief that Boyce wasn't here, I read the sheet, paraphrasing. "The male fertilizes the eggs by . . ." Son of a bitch. "Uh . . . climbing onto the female, wrapping his front legs around her, and squirting sperm over the eggs, after the female lays them."

We looked at each other from behind two sets of goggles. I was surprised mine hadn't steamed up yet.

"Kinda sucks for him, huh?" she said.

Don't think about putting your arms around Melody Dover. From behind. Jesus H. Christ.

• • • • • • • • • •

With Boyce out sick, I was back to walking to and from school. His rebuilt Trans Am might have been a loud, ugly, potential deathtrap—

but it was wheels. I was four months and a few driving hours away from my license. Grandpa and I located empty dirt and minimally paved roads inland every Sunday afternoon or evening so I could practice, taking the ferry to get there. He was close to determining that I was ready to drive on an actual road.

I'd hid my face to roll my eyes, and I definitely didn't tell him Boyce had been letting me drive the Trans Am whenever he'd had one too many beers or taken too many hits of a pipe or joint and I was relatively sober. He'd have probably ripped up my permit right then and there, and I'd never get behind the wheel of that old Ford alone.

There was only one reason I wanted that truck.

As if Melody would want to ride in that rusted POS instead of Clark Richards's snowy white Jeep—the one he got for his sixteenth birthday, a year ago. I'd heard him bragging about what Melody had done with him in the backseat of that Jeep, and his words made me furious and harder than hell. Furious because he shouldn't share that shit with a bunch of dumbasses around a fire on the beach. Hard because I wanted her to do those things with me.

Kicking the arm off a cactus as I stepped from the road into the yard earned me a sharp spine right through the toe of my black Vans. "Ow! Fuck!"

That was when I noticed Grandpa's truck parked next to the house. Along with Dad's SUV.

The front door was unlocked, although that could just be Grandpa forgetting to lock it. Dad and he had gone round and round about security and leaving the house unlocked—Grandpa insisting that he'd never locked the *damn house* in all his *damn years* of living there, and Dad insisting that it was no longer 1950.

When some out-of-towners broke into Wynn's Garage and stole an assload of tools, Grandpa conceded, sullenly. Sometimes he forgot to lock up, though.

"Grandpa?" I called, shutting the door behind me.

The interior of the house was dim after the bright, cloudless afternoon outside, even when I pulled off my sunglasses. At first, I didn't register that Dad was sitting on the edge of the sofa, hands grasped between his knees. He was staring at the threadbare rug under his feet.

He was hardly ever home this early in the afternoon, and if he was, he was working at the table, not sitting on the sofa. I frowned. "Dad?"

He didn't move a muscle. Didn't look at me. "Come sit down, Landon."

My heart thudded, the pace escalating slowly like an engine warming up. "Where's Grandpa?" I dropped my backpack to the floor, but didn't sit. "Dad?"

He looked up at me, then. His eyes were dry, but red. "Your grandfather had a heart attack on the boat this morning—"

"What? Where is he? Is he in the hospital? Is he okay?"

Dad shook his head. "No, son." His voice was gentle and quiet. I felt like he'd struck me with the unyielding words, sharp and irrevocable. "It was a massive attack. He went quickly—"

"No." I backed away from him, swallowing thick tears. "Goddammit, *NO*." Retreating to my room, I slammed the door and didn't come out until after Dad went to bed.

Barefoot, I padded into Grandpa's room—lit with the moonlight streaming through the half-open curtains. My fingers trailed over the items resting on his night table: reading glasses folded on top of a leather-bound Bible and a copy of *Leaves of Grass*, a half-full glass of water, a Timex watch with a scratched face, laid flat. On his dresser was a stack of folded shirts and a faded photo of my grandmother, holding a baby—my dad. The frame was old, tarnished, and bent on one corner.

In the kitchen, I took a lidded container of cold macaroni and cheese from the fridge and ate it without heating it first.

The funeral was short and sparsely attended—Dad, me, a group of old-timers, and a few other fishermen Grandpa knew, who'd been friends and neighbors. Dad wore the one suit he'd kept—still sharp and perfectly tailored, though it hung a little looser on him than it had the last time he'd worn it, at Mom's funeral. He'd lost weight. He was more muscular, but also gaunter. I didn't have a suit and didn't have time to get one, so I wore a black henley and black jeans for the service.

He was buried next to the wife who died thirty years before him. *Ramona Delilah Maxfield—Beloved Wife and Mother*, her headstone read. I wondered what Dad had ordered carved into my grandfather's marker, but I didn't ask.

The next day, Dad gave me two things from my grandfather: a heavy brass pendant with a Celtic symbol that supposedly represented the Maxfield name prior to the twelfth century, and the key to the old Ford truck.

I transferred the symbol, enlarged, to a sketch. I would have Arianna ink it on my side, at the edge of my rib cage. I slid the Ford key onto the ring holding my house key and a compass.

I had the truck I'd wanted, a thousand-year-old symbol of my heritage, a secret recipe for brownies, a pocketknife, and memories of my grandfather I'd have never had without the loss of my mother.

I couldn't make sense of these things or their value to me, when every one of them was linked to the loss of something I didn't want to lose.

LUCAS

I arrived as Heller was collecting the quizzes. As I slid into my seat, he asked to see me after class.

"Yes, sir," I answered, working to keep my gaze from sliding to Jacqueline, who was eavesdropping none too subtly, head angled, chin at her shoulder. My breath went shallow, knowing he could say one sentence—hell, one word—*Landon*—that would tell her who I was.

I wanted her to know.

And I didn't.

She didn't look my way again until the end of class, when I'd moved down front. As Heller answered a student's question, I took the opportunity to find Jacqueline in the mass of exiting students, but she was still in her seat. Looking at me.

Her eyes were dark, due to the distance between us and shadows cast by overhead lights. I couldn't make out the perfect blue I knew they were. I couldn't smell her sweet scent. She wasn't laughing or even smiling. She was just a pretty girl.

But I couldn't see anyone else.

"Ready?" Heller asked, stuffing lecture notes into his portfolio.

I wrenched my attention from Jacqueline. "Yeah. Sure. Ready."

He arched a brow at me, and I followed him from the room. "Sure you aren't working too hard, son? You seem a little preoccupied lately."

He didn't know the half of it.

• • • • • • • • • •

This was not my day.

First, Gwen arrived in the first bad mood I'd ever witnessed her have. She was like a completely different person. She was like Eve.

Who was also working the afternoon shift.

I had no idea when Jacqueline would show up, if she would show at all, but I knew—as Landon—that late Friday afternoons were when she scheduled her high school music lessons. She'd either be here any minute or not at all. When Heller showed up, ordered a venti latte, and parked it in a chair in the corner, I selfishly prayed he would slam his drink and go home.

He pulled out the *Wall Street Journal* and started at page one.

Not five minutes later, I heard Eve's familiar, barely civil greeting: "Can I help you?" with a double shot of attitude. I glanced up to see Jacqueline, chewing her lip as though she was reconsidering her decision to stop by.

"I've got it, Eve," I said, stepping up to the counter.

As I got her coffee and refused to let her pay, my coworkers continued to scowl at her, though I couldn't imagine a single reason *why*. Choosing one of the bistro tables on the opposite side of the café from Heller, she pulled out her laptop.

"What the hell?" I finally asked Gwen, stepping into her viewing path. "Why are you staring at her like you're trying to reduce her to ashes?"

She crossed her arms and stared up at me. "Please tell me you don't actually *like* that girl, Lucas."

I flicked a glance at Heller, who'd not moved except to turn the page of his paper. "What do you mean? Where'd you get that?"

She pinned her lips together, grimacing. "You're more transparent than you think. And also, we think she's playing you."

"*What?*" Thank God no customers were at the register and Jacqueline was too far away to hear this cracked conversation.

"It's true," Eve hissed, appearing next to Gwen. "Her friends came in here again the other day—you know the two I mean? The sorority chicks?" Her words said *sorority chicks*. Her tone said *disease-infested hookers.* Good God. I was giving her five seconds to get to an argument I could squash.

I nodded once.

"Well, I couldn't hear everything they said over the damned steamer, but I heard your name and her name and the fact that she's using you to be her . . . ugh . . ." She made air quotes. "*Bad-boy phase.* I've never heard anything so fucking *lame.*"

My brows rose. Bad-boy phase. Right. "You are both insane."

Eve crossed her arms. "Um, no. We're not. They're plotting the whole thing out and she's just following along. You're supposed to be like—a rebound stud to help her get over some other guy. So—for a million dollars and a chance to advance to the next round: do you *like* her or do you just want to screw her?"

They stood there like shoulder-to-shoulder crazy.

Rebound.

"This is not your business."

"The hell it's not." Eve poked me in the chest with one black-lacquered fingernail. "You're our friend, and we aren't letting some stuck-up bitch play you."

My jaw clenched. "Do. Not. Talk about her like that."

They looked at each other.

"Crap," Gwen said, as Eve said, "Well, fuck."

• • • • • • • • • •

After an hour, Jacqueline and Heller left, minutes apart. Before leaving, he stopped at her table, telling her how pleased he was that she was catching up—which I only knew because that was the topic he'd wanted to discuss with me this morning after class.

Then he stepped to the counter to talk to *me* about *her*—while she watched—and I remembered an old saying my grandfather had been fond of quoting: *Oh, what a tangled web we weave when first we practice to deceive.* I was getting a taste of what *tangled* meant.

The rest of the afternoon was so dead that our manager asked if anyone wanted to go home, and I volunteered. Eve and Gwen shared yet another pointed look. I'd never requested to be cut before.

Gwen followed me to the back and stopped me as I shrugged into my jacket. "Lucas?"

Turning, I sighed. "Yeah?"

Lips pursed, she laid her hand on my arm. "I know Eve can be a little harsh . . ."

I smirked. "Really? I hadn't noticed."

Her eyes crinkled at the corners when she smiled, and the Gwen I knew reappeared. "But we both care about you. We don't want to see you hurt."

I zipped the jacket to mid-chest—a soft, dark chocolate leather that I wouldn't have been able to afford on my own. Charles and Cindy gave it to me for my birthday my freshman year. It had been a little oversized then. It fit perfectly now. "I'm a big boy, Gwen. I can take care of myself. I have for a long time."

"Yeah, I know. Just . . . be careful. Some things aren't worth the pain, whether you can survive it or not."

She never said much about her baby's father, but I knew she was speaking from experience. I could hardly compare Jacqueline Wallace to a guy who was too much of a selfish prick to man up to being a father. But what I knew about Jacqueline wasn't mine to tell.

"Thanks, Gwen. I'll be careful," I told her.

Total lie.

I made a sandwich when I got home, sharing turkey slices with Francis, as I had the day he'd first shown up three years ago. I'd only been in the apartment for a month when Francis moved in, uninvited.

Even with the Hellers living on the other side of the yard, I'd had an unexpected sense of isolation. My father and I hadn't spoken often when I lived with him, but he was there, in the house. It wasn't talk I missed as much as the presence of someone else.

"What do you think?" I asked him now, tossing one last slice of turkey in his bowl. "Should I become her *bad boy*? I'm certainly quali-fied for the role." I picked up my phone and pulled up her contact info. "Speak now, or forever hold your peace."

He finished his turkey and started on a bath.

"That's tacit agreement," I said, texting Jacqueline an apology for not saying good-bye this afternoon.

It was awkward with Dr. Heller there I guess, she answered.

She had no idea what an understatement that was.

I told her I wanted to sketch her. Waiting for her answer, I watched the screen. *You want a bad boy, Jacqueline?* I thought. *C'mon, then. Try me.*

Okay, she said.

I told her I could be over in a couple of hours and got her room number.

She'd emailed Landon—ironically, *during* the hour she sat in Starbucks—thanking him for insisting she do the worksheet. Ninety-nine percent sure she'd aced the quiz Heller gave this morning, I wanted to email her back, but I didn't. She wouldn't be hearing from Landon tonight.

· · · · · · · · · ·

Her building was all too easy to get into. A simple, "Hey man, hold the door," to one of her fellow residents was all it involved. I took the back stairwell to her floor, my whole body burning.

I hadn't lied. I wanted to sketch her. Possibly, that's all I would do. Tonight.

I knocked softly, ignoring the other students hanging out in the hallway. She didn't answer, and I couldn't hear any movement inside her room. But when I knocked again, she opened the door as if she'd been standing right on the other side of it, debating whether or not to let me in.

Her sweater was a lighter blue than her eyes, accentuating them further. Dipping to a cautious V in the center and following her curves without adhering to them, the soft knit begged to be stroked. I vowed to answer that entreaty.

Entering her room—the door snapping shut behind me—was like closing a door on my conscience. That didn't keep it from tapping from inside my skull, though—a muffled but unremitting reminder that this girl was a student in Heller's class, off-limits. Further, she was getting over a breakup, which left *her* vulnerable in one way . . . and me in another.

Worse still, she had no idea of my conflict. I tossed my sketchpad on her bed.

Hands in my pockets, I feigned fascination with the room décor and felt her stare trace over me—from the worn shitkickers on my feet to the nondescript hoodie and the ring in my lip. Part beach bum, part redneck, part perfected *don't fuck with me* front—I was nothing like her preppy ex, for all that I could have been him, once upon forever ago. I thought nothing of what I wore then, or what it cost. The labels Kennedy Moore and his upper middle class *bros* sported wouldn't have impressed my middle school comrades, whose parents were influential lobbyists, senators, and CEOs of multimillion-dollar associations.

I'd never be intimidated by a boy flaunting his parents' money; I knew how fast it could all disappear, especially when it wasn't yours to begin with. This was a truth I'd learned, and learned hard: If you wanted something out of life, you had to depend on yourself to get it. And to keep it.

As Jacqueline's gaze ran over my face, I continued my sham inspection of her dorm room while in my head, I visualized the distracted expression she sometimes wore during Heller's lectures: eyes unfocused and unmoving, fingers tapping against her leg or her desktop, plucking invisible strings.

I had been drawn to her for weeks but kept my distance until the night I became her protector. Like that Chinese proverb that says if you save a life, you're responsible for that person forever—I couldn't seem to let her dust herself off and go on. Not when I didn't believe for one second she had the tools to protect herself. Maybe I hadn't saved Jacqueline's *life* that night—but I'd saved her from something that would have stolen a piece of her soul. I was consumed with watching over her, and to do that effectively, I needed to know her better.

At least that's the trumped-up story I told myself.

I caught her eyes on mine as I turned, and let my gaze skip to the small speakers on her desk. She was listening to a band I'd seen last month. I asked her if she'd gone to the show, and surprisingly, she nodded. I hadn't seen her there—but then, I hadn't known to look for her. I gave her some excuse about alcohol and how dark it was. If I'd known she was there, no amount of beer or darkness would have kept me from finding her.

Best not to disclose that.

I pulled off my cap and hoodie, tossing them on her bed and attempting to compose my expression before turning back to her. She'd probably been there with her boyfriend, anyway, while I'd gone with Joseph.

"Where do you want me?" she asked, and my mind blanked momentarily and then filled with images I couldn't say. She blushed as though she heard them anyway, her lips falling open, unable to take back the coquettish question she'd obviously not meant as a seduction tactic.

I cleared my throat and suggested the bed, matching her unintentional come-on with one of my own. Shoving my hoodie and cap off her comforter as she sat, I reminded my resurrected hormones that there were a million reasons Jacqueline Wallace was not for me, starting with the fact that I was basically lying to her about who I really was, and ending with the knowledge that girls like her didn't fall for guys who looked like me.

But she didn't have to *fall*, did she, for me to be the boy she slummed with? Her bad-boy phase. Her rebound. God help me, I was all too willing.

She stared at me with wide, apprehensive eyes, and I wanted to calm her, to gentle her with my hands. Instead, I found myself telling her we didn't have to do this if she didn't want to. I waited for her to release that pent-up breath she was holding and tell me this was a mistake. Part of me hoped for those words, because then I could back-pedal before I made the monumental mistake of compromising my integrity in too many ways to count.

But I wouldn't leave unless she told me to. Not while my head was full of nothing but wanting to move closer to her.

"I want to," she said then, softly, her body still rigid, like one of my wooden sketch models—bendable at the joints but otherwise inflexible. Her declaration didn't correspond with her posture, but I didn't know which was valid—her body or her words.

"What position would be the most comfortable for you?" I asked, and she blushed again, harder than she had a moment before.

I bit my lip and turned away, parking my ass on the floor several feet from her, my back against the only blank section of wall in her room. Opening the pad against my knees, I took a slow breath through my nose and cursed myself for sending that text. Even though my request to sketch her was no ploy, this private proximity was nothing short of hell. In one crashing moment, I realized that I wanted her more than I'd ever wanted anyone before. This desire had been building for weeks, and I'd left it unchecked, because she had a boyfriend, because she was a student in a class I tutored, because she was impossible, unattainable, a fantasy and nothing more.

Then there was that night—a night that must terrify her, still— but I'd kept it from being so much worse. My hand gripped the pencil. I couldn't credit myself for saving her and then take *her* as the prize, not under false pretenses, not when she could never be mine.

But then, she had false pretenses as well, didn't she? I could give her what she wanted.

I told her to lie on her stomach and face me, and she obeyed.

"Like this?"

I nodded, and my head swam. *Goddamn*—what had I done to myself? I had to touch her.

Unmoving, she watched as I tossed the pad and pencil to the side, coming up on my knees and closing the distance between us. She closed her eyes when I pulled my fingers through her hair, arranging it to reveal the curve of her jaw. A tiny, solitary freckle became visible just under her chin, and I forced my hand away to keep from stroking a finger over it. She opened her eyes, and I wondered if she could see the battle raging inside my skull and beneath the surface of my skin.

We were both silent while I sketched her. I knew she was watching me, though she couldn't see what I was drawing. I felt her gaze but didn't return it. Minutes later, her eyes drifted closed and she went very still. I finished the sketch and wasn't sure what to do. On my knees again, I approached the bed, sat back on my heels, and watched her for several minutes. Her breathing was deep and even. I put the pad and pencil aside and struggled not to touch her.

"Falling asleep?" I whispered, finally, and her eyes opened.

"No," she said, though I knew she was mistaken.

I didn't correct her. She asked if I was done and I heard myself tell her that I wanted to do another. When she agreed, I asked her to turn onto her back. She obeyed. I told her I wanted to arrange her, and she consented. My heart drove life through my veins as if I was waking up from a years-long coma. Everything was bright and detailed. Raw and sensitive. I wanted her so badly it hurt.

At first, I thought to arrange her as though she'd tumbled from the sky and landed on her back—an angel dragged to earth by her broken heart. But as I took her wrist and angled her arm over her head, I pictured her in my bed. Heart pounding, I moved her opposite arm—first to her stomach, and then above her head, with the other. I crossed her wrists and imagined her laughing and daring me to tie her up, clear as a memory. *Goddammit.*

I had to stop touching her or I was going to lose my mind, so I sketched her as she was, concentrating on lines and angles, shadows and reflections. My pulse subsided to a steady rhythm. My breathing returned to normal.

My gaze moved to her face. To her eyes. Which were wide open, watching me.

Her small hands, still obediently crossed at the wrists above her head, clenched into fists and then relaxed. The pulse at her throat thrummed. Her chest rose and fell faster. I was lost in the endless blue of her eyes. She seemed almost afraid, which made me angry—though not at her.

"Jacqueline?"

"Yes?"

"The night we met—" *I'm not him. I'm not him.* "I'm not like that guy."

"I know tha—"

I put my finger to her soft, full mouth, stilling her words. "I don't want you to feel pressured. Or overpowered." Even in the midst of my duplicity, I meant the words, needing her to trust me. I also wanted to kiss her more than I wanted the next breath.

"I do, absolutely, want to kiss you right now. Badly."

I was the more fearful one, because I knew she'd say no. I would prove to her that I could be trusted by leaving. I trailed one finger from her lips to her throat, down the center of her chest, and waited for her *no*.

But she didn't say it.

Her voice was little more than a sigh. "Okay."

chapter *Fourteen*

LANDON

The first time I drove solo wasn't what I'd ever dreamed it would be. I'd imagined cruising with Boyce on a Saturday night. Picking up some faceless girl to see a movie or get a burger. Grandpa sending me to the store to get milk.

Instead, I drove to the dock and caught the ferry that ran twenty-four/seven, as Grandpa and I had done many times—but I'd never been the one to steer the truck onto the ramp. I drove to the cemetery, blanking on bringing flowers and realizing when I arrived that I only had a vague notion where, exactly, he was buried. Seventy-two hours ago. That day had been a blur. It didn't feel real.

I found my grandmother's headstone and the mound of new dirt next to it.

A week ago, I was driving on a back road not far from here, with Grandpa in the passenger seat. He was telling me how he'd learned to drive at fourteen, when he quit school to work with his father and older brother. "I damn near stripped the gears offa that old Dodge afore I learned to manage it," he'd said, chuckling at the memory.

I tried to remember the last thing we said to each other, but I couldn't. Probably something to do with dinner, or chores, or the weather.

Now that I was standing at the foot of that mound of dirt, I didn't know what to do. Was I supposed to talk to him? Cry? He wasn't there. He wouldn't hear me. So these things seemed beyond pointless, unless I wanted to hear myself talk—and I didn't.

The cemetery was dotted with a few lone visitors, like me, and one large funeral service gathering. Under a big tent housing a load of massive floral arrangements, people huddled, paying their respects while seated on padded folding chairs. Whoever died had been money. I glanced at the cars lining the road near the gathering, recognizing the insignias—Cadillac, Mercedes, Audi, even a Jag . . . and Clark Richards's shiny white Jeep.

What the hell.

Scanning the mourners, I found him easily—on the front row. His dark blond hair was slicked back and he wore a black suit, white shirt, and a dark red tie. Melody sat on his left, wearing black and leaning into him. His arm was hooked around her shoulder, his face impassive. Even with the distance, Melody's miserable, crumpled posture was obvious. Her shoulders vibrated, and though I couldn't see her face or her tears, I felt her grief like a punch to the gut.

Her older brother Evan was on her right. I recognized their mother, next to Evan. The man next to Mrs. Dover was probably her husband. Immediate family accounted for, but they were all on the front row. They'd lost someone closely related.

I considered the dirt at my feet. *Dust to dust.* My throat tightened. "Good-bye, Grandpa. Thanks for the truck."

Later that night, lying in bed, I texted Melody: Are you okay? I was at the cemetery and saw you today.

She texted right back: My grandmother died Friday. Her funeral was today. I hate my family. All they care about is her money.

That sucks, I said.

Thirty minutes passed before she texted back: I'm in the fort. I needed to come outside and stare at the stars. You can come over if you want.

K. I pushed *send* and grabbed my hoodie from the hook on the back of my door.

Dad squinted up from the table where he'd spread the business ledgers and stacks of files, noting the boots on my feet and the hoodie I pulled over my head. He said nothing, but I recognized the disappointment in his tensed jaw before I turned and walked out the front door. If he'd assumed my grandfather's death was going to turn me into a model citizen, he didn't know me at all.

There was almost no wind—weird for March. Warmer than it was earlier, too. When I ducked into the fort, I pulled the hoodie off, climbing the ladder and losing my breath at the sight of Melody, sitting against a wall, her lower half wrapped in a blanket, her upper half in a thin-strapped tank.

"Hey," I said.

"Hey." Her voice was scratchy, like an old recording. She'd cried a lot, and recently.

I sat next to her, close enough to touch, but not touching. I knew from experience what not to say—*I'm sorry*. Not because there was anything wrong or even insincere about the phrase, but because there was no good answer for it.

"What was your grandma like?" I asked instead.

Her mouth turned up at the corners, just barely. She rested the side of her face on her knees and looked at me. "She was feisty. Opinionated. My parents hated that. They didn't think she was *circumspect*—that's what they used to say to each other. She wasn't dainty and discreet and easily hushed. They just wanted her to shut up, but no one could dictate to her because she held the purse strings."

That didn't sound like a woman who would have urged Melody to let a big brother or boyfriend boss her.

"She had a ton of grandkids, but I was her favorite," she said. "She told me so."

I mirrored her slight smile. "I was my grandfather's only grandkid, so I guess I was his favorite by default."

"I'm sure you would have been his favorite even if he'd had a dozen grandkids," she said.

My heart squeezed. "Why do you think that?"

We were sitting in the dark, a foot apart. Every part of me wanted to be physically closer to her, and now she was tugging on my heart. "Well . . . you're smart, and determined, and you care about people."

My lips fell open. "You think I'm smart?"

She nodded once, face still pressed against her knee. "I know you are. You hide it, though. Because of people like Boyce?"

I lifted a shoulder, one knee up and the other leg sprawled. The underside of my boot was halfway to the opposite wall. This fort was made for six-year-olds. "No. Boyce doesn't rag me about stuff like that." *Boyce only rags me about wanting a girl I can't have.* "I don't see the point—school, grades, all that. My grandpa quit school when he was two years younger than me, and my dad has a PhD in economics—but what difference did it make? They both ended up working on a boat."

She blinked. "Your dad has a *PhD*? Then why is he—I mean, why wouldn't he do something more . . ."

Lips pressed together, I turned my head to watch her stumble over this knowledge—something I'd not shared with anyone else, even Boyce. "More prestigious? Or something that makes more money?"

She shrugged, embarrassed for her impolite question, but still curious.

"He did. Then my mom . . . died." I stared at the sky. "And we moved here. And whatever he learned or did before was just a big fucking waste of time."

"So you don't want to go to college?"

"I don't know. I mean, I wouldn't know how to pay for it if I did."

I felt my face burn and was glad for the darkness. This was Melody Dover, for chrissake, and lack of money was a weakness to people like her. *Weak* was the last thing I wanted to appear to Melody.

"You could get a scholarship, maybe."

I didn't want to tell her I'd well and truly blown that to hell. My GPA wouldn't inspire admiration in institutions of higher learning. I probably wouldn't be admitted, let alone given a free ride.

I shoved my hand into my hair to push it off my face, and she reached up to trace the tattoo over the back of my wrist with one finger. I brought my hand down, slowly, and rested it between us. "I like this," she said, moving to the lick of flame over my triceps, tracking it along the cut of my biceps and up under the sleeve of my T-shirt. "And this."

"Thanks." My vocal cords failed me, and the word was a whisper. Our eyes met, lit by stars and moonlight alone.

She pulled her hand back into her lap. "Thanks for texting me tonight, Landon. And for coming over. I didn't want to be alone after this full-of-suck day. Pearl has a ten o'clock curfew, and I guess Clark is asleep—he never answered me."

I knew for a fact that Clark Richards was closing a deal with Thompson tonight and was currently getting high on the other side of town. "No problem."

LUCAS

She said okay.

I dropped the pad onto Jacqueline's floor and pressed her to the mattress, carefully, but with no hesitation, the tips of my fingers tracing the pale veins at her wrists. Her heartbeat vibrated under my fingertips, ticking almost double the count of seconds in a minute. My fingers followed those blue trails until they vanished into the crook of her elbows, her skin too fragile and soft to be real.

"You're so beautiful." I may have spoken the words aloud or inside my head. I wasn't sure which.

My lips closed over hers, more carefully than I'd ever kissed anyone. I was terrified to startle her. Afraid she would retreat and never trust me with this chance again. Afraid she would equate me with that asshole who hurt her—who would have hurt her so much more.

I shoved him from my mind as though I'd pushed him from a cliff. He was not a part of this. I wouldn't let him in.

I touched my tongue along the seam of her lips—a quiet inquiry and a promise to withdraw if required. But she opened her mouth, and my blood ignited, rolling below my tattoos like tiny ribbons of fire. Her tongue touched mine—a connection I hadn't imagined would be allowed, and one that incited an ache for more. I swept my tongue across hers and she sighed and trembled beneath me.

I placed one hand over her wrists and one at her waist, as if I could ground her to this moment. Exploring her was suddenly all I was meant to do in this life. When I sucked on her plump lower lip, so unbearably sweet, her breath caught. My tongue drove into her mouth, harder, seeking more of her, and her hands turned to fists beneath my hand. I released her instantly, fearing I'd frightened her with the intensity of what I felt, praying I hadn't—but her eyes opened, and I read nothing there but wonder.

I placed her hands around my neck and sat up, pulling her into my lap as her hands wound into my hair and *God almighty* she could have asked anything of me in that moment and I'd have granted it.

Her head fit into my hand as I inclined her back, tipping her chin to kiss that freckle I'd noticed while sketching. My lips moved lower, so slowly, my entire body on alert for any sign of *too far* from her. Her chest rose and fell, the soft pant of each breath echoing into the room and blending with mine above the music from her laptop that had faded to the background. I knew the songs but couldn't have said or cared what they were as my free hand wandered beneath her sweater.

I skimmed greedy fingertips over her ribs and up over the silky fabric of her bra, pushing her sweater higher. Her accelerating breaths feathered over my face and fanned my hair as I ran my tongue along the curve of her bare skin, just above the cup.

The tiny clasp was in the front. One press between my thumb and index finger followed by a half-inch slide would open it, but my brain won out. This would be too far. My conscience whispered from the other side of the door that I was kidding myself with this mental pretense of gallantry. This *entire night* was too far, and I damned well knew it.

I should leave, I thought.

And then she laughed. Not even a laugh, really—more like a strangled giggle, ricocheting through the room at the strangest possible moment.

"Ticklish?" I asked, because I couldn't imagine another reason for her to laugh at such a point. She bit down on her lip, much too hard. I wanted to object that she was injuring a part of herself I was prepared to spend the next hour adoring. I'd dreamed about her lips, her mouth, her tongue—I didn't want her putting any of them out of play. She shook her head, *no*, and I stared at her lush mouth and asked, "You sure? Because it's either that . . . or you find my seduction techniques . . . humorous."

She laughed *again*, belatedly covering her mouth.

I wasn't about to let her get away with hiding those lips from me. Aloud, I mulled over the idea of tickling her, just to dismiss her hysteria, and her eyes widened.

"Please don't," she begged, as if I would. Any fingers I stroked over her body would be an entirely different sort of touch, and I'd be damned if she'd laugh again, as adorable and weird as it was.

Drawing her hand away from her lips, I placed it over my heart and captured her mouth with mine—giving her no time to become anxious, giving myself no time to deliberate. She moaned softly, driving me out of my mind.

I pulled her sweater back down, but I didn't need to see her to feel her, and my imagination filled in every visual void. Caressing the soft skin of her abdomen, moving north, lazily—two inches up and one back, my hand finally cupped one breast, full and perfect. She gasped when my thumb grazed over her nipple and I felt it harden instantly through the thin fabric of her bra. I pinched it gently, reveling in her responsiveness, before paying equal attention to her other breast.

I could draw her from touch alone, without ever seeing her naked body. She'd have areolas the size of quarters, I'd guess—rosy pink nipples straining toward my mouth if I arched her further over my arm and licked each of them, once, blowing gently across the surface of her skin.

God. Damn.

As if she read my mind, she moaned, opening wider, and my tongue delved deep, probing every inch of her hot little mouth, stroking her tongue rhythmically. Growling my pleasure when she sucked on mine, I tightened my arm around her, exerting every ounce of willpower I had to keep from pulling her astride my lap, tugging her sweater over her head, sliding her bra off, and sucking her into my mouth while she molded her heated core against my rock-hard, all-too-willing erection. What exquisite torture that would be.

She hummed in my arms, giving herself over to kissing me, having no thought, I'm sure, that I was imagining so much more than these heated kisses, as powerful as they were. I stroked her throat with my fingers, like putting my hand to a train track and feeling the rumble of a train I couldn't see yet, coming fast. Abandoning her lips momentarily, I sucked soft little kisses along the front of her neck—not forceful enough to leave marks, but hard enough to leave her dizzy. Hard enough to give her a sample of what I could make her feel.

Sliding my hand around to the base of her spine and pulling her closer, I teased my fingers into the back of her jeans while I returned my mouth to hers, kissing her slow and gentle to slow and deep, slow and deep to fast and tender, fast and tender to hard and deep—reeling her in, bit by bit.

Her hand massaged and pressed. My skin burned and my muscles leaped under her palm as if prepared to do her bidding, whatever it was. I was only in charge because she allowed me to be. My command was illusory. If she said stop, I would stop. If she leaned to my ear and said *Take me, now,* I would, knowing it was too soon and would be a mistake. I would do whatever she asked, however she asked it. I would be her bad boy, if that's what she wanted. If that's what she needed.

I wanted to make it good for her. *So good.* But not this time. Not yet. Stretched out on her narrow mattress, without removing a single item of her clothing, I'd driven us both to the brink of crazy. One tap and we'd go over the edge. Her languid posture and heavily lidded eyes told me she was kiss-drunk and pliant. She would follow my lead.

"I should go," I whispered.

Her forehead creased. "You want to go?"

No, beautiful girl. I want to pin you to this mattress and please you in every goddamned way possible for the rest of the night.

"I said I *should* go." I pressed a kiss to the corner of her mouth. Her lips were swollen and wet, and if I didn't stop looking at them I wasn't going to make it out of here. Moving to nuzzle her ear, I said, "*Should* is different than *want*."

She sighed in response. "Can I see the sketches, then?"

"Mmm, sure." My body protested the separation as I lifted from her to sit up, taking her hand and pulling her up as well. If she'd re-mained lying there, her hair all around her face, her clothes askew, my shredded self-control would be thrown out the window. Forcefully.

I grabbed the sketchpad and sat next to her on the edge of the bed.

I showed her the two sketches—each undeveloped, in need of fine-tuning. Despite that, she seemed impressed. I told her I would probably redo them in charcoal and tack them to my bedroom wall. Her response was comical astonishment, especially when I added, "Who wouldn't want to wake up to this?" I bit the inside of my cheek to maintain my blank expression.

Too late, I realized I'd not washed my hands after sketching her, before touching her. If I removed that sweater, she'd undoubtedly be covered with swipes of gray, as if I'd marked her as mine. My body tightened in response to that thought. I leaned against her door and pulled her up and against me as I kissed her one last time. When she came onto her toes and pushed into me, I knew she was five seconds from being flat on her back in the middle of that bed.

"I have to go now, or I'm not going." I groaned.

She said nothing—no *yes, go*, but also no objection to my leaving. I dismissed what I saw in her eyes—a moment of hesitation that said I could be more than the rebound her friends meant me to be. Imag-ined, no doubt. I kissed her forehead and the tip of her nose, but not her tempting, luscious mouth, murmured, "Later," and left her room, my thoughts disordered and my body on the verge of rioting.

chapter *Fifteen*

LANDON

Having grown up in a small, private school, I knew something of small towns. The way nothing ever remains a secret. The way secrets spread like wildfire. The way that fire doesn't die out until a bigger fire consumes it.

Over spring break, four college girls rented a house on the beach—a Richards property. Clark's father sent him over to deliver the keys when they arrived. Word was, he stopped by with a couple of his bros from the varsity baseball team, and they hadn't left for an hour. That might not have been a big deal—but they returned that night with another guy. And nobody left until the next morning.

At least one of those guys couldn't resist bragging about the alleged orgy trade-off—not that anyone could blame him for talking. Strip poker with Cuervo shots and college girls, two guys and two girls adjourning to each bedroom and multiple partner swaps? Most guys are going to talk. And talk. And talk.

Some aren't content to stop there. Some want to take pics and video clips as proof and send them to friends, usually when they're too drunk or high to realize that a buddy with a long-term girlfriend was in one of those videos. The one where a mostly naked girl straddles him in a chair, moving and moaning in such a way that no imagination is required to know what's going on.

Boyce and I saw the video early the next day.

Melody had seen it by the time Clark went to her house the next night. There was a huge fight, and her mother threatened to call his dad if Clark didn't calm down and leave. He nearly flipped his Jeep at the end of their drive, peeling a sharp right and leaving a parallel set of rubber stripes.

I wanted to deck him when he showed up at one of the bonfires dotting the long stretches of sand three hours later, acting as if losing Melody was little more than a minor annoyance. Boyce told me Clark had screwed vacationers before—he just hadn't been caught. "Some guys think it doesn't count if it's with some chick who's short term. It's a temp fuck." As if to illustrate Boyce's statement, Clark paired off with an unfamiliar girl five minutes later. This one looked thirteen and wide-eyed as a baby deer.

"Whoa, dude—look," Boyce said, gesturing with his cigarette.

Melody slogged through the sand, flanked by Pearl, who was carrying a cardboard box. Marching up to Clark in the flickering firelight, Melody dipped her hands into the box in her friend's arms and rained ripped-up photos and what looked like pieces of stuffed bear over his head.

"What the fuck, Melody?" Clark said, standing and letting the startled girl in his lap fall onto the sand. She crawled away like a crab.

"You. Cheating. *Bastard!*" Melody pulled a gold bracelet from the box and hurled it at his feet. It hit him in the ankle and lurched toward the water, rolling.

"Those are *diamonds*, you psycho bitch!" he yelled, leaping to grab it.

"You can't buy me!" she returned.

"Who'd want to?" he snarled, and she burst into tears, stumbling away. Pearl threw the empty box at his head—he ducked and it sailed over his shoulder—and followed her friend.

• • • • • • • • • •

I tugged the cord to the fort's door, listening hard. I thought I heard a barely audible sniffle, but it could have been a gust of wind. "Melody?" I whispered.

Her face appeared from above, her hair luminous in the moonlight, like a halo around her entire head. She squinted and then said, "Oh— Landon. What are you doing here?" She hiccupped. It had been over two hours since the scene on the beach, but she was still crying.

"Just came to check on you. Can I come up?"

She nodded. "Sure."

We sat in silence until she scooted closer and leaned her head on my shoulder. "Half my friends are saying I overreacted and half want to help me hide his body. I don't know what to believe."

I shook my head. "Overreacted? Because he cheated on you?"

She pulled her knees to her chest, curling into me, and I put my arm around her. "He came over and apologized," she said. "He said he'd only gone there for his boys—the other guys are all single. He said stuff like that isn't for girls like me to ever know about. He said he was drunk, and it was a mistake."

"And you believe him?"

"Obviously not, or I wouldn't have torn the stuffing out of Beauregard."

I snorted. *"Beauregard?"*

She giggled, hiccupping again when we both began laughing. At some point, though, her laughs turned to sobs, and she collapsed into my chest. "Why would he have sex with some skank when he has me? Why?"

I figured she didn't want me to attempt an answer to that. I also suspected nothing and no one would ever be enough for a guy like Clark Richards. Like his father, he was never going to be content with what he had. He only saw what he didn't have. And felt entitled to it.

She quietened after a few minutes, inhaling a couple of deep breaths and shuddering. "How'd you know I'd be out here?"

"When I texted and you didn't answer, I guessed."

She angled her head back and looked up at me. "You're a good guy, Landon."

I'm not, came the automatic thought.

She leaned closer, eyes open, and pressed her lips to mine. Just a brush—tentative and testing. She pulled away only inches, and our breath mingled. I leaned forward, an inch at a time, and she didn't back away. I kissed her as she'd kissed me, cautiously, slowly, lips only, neither of us closing our eyes.

"Melody?" We jerked apart—her mother's voice was close, right outside the fort's walls.

I lay flat on my back while she rose to her knees, her hand pressed to the middle of my chest, the better to feel my heart pounding. "Yeah, Mama?"

Her mother sighed, exasperated. "Come inside, now. You can't be out here by yourself. It isn't safe." Melody glanced down at me as her mother continued, "Also, Clark is now calling the landline, since you aren't answering your cell."

Her chin came up. "Did you tell him to *eat shit*?"

"Melody Ann Do—"

"Do you *know* what he *did*, Mama? How humiliated I am?"

Another sigh. "Come inside, Melody."

"Yes, ma'am." She turned to back down the ladder, whispering to me, "Wait five minutes before you leave. And thank you."

• • • • • • • • • •

I was working with Dad the next day—he'd booked a family of four for an all-day excursion of fishing and sightseeing. They were standing at the mouth of the dock when Dad and I pulled up. One girl, about my age, was scowling, arms crossed over her chest. Another one, around Carlie's age, was bouncing foot to foot, her face flush with excitement.

"Holy shit," I said under my breath, already feeling grouchy.

"Can it," Dad said, directing a courteous look toward the four of them. He wasn't ever outgoing, so it wasn't like a night-and-day transformation, but his boatside manner was polite and patient, even when explaining and demonstrating the same things a million times.

I hadn't heard from Melody—but that was no surprise. It had only been eight hours since I jumped down from her fort platform and walked home, so high from her kiss that I could hardly sleep.

But I'd have no cell service until we docked tonight, plus a bitchy teenaged girl and a hyper younger one to deal with. I predicted a long, miserable day.

I was right, but not necessarily for the reasons I'd assumed. The kid actually listened to my instructions and made the biggest catch we'd had all year—though hooking a big one is mostly luck and boat placement, not the skill of the guy with the pole. No one mentioned that shit to her. Dad's motto: "It's our job to make sure the client thinks it's all him." He helped her reel it in while her parents cheered.

The older girl had straightened off her parents' car when I got out of the SUV, pulling on her earrings, fiddling with the strings on her cutoff shorts, fidgeting with her hair—putting it up and taking it down. That shit continued *all day*. She was glued to me, too, asking idiotic questions about my tats—which I'm not in the habit of explaining to anyone, especially not random strangers—and using those inquiries as an excuse to touch them. She wondered what kids who lived here did for fun, eyeballing me like she expected me to invite her along to do whatever that was—and I mean *whatever* that was. Most awkwardly: she took pics of me with her phone. I suspected she was texting or posting them and felt weirdly violated.

That boat felt more confining than it ever had, and I thought about people in emergency lifeboats, stuck at sea for days. I would jump ship after seriously contemplating shoving her overboard.

As soon as we docked and my feet hit land, I turned on my phone. I had a message from Melody, asking if I was busy today. She'd sent it hours ago.

Bumping knuckles with the kid and cold-shouldering sexual harassment girl, I called, "Great fishing, guys!" to the parents, and then I climbed into the front seat of the SUV.

Me:	Hey. Out on the boat all day. Working. No service til now. Just docked.
Melody:	I was afraid you were mad because of what I did.
Me:	What??
Melody:	The kiss.
Me:	I'm the opposite of mad, whatever that is. Fort tonight?
Melody:	Can't. Staying over with Pearl. Working tomorrow?
Me:	No. Dad will be gone all day. Come over.
Melody:	K

As soon as Dad left the next morning, I cleaned the bathroom, straightened the kitchen, and put away piles of clothes that were usually shoved to the side of my bed or haphazardly folded on the shelves. I made my bed.

Melody's knock was unsure. Quiet. I rubbed nervous palms down my sun-faded board shorts and took a breath before opening the door.

"Hi," I said, admitting her and closing the door behind her. Locking it.

"Hi," she said, tucking a long strand of hair behind her ear.

She followed me to the kitchen, where we sipped at sodas and made sandwiches we nibbled but didn't eat. We barely spoke.

Finally, she cleared her throat. "You said that you'd draw me, once. Want to do that?"

I nodded. "Sure. Yeah." We stuck the dishes in the sink and I opened the pantry door and clicked on the overhead lamp. "Where do you want——?"

"In there is good," she said. "If that's good for you."

I hope she didn't expect an answer to that question, because every-fucking-thing about this day was good for me.

She kicked off her flip-flops and we climbed onto the bed. I reached for my pad and pencils and she leaned back on her elbows. "So do you arrange me, or do I strike a pose, like this, or what?"

No way I could touch her and then draw. "Just get comfortable. It'll take me awhile. You don't want to try holding an awkward position." Like the one she was in, her perfect tits straining against her fitted top, creating gaps between the buttons and pulling the hem higher to display the strip of tanned skin above her shorts.

She turned to arrange pillows at the head of the bed while I sat against the wall. She lay on her side, half sitting, half reclining into the mound of pillows, her hair rippling across the surface like a gold waterfall. Pulling one leg into an angle, she straightened the other until our toes touched. I waited for her to still. Her eyes on mine, she unbuttoned the top two buttons of her shirt, showing off the white, lacy bra beneath.

"Is this good?" she asked, her voice quavering and soft.

My hands shook. *Fuck.* I sucked in a slow breath, and then another, regaining some self-control. "Perfect," I said, and she smiled.

Neither of us spoke. There were no sounds but an occasional throat clearing and the scratch of my pencil. Her foot swept over the top of mine when she shifted, and I pressed back reflexively. Finally, I stared at the sketch, and then handed it to her.

"Oh, my God." She looked from the pad to me and back to the pad.

"I knew you were good . . . but this . . . is amazing." She examined herself, stretching out both legs and assessing deficiencies. "I don't look like this in real life, though. This is gorgeous."

I took the pad from her hand and placed it on the lowest shelf, just over our heads. "Trust me. You look better." I moved next to her.

Not meeting my eyes, she reached out to trace my tattoos—her touch nothing like the gratuitous strokes from the girl yesterday, who seemed to think that touching me was part of the package deal her dad paid for.

"Do you want to kiss me again?" Melody asked. Still not looking at me.

I leaned over her, skimming one hand just under her shirt to her bare waist and waiting until she raised her eyes to mine. Repeating the careful, experimental kiss we'd shared two days ago, we kept our eyes open, the touch of our lips seemingly halfhearted. And then her hand twisted in my T-shirt and she pulled me down. My knee slid between her legs and there was no hiding the hard length pressed to her thigh. She closed her eyes and opened her mouth, and I didn't waste time weighing variables because I couldn't think. Driving my tongue into her mouth, my eyes closed and my hands wandered over everything I could reach.

I loosened the last three buttons of her top and we sat up, attempting to keep our mouths fused while she shrugged out of it. My T-shirt joined her shirt at the foot of the bed. When she reached around to unhook her bra, I watched, eyes consuming her hungrily. I reached to slide the straps down her arms, and she trembled as my thumbs traced her curves. Her dancer's limbs, lithe and athletic, contrasted with the supple fullness of her tits. Tossing the bra toward the end of the bed, I lay down and pulled her on top of me, high enough to tongue her nipples while cupping her ass to keep her close. Arms straight, she braced herself above me.

When Melody's whimpers became dazed cries, I sucked a nipple into my mouth, and she screamed and bucked against me. Rolling until my hip hit the wall, I dragged her under me on the narrow mattress, nudged one thigh between her legs and pressed. She clawed my arms and kissed me wildly.

Then her hand slipped into my shorts, and I lifted just enough to give access, lost to the soft, warm grip of her palm and fingers. Going to one elbow, I pulled her with me and thrust my hand down the front of her shorts. "Jesus Christ, Melody," I gasped, fingers sliding into her so easily. She came seconds later, quaking against me, and I followed.

Drifting back to reality, we slowly pulled our hands from inside each other's clothing. I grabbed my T-shirt and used it to clean her hand and then mine. I wanted to suck on the fingers I'd thrust inside her, wanted to know how she tasted, but I was oddly shy in that moment. Cocooning us inside my comforter, I drew her close and we lay staring at each other until we fell asleep.

When I woke, she was gone. She'd taken the drawing with her.

LUCAS

I didn't email Jacqueline until Sunday evening—four short sentences, all instructional, no flirting. She responded in kind, but referred to my weekend. I couldn't stop myself from telling her that my weekend was good—*especially Friday*. How was yours? I asked.

Three words stuck out of her short reply—*good, lonely,* and *productive*.

We all need our moments of solitude, but this girl should never be lonely.

I pulled out a heavy sheet of paper and my charcoal pencils, chose the fully reclining pose—on her back, arms above her head. As I re-sketched her lean limbs, each stroke across the paper evoked the kisses and caresses that left my body craving more of her. I smudged the shadows under her breasts with my finger, recalling her soft skin and the way she allowed me to touch her. Despite my need to keep a wall between myself and her, it was crumbling faster than I could rebuild it.

In my bedroom, I tacked the drawing to the wall, across from my pillow.

By the end of economics Wednesday, my desire to tell Jacqueline the truth about who I was was warring heavily with my desire to continue the game we'd begun—the one where I was the sexual mercenary who helped her get her groove back. It seemed the ideal scenario—I got to be with the first girl to rivet my attention in years, and she got to spread her wings, forget her self-important ex, and reclaim ownership of her own body.

I silenced the voice in my head telling me that none of this was enough.

Jacqueline appeared to be having second thoughts, too—she didn't email Landon or text me all week. She didn't come into Starbucks, and she only looked back at me during class a couple of times. On Friday, her ex approached her at the end of class. He smiled down at her, one hand in his pocket, confident in his charm.

I couldn't see her face as they spoke, though her posture seemed taut. Wanting to wipe that smug smile right off his face, I left the classroom before I did or said something stupid.

Friday afternoon, I got an email from Ralph Watts, the assistant chief of campus police. Watts was responsible for university-sponsored self-defense lessons the department offered a couple of times every semester. After I'd seen the flyer on our bulletin board last fall and asked him about it, he sent me to a training and certification program. I'd volunteered to assist twice now—donning padding and consenting to be punched and kicked by female students, faculty, and staff who sacrifice three Saturday mornings to learn basic self-protection.

> Lucas,
>
> Sgt. Netterson was supposed to assist the next self-defense class, but she snapped her collarbone in some wall-climbing mishap last night. I know it's short notice, but if you can make it—I need you, starting tomorrow morning. Plus two more sessions after Thanksgiving break, if you can do those. If you can only do tomorrow, that'd still be a huge help. Let me know asap.
>
> Thanks,
>
> R. Watts

For once, I didn't have a ten-to-three-o'clock Saturday shift scheduled at Starbucks. I wrote Watts back and told him yes, for all three Saturdays.

I also got an email from Jacqueline. Nothing flirtatious—just her research paper for Heller, which I'd promised to go over before she submitted it.

I couldn't be displeased when I didn't *want* her to flirt with *Landon* . . . Right? I emailed her back, telling her I'd look it over and have it to her by Sunday.

Minutes later, *Lucas* got a text from her: Did I do something wrong?

I paced the apartment before replying that I'd just been busy and added a casual, What's up? So indifferent, when I felt anything but indifference where this girl was concerned. Instead of seeming slighted, she replied with curiosity about the charcoals I'd said I was going to do of her sketches. I told her I'd done one and wanted her to see it. She replied that she'd like that.

So I told her I was out and would talk to her later.

"Goddammit," I muttered, tossing my phone on the counter and pacing to the sofa. I pressed the heels of my palms into my eyes, but there was no blotting out the memory of her beautiful surrender in my arms a week ago. *She trusts me.* There was no triumph in that knowledge because I was giving her the embodiment of mixed signals—not to mention giving them as two different people.

"I am a lying asshole," I told Francis, who yawned.

· · · · · · · · · ·

Standing in a chilly activities building classroom at nine A.M. on a Saturday morning, the last thing I expected to see was Jacqueline Wallace. While Sgt. Don Ellsworth directed our twelve attendees to sign in and Watts handed out packets, I was lacing my low-rise taekwondo shoes and setting up the mats. I slowed when I recognized Jacqueline's redheaded friend come through the door and went immobile when Jacqueline entered right behind her.

I'd considered suggesting the course to her, but didn't think she was ready yet—especially if she hadn't told anyone else what happened that night. If she attended too soon and felt intimidated or overwhelmed, she might not come back.

But she must have told her friend, who didn't move farther than a foot away from her, stroking a reassuring hand over her shoulder blade or guiding her firmly by the elbow when she looked ready to bolt out the door. Jacqueline was absolutely ready to run when she looked up and saw *me* flanking Lieutenant Watts. Her eyes tearing from me to the packet she gripped in her white-knuckled hands, she said something to her friend under her breath. One hand on her leg, her friend murmured something back.

Watts began his anxiety-dispelling opening speech, where he introduced himself, and then *I bench-press three hundred pounds* Ellsworth and me in his usual way: "This feeble-looking guy to my left is Sergeant Don, and the ugly one is Lucas, one of our parking enforcement officers." As everyone snickered, he praised them for giving up a Saturday morning to attend the session and then gave an outline of the three-week program.

After fundamental principles were discussed, we moved to choreographed demonstrations of attacks and blocks, so the women could get an idea of the moves we would be teaching them. In slow motion, Ellsworth performed the hits and I defended as Watts detailed weak spots of the attacker—some obvious, like the groin, some not, like the middle of the forearm. He stressed the goal of the attacked: *escape*.

Everyone broke into pairs to practice individual moves, while the three of us circulated to make sure they were executed correctly. Not wanting to stress her out further, I let Ellsworth take Jacqueline's side of the room, but her navy yoga pants and white T-shirt were continually in my peripheral vision. I watched for signs of distress all too common in survivor attendees. I knew which scenario would trigger memories of her particular assault, and I dreaded its approach.

Thanks to her friend, whose name was Erin, she did well with the hand strikes, yelling, *No!* with each one, as instructed, and grinning when she nailed the hammer strike block.

We finally came to the last defense move of the day. I couldn't assess her reaction while we demonstrated it, but once the group broke into pairs again, her stiff posture, wide eyes, and the shallow rise and fall of her chest were clear enough panic indicators. Erin held her hand as they spoke in low tones, heads together. Jacqueline shook her head but didn't release her death grip on her friend's hand. More murmuring ensued, and then they moved to the mat.

Erin lay on her stomach, and Jacqueline knelt over her. Her hands shook when performing the attack. Instead of trading places, they kept their positions and did the move twice more. Unable to take my eyes off them, I barely observed the pair I was supposed to be monitoring. When they switched places, I felt her panic from across the room and feared she might hyperventilate and pass out.

C'mon, Jacqueline, my mind urged. *You can do this.*

A surge of pride flowed through me when she went through the motions, pushing herself to perform them accurately despite her distress. As they rose to their knees afterward, Erin praised and embraced her, and I breathed a sigh of relief, even if Jacqueline didn't look in my direction in the last minutes of class or when she went out the door.

I didn't want her fear, or my presence, to keep her from returning. I wanted to make sure that didn't happen.

That night, before I could talk myself out of it, I texted her, asking if she still wanted to see the charcoal. She answered yes, so I told her to pull her hair back and wear something warm, and then I hopped on my Harley and went to get her.

Outside her dorm, I leaned on the bike and watched the door. People were coming and going all around me, but I couldn't pay attention to any of them. When she emerged, I was struck again at our differences. I made enough money now to buy non-thrift-shop threads, but my style hadn't changed much. This girl was a blend of classic and trendy but expensive clothes—they were a second skin she wore comfortably. She slowed, looking for me while buttoning a little black coat that could have come right out of a definitive 1960s film, the type my mother had loved.

It didn't take her long to spot me.

Her step faltered and I wondered why. I wanted to sweep her up and kiss her as if there'd been no break since the last time I held her. I wanted to erase her friends' designation for me—her *bad-boy phase*— an inconsequential segment of time between two sensible, valid stages: Kennedy Moore and whoever came next.

"I guess this is the reason for the hair guidelines," she said, inspecting the helmet I handed her as if it was a complex, alien thing. She'd never been on a motorcycle before, a fact that sort of turned me on. Like I needed help with that.

She gazed up at me as I settled the helmet on her head, adjusting and fastening the straps. I lingered over the process, mentally devouring the sweet lips I could still taste when I closed my eyes and gazing into her eyes, deep and blue as the open ocean.

The care I took on the drive over escaped her, I figured, since she buried her face in the middle of my back and held on to me around corners as if she'd be flung to Oklahoma otherwise—not that I'd ever complain.

By the time we arrived, her hands were freezing, so I took one and then the other between mine, gradually rubbing warmth back into them. I wondered how she played an instrument the size of an upright bass with such small hands, but I bit my lip just before voicing this aloud.

She'd only told Landon about the instrument she played.

Prolonging my guilt trip, she asked if my parents lived in the house on the other side of the yard. "No. I rent the apartment," I told her as we climbed the steps and I unlocked the door.

Francis didn't appear impressed or concerned that I'd brought someone home with me. He merely stalked from the sofa to the door and out, as if giving me a few moments of privacy. Jacqueline laughed at what I'd named him, musing that he looked more like a Max or a King. I explained that my cat had enough of a superiority complex without me giving him a macho name.

"Names are important," she said, unbuttoning her coat slowly.

A chill ran down my spine at her words and the possible dual meaning behind them, but it disappeared with the hypnotic draw of her small fingers, slipping buttons through buttonholes at a pace that mercifully drove everything else from my mind and affected my heart rate directly. When she finally released the lowest button, my patience was going up in flames. I slid my thumbs inside and along her shoulders, tugging the jacket gently down her arms.

"Soft," I whispered.

"It's cashmere," she whispered back, as though I'd asked.

I wanted to pull her close, run my hands over that sweater, and kiss her breathless. I wanted to stroke my tongue along the tapered arch of her ear, frame her pretty face with my hands, and taste her plum-ripe mouth. Her eyes dilated slightly in the dimly lit room, and she stared up at me, waiting. Every muscle in my body strained toward her, wanting her. But I had something more important to tell her, and I blurted it out before I lost my nerve and reached for her instead, noble intentions be damned.

"I had an ulterior motive for bringing you here."

chapter

Sixteen

LANDON

Those of us who dislike crowds were spoiled after the last few months of mild winter weather and fewer tourists. But during spring break, there's no such thing as a deserted beach here.

After barely graduating last year, Thompson senior started getting into more extreme shit—selling and using—while Rick slowly took over the weed, gelcaps, and little purple pills arm of his big brother's enterprise. His livelihood depended on buyers, so crowds were good.

"Dumbass smokes through half his profits though, man," Boyce said. From one of the rocks overlooking the beach, we watched Rick circle through the crush of bodies. He was selling a good time in a baggie, and business was thriving.

"Or gives them away." As if to illustrate my point, Brittney Loper circled her arms around him from behind, pressing her chest into his back and speaking into his ear. Without stopping his conversation with a couple of potential clients, he brought her around front with one arm and transferred a small baggie from his hoodie pocket to the front pocket of her jeans with the other.

She leaned into him and kissed him while the two guys glanced at each other. One of them said something, Rick shook his head and turned Brittney around, snaking an arm around her rib cage. The guys stared at her ample cleavage. She stuck a hand out and each of them shook it. Cash and baggies swapped hands, and Brittney walked off down the beach between the two out-of-towners.

"Man, that girl lives dangerously," Boyce said, taking one last drag on his cigarette.

"Seriously." I tossed back the rest of my beer and chewed the corner of my lip. After a minute, I added, "I'm thinking about getting my tongue pierced."

He made a pretense of shivering. "Damn, Maxfield, why the hell would you do that?"

Boyce had no piercings and only one tattoo—*Semper Fi* above an Eagle, Globe, and Anchor emblem on his shoulder, in memory of his only sibling, a marine who died in Iraq. "I didn't know how much I hated needles until then. Burned like a motherfucker," he'd told me once. "If I hadn't been doing it for Brent, I'da told Arianna to quit with the damned bird's head."

"I heard a tongue stud makes it better for the girl when you go down on her," I answered.

He crooked an eyebrow, his beer halfway to his mouth. "That so?" He took a swallow. "Even still. Maybe if it made it better for *me* . . ."

I shrugged, smirking. "If it's better for her, it's better for me."

He peered at me. "That sounds suspiciously like you're fuckin' someone you care about, Maxfield." I said nothing, and after a few seconds, he groaned, head falling back. "Oh, man—for real? Shit. Why don't you ever listen to the Boyce of reason?" I grunted at his pun and shook my head as he sighed. "You know when *I'm* the one talkin' sense, you're in deep shit." He scanned the crowd. "So where is she?"

"Houston for a couple nights. She and her mom go shopping every year during spring break."

Boyce dropped his cigarette butt into his empty bottle. "Watch your back. You know Richards is a grade-A dickhole."

"I don't think he gives a shit."

"About her? Probably not. But he gives a shit about appearances, and he doesn't like to lose."

"Neither do I." My phone vibrated and I pulled up a text from Melody, along with two dressing room mirror selfies of lacy nothings—one black, one red. I lay back on the rock, staring. "Holy, holy shit."

Melody: Lingerie shopping. This? Or this?
Me: BOTH. EITHER. Is this a trick question??
Melody: I'll be wearing one of them Friday, if you still want to go out.
Me: A. Of course I want to go out. B. You can't go out in that, unless you want me to kill the first guy who touches you.
Melody: Under my clothes, silly. You'll know, but no one else will. ;)
Me: I'll never make it through dinner.

"What? Is she sexting you?" Boyce asked, reaching for my phone. "Lemme see."

I shoved it in my pocket. "Nope. That's all mine."

"Lucky bastard."

I shook my head, sitting up. "I thought you guys couldn't stand each other?"

Spreading his arms, he asked, "Who's gotta stand her to appreciate her naked?"

I narrowed my eyes. "You'd better hope that never happens."

He put his hands up. "All right, all right—keep your shorts on."

I took a deep breath, hand on my phone inside my pocket. My fingers itched to pull up those photos and study every detail. Meticulously. "I need a beer or five."

Boyce hopped down to the sand. "On it, bro. Let's go."

• • • • • • • • •

Melody's parents were less than thrilled to see me at the door Friday to pick her up, or the old blue-and-white Ford F-100 at the end of their curving pebbled walk. I'd worn boots, jeans, and a snap-front western shirt I'd taken from Grandpa's stuff before Dad gave the rest of it away. The shirt was faded blue, soft as hell, and way older than me. There was a tear by the cuff, so I rolled the sleeves and pushed them up to my elbows. I forgot about my tattoos until her mom focused on them two seconds after opening the door—once her eyes unfocused from my truck.

Fingering the necklace at her throat as though I might snatch it off and run out the door, she spoke through clenched teeth. "Landon. Hello. Melody will be down in a minute."

Her father was less subtle. One glance at me, and he turned to his wife. "Barb, may I see you in the kitchen?"

"Wait here, please," she told me. I nodded.

Melody came down the stairs a moment later wearing a short red sundress with boots, and my mouth went dry, immediately imagining those red lacy things she'd promised to wear underneath. I knew every detail of them except how they'd feel to the touch, because I'd stared at those photos for so many hours that they were all but burned into my retinas.

"Ooh, cool vintage shirt," Melody said, running a hand down my chest. My whole body responded to her touch, everything constricting at once. I was in deep shit with this girl.

We could hear her parents arguing in the kitchen. "Did you approve her going out with that Maxfield boy?" her father said.

"Of course not—"

"What the hell were you thinking? What happened to Clark?"

Her mother's answer was inaudible.

Melody rolled her eyes. "*God*. Let's get out of here."

She got no argument from me.

We took the ferry and drove to a Peruvian seafood joint for ceviche and fish tacos.

"So you like working on cars?" Melody asked, sipping her iced tea.

I'd hung around Boyce a few times when he was working at his dad's body shop. He liked the grease under his nails, the smell of the exhaust, and getting his hands dirty while diving into the bowels of the machine under a hood. That wasn't me. "Kinda, but not really. It might be cool to *design* cars. I mean, I like figuring out how mechanical things work, but only so I can use that knowledge to build something else. Once I know how it all connects, it's not that fascinating anymore. When I was a kid, I took stuff apart all the time—radios, clocks, toasters, a doorbell chime . . ."

She laughed. "A doorbell?"

"Yeah. I made my mom nuts with that one. I got it back together, but she said it always sounded like a wounded moose after that."

She smiled. "So that's what some of those drawings on your wall were. The mechanical stuff. I thought maybe you were like, into steampunk or something."

"That's cool in fiction." I shrugged. "But I'm more into sketching new technologies."

She took my hand and traced the tattoo across my right wrist. "What about your tattoos? What do they mean?" When she started to turn my hand over, I threaded my fingers through hers instead. I wasn't ready for her to discover those camouflaged scars.

"Enough questions about me. What about you? What do you like to do?" I arched a brow and leaned closer. "Besides sending me pics that drive me crazy for two days straight."

Lips pressed together, she grinned and then stared at the table, shrugging one mostly bare shoulder and swirling a fingernail in a pool of condensation. "I dunno. I like fashion. I like being a part of the dance squad." She peered up at me and chewed her lower lip. "I kind of like history? Like, art history?"

I nodded. "That's cool."

She looked dubious. "You think?"

"Yeah—but it shouldn't matter what I think." I squeezed the hand I held. "If you like it, you like it. Is that what you want to major in when you go to college?"

She sighed. "Maybe. But my parents expect me to do something like be an accountant or a doctor. They got all excited when Pearl and me got to be best friends, because Pearl wants to go to medical school. But I'm not like her."

I couldn't help the smirk that stole across my face.

"What?" She frowned and started to withdraw her hand.

I clenched my fingers tighter and smiled. "Nothing! I was only remembering how super-excited you were to do that frog autopsy. *Not.* I'm thinking medical school might not be in your future."

She rolled her eyes and sighed. "Seriously. I couldn't have given two shits to slice that thing open, and Pearl was pissed she was out sick that day because she missed it. You did okay with it, though."

I shrugged. "I was only interested how the stuff inside worked."

"Like the doorbell and the radio?"

Nodding, I said, "Speaking of radios—do you wanna go park somewhere and listen to music?"

• • • • • • • • • •

Leaving the windows rolled down so we could hear the radio, I pulled two sleeping bags, a quilt and a pillow out of the toolbox in the truck bed.

"The cemetery, huh?" Melody peered around as our eyes adjusted to the meager light cast by the moon and a sky full of stars. "It's kinda spooky here. Like maybe all the ghosts are spying on us."

I watched her through the fringe of my hair. "The beaches are full of drunk tourists. No one in here is going to bother us. Unless you mind those ghosts watching me kiss you."

She twisted her lips and smiled. "Guess I don't mind that so much." She pulled her boots off and climbed into the truck bed, and I followed suit.

Five minutes later, I sat back on my heels, regretting the fact that I didn't dry-run this at home first. The truck bed's ridges cut through the meager layers of cloth. It was made for hauling stuff, not making out. "Not the most comfortable surface . . ." There was no way I could lay her down on this. *Dammit.*

"It's fine."

I shook my head. "It's not."

Pushing my chest until I lay back, she scooted up beside me, on her knees. "It is."

I decided not to argue, especially when she unsnapped my shirt—not all at once, but one maddening click at a time, her hands smoothing over my pecs, tracing the rose tattoo before moving down over my abs, which hardened—like every other part of my body.

She untied the shoulder straps of her dress. The fabric slipped down to reveal the red lace I'd dreamed about, asleep and awake, ever since she messaged me those pics. As the dress fell to her waist, I was thankful for a full moon and cloudless sky. I rose to one elbow and reached a finger to the shadowed crease of flesh barely covered by the lace.

"Can I touch you here?" I asked, staring into her eyes. She nodded. "And here?" I sat back up, moving both hands to her waist and gently pressing the dress down over her hips when she nodded again, her breathing becoming erratic.

She stood and let the dress drop to her feet. My mouth went dry as she kicked it behind her. Her sheer red push-up bra and panties hid absolutely nothing. Even in the semidarkness, it was better than the pictures on my phone. Going to her knees, she pressed me flat again, straddling me. My hands gripped her thighs.

"Still think it's too uncomfortable?" she asked.

"Um. *No.* I think I could pretty much lie on hot coals right now and not notice. A bit of bumpy sheet metal is nothing."

One of her bra straps fell of its own accord, and I reached to pull the other one down. Her tits were close to spilling from the barely there cups. "Holy fuck," I said.

She leaned close and unzipped my jeans. *"Yes."*

We left the lacy things on. I felt the soft scuff of it against my chest as she leaned to kiss me. I felt it against my palms on her ass, my fingertips touching the bare skin just below it. And then I couldn't feel anything but where we joined. She gasped my name minutes later as I angled my hips up to meet her and it was like there were fireworks all around us.

"I think I'm falling in love with you, Melody," I whispered when she'd fallen asleep, her ear pressed to the rose tattoo above my heart.

LUCAS

My ulterior motive terrified Jacqueline as much as I feared it would. I wanted to show her the ground defense move here, where no one was watching—the one she'd not been able to do without quaking this morning—and teach her to do it without a second thought.

Knowing she could do this would bring her power. If she'd have been able to do this move that night and escape that truck, he might have been too drunk to chase her down. If I hadn't been there, it would have given her a chance to get away from him.

I still couldn't think about seeing him on top of her without red edging my vision, followed by crushing guilt for not immediately following him out the door the second he left the party. I'd allowed my insecurity over my desire for her to blunt my perception that something was *off* about him. Monumental mistake. I swore I would not make it again.

Focus.

"Trust me, Jacqueline. It works. Will you let me show you?" I held her hands in mine—they'd gone cold again—and watched a swarm of emotions hurtle across her face. Fear was foremost, and I prayed that her fear stemmed from those memories and not from me. If she couldn't trust me with this, I couldn't reach her. I couldn't help her. *Trust me.*

She nodded—the barest inclination of her head.

I brought her to an empty space on my living room floor, going to my knees with her, our eyes connected. If I read her wrong . . . I couldn't think about the consequences of that. I knew this girl. I trusted my instincts that this was right. "Lie flat. On your stomach," I told her, and she complied.

I reminded her of everything Lieutenant Watts said in class, knowing that she'd missed some of it when she'd mentally checked out. I'd watched her do it. "The key is to get away," I said, and she nodded.

I asked if she remembered the moves, and she closed her eyes and shook her head, as if she was ashamed. I took a deep breath and forced my fists to loosen. My rage at the degradation forced on her would not help *her*, and that was all that mattered. If this was going to work, she'd have to go through it several times. It needed to be a programmed response that her body simply executed, without a lot of thought.

"If you find yourself in this position, you want to do these moves automatically, without wasting time or energy trying to buck him off."

When she went stiff, I asked, "What?" I searched my words for the one that could cause that response and came up empty.

"That's his name. Buck," she said, her voice thin as a thread.

I found myself fighting for control again, and I knew that it would be best if I never ran into *Buck* on campus—or anywhere else. There was a high likelihood that he wouldn't live through a reunion. "I will remember that."

The move was one of leverage, backed up by simple physics—something very clear to me, but not necessarily so to most people. Dislodging a bigger, stronger foe meant impairing *his* leverage first. I had her perform the move without my weight on her, and then I suggested trying it with me holding her down, promising that she could say the word and I'd let go.

She was so clearly panicked, her shoulders rising and falling beneath my hands. She shut her eyes to hide tears I'd already noted. *Goddammit*, I wanted to murder that son of a bitch.

I was careful each time, but increased the pressure as she gained confidence, until finally I put my full weight on her. She got flustered and pushed up with her hips instead of rolling to one side—which she'd been doing perfectly moments before. I reminded her to fight that inclination. "Yes. Okay." Her voice was noticeably stronger, and I locked onto that.

"Ready to try it for real?" I asked, watching her closely. She nodded. "I won't hurt you, but you'll feel the force behind it more than before. It will be fast and hard—are you sure you're ready for that?" She nodded again. Her pulse thrummed, just under her ear, and I prayed she could do it. I had to know she could. *She* had to know she could.

I grabbed her shoulders and shoved her down, and one arm shot up over her head, but she couldn't get the other one under her. She struggled, and I waited for her sign of *uncle*, but it didn't come. Instead, she switched arms, pushing the one beneath her above her head and shoving the floor with her free arm, propelling me off.

I lay on my side, amazed and laughing. "Shit! You swapped sides on me!"

She smiled, and my gaze swung to her lips.

Mistake.

I told her this is where she'd get up and run, but she didn't take the hint.

"Won't he chase me?" she asked, and I gave the answer Watts always gave—that most rapists don't want to chase a screaming, fleeing target. They don't want a challenge. I knew from experience as a guy that *Buck* probably wasn't one of these, though I would not say this to her. In all probability, she knew it already.

"I was supposed to show you your portrait, I think," I said, taking her hand as we lay on our sides, facing each other.

In a small, teasing voice she asked, "So it won't seem like you brought me here under completely false pretenses?"

I admitted that I wanted her to see the charcoal sketch, but that fact was secondary to what we'd just done. I asked if she felt more confident, and she said, "Yes."

Her hand gripped mine. My thumb lay across her wrist, and I was soothed by the steady rhythm of her heartbeat. The expression in her eyes—the faith and the expectation—was too strong to ignore. I brought my free hand up to her face. "I did have one other concealed motive for bringing you here." Slowly, carefully, I angled toward her and leaned in, staring into her eyes, measuring her response.

When my lips touched hers, she shut her eyes, kissing me back, parting her lips, inviting me inside. I stroked my tongue across hers, gently. Exploring her mouth was all I wanted to do—sucking her full lower lip, so sweet, and then the upper, my tongue tracing the heart-shaped curve before diving back inside and teasing across her teeth.

She gasped, and I released her hand to tuck her to my shoulder, my hands skimming down to her hips and holding her close. There wasn't a millimeter of space between us, but I couldn't get her close enough. I kneaded her hip and she pressed into me while my fingers meandered across the base of her spine.

I felt her hand on the bare skin of my abdomen just before she leaned up on one elbow and asked to see my tattoos.

When I found that she'd unbuttoned my flannel shirt without my notice, I laughed softly and her cheeks flushed a rosy pink. Chucking the shirt, I pulled the thin thermal I'd worn underneath over my head and tossed it aside, too, reclining and letting her eyes and fingers peruse the ink beneath my skin.

My first tattoos—the ones ringing my wrists—were seven years old. I'd added a few since then, but not many since I left home, and nothing at all in the last couple of years. Tattoo artists are like doctors. You have to trust them—not just their skill with the needle, but their ability to read you, personally. To know what you need, and what you don't. I'd never found anyone I trusted as much as Arianna.

I waited for questions that didn't come, as if Jacqueline knew they were more than body art to me. As if she knew their significance to me ran deeper than the ink.

Finally, her fingers brushed lightly over the hair trailing below my navel, and I was instantly ready to answer that touch—an answer she might not have meant to invite. I sat up. "Your turn, I think." I wanted that sweater off. I wanted my fingers roaming over her, exploring.

She frowned. "I don't have any tattoos."

Big surprise, Jacqueline. I smirked. She had no idea what I meant, and I wasn't about to explain it bluntly while reclining on my living room floor. "I figured as much. Would you like to see the drawing now?"

The emotions flickering across her face were amazingly readable—confusion in the slightly puckered brow, desire in her dilated eyes. There was a touch of indignation, as well—but I wasn't sure why. As she reached up and took my hand, her grip secure, one thing was certain. She'd accepted me as the bad boy her friends wanted her to have, and I would be an idiot to fight it.

I led her into my room and turned on a lamp as she examined the room and my wall of sketches. I'd not brought many girls to this apartment, and even fewer to my bed—and I didn't bother with the lamp when I did. I knew the room by feel—the placement of the bookcases and desk. The night table where I stored drawing pencils and a small sketchpad, glasses for late-night reading or studying, and condoms. Finally, the bed, where all that was required was finding the center of it. Pitch-black darkness—I led, they followed.

Or we just never left the sofa.

That was not for Jacqueline.

"These are amazing," she murmured, and I waited, watching her eyes scan over the wall, letting her find her sketch, knowing she was hunting for it. When she spotted it, she sat, staring. I lowered myself next to her, all too aware that I was already half undressed.

She turned and watched me, and I had never wanted to read someone's mind so badly. *Your turn, Jacqueline,* I thought, wondering how far she'd want me to go. I didn't want to go one centimeter beyond it. Or stop one centimeter too soon.

I leaned over to run the tip of my tongue over her ear, following the curve and sucking her diamond stud into my mouth. My tongue pressed against the post in the back and ran lightly over the flesh behind her ear, and she moaned softly. I nuzzled her hair aside and kissed her neck, licking her skin lightly after each kiss, lower and lower until I met the wide neckline of her sweater.

Going to one knee on the floor, I pulled off her boots, returned to the bed, and removed mine. I lifted her directly to the center of the mattress, rising over her and waiting until she opened her eyes. She blinked slowly, one hand lifting and grasping my arm, drugged with my kisses and craving more. Exactly as I wanted her.

"Say stop, whenever you want to stop. Understand?"

She nodded.

I asked if she wanted to stop now, and thanked God when she shook her head *no*. She gripped both my arms when I thrust my tongue into her mouth, unraveling me when she sucked it deeper still. I pulled away just long enough to tug her sweater over her head and toss it away, returning to run my fingers and mouth over the beautiful arc of her breast above the black satin of her bra.

Her hand against my shoulder stilled me, and I shook myself internally. *Stop.*

I drew back, but before I could interpret what she needed, she sat up and slid one leg to the other side of my hip and leaned over me, into me, and I dragged her down to kiss her, my hands smoothing over her shoulders and down her back. She rocked against me and there was no containing the groan that movement yielded, a coarse rumbling deep in my chest that spurred her on. Mouth angled and open, fostering intense, mind-blowing kisses, she rocked forward again, and my fingers found and freed the hooks of her bra and tugged the straps down. Grasping her waist, I pulled her higher and sucked a nipple into my mouth. *Goddamn* if she wasn't sweeter than anything I'd ever tasted.

Her arms wobbled as she panted her satisfaction, and I rolled her under me, sweeping my tongue over the other breast, teasing the nipple to a hard nub before sucking it deep. My fingers forked into her hair at the nape, holding her mouth to be kissed as I stroked my opposite palm down her side and returned my mouth to hers. When she arched against me, I unbuttoned her jeans and pinched the zipper between my fingers.

Breaking the kiss, she gasped, "Wait," and I went motionless, watching her. She panted, looking up at me, a worried crease touching her forehead.

"Stop?" I asked, and she nodded, catching her swollen lip in her mouth. "Stop everything, or just go no further?"

She paused before answering, and I wanted to tell her how far I would go to give her exactly what she needed—that I would do, or not do, whatever she wanted from me.

Her answer was almost inaudible. "Just . . . just no further."

My body geared up for a battle of restraint, but my mind rejoiced. "Done." I pulled her back into my arms and kept my hands and mouth above her waist or over her jeans, clasping her hips to drag her along my thigh, creating strokes of friction and employing the benefits of gravity. She minded none of it.

I turned her onto her stomach and moved her hair aside to kiss the nape of her neck, and she sighed, relaxing. The soft hairs tickled my nose and I smiled, running my tongue over the small rise of each vertebra, moving lower as I knelt over her, massaging with long strokes of my hands—over her hips and thighs, to her calves and back up. I squeezed her hip and she giggled, so I pressed a kiss to her mid-back and flipped her over, sucking a nipple into my mouth. Her laughter cut short and she plunged her hands into my hair and held me, trembling.

Sliding to her side, I didn't have to coax her to follow—she turned with me, alongside me, dipping her knee between my legs as we kissed. My hand inched from her hip to her thigh, prodding her, begging just enough room to sink between us. She shifted and I slipped my fingers between her legs. "This okay?" I asked, and she nodded and pressed against me, her small fingers tight around my bicep.

I stroked the tips of my fingers over the denim and she moaned in response. *Come, baby,* I urged silently and leaned over to kiss her, stretching her mouth wide and sinking into her. Heat radiated from her body against my hand, and I knew her imagination was filling in the blanks as my tongue thrust into her warm mouth and my fingers found the exact spot to orbit in gentle, measured circles, the exact pressure that tumbled her over the brink.

When she fell, she tore her mouth from mine and muffled her cries against my shoulder, her nails scoring my arms. Her breathing slowed and softened, and she shuddered one final time as I withdrew my hand.

Moments later, she touched her fingers to the button of my jeans. Without raising her eyes, she said, "I should, um . . ."

I tipped her chin and stared into those blue, blue depths. "Leave me something to anticipate," I whispered, kissing her gently.

chapter Seventeen

LANDON

"You were just a rebound," Clark Richards said, Monday morning, right before the homeroom bell rang. "Don't you get it, Maxfield? Yeah, I fucked up—but I came to my senses. She's mine. Girls like Melody don't stick with guys like you, freak."

Guys like you.

Under his arm, Melody stared at the hallway tiles and said nothing. No explanation. No *see ya*. Nothing.

"Want me to kick his ass?" Boyce asked when I threw a metal, lidded trash can in the men's room ten minutes later, denting a stall door and nearly knocking it off its hinges.

Hands gripping the sink's edge and swearing I would not cry or puke or scream the obscenities rolling through my brain, I shook my head, once. Clark Richards was just being the dick he'd always been.

Melody was the one I let inside. If anyone's ass should be kicked, it should be mine.

• • • • • • • • • •

I woke up in my bed the next day with no idea how I got there. My phone was dead, so I didn't know what time it was, but there was light under the pantry door and the house was quiet. The previous school day was a blur, and the hours after dark, blank. I closed my eyes and concentrated.

Boyce and I had skipped out after shop and he drove to the beach, which was still littered with remnants of spring breakers—wrappers, baggies, cans, the occasional abandoned beach towel or bikini top. The sky was light gray. Overcast. We sat on the rock near one of our usual hangouts and stared out over the water.

Boats motored across my line of vision, but my eyes wouldn't follow anything. A family with a blanket, picnic basket, and cooler had staked out a spot near the water. Brother and sister were the same size—twins, maybe. Preschool age. They kept daring each other to submerge in the still-cool water. They'd each taken a few turns darting up to it. Neither got further than their ankles before tearing back out like there were ice cubes in the water.

"My offer to kick his ass stands, man." Boyce took a drag on his cigarette.

I shook my head. "She's not worth it." The words were untrue. I knew it, but it didn't matter, so I didn't correct them.

I couldn't fathom what she had wanted from me. Was I only a ploy to make him jealous? Get him back? Had she wanted to escape her life but wasn't fearless enough to actually do it? Or maybe it was more straightforward than that. Maybe I'd imagined anything between us, and I'd never been good enough for her. I was filler, nothing more.

"Still thinking about getting your tongue lanced?" Boyce asked. The smoke from his cigarette cleared suddenly from a gust off the gulf that lifted my hair and dropped it forward. I twitched it out of my eyes. Boyce's military-short hair didn't move.

The little kids by the water threw their hands in the air and squealed, chasing each other in circles. It was hard to believe that I'd ever been that small. That young. That happy and clueless. They had pain ahead. Heartbreak. Loss. They didn't know and I didn't want them to—but at the same time, I hated that I hadn't known. I'd taken everything for granted—my mother, my friends in Alexandria, play-ing hockey. I dreamed about the future because that's what people persuade you to do when you're a kid, but that's the biggest lie of all—that you can plan. Reality is, you have no fucking clue what's coming and neither do they.

A few weeks ago, Grandpa was teaching me to drive on Sunday afternoons. He was there every night to make dinner and buffer the sour desolation between Dad and me. Yesterday, I thought I was falling in love with Melody Dover. Now he was gone, and so was whatever ignorant, naïve thing I'd felt for her. And I should have known better. I felt like the stupidest fuck alive because *I should have known better.*

"Fuck, no," I answered Boyce and downed the last of my soda. "Lip, I think."

Boyce made a horrified face. The guy wasn't afraid of anything—except needles. It was kind of hilarious.

I pointed at him. "That right there—that's why. Everyone who looks at it will have that reaction."

"So . . . you're doing it to tell everyone that you're certifiable and like pain?"

"Okay." I offered my empty can and he dropped his cigarette butt into it. Boyce was inexplicably anti-litter—an odd, singular holdover from his days as a Cub Scout. Before his mother quit this town, his father, his brother, and him. Before his dad started using his sons as punching bags, and things like scouting were no longer an option.

"Huh. Makes a weird sort of sense. I like it."

He got a text from Rick, who'd skimmed enough off last week's merchandise to party tonight for free. "Thompson's got molly and weed out the ass. He says bring beer. Up for it?"

"Fuck yeah. Why not."

How Boyce typed anything coherent with his Neanderthal thumbs was a mystery, but they flew over the surface of his phone. "*Score.* We've got a few hours to kill. Let's go get your truck from the lot and get some food."

I'd forgotten about the truck. It was alone in the school lot when we arrived, with *FREAK* key-carved into the driver's door.

"That's it," Boyce said, staring at it. "I'm kickin' his ass."

I didn't care what Clark Richards did or said to me, but my truck was an extension of my grandfather, and he'd disrespected him. "Get him invited tonight, Wynn."

Boyce had an evil grin that was all too familiar from my ninth-grade memory vault—if he'd sprouted horns and a villain mustache along with it, I wouldn't have been surprised.

"Thatta boy, Maxfield," he said, thumbs flying, texting someone. "Consider it done."

• • • • • • • • • •

According to the bathroom mirror, I'd had a hell of a night. Black eye. Swollen nose. Bruised jaw. The wall clock in the kitchen said it was early afternoon, so school was officially ditched for the day. I plugged my phone in, drank a Coke, started coffee, and went to take a shower while it brewed.

My ribs were sore and bruised, too, and my knuckles were scuffed raw. I smeared ointment onto everything still bloody after the soap and water, before pulling on dark gray sweatpants and a red-and-white base-ball tee, wincing from the sharp pain in my side the whole time. Deep breaths were agony and coughing was worse. I weighed the possibility of a cracked rib. Head in my hands at the kitchen table, I stared into my empty mug and tried to recall how I'd gotten that particular injury.

When we'd gone to buy beer, our usual clerk had been out. The woman across the counter wasn't willing to give us the benefit of a doubt that we were older than we looked. "Scram," she said, heaving the twelve-pack of Bud Light to her side of the counter. Her mouth hadn't moved from its disgruntled, horizontal line.

In its stead, we nicked a bottle of the Jim Beam from Bud Wynn's closet.

"You sure about this?" I asked Boyce, who'd be the one paying for it, one way or another.

Boyce shrugged. "Maybe he'll forget he had it."

I arched a brow. "Right." His father was one mean-assed alcoholic. And he never forgot anything.

Mateo Vega, one of Boyce's buddies, was the first to greet us when we hit the beach. The three of us exchanged greetings, Vega tipping his chin when Boyce asked if Richards was there. "Yeah, man—saw him five minutes ago." Boyce asked something else I couldn't hear, though I was pretty sure it had to do with whether or not his girlfriend had tagged along. Vega shook his head once. "But he brought a couple bros from the team," he warned.

"Gotcha," Boyce said.

We handed the bottle to Thompson and scored enough shit to get us both seriously fucked up. "I don't wanna roll until I find Richards," I said, unaware until I said the words that I *needed* to beat the shit out of him, and I didn't want anything dulling the rage.

Ten minutes later, I got my wish. Richards was parked on a cooler with a blue cup in his hand. Once I saw him, I didn't see anything else. Not his friends, not mine.

Boyce: You up?

Me:　　Yeah. Trying to remember last night. You at school?

Boyce: Yeah. Richards is out today too. Man you POUNDED him. I knew you had it in you but holy shit.

Me:　　Do I have any possibility of a cracked rib?

Boyce: Shit. Maybe. I'll be over after school.

I poured another cup of coffee and opened the door to Grandpa's room. It already smelled musty. Sunlight filtered through tiny gaps in the ancient metal blinds, which were rusted in a few places where the paint was scratched. Dust motes drifted in the beams, disturbed and swirling from my entry. The furniture was stripped bare—no sheets on the bed or glasses on the night table. Dad had stacked a few ledger boxes against a wall. The years were labeled in his jagged scrawl.

It hadn't occurred to me that I could ask to move into this room instead of remaining in the pantry. Evidently, it hadn't occurred to Dad, either.

I sat on the edge of the bare mattress and sipped a second cup of coffee, my head clearing little by little. After my fight with Boyce, Grandpa had taught me the proper way to make a fist and throw a punch.

I'd stalked straight to Richards last night and yanked him up, fisting both hands in his shirt. He dropped his cup and jerked free, stumbling back a step. If his friends moved to defend him, Boyce and Mateo convinced them to stay out of it. No one interfered.

"W-what the fuck, Maxfield?"

I stepped closer and leaned into his space. "You're a cowardly fucking pussy, Richards."

He drew himself up, eyes shifting to the gathering audience, and laughed. "Whatsa matter, freak—upset because my girlfriend didn't wanna suck your dick?" He shoved me back with both hands, or tried to.

I felt my mocking half smile shift into place. "Oh, she sucked it all right."

His eyes blazed wide and he swung a fist that glanced off my jaw. I drew back and punched him in the mouth, his teeth scraping my knuckles. He tried to land a body blow, but I blocked it with an elbow and belted him in the gut, and he gave a satisfying *oof*. We separated and circled each other.

"You're a sore loser, freak," he panted. "You need to learn not to get between another guy and what belongs to him." He repeated the hit to my jaw with the same glance-off result.

I laughed, the sound caustic. "You think this is about *Melody*?" I didn't expect the spear of pain that shot through me from saying her name. He took advantage of my pause and landed a better blow. My nose crunched and I saw stars. He moved in for another hit but I ducked and drove into him, knocking him flat in the sand.

"Of course it's about *Melody*," he said. We rolled and punched each other a couple more times, each landing solid enough hits to draw blood. "You want what you can't have and will never be good enough for."

As soon as we were on our feet, I swung too wide and missed. He tackled me and I landed on the ice chest, but I took him with me and used his momentum to throw him back over my head. Before he could get up, I jumped on him and punched him twice.

"I don't give a *shit* about her, you conceited fucking *dickhole*." I hit him once more and his eyes unfocused. Before I could knock him unconscious, I felt hands hauling me up and off him and he struggled to rise with the help of his friends. Clutching my side and panting shallow breaths, every one of which generated shooting pain, I pointed a finger at him. "But you touch my truck again and I will *end* you."

• • • • • • • • • •

When Boyce showed up, he brought, of all people, *Pearl*. I had no idea they were on speaking terms. "I won't be a doctor for ten years, you know," she said, glaring at Boyce. "He should go to the ER. I don't see the big deal. It's not like he's got knife wounds from a gang initiation."

Boyce sighed. "You're here. Just look?"

"*Fine*." She rolled her eyes and turned to me. "Lie down on the sofa."

After pressing in several places—painful but not excruciating—and listening to my lungs with a stethoscope borrowed from her step-father's dresser, she said she didn't think anything else was injured. "You may have fractured a rib—but there's no treatment for that. It just has to heal. It'll take six weeks. No *fighting* and no *roughhousing*." She leveled a scowl at Boyce.

"What? I didn't do it. And shouldn't we like, tape him up?"

"I'm sure you encouraged it. And no." She looked at me. "Take deep breaths as often as possible and cough several times per day, to make sure your lungs stay clear." Turning toward Boyce, she stored the stethoscope in her purse and said, "Taping him up would keep him from doing those things. He could use an ice pack for the pain—you can make one from a Ziploc and ice—crushed, if possible."

Boyce said, "On it," saluted, and headed for the kitchen.

"Thanks for coming over," I said, still confused. Pearl and Boyce never spoke at school unless required to in biology, and though he clearly lusted after her, she'd never seemed the slightest bit interested. Plus, I'd just beat the shit out of her best friend's boyfriend.

As Boyce dug ice from the freezer, she sat next to me on the sofa, her dark eyes level with mine. "For the record, I was wrong about Clark. He's a jackass, and I can't believe she took him back." She sighed and stared out the front window. "He's the devil she knows, I guess."

LUCAS

When I dropped Jacqueline off at her dorm, I wasn't paying attention to anything but her. Not until she reached the steps—at the top of which her ex stood, his gaze alternating between the two of us. She didn't see him until she nearly walked into him.

I didn't move except to cross my arms and watch his body language closely, and hers.

As they spoke, he continued to flick occasional glances at me over her head until finally, she turned and waved, as if to tell me she was fine. I wasn't leaving, because her body language said she was agitated—hands on her hips as they spoke, and then arms crossed defensively. They were too far for me to decipher words, but the tone of their voices drifted just far enough to reach me. Hers was irate. His was placating.

I knew her well enough to know that *placating* wouldn't be welcome.

Two words I did hear her say, clearly: "It's. *Jacqueline.*" With this, she uncrossed her arms, her hands curling into fists at her sides.

He stepped closer and she didn't move, but when he raised a hand to her face and she stepped back, I propelled off the bike and up the walk. She swiped her card and slung the door open, and he followed. I grabbed the door just before it closed, as Jacqueline whirled on him, her mouth open. She stopped when she saw me.

"You okay, Jacqueline?" I asked, stepping next to her as I examined him for signs of aggression. He oozed condescension above everything else—increasing when he recognized me as the guy who'd repaired the AC at his frat house. "What would administration think about you sniffing around the students?" he sneered, and it took every ounce of self-discipline I had to keep from reacting.

I turned to Jacqueline, dismissing him—the one thing guys like him can't easily swallow, and the one response to which I could give free rein.

She told me she was fine, her eyes sliding to the gathering audience I was just beginning to notice. Something about this girl made everything else disappear for me. At times that was ideal, while others it could be hazardous.

Then Kennedy Moore gestured to me and said exactly the wrong thing. "Are you hooking up with *this guy*, too?"

"Too?" she asked, her voice so vulnerable, and I wanted to punch him in the mouth to stop the ugly words before he said them.

"In addition to Buck," he said.

Her mouth fell open, whatever she'd meant to say emerging with no sound.

Moore grabbed her arm and started to steer her away, and without a second thought, I wrenched his wrist and removed his hand from her. I wanted to snap it.

"What the fuck?" He puffed up, and I knew in that moment that he wasn't done with her. He thought he could win her back—or maybe he knew he could.

But Jacqueline steeled her jaw, laid her hand on his arm, and told him to leave. He argued—stressing his belief that I was a *maintenance man*—which I couldn't refute without placing Joseph in danger of losing his job.

"He's a *student*, Kennedy," she snapped. He said something about speaking with her next week, when they were home. She didn't reply, her expression unreadable.

I knew the comment about Buck had unnerved her, but not for the reasons he intended. He spoke as if she should worry about a bad reputation, which was bullshit. The idea that people might be gossiping about her *hooking up* with the asshole who'd assaulted her made me want to find and beat the utter shit out of him all over again.

Moore glared as if he could intimidate me. I hoped he wouldn't be stupid, because he'd be much less trouble to put down than his rapist cohort. He seemed to think his resentment was threatening, but his stance was completely untrained and left him wide open. Two hits and he'd be on the ground. He'd probably never even been in a real fight. I held his stare until he turned and went through the door.

Jacqueline touched me then, and my body unwound. She teased me about my multiple jobs, and I told her the maintenance thing was rare, and the self-defense gig was a volunteer position.

"I guess we should add one more, huh?" she said, and I stiffened, thinking *economics tutor* while fighting to keep my expression vacant. "Personal defender of Jacqueline Wallace?" she said. I swung between relief and disappointment. I didn't want to tell her, but I wanted her to know. "Another volunteer position, Lucas?" She leaned closer, playful, hypnotizing me with those eyes. "How will you have time for studying? Or anything fun?"

I reached out and tugged her to me. *Goddamn*, this girl made me *want*. "There are some things I will make time for, Jacqueline," I whispered, kissing her neck—the sensitive space near her ear that made her go weak when I barely touched my lips to it. She hummed softly when I licked and sucked the delicate skin, careful not to mar it with a bruise. She was a sensual but private girl. Marks would only be welcome where they'd be hidden to anyone but her.

For now, I kissed and released her.

∙ ∙ ∙ ∙ ∙ ∙ ∙ ∙ ∙ ∙

I emailed Jacqueline my notes on her research paper, noting the fact that she was caught up, though I'd continue to send her worksheets the last two weeks of class. I also let her know I'd be going home Wednesday—where there was no Wi-Fi, so I'd be virtually unreachable. *As Landon.*

If Grandpa could see me now, he'd shake his head and sigh heavily. And if he could reach me, he'd cuff my ear and call me ten kinds of idiot.

She replied to the email to tell me her parents were going skiing, but she was going home anyway and would be there alone. In all the scenarios I'd ever imagined, this girl having parents who'd do something so oblivious wasn't in them.

I'd be hitching a ride in the Hellers' SUV for the four-hour trek to the coast. They'd rented a beach house and planned to make Thanksgiving dinner there. I would stay with Dad and have a few days of silence, except for the dinner we would share with Charles and Cindy, Carlie and Caleb.

Cole had snagged himself a girlfriend at Duke and had decided to go home to Florida with her for his first break, instead of coming home. His father ragged the hell out of him for a week about mothers-in-law and being whipped and texted questions like, "Where are you registered?" Cole vehemently denied impending marriage or in-laws while Heller laughed his ass off at every infuriated text from his oldest son.

I wished I could tell Jacqueline.

• • • • • • • • • •

Predictably, the altercation with Kennedy Moore renewed my antagonism and tapped it a notch higher. Monday's class was torture, between failed attempts to either ignore him or at least resist firing telepathic insults at the back of his head. When he turned and smiled at Jacqueline at the end of class, I left the classroom before I walked down the steps and put a dent in his toothpaste-ad-worthy smile.

Leaning on the wall by Jacqueline's usual escape door, I watched her emerge with the guy who sat next to her in class. He'd attended one or two of my sessions at the beginning of the semester, three months ago. They both seemed to notice me at the same time, and I could have sworn they were discussing me as they approached. After wishing her a good break, he headed toward the opposite exit, and I examined Jacqueline's face for signs that he'd told her I was the class tutor. Her expression was jumbled as she stared up at me, her forehead holding the slightest crease. Unable to read her, I fell into step as she passed, pushing the door open as we exited together. Her elbow brushed against me and her now-recognizable scent revived my memories of Saturday night.

"Can I see you tonight?" I asked.

"I have a test tomorrow in astronomy," she said. She would be studying with classmates all evening. Nothing strange about that, except for the brief pause that made it seem more pretext than reason.

Dogged by a nagging sense of exposure, I scanned the mass of people, looking for the source. Intuition told me that source was right next to me—but that had to be wrong. "Tomorrow night?"

"I have an ensemble rehearsal tomorrow," she said, and the buzzing in my ears increased. She talked about missing practice Sunday morning and packing her bass for the break—familiar ground—but my brain faltered, comprehending that it was familiar for *Landon*—not *Lucas*.

I was sprinting headlong into a concrete wall, and I had hit that wall before, hard. I didn't have to feel the wretched crunch of everything shattering to know how it would feel. I needed this break. I needed the waves on the shore, and my dad's silent presence. I needed to see if I could break this obsession.

Staring into her eyes, I asked her to text me if her plans changed. With every speck of willpower I possessed, I said, "Later, Jacqueline," and walked away without touching her or kissing her good-bye.

chapter *Eighteen*

LANDON

I thought hitting Clark Richards would make me feel better—and it did. It felt too good, if there's such a thing as too good. Every blow I landed, and even the hits I took, numbed and transformed the pathetic freak I'd been, bringing to life an unfeeling motherfucker in his place.

My fight with Boyce last year rattled that cage, but hammering the shit out of Richards's face was the watershed moment. I'd found something better than combining molly and weed, better than alcohol, better than sex for smothering the voices in my head—because even when those things worked, and they sometimes did, the voice I still heard was my own, and it would never let me completely forget. Ever.

• • • • • • • • • • •

"I'll only be gone three days," Dad had said, his hands cradling her face. "We see Charles and Cindy this weekend, right? We'll plan that Christmas in Rio trip you and she have been harping about for years."

She pouted at him with a fake scowl. "Oh, *harping*, eh? Maybe you can just stay home, Mr. Grinch."

He slid his hands down her shoulders to her elbows, loosening her crossed arms and pulling her hands to his chest before towing her close and tipping her chin. "You can't leave me behind, Rosie," he murmured. "Not after last night." He leaned down to kiss her like I wasn't sitting twenty feet away.

"God, you guys, *get a room*." I clutched the controller in my hand, eyes resolutely staring at the screen and my skateboarder guy doing ollies over spaces between buildings, aerials off walls, and slides down escalators—stuff that would kill me in real life. I tried closing my left eye so I couldn't see my parents, who were standing by the door, saying their long, mouth-sucking good-byes.

"This is why we bought you a television and game console for your room, son. So your mother and I can enjoy . . ." He smiled down at her. ". . . the rest of the house."

I hit *pause* and lay back into the sofa cushions, both hands over my eyes. "Oh man. *Seriously?*"

Mom laughed. "Stop teasing him."

"I can't. It's too easy," Dad said.

Sighing, she straightened his perfectly straight tie. "I was actually thinking that we should visit your dad this Christmas. He's always alone, Ray . . ."

My dad's relationship with his father was the definition of complicated. "He chooses to be alone. He likes it."

"But honey, he's so happy when we visit. He adores Landon, and he won't be around forever."

My mom's parents had been in their early forties when she came along—a surprise baby long after they'd accepted the idea of being childless. Prominent professors in analytical fields, they'd spoiled their curiously artistic daughter rotten—her words. They were both gone by the time I was five or six. Mom missed them a lot, but I barely remembered my grandmother, and couldn't remember my grandfather at all.

Grandpa—Dad's dad—was the only grandparent I had left.

"He just thinks he's finally got a sucker to take over the Maxfield *family business*," he air-quoted, "because Landon likes to go out on the boat with him. Plus, we just saw him a couple of months ago, in July." In spite of these claims, I heard the surrender in his voice, caving to whatever Mom wanted. He pretty much always did. "When I escaped that town, I never intended to go back at all. And here you are making me go every summer. And now Christmas?"

"Because it's the right thing to do. And because you aren't a sulky eighteen-year-old boy anymore—you're a grown man."

He kissed her again, wrapping his arms around her and growling, "Damned right I am."

"Minor in the room. Right here. On the sofa. Having his innocence corrupted. *By his own parents.*"

"Go get ready for school, baby boy," Mom said, calling me the thing she only said in front of Dad or when we were alone. Thirteen-year-olds couldn't have their moms saying crap like that in front of friends or the general public.

I shut down the game and my parents were *still kissing.*

"Gladly." I made blinders with my hands as I passed them.

"Hug your father good-bye first."

I did a one-eighty at the base of the staircase and leaned into him for a quick hug. He patted my shoulder and looked down at me, still inches taller, though I was gaining on him.

I'd picked Mom up the other day just to prove I could and she squealed and laughed. "I used to change your diaper!"

I grimaced. "Mom, really—*that's* the memory of my infancy you want to evoke?"

She poked me in the chest and slanted a brow. "Unless you want me to bring up how I fed you?"

I put her down. "Eww, *no.* Ugh."

"Do well at school and practice hard for that game this Sunday against those asshats from Annandale," Dad said. "I'll be back Thursday." He ruffled my hair, which he knew I sorta hated—and that's why he did it.

I twisted out from under his hand. "Good use of asshat, old man. Your vocab is improving."

He smirked. "All right, big guy." He took my shoulders and looked me in the eye. "You're the man of the house while I'm gone. Take care of your mother."

"Okay, Dad. Will do." I saluted and ran up the stairs, thinking about the game this weekend, and Yesenia, who I planned to ask out before the end of the day, if I could man up enough to do it.

LUCAS

The temperature at the beach was in the seventies, the average for this time of year. The Hellers dropped me off at Dad's before heading to their vacation rental with a thawing turkey and a box full of yams, green beans, bread crumbs, and cranberries. "We'll see you tomorrow," Cindy told us. "We'll eat around one o'clock. And if the turkey isn't done yet, we'll be *drinking* by one o'clock."

Boyce: You here?
Me: Yeah. Give me a couple hours.

I dropped my duffle bag on the bed. The room had never seemed smaller. It was like a cocoon. I'd emerged from it and flown away over three years ago, and now it was just a tight, outgrown place, both familiar and odd.

The blank wall was full of thumbtack holes, and the shelves opposite were mostly empty. Dad hadn't moved the light fixture back to the kitchen—it still hung near the ceiling, casting its indirect illumination over the space. A few old textbooks were stacked on one shelf, along with Grandpa's Bible and a high school directory. There was also an envelope that hadn't been there when I visited last. It contained a dozen or so snapshots I'd never seen before.

One had been taken on my first day of eighth grade, after I got out of the car in my new uniform. I'd outgrown every item of clothing that fit me three months before. I smirked at the camera—at my mom—as a guy on the sidewalk behind me photobombed, tongue sticking out the side of his mouth. Tyrell. Hated or loved by every teacher, he was one of the funniest guys I'd ever known. In the background, nearer the school building, a trio of girls stood talking. One of them faced the camera, dark hair in a ponytail, dark eyes on the back of my head. Yesenia. She was probably about to enter law school now or begin an internship in accounting or apply for master's degree programs in film or sociology. I hadn't known her well enough to know her interests or ambitions, beyond her interest in me. At thirteen, that was all that mattered.

I sifted through the other photos, pausing at one of Mom, painting, and another of the two of us clowning in the backyard. I pressed the ache in the center of my chest and put them all away to study later, musing that Dad must have left them in here for me. Maybe these images had been on a memory card in an old camera he'd finally checked before throwing it away.

In the kitchen, there was a bag of spinach in the fridge and a bowl of fruit on the kitchen table. I wasn't sure if Dad had turned over a healthier leaf, or he was deferring to what I'd want to eat while I was home.

"How's school?" he asked, pulling a beer from the fridge, his hair wet from a shower. He'd been out on the boat before we arrived today, of course. I assumed he would take tomorrow off completely, but was afraid to ask. It would hurt Cindy's feelings if he didn't.

"Good. I netted a spot on a research team next semester. A project with one of my professors from last year. There's a stipend."

He sat at the small, ancient table—the varnish long since worn away, the wood scratched to hell. "Congratulations. So—engineering research? Race car design?"

My mouth twisted. My interests had morphed beyond race cars since high school—not that he knew that. This exchange had to be the longest conversation about my academic goals we'd had since Mom died. "No—durable soft materials. Medical, sort of. Stuff to be used in tissue engineering."

His eyebrows rose. "Ah. Interesting." He stared out the window over the table, which had the best view of the gulf, except for the view from Grandpa's room—where no one lived. I was about to leave the room to shower and unpack the few things I'd brought when he asked, "Dinner plans?"

"I'm, uh, going out with Boyce in a bit." I took a beer from the fridge and popped the cap off with the edge of my unopened pocket-knife.

"Got your key, still?"

"Yeah."

He nodded, eyes never leaving the window, and we lapsed into our customary silence.

• • • • • • • • • •

Boyce and I chose a booth near a window. There was one halfway decent bar in this town, and we were in it. It was too loud and too smoky, and I missed the beach hangouts he said were overrun with high school punks now. We had to laugh, because we *were* the high school punks not that long ago.

"Still got the Sportster?" he asked. In the last few months before I left town, the two of us had rebuilt the badly maintained Harley his father had accepted as payment for repairs from one of his drinking buddies. When I needed to sell the truck to pay my first semester of college tuition, Boyce had somehow talked him into selling the bike to me cheap.

"Yep. It'll do a few more months, until I graduate." I thought about Jacqueline's arms, locked around me, her hands clasped low over my abdomen. Her chest pressed to my back. Her thighs braced around my hips. "I'll probably keep it, though, after I buy a car."

The waitress brought our drinks and a basket of assorted fried stuff. Boyce picked out a beer-battered avocado slice and dipped it into the salsa. "Seen Pearl lately?"

I shook my head. "Not in a few months. She was doing well, I think—probably applying to med schools now. You're more likely to run into her than I am, though. There's like fourteen times as many students there as there are residents here, and I know she visits her parents often."

"True." He sipped his tequila.

"So—you've seen her?"

His mouth kicked up on one side. "A few times."

I shook my head, smirking. "You two have a strange relationship, Wynn. One of these days, you're gonna have to tell me about it."

"Whatever, man," he said, dismissing the subject of Pearl Frank. "Any new adventures for you? Threesomes? Orgy parties? Cougar professors sexually harassing you?" He waggled his brows, hopeful.

I ran my teeth over the ring in my lip and shook my head, laughing. "You know I'm studying or working all the time."

"Yeah, man—your hundred and one jobs. You can't tell me you don't take T-and-A timeouts, just to break the monotony." He glanced behind us at the growing crowd. "You're too damned picky or I'd suggest one or two of the girls in this bar. What about that tutor job?

Any hot chicks needing supply and demand demonstrated at close range?" I stared into my beer for one second too long, and he slapped his hand on the table and leaned closer. "Maxfield, you son of a—"

I put my head in my hands. "I'm kinda getting over something. Or trying to."

He was quiet for about five seconds. "One of those students you tutor?"

Fuck me—how did he know that? But Boyce always knew. I nodded.

"Hmm. Knowing you—and I do—that sucks ass. If it was me? I'd be all over that shit. Just as well I'll never be anyone's tutor. Or boss." He tossed back the last of his tequila and signaled the waitress for another round. "See, *me*—I need to get hired by some hot chick so *I* can be the one being harassed."

In one flash, I imagined Jacqueline and me swapping positions—if she were the tutor and I were the student. If I'd been a high-school-senior bass player to her college-girl bass tutor . . . Every muscle in my body contracted and hardened. *Goddamn*, I would seduce her so fast her head would spin.

The waitress thumped our second round down and Boyce laughed and clinked his shot glass to my frosted pint glass. "To whatever you're thinking, dude. That's the look of a guy who's gonna get him some. Anything I can do to help?"

I shook my head, startled at the intensity of that one-minute fantasy.

That's what it was, of course. A fantasy.

Two more weeks of economics classes. Two more self-defense modules. Over.

· · · · · · · · · ·

When Boyce was driving me back last night, I caught the altered sign of the Bait & Tackle, which had added "Coffee & Wi-Fi" to its name. I could imagine old Joe painting the sign extension himself—which is exactly how it looked. I thought about stopping by, signing into my campus email to see if Jacqueline had written to me. To *Landon*.

Once I thought about her—home alone, parents skiing, dog boarded, I couldn't stop worrying. I reminded myself that we'd traveled in opposite directions for this break. She went four hours north while I'd meandered four hours south. If she was in trouble, there was nothing I could do about it.

If she was fine, I could relax. All I had to do was check.

But I'd left her standing in front of the language arts building three days ago, when I'd made the decision to suspend this craving, at least for the break. If I texted her now, everything would start all over. That wouldn't be fair to either of us.

Then Caleb fell asleep on my bed after eating at least two pounds of turkey and double helpings of everything else. Dad, Charles, and Cindy were all glued to a closely contended football game I couldn't focus on at all, and Carlie whined, twice, *"I'm so boooorrrred."*

My convictions vaporized and I volunteered to accompany Carlie on an exploratory drive around town. Her father happily surrendered the keys to his SUV. We rolled down the windows and I submitted to a pop station in exchange for stopping at the Bait & Tackle & Coffee & Wi-Fi.

"That's a mouthful," Carlie said, one brow angling with the sort of superiority only a sixteen-year-old girl can deliver. Once inside, she observed, "This place is like a stage set. Are they for real with these flowery chairs?" Her opinion of the coffee: *"Blech.* It tastes like *fish."*

She checked out the souvenir shelves while I signed on and encountered a dozen useless emails, but nothing from Jacqueline. Landon had no plausible excuse to write to her. There was no worksheet to send. No upcoming quiz. So I described the new-and-improved Bait & Tackle, and above my usual signature, LM, I added a casual: You're locking and alarming your house every night, right? I don't mean to be insulting, but you said you were going to be home alone.

I stalled for fifteen minutes, but she didn't answer.

Carlie, all out of pithy observations on the décor, purchased a bright pink T-shirt with *bait* written across the chest—which her mother would probably confiscate immediately—and a snow globe containing sand-colored "snow" and a tiny replica of the original Bait & Tackle, sans coffee and Wi-Fi.

"C'mon, Lucas, let's go sit on the beach," she said. "If there are cute boys my age in this town, they are definitely *not in here.*" I decided not to inform her that cute boys her age would be unlikely to come anywhere near her if I was there.

Six hours later, my phone's screen cast a greenish light in my pantry cocoon. My willpower was depleted.

Me: When will you be back on campus?

Jacqueline answered seconds later: Probably Sunday. You? I took a breath, relieved. She was okay. I told her I'd be back Saturday, and out of nowhere I added: I need to sketch you again, and told her to text me when she got back.

Friday, Dad and I took Charles and Caleb out on the boat while Carlie and Cindy sat on their rental's porch, drinking virgin daiquiris and reading. After we got back, I borrowed Dad's truck and headed to the Bait & Tackle. Jacqueline had replied to Landon's email minutes after we'd texted. My smile over the fact that she was engaging the security system every night didn't last long.

I spent the day at my ex's, she wrote. He wanted to see her Saturday to *talk.* I could guess what kind of *talking* he wanted to do. I shut the laptop without replying.

• • • • • • • • • •

When Caleb announced that he had a science fair project outline due Monday—and he hadn't chosen a subject yet, the Hellers decided to head back Saturday morning. Dad had booked an all-day fishing tour anyway, so we said our good-byes before dawn, and I was back home by noon.

I pulled up Jacqueline's email again, imagining that she might spend the evening—if not the night—with Kennedy Moore. He'd treated her like she was expendable, replaceable, when she was so far from either. She was stronger than she knew, but her relationship with him had made her weaker. She'd accepted his view of her. She'd followed his dreams, and not her own. She'd let him change her name, and who knew what else about her.

I hit *reply*, and told her it sounded like he wanted her back. Then I asked: what do you want? I wondered if anyone ever asked her that.

The Hellers went out to dinner and a movie, followed by a holiday lights procession through gated neighborhoods in the hills on the south end of town that were filled with grandiose mansions decorated by professionals. Bowing out to do laundry, I told myself I wanted to be alone. I made a cilantro lime marinade for the red snapper I'd caught yesterday, stuck it in the fridge, and went for a run. Jacqueline Wallace was on a perpetual loop in my mind. The thought of her with Moore woke a violent part of me I thought buried and gone. It made sense to fight to protect her, but I couldn't kick someone's ass because she chose him over me. Fuck if I didn't *want to*.

Joseph: Survive T-day? How bout them Cowboys!?
　　　　I'm not allowed to say that again to Elliott, upon penalty
　　　　of something called kinky boots—not my kind of kinky
　　　　btw—on replay all the way home from Cleveland.
　　　　It's a long damn drive.

Me: Survived. Home. Go Cowboys. Your bf is controlling,
        dude.
Joseph: Tell me about it. I'm fucking whipped. :P

When my phone buzzed again, I assumed it was more from Joseph, but no. It was Jacqueline, saying: I'm back. So of course, I invited her over for dinner.

· · · · · · · · · ·

Preparing my own food was something I'd done for so long that it didn't seem odd. As a child I'd played culinary assistant to my mother, to whom cooking was another art form. Once Grandpa died, I cooked for Dad and myself out of necessity. It was that or a steady diet of toast, fish, and eggs. We'd have both contracted scurvy before I got out of high school.

Cooking a full meal for anyone but myself had become rare. I lived alone, and Carlie had been right a few months ago—I generally didn't have anyone over. I didn't have time for a circle of friends, and I didn't do dates. I barely did hookups.

Inviting someone for a home-cooked meal boasts culinary confidence and encourages a level of expectation, but I was no chef. I bypassed gourmet recipes and anything with complex steps. I prepared simple meals in unassuming ways.

I had no idea what Jacqueline liked or didn't.

"I've never had a guy cook for me before," she said, leaning her elbows on the opposite side of the counter, watching me chop veggies and drizzle basil vinaigrette over them. Her inexperience with college-guy cooking boded well for the snapper and baked potatoes. Once everything was in the oven, I set the timer and led her to the sofa.

I wanted to know what conclusions she and her ex had reached, but

I wouldn't ask. She was here, and I couldn't think about her going back to him.

Taking her magical hand in mine, I examined every millimeter of it. I traced the lines in her palm, the sensitive valleys between fingers and the arching whorls on the pads of each one. She kept her nails short so she could play her bass, pressing and plucking strings, without impediment.

Landon knows that. Lucas doesn't.

I had to tell her. I had to tell her, soon.

Pulling her onto my lap, I leaned her into the corner cushions to tip her head back and kiss her neck, buzzing with need when she swallowed, tracing the path of those tiny quivering muscles with my tongue as her pulse and breathing sped. I unbuttoned her white blouse—one button, then two, following the path of each inch of newly gained territory with my lips, halting at the top of her bra. If I unfastened her any farther, our dinner would be burned to soot.

One of her hands was trapped between us, splayed against my chest. Her free hand gripped my bicep, the thick knit bunched beneath her palm. When my tongue began to stroke the just-visible curves between her breasts, she kneaded my arm like a kitten and purred like one, too. The weight of her was just right, her rounded hip pressing into the saddle of my lap. I fought to slam the door on my rampaging contemplations—like how her soft, naked body would feel in my hands. I wanted to turn her around, feel the heat of her pressed against me—

The timer began to beep, and Francis added his eager meow to the alarm.

I'd never been so turned on and willingly ready to starve in my life.

"Time to eat." Those words discharged another surge of reckless, uninhibited thoughts concerning Jacqueline's lovely body.

Her disoriented, frustrated groan was a mind-blowing sort of music to my ears—a refrain that told me, clearly, she wanted me. *What she knows of you,* my brain clarified. Even possessed with lust, I couldn't break away from my conscience.

Over dinner, I mentioned that I'd cooked for Dad and myself before leaving for college.

"You cooked? Not your mom or dad?" Her gaze was steady below faintly creased brows.

"My mom died when I was thirteen." I tried to make light of the fact that I did the cooking after that—like I was just making sure Dad and I ate something besides toast and fish.

"I'm sorry." Her genuine sympathy surfaced in the quiet concern of her voice, and I felt pulled apart by contradictory desires—follow my characteristic restraint where the subject of my mother was concerned, or tell her everything. As usual, the words roadblocked in my throat. I nodded and said nothing.

While we ate, Francis consumed his body weight in snapper and yowled to be let out after. Bolting the door behind him, I imagined he'd need a jog around the neighborhood rather than a hunting expedition tonight.

I walked back to the table and took Jacqueline's hand. She rose and followed me to my bed, where we lay, eyes locked, like it was old habit to do so. I reached to touch her, to confirm that she was real and not a cruel fabrication of my heart. Her skin was so soft, and her face became more beautiful every time I saw her. She scared the hell out of me, but I couldn't stay away from her.

I unbuttoned her blouse the rest of the way, slowly, eyes on hers, ready to stop the moment she signaled me to do so, regardless of what we'd done before. She swallowed thickly, nervously, as I bared the curve of her shoulder and leaned to touch my lips to it. Her warm breath in my ear, she shoved her cool hands under my shirt, palms sliding across my abdomen and wandering higher. I couldn't tear my shirt off fast enough.

Sliding one leg between hers, I pressed my thigh against her firmly and drove my tongue into her sweet mouth when she gasped, my need for her overriding my need for oxygen. She rewarded me with a subtle moan and arched against me, her hands sliding over my skin, stroking over the poem inscribed on my side that I finally understood fully. My brain was a riot of want and fear. I'd never been so terrified of my own desires, because they went well beyond her body. I shook to my core, my soul curving around her protectively as my mind strove to determine the logical calculation that could make her mine. I wanted to be hers as much—*more*—than I wanted to possess her, when I knew damned well that neither was possible.

She moved above me, her hair tumbling over her shoulders, the silky tips brushing my chin, her blouse and bra sliding away with strokes of my appreciative fingers. I shoved my reservations to the side for these surrendered, short-lived moments, worshipping her with murmured supplications and whisper-soft caresses. I felt certain my skin's nerve endings had multiplied in the prior week, because every place she touched me with her mouth or fingertips, I burned.

Since I had no plan to push past Jacqueline's former point of resistance, the hours we spent in my bed were hotter than I'd ever imagined making out could be, and kissing her was a luxurious, sensory indulgence all its own. As my body accepted this, I lingered over every stroke of my tongue, coaxing her along with my mouth alone and pinning her hands flat to the mattress so she couldn't touch me. She arched and twisted beneath me, winding her legs around mine, telling me with every whimper and hum that her body was the instrument I knew how to play, and play well.

When I finally released her hands, she shoved her fingers into my hair as I kissed down her chest and across her belly, swirling my tongue into her navel while gripping her tightly between her waist and hips, as if debating whether to remove her jeans. She scraped her nails across my shoulders, and I knew if I touched the button just below my chin, she would tell me yes. Every provocative touch of her fingertips, her lips, her tongue, and every sound she made built both my craving and my contentment—which made no logical sense, but I didn't care.

I slipped back to her lips, slowly, pressing my weight into her, attending to every part of her body that demanded my notice on the way up. She trembled and held on to me when I pulled us to our sides. "I should get you back."

Tucked to my chest, her fingers were entwined with mine, and though she nodded, she tightened her grip on my hand and didn't move an inch from her position in my arms for several minutes. I felt a compelling desire to preserve the moment, as if final grains of sand were streaming through the neck of an hourglass, and all I wanted to do was tip it onto its side for a few more precious seconds.

We dressed without speaking, and I buttoned up her blouse, lingering deliberately over each button, and then leaned to kiss her one last time.

I was about to bring the Harley to life when Charles emerged from the back of the house with a kitchen trash bag. I couldn't move, my eyes tracing his steps from the door to the bin, and back to the door. I willed him to go inside without turning around, but I knew he wouldn't. His hand on the doorknob, he turned and looked straight at me. Straight at Jacqueline.

"Landon? Jacqueline?" he asked, as if he couldn't believe his own eyes. Or just wished to God he was wrong. He sighed and told me to meet him in the kitchen when I returned. I nodded once, and he went inside.

Jacqueline said nothing at all. I didn't know if she'd been shocked into silence or if she'd sensed this impending finale, as I had. The ten-minute journey to her dorm seemed like ten seconds, but it was long enough for me to realize one clarifying truth about my dual persona and Jacqueline: she already knew.

chapter Nineteen

LANDON

After spring break, my truancy scaled new levels of don't-give-a-fuck. Mr. Quinn was disappointed in me—he'd told me so every time he handed back a failing or near-failing test or sent me to detention for skipping. But there were some days I just *wasn't* going to sit across a table from Melody Dover.

Ditching class eventually results in in-school suspension, because in public school, a body present and accounted for means money from the state. Exiled to a secluded room, you're given a shit ton of work that no one can make you do. A front office secretary babysits you. You're allowed to sleep all day, though they occasionally jostle your shoulder and tell you not to sleep. All of this, of course, is *for your own good*.

The last time she sentenced me to ISS, Ingram informed me that one more unexcused absence would result in my expulsion, and even an excused absence would result in my being held back a year instead of being promoted to the next grade. No fucking way I wanted to be stuck there for an extra year. In the last month of school, I had to attend every class, which blew. I passed by the skin of my teeth, Grandpa would have said.

I worked for my dad on the boat, but he handed me cash that didn't amount to minimum wage, so I supplemented with a second job. Rick

Thompson had become one of the most sought after guys in town. His popularity was due to two things: drugs, and girls he called *party favors*—who brought in business and were paid in drugs. Thanks to frat guys, teen guys looking for something *non-family* to do on their family vacations, and grown men who were stupid enough to be lured by high school girls, Thompson made serious bank.

He began allowing for lines of credit from locals. Now and then, somebody either got in too deep or resold in his territory without giving him a cut.

That's where Boyce and I came in.

Boyce had mostly quit picking on girls and smaller kids, though that had little to do with becoming more perceptive. The first got him laid more often—obvious incentive, and the second was due solely to the fact that I didn't like it. His prior bully reputation preceded him, though, and after my Hulk-out during the fight with Richards, the added benefit of mental instability made me almost as menacing as my best friend. Luckily, Thompson didn't have many problems, so most of the time, we were just there to make sure people did what he wanted them to do—pay him.

In return, he paid us. Sometimes in drugs, sometimes in money. All we had to do to be on his payroll was be intimidating and beat the shit out of the occasional dumbass. Boyce, bigger than me, typically handled the first. I handled the second—and I enjoyed it.

• • • • • • • • • •

"You don't have to be in here," I said. "We don't need you fucking fainting or some shit."

Boyce threw his hands in the air, as if he hadn't made gagging sounds while Arianna lined up the huge curved needle. "If you don't want me to stay, I won't stay," he said.

I stared at his paler-than-usual face with a straight-up blank expression.

He rolled his eyes and went back out front.

Five minutes later, I had a ring through my lip.

"Sexy ma-aaan," Boyce sang while I paid. He was fine once the needles were put away.

"Want one, Wynn? I'm paying."

"Fu-uuuck no-oooo," he sang, adding a hip-swiveling dance move. "My sexiness is a Wynn-win without pokin' holes in my *ski-iin*."

Arianna shook her head and handed me my change.

"Oh, God. Stop," I said.

"See what I did there?" he asked, unrepentant.

LUCAS

"You already knew, didn't you?" I couldn't look at her.

"Yes."

I wanted to know how long she'd known and how she found out, but neither of those things were important. I made myself face her anger. "Why didn't you say anything?"

"Why didn't *you*?"

I couldn't blame her. I couldn't answer her.

She wanted to know how it was that I went by two names.

"Landon is my first name, Lucas the middle. I go by Lucas . . . now. But Charles—Dr. Heller—has known me a long time. He still calls me Landon." My throat narrowed when I searched for the words to explain why I'd made that change, so I said nothing. The fact remained that I could have told her and hadn't.

"You *lied* to me." Her eyes snapped blue fire.

I stepped off the bike and took hold of her shoulders, desperate to make her see that I'd never meant to hurt her. I insisted I'd never called myself Landon—that was her assumption, but *Jesus Christ* if that wasn't the most spineless excuse I'd ever voiced. I had known all along what she believed to be true, and I hadn't corrected her perceptions.

She shrugged out of my grasp and I looked into her eyes. The betrayal there sliced me open. *I had to let her go.*

"You're right, this was my fault. And I'm sorry." My hands shook and I knotted them at my sides. I steeled myself and took a breath. "I wanted you, and this couldn't happen as Landon. Anything between us is against the rules, and I broke them."

I had to make this right with Charles—first and foremost, for the inviolability of her grade. She'd done the work, and I couldn't let her be punished for my deception. My desire to restore the trust of the man who'd been my savior in my darkest hours was secondary. I couldn't consider, now, what I would do if I'd lost that trust entirely.

"So it's just over," she said, and I came back to myself.

"Yes," I answered, bleeding out at her feet. My ears were ringing. I knew I'd spoken the word, but I couldn't hear it.

She did.

She turned and went inside, and when she'd disappeared, I went home to face the consequences of what I'd done.

I wanted you . . . I wanted you . . . I wanted you. I heard the refrain of my words all the way, like a vinyl track with a scratch, repeating. And then hers: *It's just over . . . over . . . over.*

It was nearly one A.M. when I slipped through the back door. Heller sat at the kitchen table with a cup of tea, his gradebook, and Jacqueline's paper. The only light came from the stovetop and the small lamp over the table. The rest of the house was silent.

I took a seat across from him and waited. In all the times I'd cooled my heels across a desk from a frustrated teacher or my small-minded principal, I'd never felt this bone-deep remorse, or this exhaustive disappointment with myself.

As soon as I was seated, he asked, "Did you assist her in producing this paper?"

I shook my head. "I offered her research sources, and I checked her conclusions and citations. But she wrote the paper."

"Same as you would have done for anyone I'd assigned this project to."

I sighed. "Yes, but——"

"Son, let me help you unhook yourself where I can." He grimaced, our eyes connecting. "If I'd assigned this paper to another student in the class, would you have given that student the same help?"

I nodded. "Yes."

"Did she ask you for additional advantage or any kind of grade revision because you two were . . . involved?" His eyes didn't leave mine.

I licked my lip, and sucked the ring into my mouth. "She . . . didn't know I was the class tutor."

His frown intensified and he squinted, confused.

"I met Jacqueline outside of class, before you assigned her the makeup work and gave her my email address. She knew me as Lucas, but you called me Landon. I never met her in person as her tutor—we conducted all of that through email, because our schedules didn't work for meeting up."

He quirked a brow and my face heated.

"Um, during regular, daytime hours."

"So you didn't know, until I asked you to assist her with catching up, that she was in the class——"

"I knew."

He sighed. "She thought you were in the class—but didn't know you were the tutor."

I nodded.

He pulled off his glasses and closed his eyes, heaving a sigh. "So you conducted this entire dual—*relationship*—lying to her about who you were. And she didn't know until tonight."

"Right." I swallowed, but the guilt didn't go down easily. I hadn't intended to lie *additionally* tonight, but this lie protected Jacqueline. I didn't know why she hadn't confronted me once she knew or suspected. I didn't even know how long she'd known. But it wouldn't look good that she'd known and continued the relationship.

I had no choice but to protect her—doing so had become a necessity, like breathing.

"Landon"—he waved a hand and corrected himself—*"Lucas— why?"*

How many times had I asked myself this question? "At first, it was because she was afraid of me—as Lucas. But not as Landon. Through email, she took me as you'd presented me—a knowledgeable upperclassman who would help her catch up in class. She was funny, and smart, and as Landon, I didn't . . ." I frowned at my hands. "I didn't *scare* her."

He cleared his throat. "Not to disaffirm your feelings . . . but she didn't look all that *frightened* of you a few minutes ago."

My lips pinned into a flat line.

"Is there anything else you'd like to confess, before I decide what to do about this?"

Shit, I thought, as one more indiscretion popped into my head. "The quiz—I didn't *tell* her about it, per se . . . but I may have *hinted* that you were giving one."

He covered his eyes with his hand and sighed. "All right. I'll speak with her Monday—"

"Charles." I leaned into the table, clasping my hands in front of me like a supplicant. "This is my fault. All of it. She did nothing out of line—she's worked hard to catch up. She wrote that paper unaided, as you wanted. If she'd have had a problem doing it, I might have been tempted to cross a line to help her. But that wasn't the case. Please don't penalize her for my bad judgment."

He angled his head, gaze softening. "You admire this girl quite a bit, don't you?"

I gave one quick nod.

"You put her in a bad spot here, son. If I hadn't known you all your life . . . I could be making a disciplinary decision for each of you based on how the situation looks. Appearances often carry more weight than the truth—but I think you know that." He sighed again, laying a palm over my tightly gripped hands. "Well. Can I trust you to limit yourselves to appropriate tutoring interactions for the last couple weeks of the semester? I need your word."

I nodded again, my eyes stinging. I wasn't worthy of his forgiveness. "Yes. I promise. I'm sorry I let you down, Charles. And her."

He patted my hand before gathering the papers. "I'll admit I'm frequently wrong about women—but it seems to me that lying to avoid present hassle just to postpone it for later is a bad idea. Lies have a way of compounding the problem—or coming back to bite you in the *nuts*, as Caleb would say."

We both chuckled. "I guess I agree with Caleb there."

"Yeah, he's pretty smart now. Give him a year or two. Once puberty whacks him hard enough, it'll flush half his brain cells right down the tube."

• • • • • • • • • •

I didn't look at Jacqueline Monday when she entered class. I didn't look at her, if I could help it, all during class. I didn't look at her when Heller said, "Ms. Wallace, please see me for just a moment after class."

Benjamin Teague glanced over his shoulder at me, though. A moment later, leaning close to Jacqueline, his head inclined in my direction, asking a question. She shook her head, but didn't turn around.

I continued sending her the worksheets, my emails limited to: New worksheet attached, LM. She didn't reply; I didn't expect her to. I didn't watch her enter or exit class, except to note that Moore escorted her out, and followed her from the building as well. She didn't look at me, and I couldn't blame her.

I allowed myself a few unguarded assessments of her during class Wednesday and Friday. She paid full attention to the lectures—no fidgeting or glancing over her shoulder. Except for taking notes, her hands were still. She was like an enchanted being who'd suddenly found herself earthbound and bereft of her magical powers, when nothing could be further from the truth. She'd conjured love in the heart of a man whose soul had been frozen for years, anesthetized by too much pain and guilt to bear.

· · · · · · · · · ·

Jacqueline and Erin went to Ellsworth's line when it came time to practice kicks. I didn't watch her, but I was tuned to her frequency. I could hear her voice above everyone, even when she was no louder than anyone else, yelling, *"No!"* as she landed a knee strike or kick, or laughing with her friend.

When Watts announced a break, I couldn't stop myself from finding her, drinking her in. She looked up and our eyes connected, and everyone else vanished. There was only Jacqueline, standing on the other side of the room, her eyes a cloudless sky and her face flushed pink from exertion. Catching sight of her in that moment was like glancing out a window and happening upon a sunset—inadvertent, breathtaking, never before and never again.

Erin took her arm and steered her out into the hall to the women's locker room or the water fountain, and I shook myself from my stupor to help Ellsworth arrange the equipment for the next round of drills, and then we padded up.

"Make sure you get that shit on tight," he reminded me. "Fairfield got nailed in the junk last fall after some sloppy padding up. We're teaching these ladies not to hold back and they *don't*. I don't think he could stand for a full fifteen minutes, poor bastard. I laughed till I cried, of course."

When called back to order, the women separated into two groups, prepared for the bear hug assault, which was just what it sounded like. Then Watts said, "Don, Lucas, let's have you two switch off, mix up the attacker tactics."

This landed Jacqueline in my line, as well as my department admin, who volunteered to help demonstrate the move—a series of possible defenses against being grabbed in a full body hug. Little wonder Jacqueline looked freaked and ready to make a dash for the door. I felt no different. I would have my arms all the way around her, in front of everyone, within the next few minutes.

I explained the moves—head butt, shin scrape, instep stomp, elbow to the midsection, and the hands-down class favorite every time, the balls-grabbing-twisting-yanking *lawnmower*. Watts came over and used me to demonstrate. "Reach back and grab the goods, twisting and pulling straight out like you're startin' a lawnmower."

He ended with, *"Vvvvrrroom!"* The women howled with laughter, and I bit my lip and probably reddened when Watts asked them to please dramatize that move without fully enacting it, to ensure Ellsworth and I remained capable of future fatherhood.

One by one, the six women in my line took turns facing the others while I came up behind them and grabbed all the way around, banding my arms and pinning theirs. They used whichever of the defenses they wanted to use, most doing a facsimile of the lawnmower at the end, complete with sound effect. Jacqueline's friend, Erin, performed every single defense, full throttle. I smiled, imagining her attacker on the ground *begging* her to run away. Her group cheered while she asked, completely serious, if she should kick him before running away.

I liked this girl.

Finally, it was Jacqueline's turn. I knew that her nervousness was because of me, and I was determined that she not be at a disadvantage because of that. She needed to learn these moves. She needed to feel the power behind performing them. She needed faith in herself, and it was my job to give that to her.

When my arms surrounded her, she froze. *Dammit. My fault, my fault, my fault.*

"Hit me, Jacqueline," I prompted softly. "Elbow."

She obeyed.

"Good. Foot stomp. Head butt." I led her quietly, and she followed. "Lawnmower." She did the move, without the sound effect employed by the others.

I released her and she stumbled toward her group, who were cheering as if she'd medaled in an Olympic event. Erin enveloped her in a protective embrace, and I decided she was the worthiest friend my girl could have.

My girl.

The front bear hug rendered me dumbstruck. Even with the padding and the audience and the objective behind the interaction, I looked into her eyes, inches away, and felt my desire for her like a kick to the gut. Luckily, my body went on autopilot to imitate a full-body frontal assault, and she did the defense moves without prompts, attuned to the voices of her group's enthusiastically shouted directives and calls of encouragement.

One more week of economics classes.

One more self-defense module.

Over.

chapter *Twenty*

LANDON

"See, Standish, here's the deal . . ." Boyce sometimes sounded like a long-suffering parent, which in a way was just meaner. It made people think things weren't as serious as they were. "You've gotten yourself into some deep shit, dude."

I rolled my eyes, arms crossed over my chest, one hip braced against a chipped sink.

Eddie Standish faced Boyce but eyed me from the side without turning toward me, like a bird. The better to track where I was . . . without looking me in the eye. "I just need a little more time, you know?"

"Ah," Boyce said, pursing his lips. "See, that's the problem. Your time—it's kinda run out."

Standish blinked and his face went blotchy. Jesus, I hope he didn't cry. I hated when they cried. "Run out? Whaddaya mean, run out? Y'all know me. Thompson knows me. Can't I like, have an extension?" He turned away and ran both hands through his hair, tugging it—but when he turned back, it was like he'd put on a mask. "C'mon, Wynn. Don't be a dick." A superior, better than thou, *I'm about to get my ass handed to me* mask.

Wynn looked at me. *Is he doing what I think he's doing?*

I shrugged. *Yeah, man.*

A lowerclassman came through the bathroom door then, took one look at the three of us, and backed straight out, eyes bulging.

Wynn angled his head and walked up to Standish. "So *I'm* the dick, eh? Not the guy who's two hundred—is it two hundred, Maxfield?"

"Yep."

"Two hundred bucks in debt for shit he traded for pussy." Boyce laughed, and Standish laughed, too. *Idiot.* "I could make a comment here about the fact that Maxfield and I don't have to pay for pussy— ever. I could comment about how sad and pathetic it is that (a) you have to pay to get laid or that (b) doing so narrows the field to girls who'd do a guy for free shit in the first place, but I won't."

Boyce stared at his feet, fingers on his chin, tapping—which meant he was about to turn philosophical. *Fuck.* I had a class to get to.

"Now, I've got nothing against a girl who enjoys her body in the same manner I do mine, though there is a difference between bein' a slut—like me—and bein' a prostitute." Boyce peered back at Standish. "I don't judge them. A girl's gotta do—et cetera, et cetera. But guys like you—who only get it when you pay for it? *That* is just tragic. In a really humorous sort of way, when you want to turn around and call *me* a dick."

There was a pause as Standish absorbed this. "I don't really give those bitches any of my shit, man," he said, laughing nervously, like we were all tight. "I just *tell* 'em I'm gonna, then go ahead and fuck 'em. What are they gonna do? Cry rape? They're addicts and whores." He looked between us, swallowing. "I—uh, I traded most of the shit for a carburetor."

"I really wish you hadn't said that," I said, my voice low.

"Standish, *dude* . . . First, tradin' a substantial amount of shit for car parts? *That's dealing*, dickwad. In Thompson's territory." Boyce glanced at me. "And as for that other thing? You just fucked yourself, man. My friend Maxfield, here—he's got issues with the r-word."

I watched Standish think hard to remember what r-word he'd said. "B-but, you can't *rape* a junkie whore—"

He didn't finish his sentence. I didn't really mean to knock a tooth out—that was a bonus. I meant to motivate him to get creative with getting Thompson his two hundred dollars, and I meant to make it so he couldn't speak or eat normally for a month. Done and *done*.

He paid up the next day. Boyce heard he pawned his dad's Rolex, and he lost twenty pounds he was already too scrawny to lose with the forced-liquid diet he was on for six weeks.

The hitch came from the fact that we were on school property when Standish acquired his motivation. Though we preferred to keep these confrontations off campus, he'd made himself scarce for days. But school was compulsory, and it's not hard to find someone when the whole student body is less than two hundred bodies. We figured out his schedule and set up an ambush—Boyce slinging an arm around his shoulders, laughing and smiling like they were bros, while steering him into the out-of-the-way bathroom.

Standish's unfortunate accident put us back on Ingram's radar. We were called to her office out of shop. Boyce guessed the lowerclassman snitched, because he was pretty sure Standish would shit himself before he'd rat us out as the guys who messed him up.

"Except for that Jekyll and Hyde act of his—maybe he *is* dumb enough," I said.

"Who and hide what?" Boyce frowned. "That's a book, right? Never mind. Just deny."

"Agreed."

We were installed in the same chairs we'd occupied two years ago, after the infamous hallway brawl no one ever admitted witnessing. Ingram narrowed unblinking eyes. "I find it interesting that you two were seen with Edward Standish just before he left this school with his

front tooth in his hand, a bloody mouth, and years of expensive ortho-
dontia *destroyed*."

Boyce staged an impromptu coughing fit to hide laughter. If there
was one thing Boyce Wynn couldn't do well—aside from reading for
comprehension—it was pretending he wasn't laughing when he was
laughing. I concentrated on maintaining a blank expression. She
couldn't expel us for beating the shit out of a guy who swore we had
nothing to do with it, and strangely, her eyewitness also retracted his
story. I was sure Boyce was behind that, but I didn't ask.

• • • • • • • • • •

We'd been out on the water for two hours before the girl in the red-
and-white-striped bikini deigned to speak to me. She made me think
of a hot little peppermint stick. Snobby, but hot. I wasn't particular
about attitude, though, because a cute girl on the boat was rare. It
made for a better view for the day than miles of water, coastline, and
fish, if nothing else.

"Guys who are like, emo or goth or whatever at my school are a
lot . . . *paler* than you. And less muscled up. I thought that anemic look
was part of the lifestyle. Or whatever."

I squinted one eye to peer at her. She'd sidled up next to me as I
prepared to bait the rod on the starboard side. We were trolling deep
today.

"*Lifestyle?*" I chuckled. "I don't really have time to establish a philos-
ophy," *sweetheart*, I would have added, if she wasn't a client's daughter.
"I just am what I am."

"And what's that?" She had a wicked gleam in her eye I hadn't noticed in the first two hours of this trip. Then again, she'd spent that
time working on a tan behind the dark sunglasses now perched on her
head while trying to ignore her parents, who were trading veiled and
not-so-veiled insults at the back of the boat.

A smile hitched my mouth on one side. "What do you want me to be?"

She rolled her eyes. "That line work on the girls around here?"

I ran the tip of my tongue over my lip ring and squatted down to snap open a bait bucket, a movement that exhibited those muscles she'd noted. "Yep."

She arched a brow. "What else works on them?"

I looked over my shoulder, where my dad was at the wheel and wasn't, at the moment, giving me the evil eye. "Why don't I teach you how to bait this hook and hold this rod while we talk about that further?" I looked over the top of my sunglasses at her. "If you really want the answer to that question, it might take a little while to itemize the data."

As I stood, she moved in front of me, bracing her feet apart to ride the gulf's undulations on deck. It was choppy out today and would have been better to go into the bay, but her dad wanted to fish in open water.

"I know all about bad boys and lures and baitin' *hooks* . . ." She put both hands together on the railing, staring out at the water. But from my position over her shoulder, she'd just pressed a perfect swell of cleavage together, almost up and out of her tiny bikini top. Lures indeed. ". . . and *holdin' rods*—what was your name again?"

"Landon."

"Nice to meet you, Landon. I'm Chastity."

I knew her name, having paid attention to her parents introducing themselves and her before we all set out on this excursion. Before it became obvious that her parents were going to spend the day at each other's throats, hissing comments or ignoring each other. Hell, her mom had even flirted with my dad. Not that he paid her any mind.

"Chastity."

We heard the words *know about* and *whore* and *jackass* over the waves and gulls. My dad was making himself as scarce as possible, considering we were all stuck on thirty-two feet of boat. Chastity and I were trapped in the middle.

"Parents having issues?" I asked.

"Dad and step-monster. And *yeah*. She's accused him of gettin' some on the side. Knowing my dad . . . it's possible. Let's not talk about them. They're boring as hell and I want to have *some* fun on this stupid vacation. And Landon, you look like fun to me." She maneuvered around the rod, gripping it, and pressed her hip into me.

"So, Chastity—is that an accurate designation or a misnomer?"

She laughed softly and leaned a shoulder into my chest, both hands sliding over the rod. "That's for me to know, and—"

"Oh, no worries. I fully intend to find out."

"Cocky son of a bitch, aren't you?"

I smiled down at her. "I prefer *confident* son of a bitch . . . but yeah. So what'd you say you're doing tonight?"

"Mmm, how 'bout *you*?"

· · · · · · · · · ·

Despite what I told Chastity about lines and local girls, I rarely screwed around with them. They wanted dates and school dances and relationships—and I couldn't have been less interested. The vast majority of the girls I messed around with were here temporarily. I met them on the beach, or at the Bait & Tackle, or somewhere in town. We hooked up in their rental condos or hotel rooms or on the beach, if it was dark and they were willing.

Chastity was game to play—but not out in public, dark or not, and not anywhere near her parents. When I picked her up, she said she'd convinced them she'd run into some friends from her school in Fayetteville. "I told them they'd drop me off by midnight, after a fish fry and s'mores on the beach."

I couldn't believe they'd fallen for that.

"Take me to your place," she urged, after we'd kissed and strolled around on the beach with a few dozen other people. "I can be real quiet. Promise."

So I did something I never did—I snuck a girl into my house. It was only ten or so, but Dad was an early riser and went lights-out early, too. His room was down the hallway from my pantry. We meandered through the dark living room and into the kitchen, avoiding every squeaky board.

Once we made it into my room, I shut the door and she whispered, "Holy shit, this is tiny. Is this a . . . a *pantry*?"

I switched on a nightlight I'd stuck in the wall and turned off the overhead light. Kicked off my battered deck shoes next to hers.

"You want to discuss my room, or . . . ?"

"I just thought everything was bigger in—"

I stripped off my T-shirt and her mouth fell open. I leaned over to kiss her, drew her tank over her head and pulled the tie at her nape, unwrapping that peppermint bikini top and spilling her tits into my hands. She scooted back onto the bed and I followed.

"You were saying?" I said, and she shook her head, pulling me down on top of her.

We woke up around one A.M., which would have been bad enough on its own, since she was an hour past curfew and had missed calls, voice mails, and text messages out the ass on her phone—which she'd switched to *silent*.

But the reason we woke up was because of Dad. I have no idea why he decided to open the door to my room. If he'd done that before, I didn't know about it. Maybe he was checking to see if I was home for some reason. But Christ, we were all wide-awake five seconds later.

"*Landon Lucas Maxfield*—what in holy *fuck* are you *doing*?" he bellowed, and then turned fully around, because Chastity sat straight up, still topless. "Jesus fucking *Christ*! Can I assume her *parents* don't know she's *here*?"

I cleared my throat as we grabbed our clothes and put them on, awkwardly, stuck on my twin bed with Dad blocking the door. "No, Dad, they don't."

"Do they know she's with you?"

I looked at her. She shook her head. "No, Dad, they don't."

"Get her back to her hotel. *Immediately. Goddammit*, Landon. *Goddammit*."

This was the most I'd heard him cuss at one time in forever. As we passed him, the muscles in his throat clenched and his face was pure fury.

I dropped her at the entrance to the hotel. She'd texted her dad that she'd accidentally turned her phone off. He was waiting just inside the lobby, scowling, when we pulled up.

"Shit," I said.

"I'll handle it. He deserves whatever he gets from me. Trust me." She turned back and leaned over to kiss me. "Thanks for making this trip way better than I thought it would be. There's a broody guy in my lit class with a few piercings. I always thought he was kinda creepy, but I may have to give him a shot now." She grinned and hopped out.

LUCAS

Sunday evening, I sent the last worksheet to Jacqueline, along with my now-standard message: New worksheet attached, LM. I wanted to say so much more, but what I most wanted to tell her couldn't be reduced to words.

Near ten P.M., my cell rang. Jacqueline's face filled the screen—a pic I'd snapped of her on this sofa. She smirked up at me like she had a secret.

We'd not communicated—aside from the self-defense class inter-actions yesterday—in over a week. More importantly, she'd never called me before.

When I answered, she said, "I need you."

I stood, dropping my pen and textbook on the sofa next to Francis, and strode to my bedroom. "Where are you?" I shoved my lace-up boots aside and grabbed the Nocona shitkickers I'd had since I was seventeen—the only footwear I bought new in high school.

"In my room."

I shoved my feet into the boots and grabbed my hoodie on the way out the door. "Be there in ten minutes."

Her answer, before disconnecting, was a near whisper. "Thank you."

• • • • • • • • • •

I got into her dorm as easily as I had last time, took the stairs two at a time, and thumped softly on her door. A tremor passed through me. I had no idea what awaited me on the other side of this door, but what-ever she needed me to be, I was ready to be it.

She opened the door, but didn't push it aside for me to enter. Her eyes filled with tears when she looked up at me.

"Jacqueline—what—"

"He did it again, Lucas—and it's my fault."

"*WHAT?*"

"Shhh." She shook her head, laid a hand on my arm, and scanned the empty hallway. I heard voices from inside her room in the same moment she said softly, "Another girl. At a party, last night. She's here. Erin and I don't know what to do next." She swallowed. "She's a freshman. She's so upset, and scared, and we didn't know who else to call. I'm sorry."

I cupped her face in one hand. "Don't ever apologize for calling me for help. I'll do whatever you need. Will she talk to me?"

She nodded. "I think so. Erin's told her that you teach the self-defense class and you're campus police. Little white lies, but she's just so scared . . ."

"I understand." I took a calming breath and composed my features. "What's her name?"

"Mindi."

Jacqueline's roommate sat on her bed, one arm tightly surrounding a girl who reminded me of Carlie—pale blonde hair, heart-shaped face—every feature small and delicate except for her huge eyes. But I'd never seen Carlie like this.

"Hi, Mindi. I'm Lucas." I approached her slowly.

"Y-you don't look like a p-police officer," she stuttered, breaths shaky, speech broken from crying.

Lip ring, longish hair, hoodie—I didn't look like the most trust-worthy guy, and I certainly didn't look official. I squatted in front of her, but not too close. "I'm actually a student. But I have a work-study job with the police department."

She seemed to accept this.

"So the thing is, we need to get you to the hospital so you can see a counselor and a doctor, and see about filing a report." Her eyes filled with tears, and I continued. "You'll need to be really brave to do that stuff, but Erin and Jacqueline think you can do it, and so do I."

"Absolutely," Erin said, holding her hand. "And I won't leave you for a minute."

Mindi sniffled and wiped her eyes with the back of her hands. "Okay." Her voice was high-pitched, like a child.

"Do you have parents nearby?" I asked, fighting to unclench my jaw. I could have ground glass between my teeth.

She shook her head. "They're in Pennsylvania. But I can't call them. I *can't*." Her hysteria escalated with each word. "They'll be so mad that I was drinking—"

"You don't have to call them yet," I said. "But there's no way they'll be angry with you." I hoped this was true. If this was Carlie, or Jacqueline . . . best not to go down that path just now. I took another calming breath. "You can talk to the counselor about how to tell them, okay?"

She nodded, mimicking my deep breath with one of her own, shuddering and gripping Erin's hand.

"So we should go to the hospital, then, Lucas?" Erin asked. "We can take my car."

"Will you be there?" Mindi asked me then, her voice hoarse. She must have cried for most of the day. I recalled Jacqueline the night of the Halloween party. The tears in her eyes. Her shaking hands. If I knew where that asshole lived, he'd be dead by the end of the night.

I glanced at Erin and she nodded. "If you want," I answered. Mindi nodded. Fifteen minutes later, the four of us entered the ER, and I found out how difficult it is to *tell*.

I fixed my poker expression in place when the details of last night's party began coming out, before we even left the room. It had been a big deal event—a formal, multi-frat party, with both Buck and Kennedy Moore in attendance—and *Jacqueline went*. She's not Greek, so there was no requirement for her to go, no expectations of her presence there.

"Erin needed me as a buffer with her ex," she offered in the backseat on the way, her voice a murmur. I hadn't asked her why she went.

Once we were alone in the waiting room, I had to know if Buck had approached *her*. "So did he talk to you? Last night?" I didn't look at her or tag the question with a name. I was certain she knew who I meant.

"Yeah. He asked me to dance."

I sat stock-still and couldn't look at her. I wasn't angry with her—I wasn't. But the thought that she'd put herself that close to him without me there scared the unholy fuck out of me. Finally, I raised my eyes to hers.

"I said no," she said, as if she was at fault for any of this. As if she was placating jealousy, when all I felt was *terror* and an unconditional, all-encompassing need to protect her.

"Jacqueline," I spoke low, forcing my jaw to release. "It's taking everything I've got right now to sit here and wait for law-abiding justice to take care of this, instead of hunting him down myself and beating the *fucking shit* out of him. I'm not blaming you—or her. Neither of you asked for what he did—there's no such thing as asking for it. That's a fucking lie argued by psychopaths and dumbasses. Okay?"

She nodded, saying nothing, and I asked if he accepted her *no*. My temper was in danger of snapping. I felt it, twisting and stretching, striving to free itself, promising retribution and vengeance I had no right to mete out. I was just this side of containing it.

She told me her ex was with her, and he'd noticed her discomfort. She told him what happened that night. "He was angrier than I've ever seen him. He took Buck outside and talked to him, told him to stay away from me . . . which probably made Buck feel weak, and that's why . . ." Her words trailed off.

Jacqueline thought Buck's resentment over Moore's dressing-down was why he raped Mindi. The sad truth was, that was possible—guys like him are weaklings who act out when they feel powerless—but what Jacqueline couldn't understand was that his actions were still *no one's fault but his*.

"What did I just say?" I told her. "This is not your fault."

I wished I could make her believe me.

• • • • • • • • •

Unless Francis had learned to make a fist, there was someone at my door at 1:15 in the morning. I glanced through the peephole with a baseball bat in my hand. And then I dropped the bat back into the corner, unlocking and yanking the door open.

"Jacqueline? Why——?" I pulled her inside and relocked the door. "What's wrong?"

She stared up at me, her eyes wide and frightened, and my heart nearly quit beating.

"I wanted to tell you that I just—I miss you," she blurted, her voice frantic, almost winded. "And maybe that sounds ridiculous—like we barely know each other, but between the emails and texts and . . . everything else, I felt like we did. Like we do. And I miss—I don't know how else to say it—I miss both of you."

The distress on her face was . . . because she missed me?

She shouldn't be here. Heller was right on the other side of the yard. I'd promised him to be *appropriate* with her for the remainder of the semester, but the desire coiling through me was anything but appropriate. It was fire and possession, adoration and need, hunger and thirst and an impossible, unbearable hope. I couldn't stand the thought of her leaving me for five minutes, let alone forever. I couldn't have her, but I wanted her so, so badly.

Her bad-boy phase. Her rebound.

I felt it like a physical, internal malfunction—the split second my control snapped. When I no longer cared what I lost outside of this moment, because I couldn't stand to lose what was right in front of me.

"Fuck it," I said, shoving her to the door and caging her with my

arms, prying her mouth open with mine and kissing her as if I could swallow her down and keep her from breaking me.

I pulled away long enough to strip her coat off and haul her to the sofa, to my lap, my hands behind her knees, spreading them into position on either side of my hips and tugging her to fit against me. My left hand pressing her closer, I cradled her beautiful face in my right and kissed her. I wanted to kiss her forever. Make love to her all night. Fuck her until she belonged to me and no one else, without care of consequences—and there were so many consequences to choose from.

I tossed the glasses I wore late at night, uncaring whether they hit the side table or flew across the room. I ripped off my T-shirt and then slowed to remove hers, my hands shaking with a gentleness I had to force. As I slid my hands to her sides, she huddled closer, slipped her arms around my neck and her hands into my hair. I kissed the side of her mouth, her sigh containing the softest little moan, and ducked below her chin to kiss and suck the fragile skin of her lovely throat— the origin of the passionate sounds and garbled words she uttered as her head fell back.

I paid particular attention to the singular freckle that drove me insane—it was like a tiny clue, put there for me to find—the *start here* on a treasure map. I lapped my tongue across it, and she pitched against me, hands gripping my hair. Fantasies exploded in my mind, too good, too perfect. I wanted her, like this—all of her.

Everything slowed.

I removed her bra, cupping her breasts and teasing them with my fingers—light circular trails around each nipple, thumbs sweeping underneath. She leaned down to kiss me, drawing my tongue into her mouth and sweeping hers across and around it, sliding her hand from my chest to my stomach to the still-tied strings on the front of my pajama bottoms—thin, soft flannel that couldn't conceal what my body wanted from her.

But I'd made a promise. *I'd made a promise.*

My hands slid into her hair at the nape and I pressed my forehead to her shoulder, eyes closed. "Tell me to stop," I breathed.

"I don't want you to stop," she whispered, her breath in my ear, temptation incarnate.

For a suspended minute, I let her honeyed words absolve me of the promise I *wanted* to break, the ethics I was trashing, the heart I was letting her slice open—mine. I rolled us to our sides, unzipped her jeans and slid my fingers down and into her, curling them up and pressing as she gasped my name and gripped my arm like she'd never let go.

I could make her love me. I could be that next man for her . . .

Ah, I knew better.

"Jacqueline. Say stop." I was begging her, unable to make myself let her go.

"Don't stop," she repeated, kissing me, and I clawed for solid ground when I wanted nothing more than to sink into her. She opened her mouth, kissing me, hinting at what could be mine if I just let go.

I promised.

Five seconds. I would pull her jeans away and take her right here on the sofa. "Say stop, please." Three seconds. I would carry her to my room, drop her on my bed, and begin with my mouth on her thigh. *"Please."* One second. I would betray the trust of the one person who'd never given up on me.

"Stop," she said.

Thank you, I said. Or wanted to say, before I fell asleep, holding her.

chapter *Twenty-one*

LANDON

When the sun went down, the temperature cooled and the light disappeared, and spring break festivities heated up.

The redhead straddling my lap took the last drag off the joint we'd shared, the embers singeing the tips of her index finger and thumb. "Ouch!" Her voice was a mousy squeak. She dropped the last bit into the sand, where it extinguished and disappeared.

"Hey!" I frowned, squinting down from my perch on a piece of ragged driftwood and toeing the immediate area like an idiot. The last thing I wanted was to find a possibly still-lit joint with my fucking foot.

"What? It was all used up anyway." Her petulant voice was grating, though I knew damned well there hadn't been enough left to pull a full hit from it.

I started to retort, but when I glanced up, she was sucking on her injured thumb. The nearly consumed joint dropped out of my mind and my thoughts veered toward other cravings. Pulling her closer, I drew her index finger into my mouth, sucking it gently while she sucked the thumb next to it, eyes lidded, just as high as I was. My jaw rested on the heel of her palm, and I sucked harder when she curled her sharp-nailed fingers into my cheek. I wanted to feel those nails scraping down my back, and I didn't want to wait or move. A short, loud fight with my dad over another round of failed classes, the long, weirdly hot afternoon, and the weed had left me sluggish and lazy, but horny. Opening my lips, I ran my tongue along the V between the finger in my mouth and the thumb in hers. She closed her eyes.

I tugged one thin cup of her bikini top down, liberating one tit. Her eyes flashed open, but she didn't pull away. If she didn't mind this, I'd see how willing she was to do me right there, twenty feet from the bonfire and the two dozen or so people drinking, smoking, and/or paired off around it. With any luck, she was as lazy and horny as I was.

Releasing her finger with a faint *pop*, I ducked my head and tugged her nipple into my mouth. She arched into me, gasping, her burnt thumb forgotten. Reaching between us, I moved the crotch of her bikini bottoms aside. She gasped again, her arms sliding around my shoulders like bands, before saying the magic words. *"Oh, God—yes. Now. Now."*

Hell, yeah. I hadn't even kissed her yet. Maybe I wouldn't. A no-kiss fuck—*that would be a first,* I thought—and I was always looking for firsts. They were getting fewer and farther between.

That's when I heard Amber Thompson scream.

Certain it was her customary attention-seeking shriek, I was determined to ignore her. There was a wobble of panic to it that I hadn't heard before, but she was likely having a paranoid delusion brought on by her dumbass brother passing her a joint. Scrawny fourteen-year-olds shouldn't smoke weed. They didn't know how to ration. The same amount that made me ready to screw this girl on my lap, find something to eat, and then fall into a mercifully dreamless sleep could freak them the fuck out.

I'd just ripped open a condom—the only one I had on me—when I heard another scream.

Goddamn Amber's useless brother. A tall can of beer in one hand and a joint in the other, he was visible in the firelight, stumbling side to side, laughing with two other guys.

The girl on my lap moaned and pressed herself against me. Clutching the condom in one fist and a thick ponytail of soft red hair in the other, I yelled, "Hey, Thompson!"

Rick glanced around once before going back to his conversation. "*Shit*, man," I said, and then tried again. "Thompson, you asswipe!" This time he only lurched in the opposite direction, to the other side of the six-foot flames.

"Why are you yelling?" Redhead whined.

Then I heard Amber a third time—but this time, her voice sounded both scared shitless and farther away. Not one goddamned person was paying any attention—except me.

Standing, I slid the warm, pliable girl off my lap and handed her the condom. I pressed her to sit down and her hands went straight for the drawstring of my shorts. In that second, I knew she thought I wanted her to blow me before I screwed her, and she was totally prepared to do it.

Fuck this night.

Gripping her shoulders firmly, I said, "Be right back." Her lip curled slightly and she blinked, confused. I couldn't blame her. Even high, I was fully aware that I'd just said the stupidest fucking thing I'd ever uttered.

Amber screamed again, thankfully not sounding any farther than she had seconds ago, and I turned and ran toward her voice—away from the bonfire, away from my sure thing for the night, cursing Rick Thompson and my conscience.

Out of the firelight, my compromised eyes adjusted slowly to discern two figures, kissing. *Great*, I thought. *Fucking great.* I'd abandoned the hottest girl I'd met in weeks to run down the beach and find out Thompson's little sister was a screamer while making out. Then the smaller figure jerked away, the larger one lunged and pinned her, and they both went down in the sand. That wasn't a *do me* scream—that was a *get off me* scream.

I took off toward them, cursing the weed buzz that made me zigzag across the goddamned sand. The last thing I was fully conscious of doing was ripping the guy up from the ground with my left hand and swinging my right fist straight into the side of his face. The initial impact of my fist to his cheekbone hurt and felt awesome. When he didn't go down right away, I hit him again. And again. And again. Until the euphoria and rage came together and spiked, and I sort of blacked out.

I broke most of the blood vessels in the top of my hand and fractured a couple of knuckles. I didn't even know you could do that. My right hand looked and felt like hell and was in a splint. Other than that, there wasn't a bruise on me.

The other guy suffered a concussion that bordered on a coma for a few hours. I could have killed him. I could have killed him, and I couldn't remember doing it.

What I did remember: Handcuffs. The backseat of a police cruiser. Getting booked at the station. A jail cell that smelled of BO and piss, but thankfully housed only me. Because I wasn't in juvie. Seventeen-year-olds are tried as adults, so they go to regular jail. As I crashed from the weed and the fight, I started shaking and couldn't stop.

"Maxfield!" an officer barked sometime later, and my head shot up. "Bail. C'mon, move your ass outta there—unless you're wantin' to stay."

I scrambled up from the bench.

I expected to see Dad. He was there, but Charles Heller was next to him. I'd forgotten they were visiting for spring break. I hadn't seen much of them while they were here. Hadn't made the time.

In the backseat on the way home, I didn't make a sound. All three of us were dead quiet. Instead of dropping us off and going back to his hotel, Heller followed Dad inside.

"I need a shower," I mumbled, and no one objected.

When I turned the water off, I heard their voices through the cardboard-thin door.

"You're losing him, Ray." There was a pause, and I held my breath. "You're my friend, and I love you—and because I love you, I'm going to tell you the truth. You've fucked this up from the beginning.

"Cindy begged you to get him into therapy, and you chose not to. We begged you not to take him away from his friends—away from *us*—and move him halfway across the country, but you didn't listen. He was in a private prep school and now he's . . . he's letting everything go. The fight tonight wasn't his first, was it? And the drugs—there must be drinking involved, too. He's using every method of escape he can. Because *you did*."

Dad murmured something.

"I know. But it's not enough. He needs a goal. He needs to see worth in himself." Another pause. I swallowed, my eyes stinging. Heller's voice lowered, and I couldn't hear what he said. I left the bathroom, towel around my waist, and didn't look at them—seated at the kitchen table—before closing myself into my pantry room.

I pulled on a pair of athletic shorts, which took three times as long with the use of one hand. It meant something to know Charles Heller cared about me. Didn't change anything, but it meant something.

A goal. He said I needed a goal. Maybe it was time I gave up on school—my jaw clenched at the thought of giving Ingram that satisfaction—to work on the boat. If I didn't end up in prison for the assault. I knew enough about bail to know I was only out until I got a trial date.

Funny, that out of all the fights I'd been in, the one I had good reason for would be the one that caught me. If Amber refused to testify, I was screwed. The guy I'd nearly killed was a rich college kid. He'd flashed enough cash last night to make Thompson's dick hard—buying stashes of whatever we had and handing it out to his friends like Halloween candy. Guys his age who dressed like he did and drove Range Rovers didn't come by money like that alone.

You got your wish, Grandpa, I thought. The boat would be my savior. My future. My way out. It was better than prison. I closed my eyes. *Better than prison. Wow, that's fucked up.*

The second my head hit the pillow, I fell asleep.

LUCAS

I couldn't resist catching Jacqueline's eyes for just a moment when she entered the classroom.

Her smile was tentative, unsure, and after last night, I couldn't blame her. When I woke to find her leaving, I walked her to her truck and kissed her good-bye. Watching those taillights recede, I knew I could give her what she wanted, once I was free of the restrictions of being her tutor. I would be what she needed, and then I would let her go.

Because I was in love with her.

At the end of class, the blonde who'd been interested in Kennedy Moore earlier in the semester was asking me about my review session. I couldn't remember her name. "It's Thursday, regular time," I answered, watching Jacqueline pack up. Talking to that Benjamin guy, who flicked a glance my way, she rolled her eyes and looked at me, too.

I got a definitive answer to how much he knew about what was going on between Jacqueline and me when he batted his lashes and said, "I'll take *Hot Tutors* for two hundred, Alex," as he left their aisle.

Jacqueline full-on blushed as he hummed the *Jeopardy!* theme song, climbing the steps toward the exit. He grinned at me before disappearing.

Neither of us spoke until we were outside.

"Does he, um, does he know? About . . . ?" My teeth grazed over the ring as she told me that her classmate was how she found out.

"He'd noticed us . . . looking at each other. And he asked me if I went to your tutoring sessions." She shrugged, as if she was beyond it.

I could imagine that conversation and how she must have felt, after Moore's betrayal, to be lied to again. "God. I'm so sorry." But words couldn't make up for those lies, and I knew it.

We walked toward her Spanish class, silent and hunched into our jackets. My old friends in Alexandria would laugh and say this sunny, late fall day was *shorts weather.*

"I noticed you the first week," I said then. Like a flash flood after an unexpected summer storm, I confessed everything—watching her in class and cataloguing her mannerisms, from tucking her hair behind her left ear to her musical fingers. I told her about the rainy day—her *thank you*, her smile, and how those two things affected me. I told her about my jealousy of Moore, before she ever knew me.

"And then, the Halloween party."

She went very still. We'd never discussed what happened that night—my view of it.

I admitted that I'd watched her leave. That I'd watched Buck follow her. "I thought maybe . . . maybe you two had decided to leave early together, without everyone knowing. Meet outside or something." My heart thumped beneath my ribs, revealing this failure to her—the fact that I'd been standing inside, debating following her at all, while a predator wound through the parking lot behind her.

As I suspected, Buck was more than a guy she just knew by name. He was someone she'd seen as a friend. "He's my roommate's boyfriend's best friend," she said, no condemnation for me or my too-slow reaction that night in her voice. From my childhood, I recalled the symbolic gesture of absolution from the priest, and I felt she'd just given it to me.

In the same moment, we realized we weren't surrounded by masses of fellow students anymore. It was past the hour—she was late to class. "I have an A. I don't really need the review," she said. I had an hour before my next class. I stared at her cold-reddened lips, running headlong into inappropriate territory. I wanted to kiss her, right here in the middle of campus.

"You never did sketch me again," she said. She licked her lips, a small brush from the tip of her tongue, and by some miracle, I jerked my eyes away instead of pushing her into the bushes and taking possession of that mouth.

"*Coffee,*" I said.

I seldom stopped by the student union Starbucks as a customer. There was a line, but Gwen and Ron were a well-oiled machine.

"Lucas." Gwen smiled tightly, refusing to look directly at Jacqueline. She was unhappy that her wise words had fallen on deaf ears, no doubt.

"Hey, Gwen. A couple of Americanos. And I don't think you've met Jacqueline."

Like an owl, Gwen swiveled her head to eye Jacqueline. "Nice to meet you," she said, her teeth clamped.

Jacqueline smiled back, as if my usually sweet coworker wasn't bristling with frostiness. "Nice to meet you, Gwen. I love your manicure—so cute!"

Gwen's nails were painted like wrapped, multi-colored Christmas gifts. They looked kind of hideous to me. But she turned her large, dark eyes to Jacqueline, enhancing the owl likeness. "Oh. Thanks. I did 'em myself."

"You *did?*" Jacqueline held out a palm and Gwen put her left hand in Jacqueline's for closer inspection while ringing up our order and swiping my card with her right. "I'm so jealous! I can't paint even one color on mine without making a mess. Plus, I play the bass, so I have to keep my nails too short to do anything fun with them."

Thank God, I thought.

"Aww, that sucks!" Gwen said, won over. I was impressed. I was also glad Eve wasn't working, because she distrusted compliments to the point that she regarded them as an attack.

Once seated at a table in the corner, Jacqueline brought up the fact that I wear glasses, prompting a legion of inappropriate musings, courtesy of my cruel, vividly detailed memory of the reasons I'd flung those glasses away.

I don't want you to stop.

"I could sketch you now," I said, and grabbed my sketchpad from my backpack as if it was a life preserver, meant to save me from drowning. I slid the pencil from behind my ear, balancing the pad on my crossed knee, and leaned back to look at her. She flushed like she could read my thoughts.

Read this, Jacqueline. My pencil swept across the page, and I envisioned my fingers sliding across her skin. I watched her chest rise and fall, as I had last night. She stared at my hands as they interpreted the curves of her body and converted them to lines and shadows on paper.

I imagined stretching her out on my bed, crossing her wrists above her head, as she was in the drawing on my wall. I would run my fingertips over her, applying no pressure. Light strokes only, raising the tiny invisible hairs, training her body to recognize my touch. To rise to it. She would hum deep in her throat, as she had last night, restless, especially when my fingers grazed over her thighs, starting at her knees and moving up.

Hell. Sketching her was a *terrible* idea.

"What are you thinking about?" I asked, in an attempt to distract myself.

"High school," she answered.

Okay. That worked. She might as well have tossed her coffee at me. I assumed she was thinking about Moore until she said, "I wasn't thinking about him."

She asked what high school was like for me, and I saw those years in a series of flashes—Boyce's unexpected friendship, Melody's dismissal, the ache of losing my grandfather, Dad and his silence, the fights, the faceless girls, and Arianna, transforming my scars and skin into a narrative of loss. I'd changed my name when I left home, but I couldn't disconnect from who I'd been so easily.

"A lot different than it was for you, I imagine," I said. She asked how, and I told her the first thing that popped into my head—I'd never had a girlfriend. She seemed skeptical, but she couldn't understand the boy I'd been. The partying and detached hookups, the hopelessness. In a few sentences, I told her about Amber, and that last fight—when rage hijacked my brain and my fists, and I blacked out. I told her about the arrest. I told her about Charles, and the way out he offered.

"He's like a guardian angel for you."

"You don't even know," I said.

• • • • • • • • • •

I sent Jacqueline the review two days before I would be giving it out in my session, after debating whether doing so crossed yet another ethical line. It was blatant favoritism. But what good was embracing my bad-boy side if I couldn't play favorites?

She wrote me back and said it felt weird to get economics email from me, as if Landon and I were still two different people. She admitted that she'd almost recommended *Landon* as a tutor to *Lucas*—who seemed like a total slacker, never paying attention in class and skipping quizzes. I was glad she didn't tell me this in person, because I laughed out loud.

She and Mindi had gone to the police station to file reports and press charges against Buck—legal name: Theodore Boucker III, which I found out when I was contacted by the detective. I gave my story of his assault on Jacqueline and our fight. Buck had informed his whole frat and anyone else who'd listen that he had consensual sex with Jacqueline in her truck, and was jumped by "homeless thugs" after she drove away— though he failed to file an assault report with campus or city police.

Tomorrow was my last class with Jacqueline. Her econ final was next week, and the dorms would shut down for winter break the week after that.

She texted: After the final next Wednesday, then what?

I clicked the screen on and off. *Then what?* Didn't she know how the bad-boy thing worked? There was no *then what*. I'd proven as much with too many girls to remember. Make out and then done, or head and then done, or fuck and then done.

Unlike everyone before and everyone after, I would worship and savor Jacqueline Wallace when she came to my bed. A first, then, for me. Make love and then done.

Finally, I texted back: Winter break. There are things you don't know about me. I told myself I won't lie to you again, but I'm not ready to put everything out there. I don't know if I can. I'm sorry.

I didn't expect an answer. I didn't get one.

chapter Twenty-two

LANDON

I woke to the smell of coffee. Weird, because Dad was almost always gone by the time I woke up. I couldn't imagine he'd cancelled scheduled excursions to discuss my arrest—he never backed out on his clients.

I emerged to find Charles Heller sitting at the kitchen table, no Dad in sight. He had a legal pad in front of him, along with his laptop and a local phone directory. He sat back and glanced up at me as I walked out into the kitchen.

"Landon—I'd like to talk to you, if you're willing. I brought toasted bagels, and I just started a fresh pot of coffee. I'll give you a few minutes to wake up, and then we'll chat. All right?"

Frowning, I nodded and went to the bathroom, digging some OTC pain meds from the cabinet over the sink. I could barely get the child-proof lid off. My hand was so swollen it looked like it belonged to a cartoon character, and it hurt like hell. Everything was awkward without the use of it, from brushing my teeth to getting clothes off or on. I pulled on a tank and board shorts—which I gave up and left untied.

After I slumped into the bench seat across from Heller, he scooted a bagel loaded with cream cheese and a mug of black coffee toward me. He removed his reading glasses and looked at me, his gaze open and persistent, searching my face, my eyes. I wasn't used to such close examination from someone who gave a shit about me. I knew I'd disappointed him. The shame was a landslide, so quick and overwhelming that I was buried in it before I could run away.

Eyes dropping to the mug in my hands, I fought to keep from tearing up and waited for whatever he had to say.

"I have a proposition, and you're free to take it or not," he began. "What I'm about to offer you isn't a gift. It's a challenge. If you don't want to take it on, no one can make you do it, and no one will try to. Understand?"

I didn't understand, but I nodded, silent.

"I've written a list of what I want from you. And next to it, I've written what I'll do, if you do these things to the best of your ability." He pushed the legal pad toward me, and I stared at it as he narrated. "First: school. I want you to start going to class, every day, every class. I want you to do the best you can, because I want you to go to college. You'll need to sign up for some challenging courses next year, to prepare, and you'll have to work very hard at pulling your current GPA up, because you've dug yourself a big hole, Landon."

I wondered if he had any idea how bad it was. I couldn't tell him.

"Second: get a job. Any job. Something that gives you a paycheck, not cash from your dad. Something that gives you experience working for someone else. Third: quit the drugs and drinking. Drugs, entirely. Drinking—well, I'd be a hypocrite if I said I was making you swear not to touch a beer again until you're twenty-one. But I want you to try, and I want you to keep control of yourself. And finally, I want you to enroll in taekwondo. If you're going to fight, you need to know how to do it right, and you're going to learn the reasons to do it, and more importantly, the reasons not to."

I swallowed, and my first thought was that I couldn't possibly do all of this. This wasn't a challenge. This was impossible.

But I wanted to do it. *I wanted to.*

"If you agree to do these things, here's what I'll agree to do: I'll pay for the martial arts classes. They saved my ass and centered me as a young man, and I think they'll do the same for you. Second, I'll pull every damned string I can pull to get you probationary enrollment at the university." My eyes snapped to his. He worked for the best school in the state. "Barring that," he continued, "there's community college. We've got a great one. You make a year of top grades there, and you should be able to transfer in. Either way, Cindy and I want you to come live with us. There's an apartment over the garage housing a bunch of junk we don't need. You'll need to get a job to pay for tuition, but your housing will be covered.

"I made a few calls this morning. I found a reputable dojang about twenty minutes away. If you accept my challenge, we'll get you signed up today. I'll take your signature at the bottom of this list as acceptance." He set a pen on top of the pad and stood. "Eat your breakfast and think it over. I'm going to go see Cindy and the kids off—they're going on home today. I'll be back in a little while."

Laying a hand on my shoulder, he said, "I've also got a call in to the detective about your assault case. Your dad and I are going to see what we can do about that, regardless of what you decide here."

He couldn't have known how scared I'd been, how desolate I'd felt, sitting in that cell. I looked up at him to acknowledge everything he'd said, and I couldn't speak. I just nodded. He patted my shoulder and was gone.

I signed that piece of paper before he'd been gone a full minute.

LUCAS

When I arrived for econ Wednesday morning, Jacqueline was talking to Moore in the hallway. The stiff set of his shoulders radiated frustration, and his tone confirmed it. "It never occurred to me that he'd do *that*."

Jacqueline spotted me over his shoulder as I moved to stand next to her. "You okay?" I asked.

"I'm fine," she said, nodding. I glared at Moore for a moment before turning to enter the classroom. He recognized me and was fitting pieces together before I was out of earshot. "That guy's in our class? And what the hell was that look for?"

He did *not* want to know what that look was for, or that I was more than capable of backing it up.

Jacqueline didn't glance my way as the two of them entered, five minutes later. Heller had begun lecturing. Moore passed me, his expression grim, and Jacqueline slipped into her seat, composed. I took an easy breath.

• • • • • • • • • •

Jacqueline and Mindi planned to file temporary emergency restraining orders this afternoon. I offered to get my shift covered so I could accompany her, but she said Mindi's parents were taking good care of both of them. "Erin says they may withdraw her permanently."

I wished for the hundredth time that I'd killed that bastard when I had the chance.

I watched my breath puff out like smoke and craved a cigarette for the first time in forever. I'd only ever smoked while drinking—and maybe that's what I really wanted. Some numbing of this. Watching what that girl—just two years older than Carlie—had to go through to report what happened to her was unbelievable. She had the support of her parents and the backing of her sorority—but the one time I'd seen her since then, she still looked hollowed out.

Jacqueline hadn't told her parents. After their disappearing act over Thanksgiving break, I could well imagine why.

When we got to her building, she turned to face me. Despite my bleak thoughts thirty seconds before, I smiled down at her adorable face—barely peeking from a knit cap, a hooded coat, and a fuzzy scarf wound several times around her neck, so high that it covered her mouth.

I touched my cold finger to her face, caressing the line of her jaw and dipping into that ridiculous scarf, revealing her full lips. "I'd like to see you, before you go home," I said.

She reminded me of her solo performance tonight, the recital she had to attend Friday, and her ensemble performance Saturday evening. I was officially convinced that music students had more outside-of-class obligations than any other majors.

"I can come over tomorrow night, if you want," she said.

Oh, I wanted, all right. I nodded. "I want."

Her eyes were impossibly big and blue, her dark pink lips begging to be kissed. *I want to kiss you, Jacqueline,* I thought. *Right here, right now, in front of God and everybody.* She would let me. I could see it in her eyes. To save us both, I tugged her scarf back into place. "You look like a partial mummy. Like someone was interrupted while winding you into your shroud."

"Maybe I did a hammer-fist strike and bloodied his nose before he could do all that gruesome mummy stuff to me," she said, and I laughed. When she leaned toward me, I couldn't resist kissing her forehead, carelessly inhaling. *Damn.*

"Text me when you're done this afternoon?" I said, stepping back.

Jacqueline: All done. TROs filed. He can't come within 1000 ft of
            either of us.
Me: Good.
Jacqueline: Heading to my solo performance. Wish me luck!
Me: You won't need it. You have magical fingers,
            remember?
Jacqueline: ☺

I always knocked on the back door of the Hellers' place before entering. Charles and Cindy had never been as demonstrative as my parents were, but you could never be too sure. I didn't want to traumatize
all of us by walking in on them when their kids were out and they
thought they were alone.

Heller answered the door. "Landon, everything okay?"

Landon. I sighed. "Yeah. Great. I wanted to talk to you about . . .
Jacqueline."

His eyebrows rose, and then he smirked. "Come on in. I'm just
making up my final exams for next week. My graduate students will
loathe me by the time they finish." He rubbed his palms together, far
too entertained by that thought. Undergrads almost always loved
Heller. Graduate students thought he was Satan—but the ones he
mentored knew their shit.

We sat at the kitchen table with a couple beers.

"Two things. One, I need to fill you in on my relationship with
her . . ."

He braced himself. "Okay."

"I told you I'd known her before I became her tutor, as Lucas.
What I didn't tell you was how we actually met." I took a breath. "She
was assaulted, outside a frat party on campus. I . . . stopped it. She
didn't want to report it."

"Jesus Christ." He pushed his laptop aside and leaned his elbows onto the notebooks spread over the table. "She was assaulted by *another student?*"

I nodded.

"Why wouldn't she report it? He's undoubtedly dangerous—"

"I'm . . . not done."

He fell silent, frowning.

"Charles, I stopped it before—before it went to the level of anything she could prove, *physically*. No bruising and no"—I ground my teeth—"no penetration. The guy is a member of her ex's fraternity. You know how those guys can be—they'd either not believe he did it, or they'd smear-campaign the shit out of her regardless. I couldn't make her do it, though honestly, I didn't try all that hard. So maybe it's my fault. Maybe I hoped that beating him bloody would deter him. It didn't."

"Oh, God. He did it again." His words were a statement, not a question.

"Yeah. He raped another girl."

"What the—"

"She's reported it, and so has Jacqueline. And so did I."

"Is he out on his ass?" His eyes blazed. "I don't want that little prick prowling around *my school*."

My lips twisted. "Rumor in PD is that administration will let him remain through finals week, if he only comes onto campus for his finals, and a member of his frat is with him at all times when he's there."

"That is bullshit—"

"Innocent until proven guilty, Charles."

"I know. *I know.*" He sighed heavily, as frustrated as I'd been. "I just—I think of Carlie, and it makes me so fucking furious—" He stopped.

I ran a finger over the scar inside my left wrist, and neither of us spoke for a moment.

"Jacqueline and the other student filed temporary restraining orders today. He can't come within a thousand feet of them, on or off campus, or contact them in any way."

He nodded, and I knew he was thinking what I was thinking: *Not good enough*. But it was something.

"You said there were two things?" he prodded.

I sucked on the ring in my lip, and he noticed. I had an unforgiving tell. I couldn't keep from worrying the damned thing when I was anxious. I took a deep breath. "I want to see if the . . . um, student/tutor separation can be lifted now? We want to hang out tomorrow night. After I give my review. At which point my tutoring duties are sort of done . . ."

He angled one brow. "Hmm. Does she live in the area, or will she be leaving campus during winter break?"

"Leaving."

"Ah, well. I'd suggest that you not go fully public until after the exam next week. But a little covert hanging out——" He aimed a devious grin my way. "I suppose you two are capable of that."

He thought Jacqueline was about to become my girlfriend——or already was. Furthermore, he looked thrilled at the prospect. I didn't have the heart to set him straight.

● ● ● ● ● ● ● ● ● ●

Jacqueline was jittery during dinner. I made pasta, which seemed to impress her, again——but I figured she was nervous about what had happened last time. There wouldn't be a repeat, but I couldn't exactly tell her that without sounding like a dick. *Hey, remember how I wanted to stop last time? Well, this time, I'm not stopping until you're done screaming my name.*

Yeah, no.

After I loaded our plates into the dishwasher, I pulled her closer and pretended to give her an impromptu self-defense lesson—taking her hands and pinning them behind her back. "How would you get out of this hold, Jacqueline?"

She told me, softly, that she wouldn't want to get out of it.

"But if you did want to. How would you?" I pressed. She closed her eyes and gave me real answers—groin strike, instep stomp.

"And if I kissed you, and you didn't want me to?"

I expected her to use something she'd learned in the class—a head butt, maybe. But no. She told me she'd *bite me*, and goddamn, I almost lost it.

I kissed her, carefully, halfway hoping she *would* bite me. Instead, she ran her tongue across the inside of my lip and over the ring, and I put her on the counter so she was above me. Wrapping her arms and legs around me, she pushed her small tongue into my mouth. I sucked her tongue in deeper, caressing it with mine, nipping at it as she withdrew.

"Holy crap," she breathed. I swept her off the counter and carried her to my bed, laying her down in the center and kissing her until she was breathless. I stripped off her sweater and she unbuttoned my shirt while I went back to kissing her. When I touched a finger to the zipper of her jeans, she said, "Yes."

I told her I hadn't tried this with anyone significant in a long time, and she misunderstood and thought I was telling her I hadn't had sex with anyone. I almost laughed, but there was nothing funny. "Not with anyone I cared about or . . . knew," I amended. "One-time things. That's all." I was worried she'd be disgusted by that. Three years with Kennedy Moore—pretty sure she'd been there with him. But I figured there was a good chance that he was it.

"That's all—ever?"

"It's not like there've been tons of them." I felt like I should cross my fingers behind my back. "There were more before, in high school, than there have been the past three years." That much was true.

Braced above her, I stared as she told me she wanted this. Wanted me. "Please don't ask me to say stop," she added.

She didn't need to worry about *that*. My only concern was taking this slow enough to please her. I wanted her to feel beautiful and desired and fully, intensely, thoroughly satisfied.

I tugged her jeans down her legs and off, allowing my eyes to graze over her lovely body while I stripped off my shirt and jeans. I swept my fingers over her, lightly—the swell of her breasts above a lacy pink bra, the tiny oval hollow of her navel above the matching pink lace—and not much more—below. She was so incredibly hot, reaching for me, tracing the lines of my biceps and shoulders, palms sliding across my abs—her tongue darting out to wet her lips.

I grabbed a condom from the night table drawer, but when I resettled over her, she was shaking. I knew it wasn't from cold, even if that's where she placed the blame when I asked. She was tense, almost panicked, and I wasn't sure why. I prayed it had more to do with inexperience than it did with what happened to her *that night*. Inexperience I could remedy. Dread or fear that summoned echoes of something as distressing as what happened to her—I wasn't sure how to combat that.

I could stop. I could hold her. If her fear didn't abate, that's what I would do.

I sat back and pulled the covers down beneath her. The sheets were cool, increasing her shivering until I pulled the comforter back up and over both of us, laying on top of her, kissing her softly and warming her with my body. I felt her muscles relax below my fingertips, her breaths coming faster, but deeper. I took her mouth slowly, gently, my hands cradling her head, coaxing her back to the heated state we'd been in when we left the kitchen. She snuggled under me, trusting, warm, relaxed.

"Better?" I asked, and she answered *yes*. "You know you can say it. But I'm not asking you to, this time."

I bent to kiss her again, and she opened for me, tangling her tongue with mine, licking my lip, sucking lightly on the ring and pushing her fingers into my hair—holding my head at the exact angle she wanted me. When she scraped her short little nails from my shoulder blades to my hips, fingers dipping below the elastic of my boxer briefs as we kissed, I knew she was ready, but I kept the pace slow, intent on appeasing every desire she had. I unfastened her bra and removed it, slid her panties down her legs, removed my boxers and fixed the condom in place, and we never stopped kissing.

One hand at her hip, I leaned into her, opening her mouth with a deep, penetrating kiss as I thrust into her and remained just long enough for us to both feel the connection fully. Warm and tight, she was a perfect fit. *Of course she was.* I kissed her chin, her jaw, the edge of her hairline right next to her ear. "Beautiful girl," I murmured, withdrawing and returning. Stroking the interior of her mouth, I told her without words how I loved her.

She gasped, fingers pushing into my hair and gripping, sucking my tongue, coiling one leg around mine and bracing her opposite foot flat on the mattress so she could arch up to meet my thrusts as I began rocking into her.

I shuddered above her—*so good, so good*, moving with her, sliding my hand over her soft body, kneading and stroking. When I took her breast in my hand and bent to suck her nipple into my mouth, she murmured my name, writhing and whimpering softly, needing this, needing me.

I rolled onto my back, taking her with me, hands at her waist, pressing her down as I surged up, guiding her until she took over and set the tempo she required, knees pressed to my hips, arms trembling. Her hair tumbled all around us as my hands slipped to her thighs, and beneath the curtain of her silky, honeysuckle hair, I mapped the curves of her breasts with my tongue, skimming the soft undersides, the full outer contours, the pectoral line down the center. She hummed so deep in her throat that I felt it with my cheek pressed to her chest.

"Come, Jacqueline," I whispered. "Come now, baby." She whimpered again, frustrated, like she wasn't quite sure what to do, so I rolled her under me, flattened her hands to the mattress on either side of her head, and thrust back into her.

"Oh, God," she gasped, her fingers curling over mine. "Lucas," she moaned, her eyes closed.

"I'm right here," I said, leaning over to kiss her as she tightened and convulsed.

I followed, never more satisfied in my life.

• • • • • • • • • •

I couldn't see anything of her below her bare shoulder, cuddled beneath the comforter—though I could certainly feel her. She was warm and soft, folded in my arms, our legs tangled. I attempted to focus on the parts I could see—features I knew as well as the patterns embedded under my skin. I decided her eyes were my favorite. They were also the most difficult to capture on paper. Impossible, to illustrate the multihued facets and the way she looked at me. Or maybe her mouth . . . I touched her lips and she stared, waiting.

So unfair, how much I wanted her. I kissed her and peeled the covers to her waist. Men are visual, as are artists, so I doubled-down on the desire to see her bare skin. Goddamn, she was so very beautiful. "I want to sketch you like this," I said, struggling not to laugh when she asked, jokingly, if it would go on the wall. I would never get to sleep if I did that. I'd either have her in my bed, repeating what we'd just done, or I'd be using my very vivid imagination to imagine her there.

"I've done several sketches of you that aren't on the wall," I said. *Oops.*

She wanted to see them, of course. I ran the tips of my fingers over her breast before pressing her closer. "Now?" I asked. *Please, not now.*

She relented, curious, I think, and I moved over her and disappeared under the covers.

I pressed kisses from her sternum straight down, progressing slowly. Her breath caught and her fingers sunk into my hair and tightened when I passed her navel and kept going. I veered to the side, sucking kisses on her upper, inner thigh, inhaling her sweet scent, blowing gently as if showing her the path my tongue intended to take. In her small hands, my long, dark hair transformed into something it had never been—reins.

Lead me, Jacqueline. Show me where you want me to go.

She did.

• • • • • • • • • •

I pulled on my boxer briefs before letting Francis in and feeding him so he'd leave us alone. I poured a glass of milk and put a few brownie squares on a plate, handing them to Jacqueline when I came back into the dimly lit room.

She held the sheet over her breasts, which was both humorous and enticing, considering the last few hours. After switching on the desk lamp, I grabbed my sketchbook and got into bed behind her, urging her to lean back against my chest. Her bare hips were pressed against what would be, in the not-too-distant future, a solid, demanding erection. For the moment, I wanted to purr with contentment, or growl, or whatever guys did when every possible need has been met.

She nibbled at a brownie as I flipped through sketches I'd done this semester—campus buildings with noteworthy architecture, mechanical sketches, landscapes, and people I found interesting. By the time we turned to the sketch I'd done of her on the rainy day, she'd finished two brownies and was starting on a third.

I glanced toward my ceiling. *Score, Grandpa. Now avert your eyes.*

I asked if it bothered her that I was watching her before she knew me, but she seemed to think she was just another of the interesting strangers I'd drawn.

"I don't know if that makes me feel better or worse," I said.

She leaned back against my arm. "I'm not mad anymore that you didn't tell me you were Landon. The only reason I was angry was because I thought you were playing me, but it was the opposite of that." Her soft fingers touched my face as the sheet drifted lower. "I could never be afraid of you," she whispered.

I transferred the brownie plate to the night table and turned her to face me, straddling my lap. As I touched, kissed, and sucked her breasts, and she ran her magic fingers through my hair and over my skin, my body woke fully.

"Should I get, um . . ." she whispered, and I nodded. She leaned to the nightstand drawer and came back with a cellophane square. "Can I . . . or is that too—?"

"God, yes—please." I'd never had a girl roll a condom onto me before. I assumed, as her cool little fingers pressed it on and down, expertly, that I was the inexperienced one in this moment. And *oh, my God*, I was okay with that.

chapter *Twenty-three*

LANDON

Landing a part-time job was more problematic than I'd assumed it would be. In a small town, with a known probated assault in my none-too-distant past, managers weren't jumping at the chance to have me on the payroll.

Plumbing the depths, I asked for an application at the very last fast-food place I would ever want to work, and still heard: "You can fill this out, but we're not really hiring right now." It was almost summer—the busiest time of year for every business in this beach town. Not hiring my *ass*. I stared at the manager's short-sleeved dress shirt and polyester tie as I took the sheet from his hand, which would take fifteen minutes to fill out. For nothing.

"Ain't you Ray's boy? Edmond's grandson?"

I turned to find one of the town's crotchety-looking old guys peering up at me. They weren't scarce around here. This one was shorter and wider than me, sporting a pair of red canvas coveralls that resembled prison threads too closely, with exception of *Hendrickson Electric & AC* monogrammed on the chest. He tipped his tray of wadded wrappers and cartons into the trash and turned back.

"Yes, sir." I stuck a hand out. "Landon Maxfield."

He shook my hand in a remarkably bone-crunching grip. "W. W. Hendrickson," he said, his local drawl shortening his initials to *dubyah*

dubyah. "Needin' a job, are ya? You don't wanna work in this crap place." He shot a look at the manager, who reddened. "No offense, Billy."

I got the feeling that Bill Zuckerman hadn't gone by *Billy* in at least twenty years. He cleared his throat and struggled not to scowl, failing. "Uh, none taken, Mr. Hendrickson."

"Hmph," Hendrickson said. "Come outside a minute, Landon. Talk to me." He motioned and I followed. "You work on the boat with your dad, I thought?" We walked up to his truck and he leaned an elbow on the bed's side.

I nodded. "Yes, sir. But I plan to go to college in a little over a year, and I'll need work experience with a reference."

"Plan to scoot on outta town like yer dad did, do ya?" he asked, but I couldn't detect any malice in his tone.

"Yes, sir. I plan to study engineering."

His bushy brows elevated. "Ah, now that's a levelheaded thing worth studyin'. I never could understand how your dad needed so much schoolin' to study somethin' done with smoke and mirrors."

I pinned my lips together, knowing better than to try to explain my father's multiple economics degrees to guys like Mr. Hendrickson.

"I'll get to the point. I'm needin' a new assistant. Before you jump at the opportunity, realize that you'll probably get zapped a time or two afore you learn which wires to avoid. And I'll be sending you into dark, hundred-and-twenty-degree attics where you'll sweat buckets, get fiberglass in yer knees and ass, and may have the occasional critter skittering across your feet." He laughed, a near-silent snuffling sound through his nose. "I had one assistant go clean through a client's ceilin' because of a hissin' possum. Landed in the middle of the livin' room, luckily."

Luckily? "Um, okay." I didn't know what to say or ask.

"Pay's a couple bucks above minimum wage. No drinkin', smokin', hanky-panky with clients' daughters—feel like I gotta mention that, you bein' a looker like yer dad and also, I been there before."

My face heated.

"I assume you know all about computers and such?" At my nod, he said, "Good. I could use some help with gettin' my books on there. Come up to the twenty-first century afore it's over. So. Whaddaya think?"

I got a job, I thought.

• • • • • • • • • •

"Well, Mr. Maxfield. Here we are—the beginning of your senior year. I must admit, I never thought you'd make it this far."

I stared at my principal and thought, *No shit. Especially when you did everything in your power to make that true.* Still, the brass balls of her to call me into her office just to say this to my face couldn't mean anything good. She thought she was above everything and everyone, and within the confines of this school, she was right.

Nine months, I told myself. Nine months and I was out of here. I wouldn't even pause to shake the dust off my boots.

So I said nothing. Merely returned her beady-eyed gaze with a flinty one of my own. She studied a slip of paper with my schedule printed on it. "I see you've signed up for calculus and physics." She glanced at me over the glasses perched on the bridge of her nose. "How . . . *ambitious* of you." Lips pressed closed, brows somewhat elevated, eyelids lowered—her entire expression displayed her skepticism that I was capable of the change I'd begun in the last few weeks of the previous year.

I wanted to flick those glasses and that condescension off her face.

Instead of responding, I repeated my mantra silently—the tenets I'd learned in my first month of martial arts, last spring: *Courtesy, integrity, perseverance, self-control, indomitable spirit.* Often, the functions of these blurred together—because each was interwoven through the others. If I failed one, I could fail them all. What good was integrity if I had no self-control?

So there I sat, waiting for Ingram to be done with me.

She wasn't pleased with my muteness—that much was all too apparent. Her thin lips twisted. "I understand one of our star students assisted you in passing your classes last spring."

Ah. Pearl.

Aside from the day she checked me for a punctured lung, Pearl Frank and I hadn't ever spoken outside of Melody's presence or *Can you pass this forward* classroom-type chatter. I almost didn't respond when she touched my arm in the library last spring and asked, "Landon, are you okay?"

With six weeks of school remaining to learn the thirty weeks of stuff I'd failed to absorb plus the new material, I was going under. But I had no desire to confess that to Melody's best friend, who also happened to be the smartest person in my graduating class.

I blinked and rolled my shoulders, popping my neck. "Yeah. Fine." I'd been stuck in a hair-clenching position for the entire hour of study hall, staring at a section in my chemistry textbook.

Her brows creasing, she gestured at the open text. "Why are you looking at that? We went over Dalton's Law last six weeks."

I shut the book, scowling and standing. "Yeah, well, I didn't get it then, I don't get it now." I loosened my grimace and shrugged. "No big deal."

Pearl's gaze missed very little. "But you're studying it now because . . ."

I swallowed. I didn't want to say it out loud—that I was making an eleventh-hour bid to alter my future. That I was afraid I wouldn't be able to do it.

"If you want, I can send you my notes from last six weeks, and you can ask me questions." Her dark eyes held a dare, not pity.

I nodded. "Okay."

"Don't be afraid to ask for help from your teachers, too. They're just people, you know." I arched a brow and she smirked. "Well, most of them."

Over the next several weeks, she saved me from failing my junior year—not just chemistry, but literature and pre-calc. Thanks to her help, my brain woke up from three years of hibernation.

"Pearl Frank?" Mrs. Ingram prompted now, as if I wouldn't remember the tutoring or who gave it. I wasn't sure how she knew, but I damned sure wasn't going to ask.

"Yes," I answered.

She hated me right now. In my first few months of taekwondo, I'd become more aware of the clues that someone was progressing from irritation to rage. Recognizing the level of likelihood that someone might fucking lose it any second was necessary for defense, after all. Her physical indications were minor, but they were there.

"I understand you were arrested last spring for assault. Plea bargained to probation, fortunately." *Fortunately* was not what she wanted to call it.

I said nothing.

Pearl told me once that Ingram was the type of leader who believed in *addition by subtraction*. "It's half genius, half cheating. They remove the lowest-scoring students, employees with bad service records, et cetera, which raises the overall score or ranking of the organization."

Finally, Ingram broke rank and flat-out glared. "Why aren't you answering me, Mr. Maxfield?"

One brow angled. "You aren't asking any questions."

Her eyes blazed. "Let me be clear. I don't know what game you're playing here, or what your business is with Miss Frank, but I don't want her valuable time wasted for your nonsense. I don't believe for two seconds that you have the essential work ethics or the life and interpersonal skills necessary to represent this school and its exemplary educational standards."

I bit my lip to keep from correcting her. According to the state, her school was far from *exemplary*.

I tuned her out as she blathered on about my lack of integrity and critical thinking skills and respect for authority. Funny how people who railed about other people's lack of respect usually weren't willing to offer any in exchange.

When she stopped, my ears rang. "Do we understand each other, young man?" She clearly expected an answer to more than that question—or a heated reaction. She was doomed to be disappointed.

"I believe so. Are we finished here, Mrs. Ingram?" I stood, casting a broad shadow over her desk from the east-facing window behind me. "I have a class to get to. Unless you want to make me late the first day." On cue, the first bell rang.

She stood, but still craned her neck to look up at me. I'd reached my dad's imposing height over the summer, and she didn't care for me looming a foot over her. I slid a hand into my front pocket and shifted my weight to one side—as close to a cease-fire as I'd give her. I wasn't fourteen anymore, and this woman was not going to trash my chances of getting out of this town and into college.

"You're dismissed. But I'm watching you."

Uh-huh, I thought, turning and leaving without response.

I wondered why in the hell someone like her would pursue a career in education in the first place, but I wouldn't ask. Everyone isn't logical. Everything doesn't make sense in the end. Sometimes you have to forget about explanations or excuses and leave people and places behind, because otherwise they will drag you straight down.

LUCAS

Saturday morning, it had been thirty-something hours since I'd seen Jacqueline. Sergeant Ellsworth and I suited up for the final module in the locker room. The two of us weren't supposed to arrive until halfway through the class, because we would serve only one purpose today: "attackers," which necessitated emotional distance from the "victims."

When we entered the room, fully padded, my eyes went to Jacqueline instantly. Along with the others, she was wearing all the protective gear. They resembled a tribe of mini sumo wrestlers. She looked up and saw me, quickly lowering her lashes and biting her lip, and I was struck with a graphic recollection of the hours we'd spent in my bed. By the looks of her shy grin, so was she.

Emotional distance. *Right.*

I wished, too late, that I'd outright asked Jacqueline to avoid going up against me. We could practice defenses together, but this was different. As the attackers, Ellsworth and I would make audible comments. We would look for openings to attack. We wouldn't release a "victim" unless a defense blow was adequately delivered—and we'd both been trained to judge that point.

This section of the class was unnerving for me. Pretending to be a sexual predator always made me crave a scalding hot shower after.

As soon as the women finished reviewing moves with Watts, they'd be ready to do what Jacqueline told me her friend Erin termed *serious junk kicking.*

"She's only excited because she can practice doing it and not hurt you guys, because of the padding," she said as we dressed so I could take her back to the dorm late Thursday night.

"Uh-huh," I said, deadpan, and she laughed.

As she pulled on her gloves, her eyes skittering away from mine, she said, "Erin was the first person I told." Her voice was so soft. "I wish I'd told her sooner."

I tipped her chin and pulled her close. "There's no right or wrong way to be a survivor, Jacqueline. There's no script." She swallowed and nodded, not quite convinced, yet, because of Mindi. "You survived, and so will she."

I was up first. As I went to the mat, I felt Jacqueline's eyes on me, and I prayed we wouldn't be paired for this. Vickie was the first volunteer, and she kicked my ass in the best kind of way. I'd expected Erin might step forward first or second, but she hung back with Jacqueline, who seemed in no hurry to go at all. During Ellsworth's turns on the mat, I watched the two of them root for their classmates, Erin screaming suggestions at the top of her lungs—"Head butt! *LAWNMOWER!* Kick him! Kick him *HARDER!*"—while Jacqueline cheered and clapped.

Finally, Erin squeezed Jacqueline's hand and stepped forward to fight Ellsworth, leaving only Jacqueline and one other, extremely timid woman who worked in the Health Center. Ellsworth eyed Erin and mumbled, "If this one kicks my nuts up to my throat, you *owe* me, dude," before he stepped out. "I'm not so sure I trust the pads with her."

If the "victim" landed a good blow, we weren't really going to feel it—hopefully. In my training class, they'd told us to find our inner thespians. Even so, when Erin nailed Ellsworth in the junk with a perfect sweep kick and he crumpled straight to the ground, I was a little worried. Eleven voices screamed, *"RUN!"* but Erin had an inner thespian of her own. After launching herself off his *chest*, she turned around and kicked him twice before running to the safe zone, where she bounced around like she'd won the heavyweight championship.

Ellsworth rolled to his feet and gave me a thumbs-up. *Phew.*

I went to the mat and waited. Gail from the Health Center stepped out, so nervous she was shaking. At this point, some might have been tempted to tell her she didn't have to do it. But she'd gotten this far. Time to prove to her that she'd learned something. Watts gave her quiet instructions, at first, encouraging her to hit harder. I went easy on her, but as she landed punches and kicks, and was cheered by her classmates, she kicked harder, hit harder, yelled *no* and *get back* louder. She was crying and smiling by the time we were done, surrounded and congratulated by the others.

For me, nothing compared to watching Jacqueline. Without direction, she executed a series of moves, and whether she landed them or not, she varied them. At one point, she appeared stuck in a front bear hug, until Erin hollered, *"NUTSACK!"* loud enough to be heard in a neighboring state, and Jacqueline brought her knee up, hard. Ellsworth went straight to the ground. She tore off toward the safety zone, where Erin tackled her in an enthusiastic hug. I was so proud of her—and I hoped to God she'd never have to use anything she'd just learned.

• • • • • • • • • •

Sunday afternoon, Jacqueline and I took a final break from studying for finals. I packed coffee in thermoses and we headed to the lake. I wanted to sketch kayakers, who Jacqueline insisted were certifiably insane to be out on the lake in these temperatures. She huddled next to me on the bench, wrapped head to toe and still shivering. I wore my hoodie, but no gloves, and I'd discarded my leather jacket because I didn't need it.

I called her a candyass for being such a cold-weather wimp, and she punched me in the shoulder. I saw it coming and could have blocked her, but I didn't. "Ow, jeez—I take it back! You're tough as nails. Total badass." I pulled her closer to warm her.

"I throw a mean hammer-fist." Her words were almost inaudible, mumbled into my chest.

"You do." I tipped her face up to mine. "I'm actually a little scared of you." My playful words were truer than she knew.

"I don't want you to be scared of me." Her words issued with small puffs of her breath, and I kissed her until her nose was warm against my cheek.

We went back to my apartment, where she reminded me of my request, weeks ago, that she leave me something to anticipate. "So, have you been . . . anticipating it?" she asked. Our clothes were askew, but we'd gotten no further than a heated make-out on my sofa with Francis for a bored audience.

Had I been anticipating her hands and mouth on me? Uh . . . yeah.

Staring at my lip—the ring sucked fully into my mouth—a slow smile spread across her face. She kissed me before sliding from my lap to her knees, between my legs. As she unbuttoned and unzipped my jeans, I was pretty sure I was dreaming. I didn't want to move and risk waking up, but I couldn't help lancing my fingers through her soft hair so I could both touch her and watch every single thing she did.

When she darted the tip of her tongue and ran it base to tip, I closed my eyes for just a moment, losing my mind with ecstasy. She leaned up to nibble me with her teeth, stroking me with her fingertips and then her tongue. I moaned, which was apparently the exact right response. As her warm mouth closed over me—*Holy mother of God*, my head fell back on the sofa and I closed my eyes again, my hands still in her hair, the heels of my palms against her cheekbones. And then, she hummed—one long, low note.

"Fucking hell, Jacqueline," I gasped.

This time, she didn't let me stop her.

• • • • • • • • • •

She texted Wednesday afternoon: *Econ final: PWNED.* Whether she knew that gamer term from video games or cat memes, I didn't care. It was too cute. *All because of me, right?* I texted back. *No, because of that Landon guy,* she returned. I laughed out loud, earning a crooked brow from Eve, with whom I was working a double shift. Gwen and Ron had two finals each today, and neither of us had one, so we'd agreed to work practically all day, along with our manager.

"I need somethin' hot-n-sweet." I recognized Joseph's voice, giving his order to Eve. He rubbed his hands together in his fingerless gloves, trying to warm them. His coat was university-issued and displayed his name. His wool cap, pulled low over his ears, sported our mascot.

She glared at him. "I'll need the *name* of your desired *drink*, sir." Venom rolled off her. This was going to be funny. Or really painful. Either way, I couldn't bring myself to step up and make it stop.

Joseph rarely came into the coffee shop, insisting it was all complete hype—overpriced and over-marketed.

He eyed Eve across the counter. "Recommendations? I'm not familiar with all the fancy-ass drinks y'all have. Like I said—I want something *hot*, and *sweet*. I'm not so sure you're the one to give it to me, though."

"*Really?* That's your line?"

His brows angled up and his mouth twisted. "Sweetheart, if you're hopin' for a line, you ain't gonna get it from *me*. You are a far, far cry from my type."

Eve sputtered, furious. "Oh, so 'I want something hot and sweet' means 'nothing'?"

"Um, *no*." His eyes were glacial. "It means I'd like a *hot* drink, as opposed to a cold one, and I'd like something *sweet*—as in *with syrup in it*. Goddamn. You got a coworker or somethin' I could order from?" He glanced over and spotted me, lips pressed together.

"Lucas, dammit, get me somethin'"—he eyed Eve—"*hot* and *sweet*."

"Salted caramel mocha sound good?"

Smiling, he said, "Hell, yeah—that sounds perfect." His smile dropped when he looked back at Eve, though he was still speaking to me. "And thank you for your professionalism." I made the drink as he handed over a bill and Eve rung him up, silently.

"See ya next week for that Air Review show," he said, taking the cup. "Elliott's sister is comin' for a visit the week after, by the way. If you wanna join us for dinner one night, I can show off my one smart friend."

"Sure thing." I laughed. "Sounds good, Joseph."

When he'd gone, Eve glowered at me and said, no inflection: "He's gay, isn't he."

"Yep."

"And you just stood there and let me make an ass of myself—"

"Eve, everything isn't about you." I tapped a finger to her nose to lessen the harsh words. "Maybe you should figure that out." I turned to wash pitchers before the next wave of finals-freaked customers deluged us.

She huffed a sigh but didn't reply.

My phone buzzed with one more text from Jacqueline, who had three more exams between now and Saturday to my one: Chinese on Saturday? I need something hot and spicy to celebrate the end of the semester. Kung-pao maybe? *wink* After the previous exchange between Joseph and Eve, I chuckled aloud again. Jacqueline and I had plans to celebrate in her dorm room, after Erin left for winter break.

Me: I think I can make hot and spicy happen
Jacqueline: *fanning* yes please

• • • • • • • • • •

"So how did you end up playing the bass?" I asked, digging in my carton for a broccoli spear. We were sitting side by side on Jacqueline's dorm room floor, our backs to her bed.

"By way of Pee-Wee football," she answered. I made a face, my imagination putting her in a football uniform, and she laughed. "One of our bass players snapped his collarbone in a game, and our orchestra teacher begged for one of the violins to switch. I volunteered. It was a bonus that my mother wasn't happy about it."

"So your relationship with your mom—not so good, I take it?"

She sighed. "Actually, I just told her—about Buck. About all of it. And she *cried*. She never cries. She wanted to come here." A frown creased her brow. "I told her I was good, I was strong, and I realized I was." She leaned her head back against her bed, her face turned toward me. "Because of Erin—and you."

My mind suggested that this was no *bad boy* trait she was praising.

I tipped an imaginary hat. "Happy to be of service, ma'am."

She smiled. "She's making me an appointment with her therapist. At first I agreed because it gave her something to do—some way to help. But when I thought about it, I was glad. I want to talk to someone about what happened. Someone who can help me deal with all of it."

Our faces were inches apart, and I could have sworn she looked sad for *me*. Maybe because I didn't have a mother. "That's awesome. I'm glad your mom was there for you."

This was not where I wanted this evening to go. I had so little time left with her.

"What about you? How did you decide to study engineering? I mean, you could have majored in art, probably."

I shrugged. "I can draw whenever I want. It calms me—always has. But I don't want to do that for anyone but me. As for art in general—I'm not really a painter, sculptor, anything else. Whereas narrowing down my interests in engineering was difficult. I wanted to do it all."

She smiled. "So how did you choose?"

"Well, skill and opportunity. I hadn't really considered going a medical route. I thought I'd be designing cars or inventing futuristic stuff like hovercraft. But the opportunity presented itself when Dr. Aziz asked me to apply, so I'm game."

I scrolled through my iTunes list for the playlist I wanted her to hear and handed her both earbuds. Unsurprisingly, she was emotionally attuned to music like no one I'd ever known—an unguarded range of feelings reflected in her eyes as she stared at me, listening. I leaned in to kiss her, and then picked her up, laid her on the bed and stretched out next to her, one arm under her head, the other flat on her abdomen.

When I reached to brush a finger over her ear, she removed one earbud and handed it to me. I dialed the playlist to a song I'd discovered just before I got my last tattoo—four lines now inscribed onto my side, a poem composed by my artistic mother for the analytical man who loved her. The song had triggered the memory of her words, so I'd searched the attic for her poetry notebook the next time I was home. I copied the lines and took them to Arianna, and she added the poem to the canvas of my body, two years ago.

Love is not the absence of logic
but logic examined and recalculated
heated and curved to fit
inside the contours of the heart

Our hands began to wander over each other—my fingers sliding under her shirt as I kissed her. She warned me that Erin could return any moment—apparently her roommate hadn't left for winter break yet. Something to do with a boyfriend who was trying to win her back.

"Why did they break up?" I asked.

I cupped her breast, about to search for the clasp—front or back this time?

"Over me," she said, and I froze. "Not like that. Chaz was . . . Buck's best friend." Her entire body went rigid, just speaking his name, and I pulled her close.

Buck was supposed to be gone, and probably wouldn't be back next semester—certainly not if Charles had anything to do with it. He knew someone on the disciplinary committee, and I was pretty sure he was going to call in every favor he could.

"I never told you about the stairwell, did I?" Jacqueline said then.

I went as taut as she was. "No."

She swallowed. "About a month ago, all the washers were full on my floor, so I went down to the second floor to see if they had any machines free." Her voice was so subdued that I couldn't shift positions and still hear her. "On the way back up, Buck caught me in the stairwell. He threatened to . . ." She swallowed again, hard, and left the blank for my mind to fill. "So I said, 'My room.' I thought if I could get him into the hallway, people would be there and they'd hear me tell him to leave and he'd have to go."

I was holding her too tightly. I registered that, but my muscles had solidified. I couldn't loosen my grip on her.

"There were five people in the hall. I told him to leave. He was furious when he figured out what I'd done. He made it look like we'd done it in the stairwell. And from the looks on everyone's faces in the hall . . . from the stories that circulated after . . . they believed him."

He didn't get into her room. But he put his hands on her. And he scared her. *Again.*

I felt the protective rage and excruciating powerlessness building and didn't know what to do with it. I didn't want to hurt Jacqueline, or frighten her, but I didn't know what to do with the anger bubbling up inside, threatening to spill over.

I pushed her onto her back and kissed her, pressing a knee between her legs. I felt her struggle and my brain screamed *WHAT THE FUCK*

ARE YOU DOING. I tried to pull back—but her hands, freed from be-tween us, stabbed into my hair and held on tight, and she opened her mouth, pulling me inside and kissing me back just as hard.

I shuddered, loving her, loving her so much I could hardly breathe. Wondering if that was how it was supposed to feel to love someone or if I was just fucked all to hell and incapable of loving correctly, because all I felt was this insane, unfillable need, this empty black hole inside my soul. I was breaking apart in her hands, crumbling to nothing.

I had to stop. This had to stop. I'd given her what she wanted, what she needed—and I was in pieces at her feet. How could she not see? I couldn't play this game anymore. I had to save what little of me re-mained.

I wanted to strip her and possess her one last time. Spread her legs and adore her. Make her cry my name and shudder beneath me. I wanted to pretend, one more night, that I could belong to her. That she could be mine. I lay over her, kissing her, and knew it wouldn't happen. Her roommate would return any minute, and it was just as well. There was no filling the space I wanted her to fill.

We slowed, lying side by side, and I began to compose my exit lines.

Then she asked about the Hellers, and my parents, and I turned onto my back and answered her questions.

And then—"What was your mother like?"

"Jacqueline—" I said, as Erin's key hit the lock.

I got up as she entered, and Jacqueline followed. Erin tried to make like she had laundry to do, but I said, "I was just leaving," lacing my black work boots and wishing I'd worn my old Noconas so I could shove my feet in and go.

"Tomorrow?" Jacqueline said at the door, arms hugging herself.

I zipped my jacket and said, "It's officially winter break. We should probably use it to take a break from each other as well."

She recoiled, stunned. She asked me why, and I became all logic, no emotion—she was leaving town and I would be, too, for at least a few days Christmas week. She still had to pack, and Charles needed help getting grades posted—which was bullshit, but she had no way to verify that and I knew it.

I told her to let me know when she was back in town, and I bent to kiss her—one quick, barren kiss. Nothing like she deserved. Nothing of what I felt. I said good-bye and walked away.

chapter *Twenty-four*

LANDON

I knew I wasn't the only student in the school without a computer, but it felt that way. I usually logged in at the library, or during my programming lab, or at Hendrickson's. I didn't have lab or work hours today, though, so I was using the prehistoric computer at Wynn's Garage.

"Buy a cheap laptop already," Boyce urged. "You work all the fucking time so I know you've got the cash, and I sure as hell know you aren't smokin' it or shootin' it anymore."

After pulling up the site where I hoped my SAT scores would finally materialize, I waited for the computer to wheeze its way to the log-in page where I tapped my password. Boyce watched for his father through the plate glass window, grimy from fingerprints, Scotch tape bits, blotches of who-knows-what, and decades of no one thinking to buy glass cleaner.

"Saving for tuition." I gave the excuse I used every time I refused to spend money on something. "And I never shot up."

"Yeah, yeah." He squeezed my bicep. "Your big, hard, virtuous arms are reserved for tattoo needles only."

I shrugged him off. "Shut up, man . . ."

Almost unattainable scores on the SAT were my only hope of

scraping my sorry ass into college past the pathetic GPA I could only raise so much. Not even a straight 4.0 this year would be enough. I'd made use of every free online pretest and every study guide in the library for the past eight or nine months. If my scores on this goddamned entrance exam weren't ridiculously high, I was screwed, and there would be no string Heller could pull to change that fact.

I hit enter, the screen flashed several times, and then there they were: the numbers that determined my future. I sat back in the chair, staring, my heart rate hurtling higher.

I'd done it.

"Ninety-eighth percentile?" Boyce's brows arched and he hooted. "Does that mean what I think it means? Shit, man. I knew you were a brain, but *holy fuck*." He grabbed my shoulders and shook them, laughing. Boyce was the only person—Heller aside—who knew how badly I wanted this escape. How much I needed it. "Dude, you did it."

I nodded, still stunned.

"Oh, man." He shoved me. "This *sucks*. I'm going to be stuck in this crap town while you run off and fuck tons of *college girls*."

I shook my head and smiled. Leave it to Boyce to zero in on the only part of college that might have appealed to me.

Belatedly, we heard a truck door slam. "Shit," we said in unison.

The bell over the door jangled right after I cleared the history, shut the computer down, and bolted from the chair, but Boyce's dad wasn't a complete idiot.

"You jackasses looking at porn again on *my computer?*" he roared, not even waiting for the door to shut behind him. Thinning hair stood straight up on his head, as though he'd received an electrical shock.

Technically, we'd only watched porn on his computer once, though I was pretty sure Boyce still did it whenever he could. We'd come to an unspoken agreement that watching it together was too weird.

"We were looking up college entrance exam scores," Boyce said, tracking his father's movements. I didn't even know he could string those words together.

"Lyin' sack of shit," Mr. Wynn growled, lunging. We slid out of his way, Boyce ducking the meaty fist that flew at his head, halfheartedly, the way you'd wave a hand at a fly to shoo it away. His dad cursed us all the way out the door.

Boyce and I had bonded over defective fathers and absent mothers, but that's as far as the parallels went. His father was an abusive fuck, where mine was silent and detached. His mother left his father—and her two sons—when he was almost too young to remember her. He'd never seemed to hold her desertion against her. *I would've ditched his ass, too, if I was her,* was all he'd ever said about it.

"Time to celebrate, my man." He steered me toward the Trans Am as his father cursed him from the door of the shop.

"Quittin' time is at *six!*" he bellowed, ignoring the fact that he'd closed up for two hours mid-afternoon to visit a "lady friend" in the next town—a person Boyce and I weren't certain existed. How any woman could find Bud Wynn attractive was beyond our powers of imagination. "You worthless piece of—"

We slammed wing-wide doors shut on the familiar tirade and Boyce turned the key, igniting the stereo, while I grudgingly acknowledged the sounder fact of my father's muteness.

LUCAS

Jacqueline would be moving home in two days. The space between us was magnetized—I couldn't think of another way to describe it. I fought her pull every second of the past twenty hours. I knew exactly where she was, and I wanted to be there. I hoped that once she was gone, once she was farther from me, I would get a respite.

Carlie and Caleb were in my apartment, playing video games. They were in that zone—the one where school has let out for two weeks, and there's nothing but eating and sleeping late and getting presents as far as you can see—because at sixteen and eleven, you can't see all that far. You think you can . . . but you can't.

I can't say their perspective was contagious, but it was fun to watch.

There was a knock on the door, but I wasn't expecting anyone. Before I could think, Carlie was up and unbolting the door.

"Who is it, Carlie?" I jumped up, going for the bat. "Don't just open the door—"

"It's a girl," she said, rolling her big, dark eyes.

A girl? What girl? Carlie pulled the door open. "Jacqueline?" I said, needlessly, because *of course* it was Jacqueline, showing up after I told her good-bye. "What are you doing here?"

She turned to tear down the stairs and without thinking I reached out and seized her arm. Her momentum swung her right into the air. I grabbed her with both hands and pulled her to my chest, my heart stopping, restarting, revving up, and then slamming like a train engine. When she wriggled like she wanted loose, I realized that a pretty girl had answered my door.

"She's Carlie Heller," I murmured, leaning to her ear. "Her brother Caleb is inside, too. We're playing video games."

She swayed into me, professing unnecessary apologies into my chest.

The last thing I could feel, holding her in my arms, was sorry. "Maybe you shouldn't have come without telling me, but I can't be sorry to see you."

I confused her. That was obvious enough. I supplied some implausible excuse about trying to protect her with this separation, and my brain scoffed—*liar*—while she told me that didn't make sense.

"Unless . . . you don't want to," she said.

Unless I don't want to? My whole body was prepared to mutiny if I allowed her to leave here thinking I didn't want her. I shoved both hands into my hair.

"Brrr! Are y'all coming in, or what?" Carlie said behind me. "'Cause I'm closing this door."

Jacqueline was shivering, and I was standing barefoot on the landing outside in the middle of December. I captured her hand in mine and brought her inside, refusing to consider Carlie's hundred-watt smile. She went back to her corner of the sofa, where Francis allowed himself to be hoisted and repositioned in a way that would've gotten anyone else on the planet a hiss and scratch.

Caleb, objecting to the disruption because he'd been kicking Carlie's ass and mine, made some surly comment and got an elbow from his sister while I placed Jacqueline in my corner of the sofa. After making introductions, I sat on the floor in front of her and wondered what the hell to do now. Uncharted territory—that's what this was. I'd given her every reason to let go, and she wasn't doing it.

Minutes later, Carlie, determined that everything go according to her romantic whims, winked at me and hustled her brother across the yard, whether he wanted to go or not. I bolted the door behind them and turned to lean against it.

"So. I thought we said we were taking a break?" I said.

"*You* said we were taking a break." She was still irritated.

I reminded her that she had to leave by Tuesday morning—the break was university decreed, after all—and she conceded.

I stared at the floor, knowing damned well what I was to her. I had to tell her. I had to put it all out there, because she had everything so wrong. I'd shielded myself too well. So well that she couldn't see the truth.

"It's not that I don't want you. I lied, earlier, when I said I was protecting you." My eyes rose to hers as she sat, silent, still curled into the corner of my sofa. So impossible, so beautiful. "I'm protecting *myself*." My palms braced against the door, and I forced out the thing I feared, and the desire that had bided its time, waiting to crush me. "I don't want to be your rebound, Jacqueline."

Her thoughts were readable, even from this distance. She wasn't sure how I knew, but she saw that I did. I waited for her to try to explain that she cared about me—because I knew she did. I waited for her to argue that she just wasn't ready now, to claim that she was giving me what she could, to ask why I couldn't be satisfied with that.

"Then why are you assuming that role?" she said instead, rising and crossing the carpet, her eyes on mine, unwavering. "It's not what I want, either."

I accepted her body, pushing into my space like she'd pushed into my heart. She'd chipped away at the wall between us until it collapsed and turned to dust at my feet.

"What am I gonna do with you?" I asked, palms cupping her face, and she said she could think of a couple things. Unwilling to wait to find out what those things were, I picked her up and carried her to my bed.

I loved her silly, furry-cuffed boots. Off they went.

I loved her blousy knit top, pink and white swirls, like a watercolor sunset my mother had painted on Grandpa's beach when I was very small. Off it went, too.

I loved her snug, curve-hugging jeans that wouldn't simply slide down her hips—they had to be tugged while she wiggled. I tugged. She wiggled. Off they went as well.

Her bra and panties were silky-smooth and matched the creamy tone of her skin. Front clasp. Bra off. The last thin scrap of fabric covered the part of her I wanted to taste, soon. Panties, gone.

She lay in the center of my bed, naked, and I was fully clothed, but barefoot. I stood, staring down at her, prolonging the moment. She squirmed, her chest rising and falling, her hands kneading the comforter beneath her.

I reached to pull my long-sleeved T-shirt off, unhurried. The squirming increased as I slid the sleeves down my arms, flexing them. I combed my hair back from my face and took a measured breath, like a light tap on the brake. *Slow. Slower.* My jeans were threadbare—I didn't wear these out, because they always seemed to threaten spontaneous disintegration. Ripped in three or four places, frayed around the hems, the seams, and the waistband, which hung at my hipbones. One button, undone. Two.

Jacqueline's chest rose and fell, rose and fell, her breasts lush handfuls I wanted to feel against my chest, against my palms and fingers and face as I sucked those hard, pebbled nipples.

As if I'd said this aloud, she whimpered, softly.

"Soon, baby," I whispered.

At the third button, I could have shoved the jeans down—they were loose enough. I paused. She panted. Fourth button. I pushed the jeans down and stepped out of them. Her eyes grazed over all of me. She licked her lips. *Yes.* Her hands clenched, tight fists at her sides. One knee rose restlessly.

Boxers down and off.

She started to rise, but I pointed at her and shook my head. *Stay. There.* Reading the silent command in my eyes, she lay back down, biting her lip.

I took my wallet from the desk behind me and removed the condom, rolled it on. One knee on the foot of the bed. Her soft skin was a feast, and I wanted to devour her. She spread her legs, just enough to welcome me. I wanted to slide the tip of my tongue from her ankle to her thigh, licking and charting an unhurried, torturous course. I wanted to taste her, but that would have to wait, because I had to possess her. *Now.* I crawled forward, my body shaking with anticipation, just as hers was.

When I rose over her, she reached for me and I paused, staring into her eyes, and then rocked into her, fully. Her arms surrounded my shoulders, fingers clutching the hair at my nape as she cried out. Sweeping my tongue through her mouth, I kissed her, holding myself still. *Mine,* I thought. *Yours,* her body answered. I began to move, and she held tight, humming and moaning, crying and pulling me inside, everywhere I wanted in. She came apart seconds later and I plunged my tongue into her mouth, stroking deeply and swallowing her pleasure, making it mine. I growled her name, shuddering, and dragged her with me as I collapsed at her side.

I love you, I thought, but heard nothing in return.

· · · · · · · · · ·

Her fingers moved over the petals tattooed over my heart.

"My mother's name was Rosemary. She went by Rose." I stared at the ceiling.

"You did this in memory of her?"

I nodded against the pillow. "Yes. And the poem on my left side. She wrote it—for my dad."

Her fingers traced the poem, and I shivered. "She was a poet?"

"Sometimes." My mother's face smiled down at me—a memory that I couldn't place now. I held on to whatever I could of her. "Usually, she was a painter."

Jacqueline made some comment about the *artist genes* and *engineering parts* that comprised me, and I laughed at this visual, wondering aloud which were the engineering parts.

She asked if I had any of Mom's paintings. I told her that some hung in the Hellers' place, since they used to be so close. I would, perhaps, show her those. Others were in storage in the Hellers' attic or Dad's.

She began questioning me about their friendship, and at first I thought she was merely curious about the long-standing relationship between the Hellers and the Maxfields.

"They were all *really* close—before."

Before was an uncomplicated word, and it would never express all I'd lost when my timeline split in two, hurling me into an *after* I would never escape. I couldn't reach through that curtain, ever, and see my mother as she was. Touch her. Hear her voice the way it should have been.

"Lucas, I need to tell you something," Jacqueline said, and there was an uneasy tenor to her voice. I turned my head, watching her face as she told me she'd been curious and had searched for my mother's obituary online.

I knew well enough what she'd found. The nightmare from which I could never wake. My heart went stone cold, and I could barely breathe. "Did you find your answer?"

"Yes," she whispered.

Pity. That's what I saw in her eyes. I lay back, eyes stinging as I thought of the news articles she must have read. I wondered if she'd sifted through the facts to see my part. My guilt.

I braced, trying to come to terms with this. No one outside the Hellers and Dad knew the details. I'd never spoken of them with anyone. I couldn't bear to even think about it—how could I speak of it?

Then I caught what she'd just said—that she'd talked to Charles.

"What?"

"Lucas, I'm sorry if I invaded your privacy—"

"*If?* Why would you go talk to him? Weren't the gory details in the news reports sickening enough for you? Or personal enough?" I shot off the bed and pulled on my jeans, my voice like ice, like a razor, cutting into my skin. My wrists burned. I don't know what I said to her and what I didn't—the details I'd never uttered aloud. It didn't matter. She knew them all.

I sat, head in my hands, struggling to breathe, reliving it—*please, God, no—*

A distant noise woke me, but I rolled back over, kicking off the sheet. I was hot, but too lazy to get up and turn on my ceiling fan. I lay on my side, staring out the window to the backyard, thinking about Yesenia, and the coming weekend. I would hold her hand. Kiss her, maybe, if I could get her alone. If she let me.

God, it was hot. I flopped onto my back. To be thirteen was to be a furnace. I burned off food and energy like a flame sucking down oxygen. *You will eat us out of house and home by the time you're fifteen!* my mother said while watching me finish off the leftovers she'd intended to reheat for our dinner. We'd ordered takeout instead. She didn't want all of hers, so I'd finished it, too.

I heard the noise again. Mom was probably up. She prowled around the house sometimes when Dad was gone, missing him. I should check on her . . . My clock read 4:11. *Ugh.* Four hours until I would see Yesenia. I could get up early, get to school early. Maybe I would catch her without all her giggling friends, and we could talk about . . . something. Like my upcoming game. Maybe she'd want to come watch me play sometime.

I turned just as someone leaned over me. Dad? But he was out of town.

Jerked from the bed, I stumbled. Something was stuffed into my mouth as I opened it to scream—I gagged and couldn't make a sound or spit it out. I thrashed and kicked but couldn't get loose. Couldn't move my wrists. I was shoved to my knees at the foot of the bed, and then he was gone. I tried to stand up, run, grab my phone to dial 911, but I was stuck.

My wrists were tied. I strained to scrape the binding loose with my fingernails, but it was too tight. Plastic. It was *plastic*. I pulled against the restraint, but it didn't budge. I tried to rotate my hands to see if I could swivel them free, or fold them and twist them free, like Houdini, but the plastic just cut into my wrists. My hands were too big. Mom said my hands and feet were like the big, floppy feet of a puppy that would be a ginormous dog.

From her room down the hall, my mother screamed. I froze. She called my name. "Landon!" There was a crash and a thud and I struggled harder, not caring if it hurt. I couldn't answer her. I couldn't tell her I was coming. My tongue shoved against the cloth in my mouth.

"What did you do to him? *What did you do to him?* LANDON!"

There were more words, the sound of a slap—an open palm against bare skin, more screams, and I heard them all but they didn't register because there was a buzzing in my ears and my blood swishing and my heart pounding. She was crying. "Oh, God. God. Don't. No. *No-no-no-no-no!*" Screaming. *"NO! NO-NO-NO!"* Crying. *"Landon . . ."* I yanked harder, pulling the bed with me, all the way to the door, my feet bracing against the floor, my legs straining. The bed ran into the dresser, wedged against the wall. I couldn't feel my hands.

I couldn't hear her anymore. I couldn't hear her. The rag in my mouth finally worked free. *"Mom! MOM!"* I screamed. *"DON'T TOUCH HER! MOM!"* My wrists were on fire. Why wasn't I strong enough to break these stupid fucking plastic bands? I screamed until I was hoarse and kept screaming.

Gunshot.

I stopped breathing. My limbs shook. My chest quaked. I couldn't hear anything beyond my heartbeat. My blood. My thick swallows. My useless sobs. "Mom . . . Mommy . . ."

I puked. Passed out. The sun came up. My wrists and arms were covered in blood. The zip-ties on my wrists were covered in blood. It was all brown, dried, itchy.

I called for my mother, but I'd screamed too much. A rasp came from my throat, nothing more. Useless. I was useless. Fucking, fucking, fucking useless.

You're the man of the house while I'm gone. Take care of your mother.

"Do you want me to leave?" she said.

"Yes," I answered.

chapter *Twenty-five*

LANDON

The number of people in my graduating class was forty-three.

That number could have easily been forty-two. I'd been one of the projected dropouts since the first day of high school. Before that, probably. In this town, there was no such thing as a fresh start; we carried our histories year to year like lists of impairments pinned to our shirts. The only reason I crossed that gym floor in a cap and gown was the man in the third row of the bleachers, sitting next to my father.

My classmates and I filed through the side door as our band—minus the senior members—played the processional. Seated in a matching cluster of royal blue, we fidgeted as Mrs. Ingram, our esteemed principal, assured us of our bright and shiny futures. I knew she was full of shit, and so were her optimistic claims. I stared at the two vertical lines set between her eyes, permanent from decades of hostile glares at unacceptable students. Those lines made her graduation-speech grin look sinister.

Many of my brainwashed classmates—those who'd scored near-perfect grades since learning to print their names—thought they'd skip off to college in the fall and perform just as well, just as easily. Delusional dumbasses. My eighth grade prep school courses were more challenging than almost anything demanded of us here. Getting into a good school wasn't winning the lottery. It was winning the right to work your ass off for the next four years.

As valedictorian, Pearl gave the expected speech about opportunities and choices and making the world a better place—she actually used that phrase: *make the world a better place.* As one of the "top 10 percent" of our class—four people—she'd earned automatic admittance into the state university of her choice, while I'd scraped up a probationary admittance to the same campus she chose. I liked Pearl more than I liked the majority of people sitting around me, and I had no doubt that she knew how to work hard. I just hoped she wasn't betting on improving the world.

On the second page of the commencement program, my name was listed at the bottom of the first column. My last name was the alphabetical midpoint of my class—student number twenty-two of forty-three. The placement was fitting. As far as almost everyone here was concerned, I was average. Mediocre. Not exceptional, but not a total fail, though some—like Principal Ingram, believed that remained to be seen.

When my name was called, I crossed the worn oak floor in front of the band, staring over my principal's shoulder at the giant fish—our renowned mascot—depicted in painstaking detail on the far wall. In mascot form, its expression was supposed to look aggressive, intent on winning, but it seriously just looked like a stupid, pissed-off fish.

I'd been determined to cross the stage staring down the bitch who'd made my life hell for almost four years. To show her she hadn't broken me, whether or not that was true.

Then, above the obligatory applause and crowd noise, I heard Cole's roar of, *"LANDOOON,"* Carlie's chirpy squeal, and Caleb's piercing whistle.

"He's fucking practiced that *all week*, dude," Cole told me this morning when Caleb demonstrated his new earsplitting skill less than five minutes after the Hellers arrived. "The only reason Mom hasn't gagged him is 'cause he's a little kid. If it was me, I'd be toast."

My principal's reign over me was done. After this moment, she couldn't touch me.

I reached for the rolled diploma with one hand and shook her cold hand with the other, as we'd been instructed to do. I stared into the camera, ignoring the photographer's appeal to smile. One blinding flash later, I dropped her hand, walking away without ever making eye contact.

She no longer mattered.

As I dropped back into the metal folding seat between Brittney Loper and PK Miller, I took one furtive glance at my classmates. Out of the forty-three of us, thirty-one would be leaving for college in three months. Some would try out for baseball or track or cheerleading and find they weren't even good enough for some shit college's second string. Some imagined themselves in student government on campuses where they'd arrive as one of thousands of nobodies. They'd be one of hundreds of freshmen during rush week, desperate for a defined peer group.

Some would figure it out and learn to survive. Some would fail out, and a few would return to this town with their tails between their legs.

I sure as hell wouldn't be one of those.

Twelve of my fellow graduates planned to remain here, taking or keeping jobs in fishing or retail or tourism or drugs. They would get married and pregnant—preferably in that order, but not necessarily.

Their spawn would attend the schools that turned them out into adulthood after thirteen years with nothing to show for it but a near-worthless diploma. Ten years from now, maybe five, some of them would ask themselves what the fuck they went to school for—why they labored through algebra, gym, literature, and band. They'd want an answer, but there wasn't one.

• • • • • • • • • •

"Maxfield." Boyce Wynn tossed me a can from the cooler, wet from melting ice. His was the last name called this afternoon, the last diploma Ingram resentfully presented. He'd be staying here, pretending this gulf was the ocean, this town his kingdom. Working for his dad at the garage, partying on the beach or driving into the city for the occasional change of pace . . . Not much would change for Boyce.

"Hey, Wynn."

He clasped my hand and we leaned forward until our shoulders bumped—a ritual hello and a far cry from the day we'd beat the unholy shit out of each other—and then became friends. My cheek still bore a scar from the solid thud of his fist, and he carried its twin at the corner of his eye from mine.

"We're out, dude." He raised his can skyward, as if he was a running back with a pigskin, saluting God for a miracle touchdown. He lowered it and took a long swallow. "We're *free*. Fuck that school. Fuck Ingram. Fuck that fish."

Laughter rose from a few bystanders—younger guys with another year or two to go. One of them repeated, "Fuck that fish," and snickered. I tried not to imagine the possible graffiti.

Boyce glanced down the beach to the outer edge of the circle. "And fuck bitches, man," he added, more quietly. I knew the direction his gaze was aimed, and on who. He was one of a few people who knew the real story of Landon Maxfield and Melody Dover.

Time can be a selective dick about how fast it heals. Two years ago, I felt the sting of humiliation whenever I heard her name or looked at her. I hadn't forgiven, and I damn sure hadn't forgotten, but by the time Clark Richards dumped her for good—the night before he left town for college nine months ago—I no longer gave a shit.

"*Shit.*" Boyce echoed my last thought and cussed the sand beneath our feet, just loud enough for me to hear. "Pearl and Melody, headin' this way." Pearl Frank was Boyce's own personal demon, still.

I nodded once, thankful for the heads-up.

"Hey, Landon." Melody's spun-sugar drawl and the fingernail drawn down my bare arm made me flinch. How could those two things have ever felt like air in my lungs?

Glancing to the side, I downed half the beer before answering. "Miss Dover."

She laughed and laid a small, soft hand on my forearm, as if my words were coy instead of contemptuous, as if she was encouraging me to continue. I wondered if she'd forgotten what continuing with me meant. I stared down into her pale green eyes, and she returned my gaze through thick lashes, sliding her hand away slowly.

Hugging herself even though it was warm out, her position invited closer inspection. She wore a black string bikini with a see-through cover-up posing as a sundress. Her blonde hair spilled with calculated imperfection from the salon-created twist she'd worn at graduation. The gold hoops in her ears and gold charm bracelet on her wrist flashed tiny diamond messages of how far out of my league she was.

Not that I needed those clues. She'd delivered that message in all its crystal clarity two years ago, and I'd learned it. Hard.

"We're throwing a spontaneous graduation party at Pearl's pool in half an hour," Melody said, after a silent communication between the girls. "Her parents left for Italy right after graduation—so they won't be around. If y'all wanna come over, that'd be cool. PK and Joey are bringing vodka. Bring whatever you want."

Melody pressed close enough for me to feel the warmth of her perfectly toned skin and inhale her still-familiar scent, something spicy and floral, artificial. This time, her fingertips stroked down my bare chest, her thumb grazing my nipple ring.

"A pool party?" I gestured with the can. "We've got a *beach*, in case you girls didn't notice. Bonfire lit, beer in hand. What would we want with a *pool*?"

"It's a *private* party. Just a few people." She wrinkled her nose at some younger guys nearby who were farting dangerously close to the fire, where there was an ongoing debate about whether *gas* was *gas*. The likelihood of some idiot catching his ass on fire was a genuine possibility. "*Graduates* only."

Pearl watched the underclassmen, too, sipping from her cup and shaking her head, a shadow of a smile on her face. Boyce slid his eyes from Pearl to me and lifted a brow—letting me know he'd be more than happy to go along with this turn of events. I shrugged. *Why not?*

"All right," Boyce said—to Pearl. "We'll be over in a bit. Don't start the party without us."

Melody rolled her eyes, but Boyce didn't notice and wouldn't have cared if he did. He only had eyes for Pearl, poor bastard.

• • • • • • • • • •

The trailer Boyce shared with his dad seemed to lean into the body shop, as though the corroded single-wide was falling-down drunk and could no longer remain upright independently. Two of Boyce's three bedroom windows opened inches from the exterior brick wall of the shop, so the notion that the trailer required the building's support was plausible.

Once inside, we hung an immediate right in an effort to avoid Mr. Wynn, who was installed in front of the flat screen taking up most of the "living room" wall. Predictably, he hadn't shown for his kid's graduation. Boyce's father: plastered in the evening, hung over in the morning, mean and cold sober all day long, repeat. He was nothing if not reliable.

"What-er you two shits doin' home during the game?" he hollered, not moving from his ragged chair, which was where he ended up sleeping more often than not. Boyce once confessed to me that he'd fought the urge to light it on fire a dozen times.

Bud Wynn's threats went mostly unheeded now. A year ago, Boyce had punched back during a beating, and since then his father had been all growl, no teeth. Now eighteen, Boyce could probably kill him, and both of them knew it. This made for an uneasy truce I would never understand.

After bagging enough shit for a misdemeanor but not enough for a felony, we were back in my best friend's Trans Am and driving to the Frank mansion on the other side of town.

"I'm going for it," Boyce announced, punching stereo buttons like he was programming a rocket.

"Meaning?"

"Tonight. Me. Pearl. Going. For. It. Wherein *it* equals her thighs spread and me between 'em." He flicked me a look when I didn't reply. "What?"

I bit the ring in my lip, hating that I had to say what I had to say. Hating that I'd rather not say it—especially to my best friend. "Just—make sure it's what she, you know—"

"Landon, fuck, man." He pulled his baseball cap off, shook his head, and stuffed it back on backward. Huffing a breath, his eyes never left the road. "Don't you *know me*? Not that I have any real, ya'know, *morals*"—he grinned—"but I mean, I hear you. I've heard you. *I got it.* I don't know what your damage is and I'm pretty sure I don't want to. But if and when I screw that superior, brainy little . . ." He trailed off, unable to call Pearl something she wasn't. "She's gonna be beggin' for it first or I won't touch her. *Okay?*"

He slid a scowl my way and I nodded once, satisfied.

I wouldn't have told him my damage if he'd asked. But he never had. My mind shifted to Melody. If she begged for it now, would I?

The answer was a quiet, decisive whisper. *No.*

"Hey, Wynn? Drop me back at the beach, man."

He dialed the music down. "You don't wanna go?"

I shook my head and he sighed. "Sure, man. Who needs a pool anyway when we've got the fuckin' *ocean?*"

"I'm not asking you to give up your final chance for a Pearl hookup."

The edge of his mouth curved into a sly smile and he arched a brow. "Oh, I'm not givin' it up. If her parents left town today—they'll be gone at *least* a week."

"Dude, we just graduated, and she's going away to college in a couple months. You've had *three years*—"

"Never say never, Maxfield. That's the cool thing about being a pigheaded son of a bitch. I do not fuckin' *ever* give up." We laughed as he U-turned at a wide-shouldered spot in the road and cranked the stereo back up, heading back to the beach.

LUCAS

Silence is never totally without sound. Something to do with the human ear, straining to hear. Even when there's nothing, there's a frequency, a hum. Like a satellite, searching for signs of life where there are none.

My father's voice was gone. *Take care of your mother.* My mother's voice was gone. *Landon!* My choked intakes of breath, grating and loud, had subsided. I inhaled. Let go a ragged lungful of air. Swallowed. Took another breath. Heard each of these actions inside my own head.

Then I heard a meow. Francis jumped on the bed and stalked straight to me. He bumped my bicep with the top of his head, and I let my hands fall from where they gripped the sides of my face. My forearms rested on my knees, elbows digging into my thighs. He bumped me again, hard, like he was trying to herd me, and I sat up.

Barefoot. Old jeans. No shirt. Bed.

Jacqueline.

I turned, but she was gone. The bedcovers were a sea of sheets, blankets, and pillows that had weathered a storm. A very good storm. And then she told me what she'd done. Pain drilled through the center of my chest and I squeezed my eyes shut and pressed my fingers against it. I would not go there again.

Do you want me to go?

My eyes flashed opened. Oh, God. I'd said yes.

I stood, found my T-shirt inside out on the floor. Righting it and jerking it over my head, I reached for socks and my boots and shoved my feet into them. Grabbed my jacket from the back of a kitchen chair and my keys from the counter.

I could fix this. I *would* fix this.

I shrugged into the jacket and headed out the door and down the stairs. Getting into her dorm wouldn't be as easy this time—there were so few people around. Almost everyone had vacated campus as soon as finals were over. I would call her when I got there. I'd have to talk her into letting me into the building. Apologize. Beg if I had to. On my knees.

I hoped to God she answered. I would camp in the back of her truck if she didn't.

I was about to swing a leg over my bike when I heard footsteps, pounding up the driveway. Jacqueline, running to me—but she didn't see me. She was staring at the bottom of the steps to my apartment. Her name in my mouth, I moved to intercept her—and then she went down, and I saw Buck, his fist around her hair. Oh, *fuck* no.

He landed on top of her, but she shoved onto her side, unbalancing him. As she scrambled away from him, he followed.

I grabbed him just as he reached for her, pitched him, and installed myself between them. I glanced at Jacqueline and saw blood coating her chest. A huge, dark circle of it, like a gunshot wound, blooming, fatal. *Fuck no fuck no fuck no*—but she was scuttling backward on her hands, and her eyes were wide. If she'd been shot or stabbed there, she wouldn't be moving.

When he stood, I saw that his face was bloody under his nose. *She had made him bleed.*

I would make him bleed more.

My eyes had almost adjusted to the dark, but the Hellers had motion-detecting floodlights, and our movements activated one of them. It popped on—a dim little spotlight for our fight scene.

Buck's dark eyes were focused and unswerving, no alcohol marring his coordination. He tried to circle around, as if I was going to let him anywhere near her ever again. I moved with him, facing him, aware of Jacqueline and her exact location. I felt her behind me as if she was part of my body. Flesh of my flesh. Blood of my blood.

"I'm gonna bust that lip wide open, emo boy," he said. "I'm not fucked up this time. I'm stone-cold sober, and I'm gonna kick your ass before I fuck your little whore nine ways from Sunday—again."

Weak words from a weak man. He didn't know he was already dead. "You're mistaken, *Buck*."

I removed my jacket and shoved my sleeves up, and he took the first swing. I blocked it. He repeated the movement—because this asshole didn't learn—and I blocked it again. Rushing me, he tried one of his predictable wrestling moves.

Jab to the kidney. Open-handed slap to the ear.

He reeled, pointing at Jacqueline. "Bitch. Think you're too good for me—but you're nothing but a *whore*."

I held my temper by a hair. He wanted it to snap, because people forget what they're doing when they allow their temper free rein. They make the stupid, critical mistakes that I didn't intend to make. My temper would remain caged until I had him down and disoriented.

When he tried to grab me again, I snatched and twisted his arm, aiming to dislocate his shoulder. He turned into it, so I didn't quite wrench it out of joint, but I landed my first satisfying, face-crunching fist to his jaw. As soon as his head swiveled back around, he got another to the mouth. He blinked, staring, seeking an exposed spot. Wasn't gonna happen.

Enraged, he roared loud enough to wake the whole neighborhood and barreled into me. As we fell, he got a couple good punches in before I pivoted, took hold of him, and used his own forward motion to land him on his head. Amazing, how many guys are too fucking ham-fisted to see that coming.

I didn't waste time admiring my handiwork. While he shook his head, trying to see straight after landing on top of his skull, I tackled him—sadly, into the grass, not on the concrete—and hit him. I thought of the terror in Jacqueline's eyes. Her hair caught in his fist. My name—*Landon*—the last word my mother spoke.

Snap.

I hit him again. One time after another. And I wasn't going to stop.

Something pulled me up and off. No. *NO*. I fought to free myself and was one second from doing so when words broke through: "*Stop. She's safe. She's safe, son.*"

Charles. I stopped resisting, and he loosened the tight band of his arms but kept his arms around me, propping me up as I began to shake. Buck wasn't moving.

I turned to find Jacqueline, but I knew right where she was. Charles let me go and I staggered toward her, fell to my knees beside her, my entire body shuddering. Her eyes were still wide, her beautiful face bruising, blood speckling her chin and cheeks.

I cupped a palm under her rapidly discoloring jaw. She flinched, and I jerked my hand away. She was afraid of me. Of what had just happened—*again*. I had failed to keep her safe.

Then she came up on her knees. "Please touch me. I need you to touch me."

I reached out and gathered her, carefully, sitting back and pulling her onto my lap, within the circle of my arms. Her shirt was stuck to her chest. "His blood?" I verified. "From his nose?"

She leaned into my chest and nodded, looking down at herself in revulsion.

She was a warrior, covered in the blood of her enemy. I wanted to beat my chest in pride, and so should she. "Good girl. God, you're so fucking amazing."

She pulled at the shirt, panicked. "I want it off. *I want it off.*"

"Yes. Soon," I promised, touching her face, avoiding the bruised spot.

I begged her forgiveness for sending her away, my heart still thrashing under her ear. I could barely hear myself speak. If she never absolved me, I couldn't blame her.

"I'm sorry for looking her up," she said. "I didn't know—"

"Shh, baby . . . not now. Just let me hold you." She shivered. My jacket lay nearby in the grass. I wrapped her in it and held her closer, letting my body settle.

The police had come, and an ambulance. They loaded Buck into the back on a stretcher, which meant he wasn't dead. Charles called us to give a statement to the officer he'd been speaking with, and I rose slowly, drawing Jacqueline to her feet. We were both unsteady, holding on to each other.

Cindy, Carlie, and Caleb huddled by the corner of the house in coats and blankets over pajamas. Neighbors were standing in their yards or staring from windows containing lit Christmas trees. Cheerful holiday lights flashed along with squad car and ambulance lights.

Charles told the police about Jacqueline's restraining order against Buck, and called me her boyfriend without a single hesitation. Backing up everything he'd said, including the boyfriend remark, Jacqueline leaned her back to my chest, held my arms in place around her midriff, and gave her account—how Buck had shoved her into the truck and shut the door behind them. How she used the moves she'd learned in the self-defense class to escape the truck.

My arms tightened around her, and I felt sick. I couldn't listen to the details. I wanted to pull Buck off that stretcher and finish the job.

When the police and EMTs left, we were surrounded by the Hellers. They offered first-aid supplies, cups of tea, food—but I assured them I had all those things, and I would take good care of her. Charles and Cindy hugged me unabashedly, enveloping Jacqueline as well, maybe because I wasn't letting her get farther than inches away from me.

When we opened the apartment door, Francis exited, pausing on the landing. "Thanks," I murmured, patting him once before he wandered down the steps and back to his nightly prowl.

In the bathroom, I inspected Jacqueline's face, stared into her eyes, and asked if he'd hit her. I could hardly get the words out. She shook her head and said he'd just grabbed her really hard.

"The spot where I head-butted him hurts more." Her fingers skimmed across her forehead.

"I'm so proud of you. I want you to tell me about it, when you can . . . and when I can stand to hear it. I'm still too angry right now." I'd been right there when she'd given her account, but couldn't handle listening to the details. His hands on her body. The pain he inflicted.

I undressed her carefully, gently, a different kind of slow than hours prior. Her shirt and bra and my shirt all went into the trash, and I lifted her into the warm shower. She was perfectly capable of doing these things herself, but she seemed to understand that I needed to do them for her. I soaped and kissed every bruise and abraded spot, hating that she'd been hurt. I braced my arms on the tile and closed my eyes when she did the same for me.

The muscles of her arms were sore, so I wrapped her in a bath sheet and set her on the side of the tub. As I dried her hair, combing tangles away with my fingers and soaking the water from each strand with a towel, she told me the last time anyone dried her hair for her was when she'd broken her arm in sixth grade, falling out of a tree. She smiled and I laughed—two things wonderfully incongruent with this night.

"I think there was a boy and a dare involved," she said.

Lucky boy.

But not as lucky as me.

I squatted in front of her and asked her to stay with me, at least for tonight. She touched my face, gazing into my eyes. Hers were worried, and full of compassion. She knew what had happened to my mother, but I needed to confess what she didn't know. I couldn't keep her under false pretenses any longer. I needed her to know everything.

"The last thing my father said to me, before he left, was, 'You're the man of the house while I'm gone. Take care of your mother.'" I swallowed, or tried to. My throat ached, striving to hold back tears that weren't going to stay dammed. I felt them rising as hers spilled over and ran down her face. "I didn't protect her. I couldn't save her."

She pulled me close and held me, and I lost it, my face buried against her heart.

Minutes later, she said, "I'll stay tonight. Will you do something for me, too?"

I took a deep breath, unable to deny her anything. "Yes. Whatever you need."

"Go with me to Harrison's concert tomorrow night? He's my favorite eighth-grader, and I promised him I'd go."

I agreed to her request, too fatigued to wonder what she was up to—because I knew her well enough now to look into those eyes and see when she was up to something. I didn't care. I would do whatever she asked of me.

• • • • • • • • • •

It had been a long time since I'd been inside a middle school auditorium.

The orchestra kids were all roughly Caleb's size, although he would have been at the small end of the scale. The boys were humorously insufferable, swaggering around in their black tuxedos, leaning over auditorium seats to flirt with the girls—all in floor-length, matching purple dresses.

"Miss Wallace!" A blond, tuxedoed kid called out from within the group, waving eagerly until he noticed *me*. His dark eyes went wide. Jacqueline returned his wave, but he looked destroyed to see the love of his life sitting next to a guy. I couldn't very well blame him.

"I take it this is one of the ones crushing on you," I said, biting my lip, keeping my expression even. If Jacqueline liked this kid, I didn't want to demean him by laughing at his mopey response to the reality that *Miss Wallace* was taken. Had been taken. Would be taken again in a few hours, if I had anything to say about it.

"What? They *all* crush on me. I'm a hot college girl, remember?" She laughed.

I angled a bit closer and told her just how hot she was, and I asked her to stay with me again tonight.

"I was afraid you weren't going to ask," she said. Silly girl.

Harrison was a brave kid, giving my girl a dozen roses after the concert. He was self-conscious as hell, blushing to match the flowers as he thrust them at her, but I admired his gallantry in the face of that fear.

Thanking him, she lifted the bouquet to her face and inhaled blissfully. She told him that he'd made her proud tonight and he stood straighter, swelling up like a puffer fish.

Beaming, he said, "It's all 'cause of you, though," which made her smile.

"You did the work, and put in the practice."

I'd made similar statements to grateful students who thought they only passed econ because of me.

"You sounded great, man. I wish I could play an instrument," I added.

The kid's eyes sized me up, and I fought the juvenile impulse to tell him he didn't really want a piece of this. "Thanks," he said, giving me an inquisitive look. "Did that hurt? On your lip?"

I shrugged. "Not too much. I said a few choice four-letter words, though."

"Cool." He grinned.

Jacqueline knew how to pick favorites.

So did I.

• • • • • • • • • •

We packed her truck with everything she was taking home for winter break and she turned in her dorm key. She was spending her last night in town with me.

"I don't want to go home. But if I don't go, they'll drive down to get me." Wearing one of my T-shirts, she stood brushing her teeth at my bathroom sink. She rinsed her mouth and watched me in the mirror. "What happened yesterday was the last straw for Mom. She wasn't this upset when I fell out of the *tree*."

My arms slipped around her. "I'll be here, waiting for you. I promise. Come back early, if you want, and stay here with me until the dorms open. But go, give her a chance."

She looked straight at me in the mirror, tearing up, knowing the card I was playing, no matter how furtively. "And you'll give your father a chance, too?"

Sneaky, Jacqueline.

I grimaced, staring into her eyes in our reflection. "Yes. I will."

She sighed, pouting. "Now that you've bullied me into leaving you, may I have my proper send-off?"

My brow arched and I moved my hands to the hem of that T-shirt, murmuring, "Hell, yes." I watched myself in the mirror—pulling the shirt up and over her head, cupping her lovely breasts in my hands, thumbs teasing the nipples. One hand slipped down to cover her abdomen, sliding into her panties, straight past the lace. Her mouth fell open as I stroked her, and her head fell back on my shoulder, but she didn't shut her eyes. *So beautiful.* I loved watching her respond to my touch. I would never get enough of this.

She reached a hand behind her hips, fingers closing around me. I growled, pushing into her hand while I pressed her body closer with mine. I leaned to kiss her neck, closing my eyes and breathing her in. "Ready for bed, then?"

"Bed, sofa, kitchen table, whatever you have in mind . . ." she answered, and I groaned.

When I regained enough equilibrium to open my eyes, they'd darkened to the leaden gray-blue of a rainy day sky, contrasting with her deep, summer blue. My bathroom mirror had become the hottest interactive video ever. "All right, then," I said, sliding my fingers into her. "Let's just start right here, baby."

"Mmm . . ." she said, her eyes drifting closed.

• • • • • • • • • •

She lay in the circle of my arms, both of us exhausted. Bathroom sink, check. Desk chair, check. Sofa, double check. I visualized waking with her in this bed in a few hours, though, and decided she had one more *send-off* in store.

Still awake, her eyes were on mine. *Hmm.*

"What'd you think of Harrison?" she asked.

"He seems like a good kid."

"He is." Her eyes followed her fingertips as they caressed beneath my jaw.

I dragged her closer and asked what this was about. "Are you leaving me for Harrison, Jacqueline?"

I expected her to roll her eyes and laugh, but instead, she gazed steadily at me. "If Harrison had been in that parking lot that night, instead of you, do you think he'd have wanted to help me?"

The parking lot. With Buck.

"If someone had told him to watch out for me," she pressed, "do you think they would ever, ever blame him, if he'd not been able to stop what would have happened that night?"

My lungs constricted. "I know what you're trying to say—"

She wouldn't let me off the hook so easily, though she trembled in my arms. "No, Lucas. You're hearing it, but you don't know it. There's no way your father actually expected that of you. There's no way he even remembers saying that to you. He blames himself, and you blame yourself, but neither of you is to blame." Her eyes were full, but they wouldn't let me go.

I held her like I was falling off the face of the earth, and I couldn't breathe—no gravity, no oxygen. "I'll never forget how she sounded that night. How can I not blame myself?" My eyes glassed with tears while hers spilled over.

Her right hand was still on my face. Pressed between us, her left hand gripped mine, grounding me. Her tears flowed into the pillow as she made me see the boy I'd been. I'd never asked my father if he blamed me; I'd assumed that he did. But Jacqueline was right about him—he was stuck in perpetual grief, blaming himself when no one else did. And I had followed his example.

"What have you told me, over and over? *It wasn't your fault*," she said.

She said I needed to talk to someone who'd help me forgive myself. I only wanted to talk to her—but I couldn't ask that of her. Cindy had suggested therapy a hundred times, swearing it helped her grieve the loss of her best friend, but I'd become adept at insisting I was fine.

I'm fine. I'm good.

But I wasn't fine. I was anything but fine. That night had shattered me. I'd walled myself in to keep from breaking further, but no defense will protect you from every possible pain. I was still just as breakable as everyone else—the girl in my arms included. But I could hope. And I could love. And maybe, I could heal.

chapter *Twenty-six*

LANDON

I hadn't been afraid of anything in a long time.

I was scared shitless, but I wasn't about to show it. This was nothing. *Nothing*.

"You ready, Landon?" Heller asked, and I nodded.

Everything I owned was piled in the back of his SUV. I didn't have any luggage beyond a duffle and a backpack, so most of my clothes had been crammed into large black plastic bags like the trash they were. I'd scrounged up a few empty boxes from the Bait & Tackle for my books and sketchpads. They stank like fish. Which meant the interior of Heller's truck and everything I owned would smell like fish by the time we got five miles from the fucking coast.

It was worth it. Good riddance. I never wanted to come back.

Holding his chipped *Fishermen Do It Hook, Line, and Sinker* mug, Dad stood, feet braced apart, on the front porch—every piece of timber comprising the whole sagging and weather-beaten to all fuck. It was a miracle that anything made of wood could survive here, and yet this place had endured, somehow, for decades—defying wind, rain, tropical storms, and the relentless salt water that permeated the whole town with its brackish scent day in and day out.

As a kid, when this place was my grandfather's house, I'd loved the annual summer visits that my dad had loathed, but Mom insisted on.

"He's your father," she'd tell him. "He's Landon's *grandfather*. Family is important, Ray."

Now Dad was staying, and I was leaving.

Within the dilapidated house on the beach, waves from the gulf were audible at all times of the day and night. When I was little, spending time here was like living in a tree house or a backyard tent for a week—lacking most of the comforts of home, but so poles apart from my real life that it seemed incredible and otherworldly. Roughing it, deserted island style.

After a day of exploring the shoreline and baking in the sun, I'd spread one of the towels Mom always bought before our vacations and left at Grandpa's place. The soft bath sheets were long enough to accommodate my entire childhood frame and wide enough to stockpile and sort the shells I collected during long, hot days on a beach that was anything but the white coast I let my friends back home in Alexandria imagine.

Staring at the huge expanse of dark sky and the thousands of stars winking in and out as though they were communicating with each other, I'd dream about who I'd be when I grew up. I liked to draw, but I was good at math—the kind of good that would have gotten me labeled a nerd if it wasn't for my skill on the ice. I could be an artist, a scientist, a professional hockey player. Surrounded by that seeming infinity of sky and sand and ocean, I thought my choices were wide open.

What a naïve fuck I'd been.

Those bath sheets were like everything else here, now. Worn out. Used up. As close to worthless as something can be without being entirely worthless.

Dad looked older than his years. He was just under fifty—a bit younger than Heller—but he looked a good decade older.

Salt water and sun will do that.

Being a tight-lipped, heartless asshole will do that.

Too far, Landon. Too far.

Fine.

Grief will do that.

He watched me load my shit into his best friend's vehicle, as though it was normal for a father to reassign his parental obligations—like the day his only kid left home for college—to someone else. But he'd been doing that for a while now. It had been up to me to fail, flail, or claw my way out of wanting to end myself since I was thirteen. Five years of surviving from one day to the next. Of choosing to get up or not. Go to school or not. Give a flying fuck about anything or anyone or not.

Heller had given me one shot at getting out, and I sure as shit wasn't going to apologize for taking it.

"Hug your father good-bye, Landon," Heller murmured as we shut the hatchback door.

"But he won't—we don't—"

"Try. Trust me."

I huffed a sigh before turning and walking back up the front steps.

"Bye, Dad." I delivered the words dutifully—something I did for Heller's sake, nothing more. He'd set his cup on the railing. His hands were empty.

I was leaving him to his silence and his solitude, and suddenly I wondered how different this moment would have been if my mother was alive. She would have cried, arms looping around my neck as I bent to hug and kiss her good-bye, telling me she was proud of me, making me promise to call, to come home soon, to tell her everything. I would have cried, holding her.

For the sake of the only woman the two of us had ever loved, I reached my arms around my father, and he wordlessly put his arms around me.

• • • • • • • • • •

I stared into the side mirror, watching the town grow smaller. *Objects in mirror are closer than they appear.* Despite an uneasy curiosity, I wouldn't look back to see if this was true. That bullshit town and the years I lived there would be out of view in five minutes and erased from my conscious mind as soon as I could forget it.

"Do what you want with the radio," Heller said, and I snapped my attention forward. "As long as it isn't any of that screaming crap Cole abuses his ears with. Can't stand that noise pollution he calls music."

His oldest kid was fifteen now. Whenever we were together, he'd ape how I dressed and what type of music I was into, following me around and mimicking whatever I said or did—not always a great idea, I'll admit. His attitude on life seemed to be: if something irritated his parents, he was for it.

I blinked like I was surprised. "What, no Bullet for My Valentine? No Slipknot?"

I laughed at Heller's agitated scowl, sure he didn't believe or care whether or not those were real band names. That was all the answer I got, besides his usual stoic sigh. I plugged my iPod into the stereo console and dialed it to a playlist I'd made last night titled *fuck you and goodbye.* The tracks were a lot less violent than the title implied, in deference to my road-trip companion. I might share Cole's attitude when it came to my own father, but not his.

I didn't see the Heller kids often—though that was about to change, since I'd be living in their backyard. Literally. My new home would be the room over their garage that had been storage for boxes of books and holiday decorations, exercise equipment, and old furniture. My memories of it were vague. When I'd visited the Hellers, I slept on an air mattress in Cole's room. Backing out at the last minute every damned time, Dad would stick me on a bus with my duffle bag and strict instructions not to do anything stupid while I was there.

I wasn't a kid anymore, and this wasn't a weeklong visit. I was a college student who needed a place to live for four years. A legal adult who couldn't afford a dorm or an apartment along with tuition. Heller told me I'd be paying him rent, but it wasn't much. I knew charity when I got it, but for once in my pathetic life, I was grabbing it with both hands, like the knotted end of a rescue rope.

LUCAS

"I'll take the first couple hours, and you can take the last two." Jacqueline slid her dark sunglasses over her eyes and grinned at me from the driver's side of her truck. "But don't nap, or we could end up halfway to El Paso. I need you to navigate."

As she backed her truck down the driveway, I waved good-bye to Carlie and Charles, sliding my sunglasses into place. "That's a completely different highway." I chuckled. "You aren't *that* bad."

She shook her head and sighed. "Seriously. Don't tempt fate. You'll be sorry. We could end up lost and driving aimlessly for our entire spring break."

When I stopped to consider the fact that Jacqueline was coming home to the coast with me, driving aimlessly for a week instead didn't sound so bad. I shook my head. "I guess I should have gotten you a new GPS for your birthday."

She wrinkled her nose. "That sounds like a sensible gift."

"Ah, right, I forgot—we don't do sensible gifts."

She'd told me that her parents had always bought each other (and her) sadly pragmatic gifts, but they'd hit a new low—buying their own gifts. "Mom got herself a new StairMaster and Dad got himself a *grill*," she told me when we talked Christmas night. "It's a big grill, with side burners and warming drawers and *who cares* because *holy cow*—buying your *own gift* for Christmas?"

I didn't tell her that seemed like a great idea to me. If she believed practical gifts were out, then I was destined for a lifetime of impracticality. *Bring it.*

We'd each had a birthday in the past two months. My gift from her: driving a Porsche 911 for a day. Massively impractical. Heller and Joseph were both massively *jealous*. I texted a pic to Boyce and he texted back: Fuck the bro code. I am stealing your woman. You have been warned.

For Jacqueline's birthday, I'd chosen one of my mother's watercolors—a rainy Paris skyline—from Dad's attic stash when I was home over winter break. I had it matted and framed for her. She went very quiet after she opened it, tears coursing down her face. I was sure my aptitude for gift-giving had just crashed and burned, and I should never be allowed to choose a gift again for anyone.

And then she threw herself into my arms, and an hour later, I shoved my fingers into her hair and kissed her. "Wait," I said. "My next birthday is eleven months away. How did *that* just happen?"

· · · · · · · · · ·

Jacqueline was curled in the passenger seat, asleep, as I confronted the fact that we were fifteen minutes away from the coast. That I was taking my girlfriend *home*, where she would meet my uncommunicative father and my frequently inappropriate high school best friend. And *oh hell*, were we sleeping in the pantry? *Shit*. I should have reserved a hotel room.

"Mmm . . ." She woke slowly at first, yawning, unfolding her legs, extending her arms, and then all at once she sat up, blinking. "Are we there?"

I nodded. "Almost."

There was a line for the ferry. Welcome to spring break at a cheap coastal beach. Where I just brought my girlfriend of three months to visit. A heavy feeling lodged itself in the pit of my stomach, like I'd swallowed an iron bar. If she hadn't woken up when she did, I might have made a U-turn before boarding. A guy in an orange vest pointed us to the leftmost ferry and we pulled over the ramp and on. Disembarking on the other side, we were five minutes from home, maybe ten because of the increased tourist traffic that infused money into this community after the slow winter months.

There was nothing unusual or extraordinary about this place to me, but Jacqueline sat up straight, eyes wide to absorb it all—the mural-coated buildings painted in sunny colors, the touristy shops and diners, the blacktopped streets that blended into yards with no curbs, the water and boats almost always visible just beyond.

"Palm trees!" She grinned. "They're so cute."

I arched a brow at her.

"I mean, compared to how they look in say, L.A.—they're tall and thin there. These seem to know there aren't many tall buildings or any hills to compete with here. They're—"

"Stunted?"

She laughed. *"Cute."*

After a few reflexive turns, I parked on the gravel drive in front of Grandpa's—now Dad's—place. Swallowing, I turned to Jacqueline. "I don't know how he'll be to you—I mean, he won't be rude or anything. He's always been courteous with clients, and I'm sure that'll be the worst—"

"Lucas." She took my hand, squeezed it. "He'll be fine. I'm not expecting hugs and a welcome party. He's a quiet guy—like you. I get it."

I scowled. *Like me?*

She turned my hand and kissed the back of it, chuckling like she could read my mind—and she probably could.

I reached my left hand to her nape, pulling her closer as we angled over the console. Threading my fingers through her hair, I kissed her, and the dread overrunning my mind calmed. She was here with me because she wanted to be. We'd talked about my dad; she was prepared. Thanks to my weekly therapy sessions, I was coming to terms with how he'd dealt with his grief, even if it had been far from ideal for either of us.

Dad might not roll out the red carpet, but he would be civil. Boyce could be a jackass, but she'd probably love him anyway. And the pantry bed was no smaller than her dorm bed—one of my favorite places in the world to be.

"Thank you," I said.

Our foreheads pressed together, I watched the fingers of her free hand trace over the inked patterns on my arm. She angled her head and kissed me again, her tongue teasing my ring. She loved to play with it when we kissed, and had pouted when I told her I'd have to remove it once I began interviewing for jobs.

"You're welcome," she breathed against my lips.

Our eyes connected and my hand came up to sweep her face. *I love you,* I told her silently. I was ready to tell her, but wasn't sure how. It wasn't something I'd ever said to a girl. Wasn't something I'd ever felt—not really. Not like this. It seemed silly now that I'd ever thought I might love Melody Dover. What I'd felt for her had been real—but it had been like standing on the first rung of a ladder compared with standing halfway to the top.

When I knocked, Dad came to the screen door with the closest thing to a smile on his face I'd seen in years. "Son," he said, taking one of the bags from my hand. "Come in."

The windows were all open, and the whole place was suffused with the briny scent of the gulf that lay across the sand, outside the back door. Dad had put a fresh coat of ivory paint on the walls and wood-work, and pulled up the old carpets to reveal battered wood floors that somehow looked a hundred times better. One of Mom's paintings was hanging over the sofa. I stood staring at it as he said, "You must be Jacqueline." She still held my hand.

"Yes. It's nice to meet you, Mr. Maxfield."

With effort, I turned away from the painting and watched as my father shook my girlfriend's hand and almost-smiled, again. "Please, call me Ray. I'm happy you've come with Landon, uh—Lucas."

That was new.

He picked up both bags and walked . . . to his room? Jacqueline followed, glancing at the scant but clean furnishings the same way she'd examined the town as we drove through—logging details and missing nothing. I turned the corner into Dad's room, but it wasn't Dad's room anymore. Grandpa's bed sat against the far wall, flanked by his night table and a new lamp. His dresser sat opposite. There was new bedding on the bed, and the walls were the barest hint of blue. Another of Mom's paintings hung over the bed, and a mirror suspended by a threaded length of rope hung over the dresser.

Dad set both bags on the floor by the bed. "I thought you two would need your own space . . . when you visit. I moved back to your Grandpa's room a few weeks ago. I can get a look at the gulf first thing in the morning now, figure out how the sailing will be for the day."

"What a beautiful room," Jacqueline said, looking out the window at the squatty palm tree cluster next to the house. The beach was vis-ible in the distance. "I love it. This is one of your wife's paintings, isn't it?" She walked closer to examine it, and I continued to stare at my father.

"Yes, it is," he answered. Turning back to me, he said, "After you went through some of her things over Christmas, I decided that she'd have been sad to think that her paintings were wrapped up in an attic instead of out where they could be seen." Dad's lips compressed and he nodded. "Well. I'll let you two rest up from your drive. Got plans tonight, I assume?"

I shook my head. "Not tonight. We're meeting up with Boyce tomorrow."

He nodded. "I'll see what I've got for dinner, if you want to eat here. Several pounds of redfish, caught yesterday. We could do something with that."

"Yeah. Sure. Sounds good."

He nodded again and pulled the door mostly shut behind him.

I sat on the bed, heavily. "Holy shit."

• • • • • • • • • •

"We never talked about Mom—sentences that began with *she would have been.*"

Jacqueline lay on her stomach and I lay facing her, my finger drawing invisible patterns onto her back.

At dinner, the three of us had talked about my impending graduation, and the research project with Dr. Aziz that had altered my entire way of thinking about what I'd learned in the past four years, sending it spinning in an unexpected direction.

Your mother would have been proud, he'd said, and Jacqueline grabbed my hand under the recently varnished table, because she knew the weight of those words.

Now we lay in bed, in the room my parents had shared whenever we visited this place during my first thirteen years. Dad was back in Grandpa's room, which he'd painted a seafoam green. Another set of Mom's paintings hung there.

The pantry was back to holding food, along with neat stacks of storage boxes housing old files. The holes in the wall had been painted over. The three-pronged lamp had been replaced with a normal ceiling fixture. I'd chuckled, standing in that snug alcove when Dad sent me to fetch a clove of garlic. I felt safe, standing there, and was struck by the realization that I'd always felt safe there. Somehow, that had been managed while everything else went to hell.

"Thank you for bringing me here." Jacqueline turned to face me in the dark, her eyes reflecting the subtle moonlight from the window. The sound of the waves pulsing across the sand drifted through the window like a slow, gentle heartbeat.

"Thank you for coming with me."

She scooted closer. "You aren't going to tell me where you're applying for jobs, are you?"

"Nope. And you know why."

"You want me to transfer to the best music program I can get into, without regard to where you'll be," she recited, her tone an audible eye roll. "But . . . I can't stand the thought that in six months—*five* months—we could be on opposite sides of the country from each other."

I had no intention of putting distance between us for the next two years—but I wouldn't tell her my plan until I'd pulled it off. There was too much luck involved, and I didn't want her to be disappointed. I traced her hairline from her temple to the corner of her jaw and cupped her face in my hand. "You aren't going to lose me. But I'm not doing to you what he did. You have dreams, and I want you to follow them. I *need* you to follow them. Because . . ." I took a breath. "I love you, Jacqueline Wallace."

She swallowed, her eyes filling with tears. "I love *you*, Landon Lucas Maxfield."

My heart swelled and I leaned over her, kissing her, loving her, claiming her. In her formal words, I heard the echo of my future—a future I was so sure of that no distance would have daunted me: *I take thee, Landon Lucas Maxfield* . . .

Luck could be earned and created. It could be discovered. It could be regained. After all—I'd found this girl. I'd found my future. I'd found forgiveness. My mother would have been happy for me. For the first time in a very long time, I didn't feel guilty about that.

Epilogue

Jacqueline was invited to transfer into three of the five music programs she'd applied for, but when she got Oberlin's letter of acceptance, none of the others mattered. Ten seconds after signing into her email, she shot off my sofa, squealing and sending Francis right under the bed. Once I was certain she was *extreme happiness* squealing and not *I see a spider the size of my hand* squealing, I opened my arms and she jumped into them.

"Congratulations, baby," I murmured against her lips, loving how blissed out she was.

She texted Erin. She called her parents. She emailed her high school orchestra director.

And then she calculated how far apart we would be when she moved, if I remained here. Two engineering firms in town were actively pursuing me, and I was considering them seriously. I'd nailed a second interview for an amazing position with one that specialized in semiconductor robotics—a design job so cool I couldn't have even imagined it four years ago, when all my energies were focused on getting into college at all.

I took her out to celebrate and refused to discuss the miles and hours and years ahead. "Not tonight," I repeated, until she relented. If we had to be long distance for two years, then that's what we'd do. But Jacqueline's admittance into Oberlin had given me a new goal.

Back in December, I had dinner with Joseph, Elliott, and Elliott's little sister, Reni, who was visiting from Cleveland, where she was a third-year med school student at Case Western. Their transparent attempts at playing matchmaker went down in flames, but they set the two of us up in a different respect. Fascinated with the details of the research project I'd be part of for the next five months, Reni told me about one of her mentors, whose field of research was bioengineering.

When I emailed her about possible job leads, she passed my résumé to that professor. He was one of the three founders of a small bioengineering startup in Cleveland. One of the others knew Dr. Aziz, and she'd spotted his name in my list of references. A week later, I got a call and a request to apply.

Luck had started the ball rolling. The rest was up to me.

"Why won't you tell me where you're going for this interview, at least?" For forty-five minutes, Jacqueline had been trying to cajole clues out of me during commercial breaks in the zombie drama we were watching. "Aren't we supposed to tell each other everything?" Her honeyed tone and earnest secret-discovering expression—wide blue eyes staring up into mine—almost made me cave. She was too good at this.

"Nice try." I smirked, and she scowled.

"I'll just ask Cindy."

"Which is why I didn't tell her, either."

She stamped her foot at that, which made me laugh until she pressed me into the corner of my sofa and said, "I love it when you laugh. You're so pretty." She wound her arms around my neck and clutched at my hair, pulling me closer for a kiss.

I shook my head and traced her lips with my tongue before diving inside. Settling in to kiss her senseless, I whispered, "Flattery will get you nowhere . . . but please, *please* keep trying."

BREAKABLE

· · · · · · · · · ·

My graduation party was a cookout in the Hellers' backyard. After not leaving home for over eight years, Dad took three days off to attend the ceremony. His appearance was also a show of faith in his best friends. Watching the three of them together, I hoped this weekend was the beginning of a new habit for him.

I hadn't told anyone my future plans yet, though Charles, Cindy, and Dad knew about the offers I'd had, and they'd exchanged knowing looks at breakfast this morning, when I told them I'd made my choice. I had one person to tell, though, before I let them in on my final decision, and that person was standing in my kitchen, packing barbeque leftovers into the fridge.

"I accepted a job on Friday," I said, and she barely responded. I wondered what was going through her mind until she finally looked up, unable to rearrange the little containers any further. My brave girl was barely holding back tears.

I led her to the sofa and pulled her into my arms. "It's a startup—less than ten employees right now. The founders are cardiology researchers developing noninvasive ways of mapping electrocardiographic activity, to help with diagnosis and treatment of heart disorders. They also want to develop better invasive devices—and they wanted someone with a basic knowledge of durable soft materials."

The crease between her brows told me I'd lost her. So I told her the pay, which would be supplemented with stock options. "If the company does well—and it *will*—the employees do well. My start date is the week after July fourth."

She looked up at me, trying to smile and not fooling me for a second. I knew what she was thinking—*twelve hundred miles apart.*

I took a breath. "So my only question is this—do I want to live in

Oberlin and commute to Cleveland, or live near Cleveland and commute to you?" I watched her shifting expressions as she realized what I'd just said. Her eyes widened and filled with tears. Her mouth dropped open and she stuttered something that sounded like *What?* "Oh—didn't I tell you that part? The company's located in Cleveland." Half an hour from Oberlin.

We would have six weeks' separation between when I moved to Ohio and when she did, but I shoved that thought away as she came into my arms. Today was my celebration, and I carried her to my room to show her all the ways I intended to celebrate.

• • • • • • • • • •

Six weeks apart had been hell.

Once my flight landed, I was ready to punch out a window to get off the plane, through the airport, and outside to Jacqueline's truck.

After lunch with her parents, the two of us were leaving on a two-day road trip back to Ohio. We planned to stop for the night just inside Kentucky, drive most of the day tomorrow, and meet the moving van at her new dorm tomorrow evening.

As always, everything and everyone else disappeared when I saw her. She leaped from the truck and met me in front of it, wearing a white sundress with a gauzy little short-sleeved cardigan over it, unbuttoned. My bag hit the ground and I pulled her into my embrace. "Miss me?" I asked, our lips an inch apart. One hand at the base of her spine, I pressed her close as the other hand slid up under her sweater to encounter bare skin.

Her little dress was backless. *Holy shit*, this was going to be a long day—pre-noon and I was already imagining closing and locking the door to our hotel room tonight.

"Kiss me and find out how much." She went to her toes, her eyes mischief incarnate as my fingertips trailed up over her shoulder blades.

Walking her backward to the passenger side and pressing her to the door of her truck, I wanted to unfasten those tiny hooks at her nape, and she knew it.

What she didn't know: I had some torture of my own to impart.

Closing that final inch, I captured her mouth with mine. I traced her full lips with the tip of my tongue and just barely swept inside as we kissed. "Mmm . . ." she moaned, her tongue darting out to tease my upper lip before sucking my tongue into her mouth. I deepened the kiss bit by bit as our tongues tangled, and suddenly she pulled away. Her feet went flat on the ground and her hands gripped my biceps under the sleeves of my T-shirt as she stared up at me, eyes wide.

"Lucas."

"Hmm?"

She stared at my mouth. "Did you . . . ? Is that . . . ?"

"Like it?" I asked, and she visibly shivered head to toe. "I knew you missed the lip ring. I figured you needed something else to play with when we kiss."

Nodding, she said, "Let me see."

Obediently, I opened my mouth and she peered inside at the little ball that sat dead center on my tongue. "Oh . . . Oh, God . . ." She licked that sweet lower lip as her eyes shifted to mine. "Is it true, what they say about that?"

A corner of my mouth tipped up on one side and one brow rose. "I guess we'll find out tonight, won't we?" I kissed her again, my tongue delving fully into her mouth. She moaned—an impatient, breathy entreaty. Breaking the kiss, my hand curled around her nape and I whispered into her ear. "So tell me, how long does that *bad-boy phase* thing last? Because I'm trying my best to prolong it."

She sucked in a breath and tucked her face to my shoulder. "Oh, *God*. I can't believe you know about that."

I tipped her chin up. Her face was pink.

"How am I doing, Jacqueline? Fulfilling your every bad-boy wish, or is there something I've overlooked? I may have a steady job and be madly, deeply in love with my girlfriend . . ." I kissed her as she clung to me. "But I have a *wicked* imagination."

• • • • • • • • • •

There used to be a point in time separating *before* from *after*. On one side lay everything good and beautiful—a dream that couldn't be touched in waking moments. Memories of my mother were trapped there, and I fought to forget them because they did nothing but hurt and condemn. The opposite side was struggle. Endurance. My *after* was raw reality, and there was nothing to do but survive it.

Then came Jacqueline. This love. This healing. This new reality where before and after were no longer divided by a solitary rift. Where every moment was a tangible memory and a promise of what was to come. Every moment was a before and an after. Every moment was a *now* to be lived—and I would savor every one, beginning this second, with the girl in my arms.

Acknowledgments

Thank you to the readers who wrote to me after reading *Easy*. Your stories were heartbreaking, inspiring, rage-inducing, and empowering. Thanks to those who told me they'd signed up for self-defense classes, sought counseling, or passed the book to a friend, a daughter, a sister, or a niece. Hugs to every single one of you.

Thank you, Kim, sister of my heart, for being my Erin.

Thank you to my grandfather, my dad, and my brother for being the kind of men who stand up for, respect, protect, and defend the women in their lives. You taught me, every day of my life, what a man should be, and how he should treat me. Because of you, I didn't settle for less.

Thank you, Paul, my amazing husband, for being one of those men. Your love and support are everything to me, and I couldn't do this without you.

Love to my parents and parents-in-law. I'm blessed and grateful to have each of you in my life.

Thank you to my brilliant critique partners and beta-readers: Colleen Hoover, Tracey Garvis Graves, Elizabeth Reyes, Robin Deeslie, and Hannah Webber, as well as my editor, Cindy Hwang. Your suggestions and input were critical to bringing Lucas to life in these pages and doing his story justice.

Special thanks to my agents, Jane Dystel and Lauren Abramo, who've dispensed essential guidance and kept me sane as I navigate this still-new career. I appreciate you both so much.

Acknowledgments

Finally, here's to everyone who has survived something devastating—something that shattered your self-confidence and distorted your world in one blow. Whether you were fierce in the face of it or fell to pieces or shoved it out of sight for years—I don't care how you got here. Every day you are stronger. Every day you are healing. Every day that you survive, you are telling that event, that person, that illness, that memory: *YOU DO NOT DEFINE ME*. Keep on.